The Temple

Tormod Cockburn

A "Mysterious Scotland" novel.

Mys.Scot

First published by Mys.Scot Media in 2025

Copyright © Tormod Cockburn, 2025

The moral right of the author has been asserted.

Print ISBN: 978-1-915612-17-5

E-Book ISBN: 978-1-915612-16-8

Cover photo: Torn red, from Getty Images Pro

licenced by Canva

For updates and free books, we invite you to join our Readers Syndicate. Either click the logo above in a digital copy or see details at the back of this book.

Mys.Scot

Dedication

For Audrey, my best friend on this journey called life.

Also by Tormod Cockburn

The Bone Trap
The Ness Deception
The Stone Cypher
This Jagged Way
The Ice Covenant
This Emerald Veil
Dark Sayings
The Crystal Armour
The Torn Isle

Chapter 1

Finlaggan Fortress, Islay - August 1493

J ohn MacDonald cast his eyes over the revised document and groaned inwardly. Almost none of the concerns he'd raised had been addressed. And still, the young king sat, enthroned in John's own chair, at the head of John's table. The monarch had called for more wine, meaning the clock was ticking. Evidently, King James was tiring of this back and forth and soon he'd start kicking over chairs.

'Well,' said James, taking a noisy sip from his refilled cup. 'Are you ready to sign?'

John fabricated a mollified expression and pasted it to his face. 'You have my land, sire. My subjects, and my title. If it's your intention to disgrace me, then I'd say this is fine work.'

'Your tenants are protected. None will be evicted. Your fleet will continue to sail in the protection of these isles, albeit under my flag. And you, sir, will have permission to withdraw peacefully to some other place, even while I harbour a desire to kick your arse.'

John made eye contact with two of the weary-looking noblemen lining the walls. 'If you wish, sire, I'll unwrap my plaid before these gentlemen and let you do it. It can be no greater humiliation than what's written in this document.'

James laughed. 'Maybe I will. And complete my satisfaction by stretching your neck from the castle walls.'

John faced his king to show he wasn't intimidated. 'And if you do, my birlinns will pirate your ships. Burn your towns. Harass you at every turn.'

The king took another long swig. 'If you do that, I'll return with an army. These tenants you seem to care so much about – they'll all be killed.'

John shook his head. 'You proclaim your desire to be king of all of Scotland. But does a man deserve a kingdom when he holds the lives of its people so lightly?'

James slapped the table so hard wine leapt from his cup. 'I do love my people. And my nation. And my throne.' He thrust an accusing finger at John. 'But to protect them from the English, your kingdom must be added to mine. I cannot face an army of jackals to the south if I have you, old dog, nipping my heels from the west.'

No one moved or spoke while the king's words echoed in the chamber.

John cleared his throat. 'May we recess, sire? I'd like to consider your latest document.'

Wine jumped in the cup again. 'No sir, we may not. We sit. Sit, and drink, until we have this agreement made, or unholy war declared between us.'

John swallowed and stared at his master for a full minute. 'In that case, sire, I'll waste no more time.' He sat back in his chair and pulled himself straight. 'I'll sign.'

'Excellent', said James, slapping the table gently this time with triumphant glee. While he sat smiling, his secretary approached and whispered in the young man's ear.

The king cleared his throat. 'If our deal is done, then there is one simple formality to be completed.' He snapped his fingers, prompting the aide to hand John a single sheet of parchment.

'What's this?'

'Formalities,' said the king with a lazy wave of one hand. 'To be appended to the treaty.'

John started reading the document and had to stifle a laugh. 'We just made a deal, sire. And now you rush to twist the knife?'

'Oh, do not fuss, John,' the king shouted. 'The treaty is agreed. This final addendum lists penalties should the isles ever rise again in rebellion to the crown.'

John's forefinger traced some further text before stabbing at the sheet. 'You'd not find this much gold in all the isles!'

The king slouched in his chair and fiercely rubbed his chin. 'Then we would extract the fee some other way.'

John kept scanning. 'Some of these towns have over one thousand souls. And you'd burn them to the ground?'

'As penalty for rebellion? Most certainly.'

John placed the document on the table and laid his hand on top of it. 'The forfeits you list only accuse one party. What consequences are due if the crown ever betrays the isles?'

'None are due,' snapped James. 'The crown never betrays its people.'

John couldn't keep contempt from his face. 'I think, sir, history would beg to differ.'

'This clause isn't negotiable. I'm showing it to you out of chivalry.'

'Then will you at least allow me the courtesy of adding my own?'

James took a long drag from his cup. 'You'd list the rights of all your former subjects, from lairds to cottars and make my throne subject to their whims?' He shook his head. 'Don't waste my time, John.'

John scowled at the document. This restitution clause was further evidence the crown couldn't be trusted. By making this treaty with James he'd hoped to lift the threat of war. Now, if he signed, the king's penalties would hang over the

Western Isles forever. He winced. The totality of his defeat was rising to drown him. Forever, he would be remembered as John, the last, *Lord of the Isles*. His name would be held in contempt because he'd surrendered and signed this damned document. In desperation, he prayed to his inner guide. 'Oh, Aura, Aura! What should I do?'

'I'm waiting', said the king.

'I need to assert justice for my people. They have a right under God to be free of you, and unshackled from this damned document, should you or your successors not keep your word.'

James laughed. 'And how would Scotland know if God was on your side or mine? If indeed God exists and cares to take any man's side?'

'Scotland would need a sign. Something remarkable and undeniable during a dark day of injustice.'

'A sign!' spat James, incredulously. 'You'd have them watch for lights in the sky? Clap their hands in delight while the sea around them turns to blood?'

John sat under the king's hard glaze. He had moments to add one redeeming clause and had no idea how he'd fashion words acceptable to the king. And wilting under the king's glare, she came to him with gentle, powerful arms, squeezing him with holy reassurance. Not his wife or daughter – they'd already fled to Selkirk. No, this was a different kind of friend. One he'd met long ago on a day when he'd plunged into water, weighed down by leather armour during a storm. She had gripped him then as she gripped him now. Reminding him he was just a man and not a saviour. A man who, despite his many frailties, was truly loved. And while she held him, she whispered her suggestion.

'Bring me pen and ink,' whispered John to the attendant.

The secretary glanced at his king, and after a nod, fetched John the materials.

John turned over the king's sheet with its penalty clause and started to scratch his response on the back. 'When you rode into my court, sire, I see you did so under a new royal standard. May I congratulate you – it's a dramatic depiction of two wild and glorious beasts. Tell me, sir, do you know what they are?'

'Waterhorses, of course. Royal beasts to dignify a king's banner.'

'And these beasts, do you know where they're from?'

James' petulant sigh betrayed his youth. 'I don't think I need to tell you where they're from.'

John nodded, focusing his attention on his fierce writing. 'Aye. Upon the greatest of all the western isles, at a place called Callanish, is a temple ruin. It is there the animals go after they've been blooded.'

'And kill any man who gets in their way.' James leaned across the table and gradually raised his voice. 'I know the old stories, John MacDonald. And now, for the pity of the saints, can we conclude this work before us?'

John finished writing and thrust the paper in the air for the secretary to collect. 'If it pleases your majesty, I insist on adding this one clause to the treaty. If you cannot agree to it, then I regret that this whole exercise is in jeopardy.'

James took the paper and read it. He fixed John with a long, suspicious glance before reading it again. Finally, the king laughed. 'On one hand, you threaten me with war, and on the other, you tickle me with a jest?'

'That is my clause, sire. Take it or leave it.'

Suspiciously, James scanned the document again. 'What is this *Torn Isle* you refer to?'

'It is, sir, what God himself will do to Scotland should you or your descendants ever embrace injustice.'

'I'm tired', said James, suddenly looking drained while he gesticulated to his secretary to return with ink. 'There', he said after scratching his name at the foot of John's clause. 'Have we made a peace between us?'

The man returned with the signed sheet, and John murmured his assent. Then with a weighty sadness, he added his name.

The king stood and adjusted his cloak before turning to address the nobles resting against the walls. 'Tomorrow, at midday, I will reconvene in this hall with John MacDonald and his fellow rebels. Together, we will sign this completed document, with the clauses hereby agreed.' James turned to face the older man. 'Then you, John MacDonald, have forfeited the Lairdship of Finlaggan, and are banished from this place, never to return.' He left an uncomfortable pause. 'Are the parties agreed?'

John pushed back his chair. Standing, he bowed before the king, and with his hand on his heart, he swore to keep the treaty's obligations. Taking a step backwards, he left his hall for the final time and walked outside under the darkening sky. This would be his last night at Finlaggan. His last as *Lord of the Isles*. Aura had guided him to write the final postscript on The *Treaty of Finlaggan*, but oh, what little chance the conditions he'd specified would ever be fulfilled. And by the heavens, what a desperate day it would be for all of Scotland if his clause was ever invoked.

John's clause appended to the Treaty of Finlaggan

"*Should the Laird of Finlaggan, upon hearing a supremacy of our citizens voice displeasure at Scotland's ruler, choose to sit upon Scotland's royal horse of old renown, and ride upon that beast one circuit of the Temple of the Isles, without being gored or cast aside, then he is granted authority to declare, The Torn Isle. This faithful proclamation, upon recognition by a sheriff of the state, grants to any island in Scotland's union the right to quit said union without penalty or recourse to arms.*"

Chapter 2

Peak of Ben Macdui - 3 years ago

Raphael stood with his arms folded, wishing he had permission to intervene. But authorisation was not forthcoming, so for now, his role was to watch Sariel go about his diabolical business.

'You know McArdle has just left Falkirk?' called Raphael. 'He is coming to this mountain.'

Sariel flicked a clawlike hand at him. 'Should hope so. I put on quite a show.'

'And you do realise you can only appoint one ambassador today?'

'Rules, rules, rules,' muttered Sariel, his attention focused on the pitiful creature crouching in the snow before him.

'If you're so intent on recruiting McArdle, I don't understand your interest in this poor fellow?'

Sariel glanced at Raphael and then back to his supplicant. 'I want to limit the time I spend in this detestable human form. This creature is my insurance policy in case McArdle refuses.'

Raphael pointed at the man crouching in the ice. Stripped to his waist, he was a lean thing of a little below-average height. 'You do know he can hear you?'

'My concern is for his loyalty, not his well-being,' Sariel drawled.

'He doesn't look well to me. I estimate you have twenty minutes before he expires. Go on, Sariel. Let this one go, at least until you discover if McArdle can be swayed.'

Sariel finally turned to look at him. 'You adore your humble *Sword-bearer*, don't you, Raphael? You seem to think he'll endure my tests?'

'I am hopeful, but that's no excuse for persecuting another human.'

'But this one REALLY wants to be my servant,' whined Sariel. 'Not as delicious as switching a *Sword-bearer* but still a worthy foot soldier.' Sariel stepped towards the man and kicked his thigh. 'Are you ready to pledge yourself?'

The man, roused perhaps from a hypothermic slumber, prostrated himself before Sariel. 'I am, my lord.'

'And what will you give me?'

'Everything, my lord. My past, my present and my future. I place them in your hands to spend at your will.'

'And what do you want in return?'

'Only to serve you, sir. To seek out your enemies and destroy them.'

'Very well,' said Sariel, sounding pleased. 'I have a job for you, and if you do it well, I can smother your earthly life with munificent rewards.'

'Thank you, sir.'

Sariel gave Raphael an ugly smile. 'Would you mind turning around? I'd rather you didn't watch this next bit.'

Raphael tightened his arms across his chest. 'No secrets in the heavenly realm, Sariel. Do what you came here to do, then send this sorry wretch away.'

Sariel bared his teeth at Raphael, then turned back to his charge. 'Stand up!'

Weakly, the man obeyed, and though he was now enslaved to Sariel and his master, Raphael still felt compassion. The man's slim body carried a little muscle but not enough to protect him from the bitter cold.

'Hold out your arms,' commanded Sariel.

Obediently, the man did so, his arms shaking with cold and fear. Sariel then extracted a short metal rod from a pocket of his robe. He shook the rod, and instantaneously, it transformed into a black lance. The demon studied it for a few seconds, then in a blur of action too fast for the human to comprehend, he struck his shivering servant above each elbow. The man screamed in pain, though to his credit, he held his ground. Staring down at his arms, and no doubt enduring the smell of his own burnt skin, he studied the shape of his two new, matching tattoos. Their blackened outlines encompassed intertwined serpents, snaking up towards his shoulders.

'Thank you, my lord,' the man stuttered.

Sariel gripped the lance across its middle, collapsing it into a short rod, then immediately extending it again. 'You are now counted among my legion. Retrieve this weapon and study it. When we next meet, I expect you to have mastered its powers.'

In his extreme discomfort, the man still seemed puzzled. 'Retrieve it, sir?'

Sariel lifted the weapon to his shoulder and launched it far from the mountaintop. 'Go fetch,' he spat. 'And do not come into my presence again until you are truly worthy.'

Buchanan Estate, Loch Lomond – Present day

It was a dark evening along the wooded bank of Loch Lomond and Freya Swanson needed to be careful where she placed her feet. With the horses fed and fresh straw added to their stalls, she closed the stable doors and walked wearily towards her house. Stepping homeward under rustling trees, made all the gloomier by steadily falling rain, she allowed herself an ironic smile. When chastised by her city friends for living on a country estate, she'd protest the reality was really quite dismal. The truth was she couldn't afford urban living, never mind a place to lodge her one small mare. Living on the Buchanan Estate solved both those problems. The gatehouse she rented was small and dark, and desperately in need of updating. But it was cheap, and she was able to offset a chunk of her monthly rent by doing what needed to be done at the stables. And that allowed her to survive on a volatile freelance income, despite the cost of travelling into central Glasgow three days a week.

Glancing across the grounds, the main house was just visible between the trees. A dozen cars were scattered on the gravelled park, and lights blazed throughout the house. Perhaps the McKanes were holding another one of their strange meetings. Of course, they were free to do what they liked; this was their land. But as she reached her cottage door, she couldn't dispel the feeling there was something strange going on. She could feel it around the estate. She felt it online. Most of all, she felt it in the office, on her city days at the *Glasgow Tribune* - a tension in the air like the early hours of an undeclared war.

Freya's Glasgow job was little more than an intern position, scraping together enough experience to justify calling herself a journalist. Tomorrow, she'd be back there, hotdesking around the *Tribune* building and praying she wasn't wasting her time.

Leaving her boots in the porch, she locked the door behind her and padded through to the kitchen to make a hot drink. Flicking on the kettle, she glanced at her mobile. Its knackered old battery was still charging, receiving its third boost of the day. Picking it up, she noticed four missed calls from an unknown number. No voicemail, she noted with a sigh. It was almost 10 pm and her plan had been for a hot bath and an early night. But hey, it could be an offer of work, so she pressed herself to hope for the best.

The number only rang once before it picked up. 'John Houston,' said a man's mild voice.

'Freya Swanson here. You phoned me earlier.'

'Ah, thank you for calling back.' Houston sounded edgy. 'I spoke to one of your colleagues and although she couldn't help me, she gave me your number.'

Freya bit her lip. Whoever this guy was, he'd been doing the rounds. 'How can I help you?'

Houston sighed. 'I have something to report. Something pertinent to public safety, and frankly, I'm struggling to get anyone to listen to me.'

'Sorry to hear that. Can you give me a quick summary and I'll see if I can help.'

Houston released a ragged breath and spoke slowly. 'There's going to be an earthquake.'

Freya allowed her body to slump back against the kitchen counter. She'd not even poured her tea, and now she'd picked up the phone to a crank. 'I'd observe we seem to have a lot of little quakes these days.'

'Yes, but the next one's going to be bigger. It's been coming for years. Pressures build up, you see, around the Great Glen Fault.'

'Okay. And you know this, how?'

'I'm the head of a public body called the Scottish Geological Society. Well … I was until recently.' He left a tiny pause, and Freya used the time to open a browser on her tablet and Google the guy's name. 'We've been developing a piece of software,' he said. 'Something designed to predict earth tremors.'

Freya watched her screen refresh. There was indeed a man called Houston associated with the SGS. 'Sure. What about it?'

'You might recall that back in July, we had a Scotland-wide event, centred around the Great Glen?'

Freya remembered. The quake had occurred five weeks ago, and there'd been days of travel disruption for an event that had basically rattled windows down the west coast. A bit overblown and pathetic really, like England experiencing snow. 'I remember.'

'There was a bit of fuss about our software because it didn't predict the event. I mean the magnitude wasn't dramatic but, considering the geographic …'

'I'm sorry for cutting across you, Mr Houston. But it's late. Can you summarise your issue?'

His voice was gentle and almost apologetic. 'I think someone has tampered with the underlying model.'

'Plainer English, please.'

Houston sucked in, then released a breath. 'Our predictive software has been sabotaged.'

Freya pinched her eyebrows. 'Sounds like a data issue. Or a software glitch.'

'No, there's a sequence of algorithms hard-coded into our model. I'm certain someone's interfered with them.'

Yeah, thought Freya. She could see why this guy had been phoning around. 'The earthquake. How big is it going to be?'

'Big. Well, bigger than the ones we've seen.'

'How much bigger?'

'Twice the magnitude, or maybe more. Enough to bring down buildings.'

'And how do you know this if your software's not working?'

'Good question! Thank you, I like it when someone asks intelligent questions. And I'll answer it by explaining that I've kept an older version of the prediction engine on my laptop. When the latest tremors weren't detected, I decided to push the relevant seismic data through this older version of the software. And as I suspected, the older version did indicate the likelihood of a significant seismic event.'

'So, yeah. A software problem.'

'And that's when I discovered the most recent data indicates an even bigger quake. Frankly, I'm concerned with the implications for public safety.'

'And when's it going to happen?'

'Soon,' said Houston. 'Weeks, maybe days. It could be hours.'

'Looking on the bright side, you've still got time to fix it.'

'But nobody's listening, Miss Swanson! No one at the Scottish Geological Society, nor anyone in government.'

'Listen, I've got the SGS website open, and it says you're on a leave of absence. That a lady called Agnes Fairbank has stepped into your role.'

'Well, that's another issue,' he hissed. 'When I started pestering some of the higher-ups, they laid me off citing work stress. Now they've brought back Fairbank from the Department of Agriculture and suddenly I'm yesterday's man.'

Brilliant, thought Freya. An unhappy boffin with a persecution complex. 'Look, I'm sorry for your trouble. And your software issues must be disappointing, but I'm not convinced there's a story here.'

'Can we meet?' he pleaded. 'Let me show you the old and new models and I'll explain why I'm certain the newest version has been tampered with.'

'Tampering is a big accusation. Perhaps the differences you're seeing are just different technical approaches to what I'm sure is a very complicated field.'

'There's more to it than that and I'd love to have an opportunity to show you. Could we meet, perhaps at lunchtime or after work? And we'd make it somewhere public so if you don't feel safe you can just walk away.'

Freya chewed on this for a moment. An old mentor had once reminded her that to find the big scoop, the dedicated journalist needed to wade through mountains of horseshit. She blushed at the irony. Horseshit was something of a personal calling. 'Okay then. There's a Greek restaurant in George Square. Do you know it?'

'I don't, but I'll find it.'

'It's a big place so we can ask for a table near the back where we won't be disturbed. I can give you one hour to convince me you've identified something that needs to be in the public domain.'

'When?'

'Friday. 1 pm.'

'That's three days away. Can't you see me sooner than that?'

'Sorry, I can't.'

'Okay. Thank you. I'll see you then.'

Chapter 3

It was the start of day three on the Fisher Street site and Gill McArdle waded through a relentless sea of mud. A glance at the uncertain sky couldn't confirm if today would be wet or dry so he did his best to count his blessings. Two days of rain had greeted his dig at the old cemetery, turning this melancholic corner of Dundee into a marsh. Unsurprisingly, neither day had revealed any artefacts of particular interest. Gill was tempted to observe that if Dundee's suburb of Broughty Ferry still had a working midden, it would have been a more productive place for archaeology than this long-dormant graveyard. But on the plus side, the urban location meant he'd mustered a small army of willing volunteers. They were working hard, eager to please him, and he'd enjoyed meeting a host of new and interesting people, from college students to retired solicitors. He'd grown to like people better since his days in academia, and if all this dig produced was a public relations boost in the magazine's home city, then that was good enough for him. And the best thing about working at Fisher Street – he was two hundred metres from his own front door.

Stomping mud off his boots on the portacabin steps, he unlocked the door and optimistically hung up his jacket. A couple of older volunteers passed his window on their way to gather tools, but apart from them, he was the first to arrive. This was an unexpected moment of privacy, and he felt a sudden urge to phone a friend. Four weeks ago, Rani had summoned him to the Isle of Lewis. They'd searched for her missing animal for several days before the pressure of work had pulled him back to Dundee. And since then, their runaway candidate horse had resolutely stayed missing. Not that he was a candidate anymore. Rani's final sighting of him, when he burst from her stable, confirmed his waterhorse transformation was almost complete. For the next two weeks, Gill had phoned her daily, anxious for news. Then their calls became less frequent. As of this morning, he hadn't spoken to her for six days.

'Hey, Gill.' Rani's voice sounded tired.

'Just checking in. How are you all doing?'

'Och, Gill. We're fine.'

'I take it there's no news?'

'Graham drives down to Callanish once a day. No sightings there, nor anything else reported.'

'Have you tried leaving out food?'

'All his favourite snacks. But he's not been back once.'

Gill chewed his bottom lip for a few seconds. 'How does an animal that big just disappear? I mean it's not as if there are forests he could hide in.'

'Vast tracks of this island are uninhabited, Gill. Remember that Callum McKellar's horse hid for a year with barely any credible sightings. But that said …' Rani's voice trailed off.

'What are you thinking?' asked Gill.

'I think we have to face the possibility Bru might be dead.'

'Seriously?'

'You didn't see him that day. The blood on his face; the agony in his eyes. If he'd been a sick animal in our care we would have faced a serious welfare question.'

Gill took her meaning. 'I'm sorry he endured so much pain.'

'Poor thing. He wouldn't have had a clue what was happening to him.'

Gill took a deep breath. 'Listen, Rani. I've never asked you this, but can you tell me something about Bru?'

She seemed to catch the tension in his voice and gave a hesitant response. 'Sure.'

'After he made his transformation … was he black, or white?'

Rani was silent for a second. 'It was almost dark, Gill, and as soon as Bru escaped from the stables he was gone. I only glimpsed him long enough to be certain of what he'd become.'

'Anything, Rani. If he's still alive, it might help us predict what he'll do next.'

'Oh, I see,' she chided. 'You're thinking that if he's black he'll be vengeful, and if he's white he'll be cute and cuddly?'

'I don't think we'd ever call a waterhorse "cute," but yeah, that kind of thing.'

'This is Bru, we're talking about. I don't see how he'd ever cause us harm.'

'I'm just saying, we need to be ready. The Minos Genetics animal was a black and we remember how dangerous he became.'

'Bru was always grey, and from what I glimpsed on the day he metamorphosed, I'd say he hadn't changed.'

Gill hung his head even though Rani couldn't see him. 'I hope so.'

'And like I said, we might never see him again.'

'I honestly think he'll turn up. Tell me, how's Amy doing?'

'She's devastated, Gill. I know lots of wee girls feel affection for horses, but she loved Bru to bits and she's not the same girl without him.'

'Well, tell her I'm rooting for you all. And let me know if there's ever anything I can do.'

'I don't want to drag you back here on a wild goose chase. Honestly, Gill, if we ever have news, you'll be the first person I call.'

At the same time Gill was starting his day on the dig site, Lillico was sitting in reception of St. Leonard's Street Police Station. A quick glance at his watch confirmed he'd been there for forty minutes.

'Pity's sake, Alex, relax,' muttered Wiley. 'This is a classic powerplay. The senior officer keeps the underlings waiting to make them sweat.'

Lillico rubbed his palms together. 'I am sweating, George. I'm wondering if these are the closing minutes of my career as a police officer.'

'Just sit there with your arms folded like a bored teenager and let me do the talking.'

'If you start lying through your teeth, sir, you know I'll contradict you.'

'Which is why I'd prefer to wrap your face with duct tape.'

Lillico rolled his eyes. 'I think, sir, for this meeting, that might give the wrong impression.'

Wiley jabbed the air in front of him. 'Leave me to exploit the ambiguities about what did or did not happen in Wigtownshire. Remember, if we make a move against Macfarlane, he'll have no choice other than to force us out. So, for now, we'll take it slowly. Smoke and mirrors, Alex. The safest place for us just now is in the shadows.' Wiley noticed the receptionist was signalling them, so he got to his feet.

'Smoke and mirrors, George. How very honourable.' But Wiley wasn't listening. He was already approaching Macfarlane's office with his hand outstretched and a willing smile on his face.

'Let me see if I've got this straight,' said Macfarlane, thrusting a forefinger in their direction. Lillico's chest rose and fell with a thinly disguised sigh. He'd already endured twenty minutes of Wiley's forelock tugging and frequent deferrals to their senior officer. 'You're saying, before implementing my legitimate order to hand over the weapons cache, you suddenly decided to move the guns to a derelict bank, thirty miles away?'

'We were getting messages left, right and centre,' said Wiley. 'Orders contradicting yours, and suggestions that a third party was trying to seize the weapons. Moving the stash to a new location seemed to be the best way of ensuring we kept them safe until your unit arrived.'

'And yet, this so-called third party found your new location. Then a gunfight ensued that resulted in the injury of one officer and the death of two civilians. Why then, after that threat had been neutralised, didn't DI Lillico hand the cache to my men?'

Wiley looked theatrically puzzled for a moment. 'That was the plan all along, sir. But then your crew was recalled before reaching Wigtown. Given the ambiguity in the chain of command, I ordered DI Lillico to put the weapons beyond use.'

'By tossing them into a river?'

'Yes, sir.'

'DI Lillico, you're very quiet. Do you have anything to add?'

'I was living in the moment, sir,' said Lillico, trotting out the line Wiley had given him. 'My goals were to survive and to stop terrorists from acquiring the weapons. I was content to take orders from DCI Wiley as he had strategic oversight of the situation.'

19

'Strategic oversight,' droned Macfarlane. 'From the safety of his office in Bathgate?'

Lillico decided to deviate from the script. 'To be fair, sir, it's a three-hour drive between Bathgate and the incident in Wigtown. DCI Wiley couldn't physically be present.'

Macfarlane didn't seem convinced. 'Tell me again how Murray McGovern came to be evacuated by ambulance from Wigtown, and not from the scene of his accident in Clanyard Bay?'

'When Gill McArdle realised McGovern's men wanted the guns, McGovern tried to injure him. In the scuffle that followed, McArdle came out on top. You'll recall, we were in the aftermath of a seismic disturbance, so resources were stretched. McArdle brought McGovern to Wigtown so he could be closer to medical aid.'

'If I can ask, sir,' said Wiley, already aware of what the answer would be. 'Has the Fiscal arrived at a decision on McGovern?'

'He's decided there's no case to answer. McGovern didn't take part in the Wigtown raid, so it appears his men were acting alone. Perhaps they hoped to sell the weapons on the black market.'

'McGovern attacked McArdle,' said Lillico, respectfully, through gritted teeth.

Macfarlane shrugged. 'We only have McArdle's word for that. There isn't a scrap of evidence supporting his claim. To be honest, I think Murray McGovern is justifiably offended that McArdle would even suggest such a thing.'

'There was a gun case in a cave,' Lillico continued. 'McGovern must have been aware his men had cached weapons for their own use.'

'Again, McArdle's word against McGovern's,' Macfarlane retorted. 'And knowing the pedigree of both men, and his many years as a subcontractor for Police Scotland, I'm more inclined to believe McGovern.'

'I'd agree, sir,' said Wiley, emphatically. 'McArdle's a slippery one; I know that to my cost.'

'Very well.' Macfarlane turned to look at Lillico. 'Normally you could have expected a commendation and even a promotion in the light of your bravery in Wigtown. However, that goodwill was cancelled by your obtuse interpretation of my orders as your commanding officer. As a result, DI Lillico, you will attend a full disciplinary hearing in four weeks' time. And I must warn you, I will not be taking your corner on this one.'

Lillico nodded to accept the rebuke but said nothing.

Macfarlane picked up a pen and hovered over an official-looking form. 'That will be all.'

Wiley thanked his superior, then in a moment of uncharacteristic generosity he held the door open for Lillico. The two walked in silence until they had left the building.

'I should resign,' said Lillico. 'See if I can preserve what little pension I've accrued.'

'Aye. And save your tarnished reputation from rubbing off on *Special Investigations*.'

'Thank you, George. As ever, your loyalty and support …'

'Och, get over yourself,' rushed Wiley. 'Trust me when I say you're not going anywhere.'

Lillico stopped and jerked a finger back in the direction they'd come. 'I basically got handed my papers in there. From the second highest ranked officer in the force.'

'Just the second highest?' Wiley dismissively flicked his chin and kept walking. 'Fortunately, I'm better connected than that.'

Lillico had to jog a few steps to catch up. 'What are you saying?'

Wiley glanced at his watch. 'Can you drive us into town? There's an old case I need to catch you up on.'

Wiley kept the car radio blaring during the long trek into Edinburgh's old town, leaving Lillico to drive in sullen silence. Entering through the Grassmarket, they turned up Victoria Terrace, until Wiley indicated he should park at the top end of the cobbled street. He slammed his door and didn't wait for Lillico while he led them up stone steps and through a slew of vennels running between the ancient buildings.

Reaching his destination, winded and coughing, Wiley lowered himself onto a stone step beneath an arch and lit a cigarette. 'What do you make of that door?' he asked, thumbing over his shoulder to indicate a thick slab of oak that was probably older than America.

'Looks solid,' said Lillico, stepping forward to run his fingers over the door's authentic metal studs. 'Who lives here?'

'A lovely chap called Harry Sinclair. Remember him?'

'One of *Lady K's* victims,' Lillico recalled. 'He was quite coy about what she stole from him. Earns his crust as a phone hacker.'

'Well, he doesn't earn it anymore because someone strangled him eight weeks ago.'

'Ah, I see. And did you work that case?'

'Aye. It was one of the things I was doing while you were busy in Wigtownshire.'

'And why did this back street murder require the attention of *Special Investigations*?'

Wiley waved his hand around the confined yard. 'Do you know where you are?'

Lillico glanced around, then shook his head.

'Goodness, Lillico. I'd have thought a man like you would know his local history. This is Brodie's Close, named after a local worthy from the eighteenth century, who was a city councilor, and a respected local lockmaker.' Wiley paused to cough. 'What people didn't discover, until it was too late, was the widely esteemed Deacon Brodie was keeping copies of all the keys he made.'

'Keys?' asked Lillico.

'For doors like this, and for all the cabinets he crafted for wealthy folk to store their stash. He played the part of the invisible burglar, slipping into houses and strongboxes using his copied keys until one night he was caught in the act.'

'Fascinating, boss, but why's this relevant?'

'Somebody fabricated a key to open the ancient lock in this even older door. Then they slipped inside during one of the endless evenings this time of year when this city shoots off a tonne of fireworks and strangled Mr Sinclair at his desk. It was this elaborate means of entry, plus the fact that I'd interviewed him before on the *Lady K* case, that put his file on my desk.'

'Did you find out who did it?'

'Not yet, though it's what we discovered in Sinclair's flat that made this an interesting case.'

Lillico nodded at the door. 'Are we going in?'

Wiley shook his head. 'I don't have a key.'

Lillico tried and failed to keep frustration from flickering across his face. This had been a long drive for a short wander in a scenic corner of the old city.

'I just wanted to show you the context,' Wiley explained. 'And I'd rather not create a paper trail that might alert Macfarlane.'

'I know he's not our biggest fan, but why would Macfarlane care one way or another?'

23

Wiley nodded in the direction they'd come. 'I'll tell you the rest in the car.'

'Sinclair was an old-style phone hacker,' Wiley continued as they drove away. 'In a modern-day rendition of old Deacon Brodie, his working day was spent raiding digital mailboxes and listening to phone messages. The murderer took Sinclair's laptop and a bank of phones hidden in a safe under the stairs.' Wiley turned to wink at Lillico. 'What they didn't find was a second laptop tucked in a secret compartment, up in the bedroom.'

'But you did.'

Wiley tapped his nose. 'An old copper's instinct, laddie.'

'Please tell me a phone hacker knew to protect his laptop with a decent password.'

Wiley chortled happily. 'His mother's birthdate, run backwards. Eliza Hemmings cracked it in an afternoon.'

Lillico shook his head at the strangeness of folk. 'Did that give you anything useful?'

'Fascinating reading,' Wiley mused. 'All sorts of interesting scraps on the great and good. But there was one particular record that caught my eye.'

Lillico nodded at Wiley to continue.

'You need to understand how a phone hacker works, Alex,' said Wiley, adopting an educational tone. 'They get the phone numbers of influential people, calling the phones late at night when the victims are sleeping, and try to crack their passwords. Once they're in, they call periodically and check the messages for juicy titbits. Anything they find helps write stories about famous people that can then be sold to a news outlet.'

'I get it, boss. Pop stars, actors and the royal family. I bet there's a bunch of folk who didn't send flowers to his funeral.'

'Sinclair had some of the juiciest material in a directory, labelled "To be opened in the event of my death."'

'Did that identify his killer?'

'Not directly. But it records text messages between Sinclair and an unidentified man planning to catch and kill Lorna Cheyne.'

Lillico remembered the incident where Lorna had battled to save the life of a friend on an Aberdeenshire clifftop. 'Any clues to the identity of the other correspondent?'

'Not directly. But it isn't too much of a stretch to imagine it was one of Lorna's other victims when she was running around pretending to be *Lady K.*'

That case had been two years ago, and Lillico had to dig deep to recall the main players.

'Let me catch you up,' said Wiley, impatiently. 'Two of Lorna's victims, Malkie Bell and Harry Sinclair, are dead. Two others, Nick Babel and Gordon Ogilvy, are in prison. Which leaves one other contender.'

Lillico caught the drift of Wiley's suspicions. 'You suspect Canmore of Sinclair's murder, and that Macfarlane might cover for him?'

'He wouldn't risk getting blood on his own hands, of course. But perhaps, whatever Lorna stole from him made the risk worthwhile.'

'Proof, George? Anything at all that links Canmore to Sinclair?'

'Absolutely none. And that's why I'd like you to use your tech skills to review CCTV footage from the day Sinclair was murdered. I doubt you'll see Roddy Canmore sneaking around Brodie's Close, but you might find something else we can use.'

Chapter 4

Gill lifted his drink and carried it to the snug in the deepest part of Broughty Ferry's Ship Inn. While the others shuffled, looking for their seats, Gill glanced around their faces, looking forward to this time together. And it gave him cause to reflect on how much they'd changed since their first encounters. Deeper, stronger, better-functioning individuals, transformed from being well-meaning souls living storm-battered lives. Charlie had been the first member recruited to the Armour Group. As a builder's labourer, he'd struggled with his mental health after years of addictive behaviour. But all that changed when the angel that had touched all their lives offered him a shield, crystalline in appearance, though supernatural in substance, and something he could manifest at will. Finally, with the means to deflect the chaos around his life, nothing scared Charlie anymore.

Ailsa had been next. Gill first met her on the Isle of Harris while undertaking his first archaeological dig for *Mysterious Scotland* magazine. He didn't see her again for several years, by which time her angel encounter had equipped her with a breastplate of the same supernatural crystal. Then it had been Gill's turn, accepting the angel's sword on an Orcadian moor, he'd found his life transformed by a flood of new understandings. Adina's experience followed Gill's when she received a crystal helmet that allowed her to navigate her complex world of artefacts and espionage. Then Lillico, a police detective whose devotion to truth, manifested as a belt around his waist. Lorna was a late arrival. The angel had delivered her gift when she was still a child, and it wasn't until her encounters with the rest of the group that her ability to physically translate herself from one location to another had been redirected from a life of crime to serve a higher cause. And finally, Solomon; she'd been with Charlie from the start, then mentored them all through the early days of their strange gifts. She was their mother-figure; the glue that held them together and magnified the impact of everything they did. She was the oldest by far and utterly fearless.

'Here we are again,' said Solomon, shaking Gill out of his reverie and sliding in beside Charlie.

'A last gathering I suspect before things kick off,' observed Ailsa.

'With respect,' said Gill, 'There's no certainty that anything is about to kick off.'

'You have your waterhorse, roaming around Harris and Lewis,' said Lorna.

'An' we a' ken whaur he's goin',' said Charlie.

'Not for definite,' said Gill, aware he was sounding defensive.

'And we have Canmore's attack on Alex, through his proxy, Chief Superintendent Macfarlane,' Solomon continued. 'I suspect we'll all suffer persecution in the coming days.'

Gill watched Lillico's dismissive body language. 'They're trying to fire me from the police, not kill me.'

'Ah, then a few days after his dismissal, the disgraced detective, burdened by remorse, is found dead in his bathroom,' said Ailsa, with mock solemnity. 'In the sorry circumstances, no one suspects foul play.'

Lillico shot her a dark look. 'If you really knew me, you'd know that's not remotely funny.'

'Then tell me,' Ailsa fired back. 'How do I get to know Alex Lillico, with his clenched buttocks and all his emotional cards tucked so very close to his chest?'

'Canmore will come for you too,' Lillico retorted. 'You live freely in Glasgow without a care in the world.'

'Canmore has nothing on me,' said Ailsa.

Lillico dropped his gaze to the table. 'He'll find a way.'

'Canmore knows Lorna stole his data stick,' said Solomon, quietly. 'And because of our links, he realises we all know at least part of his plans. That means each of us is a threat to him.'

'Super,' whispered Adina, irritably. 'I do love our little get-togethers.'

Solomon nodded at her. 'In the coming days, you, my dear, given your … overseas connections, will be particularly vulnerable.'

Adina shrugged. 'I'll deal with it.'

'I'm sure we'll all have our reactions to this trouble when it comes, but tonight, I want us to agree on a plan.'

'We can't plan for the unknown,' said Gill.'

'Decide our posture, then,' Solomon mused. 'Consider as many of our weaknesses as possible and propose some responses.'

'We could all agree to turn the other cheek,' said Lorna. 'Take whatever pain Canmore metes out to us.'

'I think,' said Solomon, 'we were given our armour for a reason.'

'I'd agree,' said Lillico. 'This doesn't feel like a lambs-to-the-slaughter moment.'

Gill this time. 'The problem is, we don't know when Canmore might launch his coup. If we stay on high alert, we'll all be nervous wrecks a year from now.'

'We cannae ken the day or the hoor,' observed Charlie. 'Aw we can dae is, be watchful, ken. Be ready tae roll wi the punches.'

'We should be dispersed as far as possible,' agreed Solomon. 'Protect ourselves and each other so that even if Canmore takes some of us out, there'll be others left to resist him.'

'Sounds a bit passive,' moaned Ailsa.

'Canmore holds the initiative,' said Solomon. 'And when he acts, we must respond. Meet him play for play. Agreed?'

She glanced around their faces until she received a nod from them all. Then, reaching into her jacket for a sheet of paper, she unfolded it on the table. 'These are the vulnerabilities Canmore might use to attack us. Help me spot any I've missed, then please, let's consider how we'll respond.'

Chapter 5

It was Thursday morning, and the sunlight beating down on Broughty Ferry was very welcome after a week of rain. It was Gill's fourth day on site with eight more left on the schedule. Today was special because he was welcoming a new volunteer to the Fisher Street dig. Zack Morabi was a tall, rangy sixteen-year-old. A little younger than Gill's typical volunteer, he'd invited Zack on the basis of his enthusiastic application. And in a rare burst of nepotism, because he was Cassy's son.

'What is this place?' asked the lad, glancing around the muddy hollow about the size of a football pitch.

'It was a graveyard,' said Gill. 'Didn't your mum tell you?'

'Aye, but I thought there'd be tombstones and that.'

'A specialist contractor came in last week to remove them. The ones in best condition will be returned to form a memorial garden once the new flats are built.'

Zack looked puzzled. 'How'd you know where the bones are buried?'

Gill beckoned to the lad. 'Come over to the portacabin for a few minutes. I'll answer your question and introduce you to the other newbies.'

With everyone assembled, Gill made introductions and placed the four new recruits into the three existing teams. Fiona was his solo professional help on this dig. As a friend, and a veteran of many *Mys.Scot* digs, he trusted her to be in day-to-day charge of the site. Under her, they'd recruited three volunteer team leaders who each had buckets of archaeological experience. Trudging in from their trenches to collect new team members, they found Gill responding to questions.

'Why's this graveyard all on its own?' asked Zack.

'We don't know exactly where it was, but many years ago, there used to be a church in this area,' said Gill. 'The centuries passed, and the church fell into ruin. We think its foundations are under one of the nearby houses.'

'So, they blitzed the church and kept the cemetery?' Zack pressed.

'Aye, because families were still using it.'

'Why would you bury bodies in this swamp?' moaned another of the newbies, a shortish, black-clad lass called Becka.

'It's not normally this bad. But the first two weeks of August were a deluge, and the ground is still saturated.'

'It's like the bloody Somme out there,' muttered Fiona.

'Part of the problem is that contractors removing the headstones churned the paths to mud,' Gill explained. 'All that coming and going with heavy equipment.'

'Are they the guys in the black vans?' asked Zack.

'No, they're a company called Lossuary. They're emptying the graves, then we're following after, making sure no archaeological details are missed.'

'You mean, we won't have to dig up any bodies?' asked Becka.

'No.'

Becka scowled from beneath a thick layer of black and white makeup. 'What, none at all?'

'This cemetery closed in 1867 because it was full,' said Gill. 'But the fact the local council prohibited more burials

32

didn't stop some families breaking in here at night and burying more bodies. That means we're discovering human bones in random places.'

Zack looked curious. 'Why would they do that?'

'The cost of using a regular graveyard for one, plus the desire to bury families together. Local estimates suggest the practice continued for sixty years. People would sneak in here in the middle of the night and bury deceased loved ones wherever they could find space.'

'You'd think the polis would have something to say about that,' said Zack.

'It was a different day. And listen, guys. If you find any bones, or anything you think might be bones, just pop in a red flag and move on. Lossuary will deal with all that stuff.'

Becka folded her arms. 'If we're not digging up bones, what then?'

Gill moved to the map behind him and traced the outline of the old cemetery. 'Aside from being somewhere to bury the dead, this was a public space in a densely populated community. People will have dropped things and buried little mementoes. Our job is to find and record as much as we can before this area is handed over for redevelopment in three weeks' time.'

'Can we keep anything we find?'

Gill studied Becka's face and realised she hadn't read a word of the briefing material he'd sent the volunteers. Biting his lower lip in frustration he resolved to keep warmth in his face. 'Tell you what, folks. Why don't I go over the basics one more time.'

By late morning, the new volunteers had bedded in and were making themselves useful. After a tea break, Gill walked them the short distance to the old lifeboat station where a

33

charitable trust had donated its lovely stone building as a place where the team could clean and store anything they found. Back on the site a few minutes later, he darted between the teams, recording small finds and liaising with Lossuary as they laboured to collect a conundrum of human bones scattered across the site. As busy as he was, he was struggling to get satisfaction from his work. There was no great mystery to be solved here, nor any likelihood of any unique or challenging finds. Instead, he was doing bread-and-butter archaeology – reading the land before the topsoil was scraped away and the site disappeared under concrete. It would merit four pages towards the back of issue sixty-three, but apart from that, the whole exercise was an act of service to the city that hosted his magazine.

At lunchtime, his wife, Salina, walked with their toddler, Josh, along the stone-paved esplanade between their home and the dig site. Receiving their delivery of coffee and fresh sandwiches, he kissed them and found them seats in a respite area served by two wooden benches. Gill cracked open his sandwiches and was soon sharing them with Josh.

'Any sign of it drying out?' asked Salina, nodding towards the maze of boardwalks and diggings.

'A bit. But once you get below a metre, the water just pools. We'll need a pump next week if it doesn't improve.'

'Any sign of anything interesting?'

'Oh, it's all interesting, Sal, but just routine. We're accumulating coinage from every era of the last four hundred years and keepsakes galore. Lots of wee things squirrelled away in a few inches of soil.'

'Like what?' she asked, while chewing.

'Toys, trinkets, rings; a veritable jumble-sale of people's memories.'

'Who's that guy over there?' asked Salina. 'Is he one of your volunteers?'

Gill turned to look in the direction she was indicating where a very old man, in a coal-black suit, was making his way unsteadily among the workings. Gill groaned. 'He's taking advantage of the open gate and just wandering in. He'll be one of the locals who's come to see how we're getting on.'

Salina stared at the man and winced. 'He's pretty frail, Gill. You'll need to catch him before he takes a tumble.'

Irritated by his interrupted lunch, Gill pocketed his sandwich before kissing them both. 'I'll be home as soon as I can. And definitely before Josh's bedtime.' Then, reluctantly, he jogged after the new arrival.

'Hey,' said Gill, catching up with the slowly moving man. 'Can I help you with anything?'

The man hefted his stick and pointed towards the entrance. 'I've just seen the notices,' he said, shakily. 'About the demolition.'

Gill prepared himself for a shower of indignation. 'The notices have been up for quite a while, sir. I don't know if you're aware, but the council is redeveloping this area.'

The man's nod shook his whole upper body. 'I know. Nothing stays the same. I was … I was …'

Gill waited patiently for him to finish.

'I was just hoping I'd have a chance to say goodbye.'

'You knew someone buried here?'

'Yes.'

'Ah, well I might be able to help with that. The council has organised for all the marked graves to be emptied. The remains have been removed to a store and the council has invited interested parties to liaise with them regarding reinterment.'

The man's paper-thin mouth twisted into a smile. 'That'll be no help to Archie, I'm afraid.'

Gill caught the man's drift. 'Is his resting place unmarked?'

The man gave a little cough and gently shook his head. 'Oh, the times my parents made me swear I'd never admit to that.'

Gill caught the whiff of a family tragedy. 'That doesn't matter now. If you know his approximate location, we might still be able to help.'

The old man studied Gill with watery blue eyes. 'But the stones … they've all gone.'

'I have detailed photos taken before the demolition team came in,' said Gill. 'If you'd like to join me in the portacabin, I'll see what I can do.'

The walk across the uneven boards took three times longer than Gill could have managed on his own but it gave the man, William Ross, time to share his story.

'My family were shipbuilders. Small things, really. Herring drifters and the like, but the Second World War hastened the end of that when fish stocks collapsed. By the time my father was conscripted to fight in Europe, we'd become extremely poor. Not that I was aware of all that as I was only six years old in 1941.' The old man produced a mischievous smile. 'There were no men around. They were either away fighting Hitler or at the fishing, so my twin brother Archie and I, plus the other lads from the street could do what we liked. One morning, I'll always remember it was the fifth of May, the day before our birthday.' He paused to wave vaguely at the sea. 'A mine washed up on the gravelled beach near the old lifeboat shed. Do you know it?'

'I do,' said Gill. 'These days I live around there.'

'Well, this great metal hedgehog was rolling about in shallow water, and some lads were throwing stones at it. Trying to make it explode I suppose. It was madness; we didn't know the power of the thing. A young police officer arrived and shooed us away.' William paused to remember.

'Robert Stirrat his name was. I knew him of course. A local fella. He was just twenty-four.'

'What happened?' asked Gill.

'He chased us off the beach, but we were wee hooligans and only ran as far as the lifeboat shed.'

'Nobody can blame you for that.'

'Stirrat was trying to get a rope on the thing. You know, make sure it didn't drift back out into the Tay and become a hazard to shipping. But something went wrong, and it went off. We were watching when it happened.' The old man shuddered. 'When the spray and steam blew away, Stirrat was just a heap of rags, lying on the beach. I turned to look for Archie and found him sprawled on the ground beside me.'

'He'd been hit?' asked Gill.

'A chance piece of shrapnel struck him on the chest.'

'I'm so sorry.'

'My mother couldn't afford a proper burial, so in the middle of the night, she left me with an aunt and carried his body to this graveyard.'

Gill left a slight pause to dignify the man's memories, then presented William with his laptop. While they tabbed through the images together, Gill waited until his new friend found what he was looking for.

'Grave 68,' murmured Gill, making a note. 'It was a fine box grave under a table-stone so I'm certain the covering will have been persevered.' He pointed at the photo. 'Do you recall where exactly your brother was buried?'

William shook his head. 'Mother always said that if I sat on the table-stone and looked east, he wasn't far away.'

'Okay then. If you can leave me your details, I'll make some enquiries and get back to you.'

Gill peered over Pete Gibson's shoulder. They were looking at an ancient hand-drawn map of the cemetery to which someone in more contemporary times had added an index. 'Number 68,' said Pete, stabbing at the drawing with his forefinger. 'That was the crypt for the Ross family until 1860.'

Gill looked up from the printed sheet and tried to relate it to the desecrated mud bath he could see in front of him. 'Sorry, Pete. Can you walk me to the spot?'

'It changes how you feel,' said Pete, bursting with enthusiasm. 'When you start looking for a named person, a cherished individual, in amongst all this history.'

'Up until this morning, this was just another job,' said Gill while they walked. 'Some ancient bones and a few trinkets scattered around. Then some old boy comes looking for his brother and you're reminded of all the love for the people buried here.'

'If we'd infinite space, we'd never disturb them, Gill. But this is a city now and cities need land.'

Gill concurred but said nothing.

'This is the one,' said Pete, touching the edge of a rectangular stone box. 'The contractors removed the tabletop stone for safekeeping.'

'Any idea why they've left this monument standing when most of the others have been felled?'

Pete pointed inside where there was an eight-foot drop to the bare earth. 'This one runs deeper than a wisdom tooth. Our job was to ensure we had all the bones. It's been left for the developer to sweep away when they level the site.'

Gill peered inside and studied the four sides of the grave disappearing into the earth. 'How deep would you normally expect these things to be?'

'The same amount of stone below ground and as above. Someone really went to town on this one.'

'And did you discover human remains?'

'Aye. Fragments within the burial chamber consistent with the names and dates on the gravestone.'

'What about outside the grave? Anything that might equate to the young Archie Ross?'

Pete shook his head. 'Nothing as recent as mid-twentieth century.'

Gill leaned against the stone box and looked east, sweeping his hand over an area a few metres square. 'He'll be out here somewhere.'

'This immediate area looks undisturbed, Gill. You might want to get your team to look closer at this ground.'

'Aye,' said Gill, knowing his teams were meant to be working systematically as new sections were released to them. However, the higgldy-piggidly quilt of old graves meant he couldn't be certain every space was being covered. 'I'm gonna get them to swing back here with radar.'

Pete glanced at his watch. 'And if you find young Mr Ross, it will be our pleasure to recover him.'

After Pete excused himself and squelched off to another part of the cemetery, Gill lingered, turning again to peer into the cramped space within the old box grave. His first theory was that a novice stone mason had gone overboard in building this crypt. He'd seen that a lot in his time, where right up to the Victorian era, builders had over-engineered their projects simply because they didn't know the true strength or durability of their materials. But looking at the smooth edges of the stones, running straight and true, deep into the earth, the construction of this grave didn't look like a rookie error. This architecture was intentional, with a double layer of sandstone slabs lining the upright portions of the box grave. He was curious, and his instinct was flaring. He cast an eye around for Aura but saw and heard nothing. But this was already a done deal - he was going to dig deeper and all he needed were a couple of willing volunteers to help him.

Chapter 6

You getting anywhere with the Brodie's Close CCTV?' asked Wiley passing Lillico's desk on his way back from lunch.

'Been reviewing your notes, boss, which are mediocre as usual. For example, I can't see where you accounted for all of Sinclair's keys?'

'The deeds to the property record two original keys in existence,' said Wiley, defensively. 'Sinclair had one on him when he died, and his girlfriend had the second. Meaning the murderer had access to a third key or managed to create a counterfeit.'

'No other routes in? Windows? Backdoors?'

'None, unless the assailant got in using other means.' Wiley drifted back towards Lillico's desk and started fiddling with a desk lamp. 'We need to discover how the killer entered Sinclair's flat. It'll either be a mundane explanation, or technological. But it could even be … supernatural. I mean, maybe we should be looking at *Lady K* for this one?'

'I believe she's on the straight and narrow, boss.'

'Oh, I forgot you took a shine to her.' Wiley flashed a rare, yellow-toothed smile. 'Well, sorry to disappoint you, because she was arrested this morning.'

Lillico felt a jolt of alarm. 'Seriously? Why?'

'New evidence concerning the death of Malkie Bell. The arresting officer called me this morning asking for background on her.'

Lillico nodded urgently while he processed this information. Then, holding up a finger asking Wiley to wait, he dived into his digital diary. 'Whether she had anything to do with Bell's death or not, I'm confident she didn't kill Sinclair.'

'How can you be sure?'

Lillico pointed at his diary. 'She was still in Stirling Prison the day Sinclair died. She was released two days later.'

Wiley scowled. 'I don't think we can be one hundred per cent certain. Especially with someone capable of all that walking-through-walls shit. So, I want you to talk to her professionally. Can you do that?'

'Of course, sir,' said Lillico, grasping the opportunity to go to Lorna's aid. 'Are you coming?'

Wiley shook his head. 'All the way to Aberdeen and back? I'm way too busy for that.'

'Anything you want to talk about?'

'Not yet,' Wiley snapped, walking away. 'When I'm ready to include you, I'll send you more of my mediocre notes.'

Lillico bit back a smile, then checked where Lorna was being held before packing up his laptop. It was unlikely he'd be back in the office that day and he was almost ready to leave when his phone rang.

Adina dialled the familiar number from memory and moved to a window where blinds gave her cover to watch Newbattle Terrace below. The phone answered quickly. 'DI Lillico.'

'Alex, it's Adina.'

'Hi there.'

'Where are you, Alex?'

'At my desk in Bathgate. What's up?'

'I'm being watched and I'm wondering if you know anything about it?'

'You think it's police surveillance?'

'Unless there's a local mafia group fitting their guys in cheap suits and boring saloon cars, then yes, I'd say police.'

'Hang on a second. Let me plug my laptop back in and I'll check the logs.'

She waited for Lillico to do whatever it was he was doing and realised she was holding her breath.

'Nothing on the system. How long have they been there?'

'The first car started shadowing me while I walked home for lunch. The second pulled up outside my house not long after I got home. There's one out front and the second out back.'

'You're certain this isn't some kind of criminal enterprise? Or action by a foreign secret service?'

'Trust me, Alex. They'd show a little more cunning.'

'Do you need me to come over? I can be there in half an hour.'

'No thanks. Just checking if you knew anything about it.'

'What are you going to do?'

'Not sure. I'll probably choose something tried and tested from my espionage handbook.'

'While we're chatting, have you heard anything from Lorna?'

'Nothing. You?'

'Just heard she's been arrested.'

'What? Why?'

'I'm off to find out.' Lillico paused. 'Before I go, is there anything else I can do to help you?'

'Make a note to phone me later,' she murmured. 'Check I haven't been murdered.'

'Are you serious?'

She laughed. 'No. If their surveillance is anything to go by, these men aren't a threat.'

'Okay, Adina. Take care.'

'You too. Be safe.'

Adina hung up. Heaving a sigh, she walked through to the kitchen while she considered how to proceed. What did her training say about your cover being blown? Act normal. As normal as you can until nothing you do can sustain your false identity. She felt a rush of anxiety. Her disguises hadn't saved her in Tehran, and now the horror of those three months rushed back at her. The beatings, the mock executions, and the bizarre experience of a good-looking man in a white open-necked shirt, walking in one day and informing her it had all been a misunderstanding. "You are free to go. Have a nice day."

But this was Britain! This was Scotland for pity's sake; that kind of stuff wouldn't happen here. She flicked the kettle on and forced her body to relax. She'd make tea, then she'd take hot drinks and biscuits to her watchers. See if a little mild-mannered generosity could reveal the reason for their scrutiny.

The drive from Bathgate to Kittybrewster police station in Aberdeen took Lillico three hours. He presented his warrant card to the desk sergeant and waited to be signed in.

'Who're you wanting to see, detective?' asked the sergeant, without looking up.

'Lorna Cheyne. I believe she was brought in this morning.'

'DI Lundy's case,' the man drawled. 'Did you want me to give him a bell?'

'No. This is a separate enquiry.'

'Oh aye. Can you give me the case number, so I keep the records tickety boo?'

Lillico obliged. 'It concerns an assault against Miss Cheyne seven weeks ago. I was the attending officer, so I wanted to update her on that case.'

The man finally looked up. 'You came three hours from Bathgate to do that?'

'I've got other business in the area.'

'Okay, grab a seat, detective and I'll have her brought up to an interview room.'

Lillico helped himself to coffee from a machine, then settled in the reception area, until he was called.

Lorna looked strained as she sat across from him. Her lovely blonde hair still curled around her face, though it needed a wash, and her pale blue eyes cast down rather than meeting his gaze. He fought back his attraction towards her and resisted taking her hand across the table. He'd a role to fulfil here; a game to play, and he had to fight to keep his face dispassionate.

Lillico laid his phone close to his body, then turned the screen to face her. 'Miss Cheyne, I was in the area and wanted to update you on the assault case you brought against Billy Whyte.'

Lorna blinked at him. 'Aren't you here to talk about this ridiculous …'

'I'm not here to talk about your current case,' he interrupted, silently tapping the table beside his phone screen. 'That's none of my concern. I simply wanted to inform you, Mister Whyte made a full confession and has begun a two-year sentence in Barlinnie jail.'

Lorna's eyes found his phone screen, then flashed up to his face. Then she glanced around her, perhaps aware of the CCTV cameras for the first time. 'I see. That's good, isn't it? Saves a court case.'

'Indeed. And now Whyte is in prison where he belongs.'

'Dangerous places, prisons,' said Lorna, cooly.

'I suppose you would know,' said Lillico before standing up. 'Thank you for seeing me, and as the saying goes, I'll see you around.'

Lorna nodded sadly and kept watching Lillico while he left the room.

Thanking the sergeant, Lillico returned to his car and drove one hour south to the village of Stonehaven. Leaving the main road, he parked up, and with hands in pockets, he ambled down to Dunnottar Castle. Stepping into a verdant gulley, he leaned into the climb that would take him into the heart of the derelict, though still formidable, fortress. Wandering amongst the ruins, he found a quiet spot where he wasn't observed. Then he waited to see if Lorna had read the full text on his phone screen.

Two minutes ahead of schedule, Lorna appeared, jumping to within inches of his face. It was still a surprise even though he was expecting her, and as soon as she appeared, they threw their arms around each other's shoulders in a ferocious hug.

'What have they got on you?' whispered Lillico.

'I've been charged with manslaughter.' Lorna pressed her forehead against his neck. 'They say an eyewitness came forward claiming I killed Malkie Bell.'

'That's a suspicious development after two years.'

'DI Lundy says they made house-to-house enquiries after new DNA evidence was discovered. How's that even possible, Alex?'

'They'll have taken a DNA sample from you in prison. And they'll have samples from Malkie Bell's body when it came ashore at Cruden Bay. The system is always looking to match these kinds of data, but like any government computer, things often run slowly.'

Lorna clutched him even tighter. 'I see.'

'This new eyewitness; did you see anyone else on the cliffs that day?'

'No one.'

'Maybe someone with binoculars, watching you from a window?'

'I'm always careful before I make a jump. The clifftop wasn't visible from the nearest houses.'

'Okay, so any witness statement could be challenged by a competent lawyer,' said Lillico, pushing her far enough away he could look into her eyes. 'But this DNA evidence is more worrying. I've got to ask, why would your DNA be on Bell?'

'We tussled,' confessed Lorna.

Lillico felt a flicker of uncertainty about what might have happened that day. 'Tussled?'

'He went for me and then he fell. In fact, we fell off a cliff together, but I was able to jump away.'

'You're sure Bell's death was an accident?'

Lorna released him and took a step backwards. 'Alex, please! The only reason I was there was to rescue Katie.'

'I believe you, but I had to ask.' Lillico winced when he saw heat in her eyes. 'When this goes to court, we can't reveal your gift. What about your friend, Katie? Did she see what happened?'

Lorna turned her head from side to side. 'I don't think Katie knows what she saw that day. She was cold and still recovering from whatever Bell used to anesthetise her.'

'Does she know about your gift?'

Lorna thrust her shoulders forward. 'Yes, Alex! My best friend knows about my gift.'

He could see he'd upset her, and now it was time to ask a tough question. 'While we're talking, can I ask you about another of your old … clients? A guy called Harry Sinclair.'

'What about him?'

'He's dead, murdered a few weeks ago.' Lillico stepped closer so he could study her reaction. 'As your friend … and as a police officer, I'm asking if you know anything about that?'

Lorna's eyes darted up and left, then back to his face. 'Haven't heard his name in years, but no, I didn't kill him, if that's what you're asking.'

'Thank you. And no offence. It's just …'

'This is Canmore's doing. We know he's coming after us, and he's trying to send me back to prison.'

Lillico gave an anxious nod and glanced down at his feet. 'What, Alex? What's wrong?'

'Adina is being followed. Strangers parked up, watching her house.'

'It's happening, Alex. Adina, me, and that man Macfarlane who's trying to get you fired.'

'I disobeyed his direct orders,' he replied. 'Then I destroyed evidence by disposing of the gun cache. Maybe I deserve to be fired.'

She squeezed his arm. 'We'll find a way through this.'

'Hope so.'

'I should go,' Lorna whispered, glancing around. 'If they check my cell, we could both get into trouble.'

She took a step away from him, but he caught her wrist. 'I believe you're a good person, Lorna. If this starts to look bad for you, you could always flee. Jump somewhere far away.'

'Might come to that. In the meantime, maybe it helps us if Canmore's people think they've taken me out of play.'

'How can I stay in touch with you?'

Lorna thought for a moment. 'I know what the inside of your car looks like, assuming you haven't changed it.'

'I haven't.'

'Leave me notes in the glove compartment. I'll check in once a day around midnight when there's no risk of me being spotted.'

'Got it.'

Lorna nodded, and finally managing a strained smile, she leaned in and kissed his cheek. 'Have you asked her yet?'

'Been kinda busy …'

'Alex!'

'I hear you. Honestly, I do.'

Lorna squeezed his shoulder until suddenly she was gone.

Lillico took a deep breath and sat down on the stump of an old wall. He still had feelings for Lorna but now sensed she was gently pushing him away. And by nudging him about another relationship that deserved his attention, she was being a loyal friend. Spontaneously, he took out his phone and texted a different friend to ask if she was available at the weekend. With that done, another woman, one without romantic complications, sprang into his conscience. Immediately, he dialled her number.

'Adina. It's Alex. Where are you?'

'Back at the museum. You?'

'Just paying a visit to Lorna.'

'Is she okay?'

'Facing what look like trumped up charges relating to a death. How about you? Do you still have your shadows?'

'When I took them a pot of tea they immediately drove off.'

'Maybe they'd made an error? Mistaken identity or something.'

'Maybe. Still think they looked like cops. I've started wondering if they could be working for Canmore.'

'Okay. If you see them again, let me know before you engage them. And mention this to Douglas. If your watchers were MI5, he'll be able to find out.'

'Aye, aye, sir.'

Lillico laughed at her mockery and hung up.

Chapter 7

By 6 pm the sky had cleared, and the settling sun was ushering in a fine evening. Dashing back to the dig site after a hurried supper and a compressed version of his normal bedtime routine with Josh, Gill was just in time to say thanks and farewell to some volunteers.

'Don't get it,' said Zack. He and Becka had their jackets on and were heading home.

Gill stepped back into the two-foot-deep trench where they'd been digging all afternoon. 'Don't get what?'

'Why yous are in there diggin' when there ain't anything on the radar.' Zack swung his arms around the site. 'And there's like a million other places you could look.'

'Instinct,' said Gill, gently inserting his trowel to take another bite out of the earth.

'And what if that old geezer is mad? He's like a hundred, yeah?'

'Closer to ninety, but yes, he's old, as you'll be one day.' Gill paused to examine the earth in his trowel then quickly discarded it. 'When you witness a violent death, the details stay with you.'

Zack folded his arms but said nothing.

Gill suddenly remembered Zack's father. 'I'm sorry. That was crass of me. I didn't mean …'

'I hear you, man.' Zack watched Gill examine another fistful of soil. 'You almost finished, yeah?'

51

Gill shook his head. 'I'm going to take the surrounding area down to the same level as inside the box grave.'

'If Zack and I stayed to help, might we find human bones?' asked Becka.

'There won't be much left of a six-year-old child from 1941, but we might find bone fragments.'

Becka yanked off her jacket and grinned at Zack. 'We'd better give you a hand then.'

The sun was low in the sky when Becka called Gill over. Brushing soil off the smooth oval dome in the ground, he looked up at her and grinned. 'Good instinct, Becka.'

'It's something then?'

'Ask yourself what made you stop and consider it.'

She shrugged. 'It looks different from anything else I've seen all day. The way it's so smooth.'

Gill tenderly patted the object. 'That's a skull fragment from a child. We'll need to confirm, but in all likelihood, this is Archie Ross.'

'That was part of a real human being?' Becka stared at the fragment. 'Now I see it, I'm not sure how I feel about that.'

Gill gave her an encouraging smile. 'If this is Archie, then you've just made his brother very happy.'

'Bloody hell,' she said, turning to call to Zack. 'We got him. Come and see!'

Zack held up a hand and stayed exactly where he was. 'Guys. I've got something too.'

Gill felt a twinge of curiosity. 'Bones?'

Zack turned and grinned. 'Nah, man. Way better than that.'

When Cassy stopped by Gill's desk at 8 am the following morning, she didn't bring coffee. Instead, she parked her tiny backside against his desk and stared off into the far distance. 'Just so I can be sure the wee fella has his story straight,' she began.

'Cass …'

Cassy hefted a forefinger. 'So, when he rolls in at half-ten, caked to his ears in mud and swinging on the arm of some Goth chick, I'd kinda like to know, were they with you?'

Gill thought for a moment. 'Yeah. We all bailed out at about nine thirty when Salina phoned and called me home. I think Zack and Becka went for chips.'

'Chips! They were high as kites. Couldn't smell booze on his breath so I guess he must have been vaping the strong stuff.'

Gill shrugged. 'The strongest thing they were drinking was teenage attraction, laced with full sugar Irn Bru. And I think it's nice Becka walked him home.'

Cassy clutched her fingers into fists. 'I don't think you're catching my parental concerns here.'

Gill bobbed his head and carried on typing. 'Your lad arrived home happy in the company of a girl he likes, and you what? Scolded him and sent him off for a cold bath?'

Cassy's eyes flicked up to the ceiling. 'Something like that.'

Gill winced. 'No wonder he didn't tell you then.'

'Tell me what?'

'Just before 9 pm, we made a find.'

'He said you were looking for a child. Gill, did you have my son handling a dead body?'

'We were looking for a kid, well, the bones of a kid. And when we found his remains, we left them in the earth for the experts to handle.' Gill paused his typing to look up. 'You remember old Pete Gibson?'

'The Merry Mortician? How could I forget him.'

'He's taking it from here and will have the remains at Lossuary by late morning. Once he's spoken to the lad's surviving brother, he will in all likelihood store the bones until the day when the two brothers can be interred together.'

Cassy folded her arms tightly across her chest. 'So, Zack and the Goth chick got high on finding some kid's bones?'

Gill shook his head and paused to dig something out of his pocket. 'No. The source of our excitement was this.'

Cassy took the small clear bag and examined the single, misshapen gold coin inside. 'What is it?'

'No idea. I'm waiting for Mhairi to arrive so we can find out.'

'Zack didn't mention this.'

Gill grunted. 'He probably took one look at your happy smiling face and decided he wouldn't tell you about his day.'

'I'll ask him about it later.'

'Do, because once you and I have signed off the final proofs for issue 62, I'm meeting him and Becka to look for more.'

'It's Scottish,' said Mhairi, pointing at a website later that morning. 'You'll need to show it to an expert, but I'd say it's a James VI Sword & Sceptre. And the date, 1601 is consistent with the age of the graveyard.'

Gill nodded. As his editorial assistant and someone with a clutch of history degrees, Mhairi was his go-to person whenever he faced a challenging research question. 'And the million-dollar question,' mused Gill. 'What was it doing under four feet of topsoil?'

'Really, Gill. There would have been tens of thousands of these in circulation. And the high value meant they were a reliable store of value so the wealthy class would have hoarded them.'

Gill picked up the bagged coin. 'In 1601, this was worth a year's labour to the average Scot, so losing one would really have hurt.'

Mhairi shrugged. 'Maybe someone buried it to repay a debt.'

'Well, that's the thing. Why was it so deep? At four feet, it clearly wasn't dropped by accident. And even if you were hiding this, you couldn't reach that depth without digging out a heap of topsoil.'

Mhairi passed the coin back to Gill. 'Without context, it'll be hard to make an educated guess.'

Gill nodded and took it back from her. 'I'm going back to Broughty Ferry shortly. I'll have another poke about.'

Chapter 8

Back in the *Tribune* building at 2 pm on that Friday afternoon, Freya tossed her bag on an empty desk and checked her emails. No apology from Houston, nor any communication to say he couldn't make their meeting. Scanning down the messages, the only urgent email was from Howard replying to her request for a quick meeting. She shrugged. Maybe Houston had found a better-known journalist to listen to his woes. In the meantime, she had other fish to fry.

'You look pissed off,' Howard said without looking up from his screen.

'Just wasted my lunch hour on a no-show.'

'You're an intern, Freya. You need to learn that no-shows are all part of the game.' He glanced up at her. 'You emailed me asking for a face-to-face. What's so urgent?'

'What do you know about waterhorses, Howard?'

'Scotland's favourite extinct animal since the bones of two specimens showed up on Orkney five years ago.'

'Actually, it was the Isle of Lewis.'

'Yeah, Lewis. Right.'

'And maybe they're not extinct after all.'

'Says who?' he asked, lazily.

Freya called up an image on her phone and spun it around so Howard could see. 'What do you reckon?'

He peered impatiently at her screen. 'Okay. Fuzzy image of a horse, running in the rain with a branch sticking out of its head.'

'There's more.' Freya tapped her screen, and three more images skipped past. 'Facebook is alive with this stuff.'

'Bloody AI hoaxes,' he muttered, turning back to his screen. 'The tabloids might be happy peddling this rubbish, but if you want to be a proper journalist, Freya, don't get distracted.'

Feeling rebuffed, Freya reminded herself why she believed this story had potential. 'There's a cluster of reports dotted across mid to north Lewis. Different people who don't seem in any way connected.'

'Someone will be orchestrating it.' He smiled darkly. 'Probably the local tourist board.'

'I still think …'

Howard snatched off his glasses. 'Look, Freya. Golden rule: if a story seems too good to be true, then it generally isn't true. If there's news here, then it stems from who's stage-managing this and why.'

'You think I should research a piece that discredits these sightings?'

'Ah, the penny drops,' Howard muttered.

'Can I have a week on Lewis researching it?'

Howard snorted. 'Absolutely not. If you insist on doing this piece, I can offer you two days to sit at home doing desk research.'

Freya's retort was crisper than she intended. 'You mean, scrape social media for rumour, and counter-speculation then conjure the resulting garbage into a story?'

'With the margins we're running on these days, that's the news business,' he retorted. 'Look, Freya, you're still new to all this. It was good instinct bringing this to my attention, but you're taking it too seriously. See it as an opportunity to write something tongue in cheek.'

Freya managed an ironic frown. 'Are there any particular aspects you want me to pursue, or are you going to save those insights until I've written my piece and you're wanting me to rewrite it for free?'

'Maybe they didn't teach you this at university, but I'd suggest you talk to anyone who claims to have seen one of these things, then find some way to discredit them. Track down the guys who found the original bones and see if they'll muster a little vitriol for the people who conjure this stuff.'

'Okay, brilliant,' she said, without really meaning it. 'I'll get on it. I'll have something for you by next Friday.'

'For Wednesday please, Freya. This kind of light-hearted material is useful for padding out the midweek editions.'

Four hours later, Freya left the office and dropped down to St Vincent Street, walking west for fifteen minutes until she arrived outside the Finnieston backpacker's hostel.

'I'm looking for Ailsa McIver,' she announced at the reception desk.

The woman, like Freya, was in her late twenties. She had long untamed auburn hair and the densest crop of freckles Freya had ever seen. 'That's me. How can I help?'

'My name's Freya Swanson. I work for the *Glasgow Tribune* and I'm doing a piece on waterhorses.'

'Uh, huh,' said Ailsa, looking down at her screen.

'Obviously, I've researched the National Museum exhibit and I'm aware you were part of the team that discovered the bones.'

Ailsa tapped at her computer and avoided Freya's gaze. 'Gill McArdle, the archaeologist who dug up the bones, was staying at my gran's guest house. I think that makes my involvement quite tenuous.'

'Nevertheless, you are amongst the names credited with the find.'

Ailsa seemed to be suppressing a smile. 'Gill was being generous. Have you spoken to him?'

'Left a couple of messages for him this afternoon, but the girl I spoke to says he's out on a dig so it might be a few weeks before he gets back to me.'

'Or the others?'

'Again, I left messages for Rani Kumar without any response. And I wasn't able to find contact details for Cormac McKellar.'

'Cormac lives off-grid,' said Ailsa.

Freya nodded. 'No address for him, or phone number, email nor any social media profile.'

Ailsa laughed spontaneously, before looking up and studying Freya with pale grey eyes. 'Which is why you've come to chat to me.'

'Bingo,' said Freya.

'Well, ask away, as long as you don't mind me breaking off to do check-ins. We'll be quite busy over the next hour.'

'Thank you,' said Freya, mustering her thoughts. 'I've read the online material, so I've grasped the facts about the day the bones were discovered. I only really have one question.'

'Go ahead and ask it.'

Freya took a deep breath. 'Do you think it's possible waterhorses might still exist?'

Ailsa's face didn't flinch. 'Do you?'

Freya shrugged. 'I think, given their size and unique appearance, they'd hardly be a secret.'

'Sounds logical.'

'And given there hasn't been a confirmed sighting of one in living memory, they've probably been extinct for thousands of years.'

'Which is what the scientists agreed,' said Ailsa.

'Meaning, if anyone saw one, that would probably be wishful thinking?'

Ailsa scrunched up her nose. 'Couldn't they exist and not look like waterhorses?'

'I assume you're alluding to the speculation about waterhorses emerging spontaneously from the local wild horses?'

'Not sure about the science behind it all, but yeah, something like that.'

'The reading I've done suggests that theory doesn't withstand scientific scrutiny.'

Ailsa looked up and waved at two lads walking through the foyer and making their way towards the dorms. 'Not sure why we're having this conversation. It sounds like you've already made up your mind.'

'I want them to exist,' rushed Freya, eager to keep Ailsa talking. 'Somehow, they'd make Scotland a more colourful place.'

Ailsa smiled, dryly. 'But the science says they're gone, so who are we to argue?'

'Thing is, there's been a bunch of reports this month about waterhorse sightings on Lewis.'

'Oh, aye.'

'And if I was a proper journalist, my boss would throw me an expenses budget and send me off to investigate.' She laughed, nervously. 'Instead, I've got two days to do it from a desk. Then I discovered, one of the first witnesses to the waterhorse bones was working less than a mile away and I'd be fascinated to hear your thoughts.'

Ailsa chewed on her response for a moment. 'If an example of those wonderful animals is alive on Lewis, maybe it exists for a reason?'

'I'm not sure what you mean. But their continuing existence would be incredibly exciting.'

Ailsa looked down at her hands. 'That's probably an understatement.'

Freya went to press her point, but suddenly Ailsa's eyes filled with alarm. She staggered and gripped the counter, looking like she might slide to the ground. Instinctively, Freya grabbed her arm and steered her to some nearby soft seating. The shock in the woman's eyes receded, even while she continued to clutch Freya's hand. 'Are you alright?' Freya asked. 'What's happening?'

Ailsa lifted one hand and waved the question away. 'I have this … condition,' she said with an embarrassed smile. 'It kinda hits me in moments of stress.'

Freya squeezed her hand. 'I am so, so sorry. Have I upset you by coming?'

'No, it's alright.'

'Can I get you some water? Do you need medication?'

'No, it's passing, but thank you.'

'Again, I'm really sorry. I'm going to go now.' Freya sat back, but Ailsa kept a grip on her hand. Freya stiffened, finding the gesture strangely intimate, while Ailsa's eyes seemed to probe her. Finally, Ailsa released her. 'If you're curious about waterhorses, then I want to give you a tip.'

'Okay.'

'The *Treaty of Finlaggan*.'

'What's that?'

'It's obscure, but you'll find it on the internet.'

Freya gave her head an involuntary shake. 'What will I do when I find it?'

'I'm not sure.' Ailsa slumped back against the cushions and drew a hand over her eyes. 'But you're the journalist, so why don't you follow your nose.'

When Freya finally left, Ailsa lingered on the sofa. Her head was clearing and now she began to wonder if she'd done the right thing. Mentioning Finlaggan was a risk, because, if this girl dived into it, the treaty could become public knowledge. The government could then act to remove it from the statute books. Biting her lip, she fretted over this for a few seconds until she was distracted by the sound of a newspaper opening and closing beside her. She turned to find Freya's empty seat now filled by a large man dressed in an open-necked shirt and the classy chinos of an Italian tourist.

'You look smart,' she observed. 'Are those Ray-bans?'

Raphael gave her a shallow shrug while he continued to read. 'Maybe. I'm just trying to blend in.'

Ailsa pushed her head back on the soft cushion. 'It's Glasgow, pal. Frankly, I think you're overdoing it.'

He smiled and his voice rumbled with amusement. 'Are you mocking me, Ailsa?'

'Never,' she said, quietly. 'It's my way of showing I like having you around.'

He smiled and turned the page.

'Is that today's paper?'

'Tomorrow's,' he replied. 'It's fluid with so much still to be decided.'

'Did I do the right thing telling Freya about the treaty?'

Raphael smiled without looking at her. 'That will depend on what she does with the information.'

'My instinct …'

'I don't want you to be scared,' said Raphael, abruptly folding the newspaper and laying it on his lap. 'When news comes from home, I want you to trust Aura.'

'What news?'

'Miss?' A voice came from behind Ailsa. She turned to find three backpackers queuing at the counter and peering at her. When she spun around to press Raphael, he was gone.

'Sorry, guys,' she said, rubbing her face. 'I'll be right with you.'

Chapter 9

Y ou've been even quieter than usual,' said Cassy. They were leaving Leuchars railway station where he'd met her off a train. 'Don't you love me anymore?'

Lillico caught the gentle mockery in her voice and laughed. 'Always love you, Cass. And my predictable defence is that I'm too busy for my own good.' He paused to make a safe turn into traffic towards St Andrews. 'Where would you like to go?'

'What are the options?'

'We could wander the old town and find a coffee shop. Or as it's a nice day we could walk on the beach.'

'I haven't been on West Sands for ages. Fancy it?'

Lillico nodded. 'Aye.'

They left his car near St Andrews Old Course and crossed the golf-links to reach a two-mile stretch of perfect sand. The tide was out and although there were a few swimmers, surfers and dog walkers, they knew this was a place they could talk in peace.

'Are you getting any sleep?' asked Cassy, as they started walking with their backs to the town.

'Not really. A bit, I mean, enough to get by.'

'Is this all because of the guy you shot?'

'That certainly isn't helping.'

'The way I heard the story, it was either him or you.'

'Gill shouldn't be gossiping about this.'

'It wasn't Gill,' said Cassy.

'Who then?'

'George Wiley.'

'Wiley phoned you?'

'Why would that surprise you?' she protested. 'In Wiley's eyes, you and I are halfway to being an item. And I can tell he's worried about you.'

'Worried?'

Cassy's shoulders dipped up and down. 'Well, he's worried to the extent you might go off the rails and that'll look bad on him.'

Lillico focused on the long-distance where a flock of small waders were skimming the waves in search of fresh hunting grounds. 'The shooter had hit another officer. He was about to finish the job when I intervened.'

'You saved the injured officer's life.'

'Let's hope my bosses agree. I've been summoned to a review tribunal in four weeks' time.'

'Is that serious?'

'Could be. In the heat of the moment, I was under pressure from two sets of orders. I had to pick one course of action and let's just say the Chief Super mightn't agree with me.'

'But you did the right thing.' She gave him a nudge. 'You always do the right thing.'

'It doesn't take away from the fact I ended a man's life.'

'I know. And you're right to face this. It's a trauma and you need to give yourself time to heal.'

Lillico grunted an acknowledgement but said nothing.

'Have you tried speaking to a counsellor?'

'No. It was barely a month ago and this is the first time I've spoken about it.'

'Huh, men,' Casy huffed.

'What?'

'You endure these toxic emotions and all you do is bottle them up.'

'I'm not a basket case, Cass.'

'No, you're not. But if you keep holding stuff in, you'll be in contention.'

'What would you have me do?'

'Just talk, Alex. Tell me what happened, blow by blow and I'll keep it a secret. At least this way, if you ever need to talk about it, you'll know I'll be there for you.'

'Will you?'

'Will I what?'

'Be there for me?'

'I'd like to be. Kinda been dealing with my own shit these last few years.'

'Because of Zack?'

'Partly. But you saw what state I was in after the incident on Ben Macdui. And watching my ex getting shot a few months later didn't help.'

'And did you talk about it?'

'Yes. I met a professional therapist regularly for a year.'

'Did that help?'

'Definitely, because she helped me see that none of what happened was my fault.'

'None of it?'

Cassy bit her lower lip. 'Okay, my son is a rascal because I didn't do a great job in his early years. And I chased his father away by constantly nipping the guy's head. But me getting abducted, and Jasper getting shot in a turf war; those weren't on me.'

'Tell me about those early years with Zack and Jasper.'

'Hang on a second, I'm meant to be sorting your head, not the other way around.'

'Lead by example. You go first, then I'll follow.'

So, for two miles, Cassy spoke about Zack's early days, and how her partner had gradually traded his career in hotel kitchens to become a low-level drug dealer. She wept freely as she recalled how Jasper had snatched her toddler away and her desperate search for them a decade later when she heard a rumour they'd moved to Glasgow.

When they were in sight of the Eden Mill building, they turned, and Lillico surprised himself by revealing to Cassy the long version of everything that had happened in Wigtown. He spoke about his guilt about shooting a man called Joey, and how the moment had troubled him ever since.

'You're so very pure,' Cassy observed. 'Most people I know would give that story a completely different spin.'

'How so?'

'Affirming themselves as the hero. Absolved of any wrongdoing because they were saving someone's life. You're honest to a fault and never bend the rules.'

'Yeah, well, you can blame my dad for that.'

'Was he a stickler for right and wrong?'

'He was a police officer. A detective inspector, like me.'

'You're a chip off the old block?'

'Not really.'

'What does that mean?'

Lillico studied their footprints in the sand as they retraced their steps back towards St Andrews. 'I adored my father when I was a kid. Wanted to be like him in every way. Grow up to be a big, tough cop like the ones on TV. Be just like him and put bad guys in prison.'

'Idealistic.'

'When I was seven, I overheard my father in our kitchen, arguing with his detective sergeant. They didn't think there was anyone else in the house and were yelling back and forth about a man they'd killed.'

'In the line of duty?'

Lillico shook his head. 'A domestic violence case. They'd been unable to secure a conviction, and when the guy was released, he came after them to gloat. There was an argument, a scuffle, and in a rage, my father killed him. It wasn't premeditated and the only witness was his partner who initially agreed to cover it up. The day I overheard them arguing, it sounded like the partner had a change of heart and my father was getting angry.'

'What did you do?'

Lillico winced and clenched his fists. 'I dialled 999 to report one murder and express my fear there'd be another.'

'Oh, Alex. What happened?'

'An armed response team stormed the house. My father was arrested, and based on his partner's testimony, he went to prison. He took his own life a few years later.'

Cassy took his hand and gripped it.

'When I joined the force, I looked up the guy dad had killed and discovered he was a right scumbag. My dad was a good police officer. Sure, he wasn't perfect, but because I'm obsessed with truth, he's not around anymore.'

'Alex, that wasn't your fault. How would you have lived with yourself if your father had killed again? Especially if he'd murdered his partner.'

'That's a road we never travelled.'

They walked in silence for the last few hundred metres, before Cassy spoke again. 'Somehow, in your mind, are you equating the guy you shot in the line of duty with your father's murder of a suspect?'

Lillico crunched a shell under his shoe. 'I just … I just find myself wondering if I could have responded a different way.'

'It's a sensible question,' Cassy observed. 'But I think you already know the answer.'

They'd reached the place where a trail led through the dunes and back to the road. Cassy grasped his hand when he slid in the soft sand, then to his surprise, she held it tightly all the way back to his car.

Chapter 10

Gill began his Monday morning with a hasty trip to the office to see the first printed editions of *Mys.Scot* issue sixty-two. Then, after dealing with any urgent correspondence, he was back down to the dig site by mid-morning. He'd had the whole weekend to ponder what might be going on here and now with a head full of possibilities, it was time to test some theories.

Near to where he stood, a little flag marked the last resting place of Archie Ross, and another one nearby marked the location where Zack found the gold coin. Leaving the three main teams to continue working around the site, he'd selected two volunteers to continue excavating around the box grave, and now Zack and Becka stood on either side of him.

'Got to be careful here,' said Gill, tugging the sides of the old stone box. 'It looks solid just now, but the more soil we pull out from around the grave, the more likely one of these pieces will fall on us.'

'Just knock it down, man,' muttered Zack.

'That's what I'm thinking. Honestly, I don't know why the contractors left it standing.'

'Maybe we could prop it,' said Becka, pointing at the nearest sandstone slab. 'Then dig them out one at a time.'

'Yeah, I agree,' said Gill, glancing around for some suitable timber. 'Let's move slow and steady like we did last week.'

The three started to work on the narrow eastern elevation but after two hours they'd dug to one and a half metres depth and there was still no sign of the bottom.

'Oh, this is ridiculous,' moaned Gill. 'This thing has deeper foundations than your average mansion. What on earth were they thinking?'

Zack stopped to peer over the lip of the sandstone. 'If we cannae bash it, can we excavate the inside? See how deep it goes.'

Gill thought about this for a second. 'We could brace the top surfaces, so it doesn't collapse inwards. How deep is it just now?'

Zack squinted at Gill. 'Couple of metres? I dunno.'

Gill clambered up so he could take the measurement himself. 'About the same as the external pit we've dug, meaning we're below the level of any human remains.'

'I guess. You wantin' me to dig inside?'

Gill stared down into the cavity. 'Quite tight for a tall lad like you.'

Gill and Zack turned to face each other, then simultaneously, they both turned to look at Becka.

'What?' she protested.

At the same moment while Gill was persuading Becka to squeeze into the confined space of the box tomb on that Monday morning, Freya was working from the relative comfort of her kitchen table. Tapping away on her laptop, her shoulders sagged when she got a terse message to call her editor about the draft she'd written on her waterhorse story.

'You sent me a history lesson,' Howard said incredulously. 'I ask you to crash the rumours of a dangerous animal roaming Hebridean moors, and you send me a sodding history lesson?'

'Howard, there's a storyline here so hear me out,' she protested. 'Unicorns have always represented kingship on royal coats of arms since the eleventh century. Agreed?'

'Yes, Freya,' he drawled, sarcastically. 'I am aware that early Scottish kings used unicorns on their royal crests.'

'And in all their heraldry, two unicorns face each other, symbolising the powerful opposing forces of good and evil. Then, during his final surrender in 1493, John MacDonald, the last *Lord of the Isles* subverted this image.'

'You quote from the *Treaty of Finlaggan*,' muttered Howard. 'Never heard of it until today.'

'And that's because it was declared long ago as *Ergo Erratum*, meaning the treaty fails modern tests for rigour and enforceability.'

'Why would that be?'

'Because it mentions unicorns, Howard. Specifically, any unicorn found wandering around a place described as the *Temple of the Isles*.'

Howard's irritation was starting to ferment into anger. 'And where's that exactly.'

'The Isle of Lewis,' yelled Freya. 'The place with the blurry horse and a stick in its head. Now do you see where I'm going?'

Howard thought for a moment. 'But that would only be significant if the treaty was …'

'Still valid under Scottish law,' Freya finished. 'I've checked, and it is.'

Howard lowered his voice. 'Meaning what, exactly?'

'It's a cancellation clause in the treaty that brought the entire Western Isles into the Scottish kingdom. If those blurry photos I saw are genuine, and there really is a waterhorse walking around Lewis, then all he needs to do is take a walk around Callanish guided by this Laird of

Finlaggan. Then the Western Isles would become a separate nation again.'

'And who's this laird?'

'Dunno.'

'Can you find out?'

'Maybe, but I've already used the two days you gave me.'

Howard left a long pause. 'Take two more, Freya. I want to see where this goes.'

'You thinking of sending me to Lewis?'

'No chance,' he replied, before hanging up.

She smiled to herself. As a news story, this would probably go nowhere, but she'd baited her editor, and this was her the first tangible evidence she was developing a journalist's nose.

Almost immediately, her phone rang again, and she decided to play for advantage. 'Have you relented? Are you sending me to Lewis after all?'

By the way, the new caller cleared his throat, she realised it wasn't Howard. 'Am I speaking to Freya Swanson?' asked a smoky voice.

'You are. Who's calling, please?'

'I'm DCI George Wiley, and I need to ask you a question about a man who was recently found deceased.'

Freya's heart raced in a burst of panic. Her youngest brother had recently passed his driving test and was already notorious in the family as a fast driver. Dreading the answer she asked the officer, 'Who's died?'

'A man by the name of John Houston. At the time of his death, he was driving on the M8 towards Glasgow. According to his diary, he was on his way to attend an appointment with you. Looking at his phone records, I noticed he didn't make many calls. But he dialled your number on several occasions only three nights before his death.'

Freya swallowed. 'I see.'

'Can I ask what your business was with Mr Houston?'

Freya pondered how much she should tell this man. 'He wanted to talk to me about a potential news story. In effect, he wanted to become a whistleblower regarding misconduct within his organisation.'

'And by that, I assume you mean, the Scottish Geological Survey?'

'Yes.'

'What malpractice had he encountered?'

'Some kind of manipulation of a computer model. We didn't get the chance to talk about it. That was the reason for our proposed meeting.'

'I see.' Wiley paused. 'Miss Swanson, I think it would be worth us having a deeper chat. Would you be prepared to attend a voluntary interview at my offices in Bathgate?'

Freya was silent. She was working her first decent story at the *Tribune* and now she had this to contend with.

'Or I can nominate a Glasgow police station if that's more convenient?'

'Yes, please. I'm at work in the city centre and Stewart Street is just up from our building. Can we meet there? I'm back in the office on Wednesday.'

'Thank you. I'll see you there two days from now at 4 pm.'

Chapter 11

By Tuesday lunchtime, Gill decided to pause excavations inside the box grave and review his options. Zack and Becka had dug courageously to reach three metres depth. But now his young crew were clambering in and out of the confined space using an aluminium ladder, and consequently, he fretted about their safety.

'Too risky,' he said when they protested. 'If one of those stones is flawed, the whole thing could buckle and crush us like bugs. We need to abandon the inside for now and get back to excavating outside.'

'We can't be far from the bottom now,' Becka protested.

'We've been saying that for two days. You guys get back to digging the western elevation while I make some calls.'

'Pizza?' asked Zack.

'Reinforcements,' said Gill.

His first call was to the office. Leaving Cassy to man the phones, Craig, Larry and Mhairi agreed they'd be down to the Ferry dig site first thing the following morning. His second call was to Rosemary Soloman.

'Solie, what are you doing after work?'

At 6 pm, Gill sent everyone home. He texted Salina to say he'd be back shortly, then waited until an upright grey-haired figure appeared at the gate. He went to fetch his visitor before leading her to the box grave.

'Know a chap called William Ross?' he asked. 'He's a local pensioner.'

'Can't say I do,' said Solomon. 'What about him?'

'His brother died in a wartime accident and was buried near his family's ancestral grave.'

Soloman surveyed the old box grave from a distance, which now looked like a cross between an elevator shaft and a WWI trench. 'It appears he took some finding.'

'Yes, but we think we've got him. William wants to keep his brother's remains in store so that someday they can be buried together.'

'Aren't people strange,' said Solomon.

'I think it's sweet,' Gill retorted.

'Folk are so sentimental about human bones.' She turned to face Gill. 'When my time comes, incinerate me and dump my ashes in the Tay on an outgoing tide.'

Gill nodded soberly. 'You don't have a grain of sentimentality in your entire body, do you?'

Solomon shrugged. 'Why am I here, Gill? Or are you just sensing your fading mortality amidst all these graves?'

'We often talk about instinct,' said Gill. 'And right at the start of this adventure, you explained the instinct I experience around dig sites is actually Aura speaking to me.'

'You were a remarkably slow study,' said Solomon, 'But I recall those conversations.'

'Well, I'm wired, Solie. I've got so many uninvited thoughts in my brain this evening, I don't know what way is up.'

'Gill, you believe in an unseen God. In front of a competent court, you could probably be declared insane.'

Gill protested silently with a single outstretched hand.

'Show it to me,' Solomon demanded.

'Show you what?'

'Whatever it is you have in your waistcoat pocket.' She smiled as she caught surprise spilling across his face. 'Do you think I'm insightful? Whatever it is, you've been fiddling with it ever since I arrived.' She stretched out her hand. 'It's clearly on your mind.'

Gill slid the gold coin from its protective wrapper and passed it to her. Solie felt its weight for a few moments before pulling out her phone and studying it through the camera. Sliding it between her fingers, she seemed to enjoy the smooth texture before laying it on her palm and passing it back. 'A precious coin dated 1601. What do you say, Gill? Shall we play a little game?'

Gill's shoulders slumped. He'd no idea what Solomon was doing. He watched as she tapped away at her phone before dropping the device in her pocket.

'What did you just do?' asked Gill.

'The *Vigil* has a private message board. Members of the different groups post questions about issues they're facing in their lives. Others in the collective read the questions and try to hear Aura and how she might be responding. I think your coin will make a useful test of the group's competence.' She indicated she was going to walk around him. 'I'm going for a stroll. Back in a minute.'

Gill gave his head a little shake and returned to the portacabin to check the following day's volunteer rosters before locking up.

'Any good?' he called out as Solomon picked her way back across to his position.

'Thin pickings,' she said, flatly. 'I have two potential images for you to consider.'

'Go for it.'

'Two people reported seeing gold at the end of a rainbow.'

'Doesn't sound like Aura,' said Gill.

'On balance, maybe I shouldn't have included the image of the coin.' She scrolled on her phone. 'The second image is more intriguing. Three people reported the sensation of looking down a long chimney into the heart of a blazing fire. Does that mean anything to you?'

Gill wasn't finding this process particularly helpful. 'Unless someone's trying to tell me I'm at risk of going to hell, then not really.'

'Well, if anything else comes in I'll let you know.' Solomon hitched up her bag and prepared to walk away. 'Only three weeks until the Read.*Scot* conference. Have you read the latest version of my keynote speech?'

'Not yet.'

'Or drafted the vision document we talked about?'

Gill walked with her; his hands plunged deep in his pockets. 'I haven't.'

'Keep it simple,' said Solomon. 'Upbeat and future-focused.'

'Sure,' muttered Gill. 'In that case, I'll not mention the bit where I might tear up Scotland.'

'While we're chatting,' said Solomon, pausing at the half-closed gate. 'I'm worried about Charlie.'

'What about him?'

'Someone is pushing little packets of drugs into his letterbox every night. I suspect they're trying to lead him astray.'

Gill frowned. 'Charlie is solid, yeah? He wouldn't go back to all that?'

'Not willingly. But there's a danger here, Gill. He was so high for so long; his neural pathways are hardwired. He's already anxious about what's happening to Lillico, Lorna and Adina. I'm worried how he'll cope if Canmore ramps up the pressure on us.'

Gill considered this and found it hard to imagine anything would worry Charlie. 'Tell him, if he needs help, day or night, he just needs to call me.'

'Thank you, I will. And while our enemy sets traps for us all, have you seen any evidence of what he has in mind for you?'

Gill thought for a second. 'Not so far. You?'

'Canmore mentioned me by name during a parliamentary debate. Declared the Read*Scot* charity to be the finest third-sector organisation in the land, and one that is brilliantly led by yours truly, Rosemary Solomon.'

'He said that about you?'

'He did.'

Gill grunted. 'Thinks flattery will disarm you.'

'He's found my kryptonite, Gill. My utter lack of personal self-worth and how deeply I crave affirmation.'

Gill's eyes narrowed. 'Really?'

She swiped a hand at him and smiled. 'Of course not. But my point is, Gill. He's coming for us. You and I included.'

That night, Gill had a bad dream. The Armour Group were running through an old graveyard, ducking and diving for shelter while someone with a rifle took shots at them. And in the dream, while the perils escalated, he suddenly spotted his son, straying onto the battlefield. Desperate to save his child, Gill sprang after Josh, grappling for him before the boy tumbled into an open grave. Immediately, he was crawling after Josh along a tunnel made from seamless sheets of close-fitting sandstone. The gunshot danger outside was gone and now he faced a new heart-racing angst. The confined space was getting tighter, and he had the sensation he was deep underground. And no matter how fast he moved or how utterly he disregarded his personal safety, his little boy kept managing to stay beyond his reach. Left and right the tunnel twisted, illuminated by a faint orange glow that always seemed to be up ahead. When finally, the tunnel came to an end, Josh had disappeared and another stone sheet blocked Gill's progress. Suddenly panicked by his innate claustrophobia, he struck out at the obstruction, battering it with his fists until finally it gave way. Instantly, he had to cover his eyes when he realised he'd stumbled into a furnace. Expecting to be burnt to a crisp, he discovered the blazing furnace wasn't warm. He heard his son laughing, and forcing himself to look, he saw Josh inside, playing with the burning coals. And then Gill woke up.

The images were gone. Grappling for his phone, he found no alarming messages from the other armour bearers. Reconnecting to his senses, he took a deep breath and heard Josh's happy muttering from the baby monitor beside his bed. It was 6.30 am, time for Gill's shift. He swung his legs out from the sheets, and after he'd raised a prayer for his friends' safety, he suddenly realised what the dream meant.

Wednesday morning came in cooler as August began to feel the tug of autumn. Gill was on site early to supervise a scaffolding team who'd come to shore up the sandstone column. Shortly afterwards, his office crew arrived on schedule, and he was relieved to see they'd taken his advice and worn solid outdoor clothing. When he saw their faces, he knew he must have fire in his eyes. He let Zack introduce everyone to Becka, then he set out his plans for the day.

'Craig, you're with me,' he said, pointing at the open mouth of the box grave. 'We're in there, digging in shifts, until we hit bedrock.'

'Sure, boss. Diggin' halfway to hell in some old grave isn't creepy at all.'

'Larry, you're in charge of logistics. I need a mechanical earthmover here with an operator ASAP. Then, when you've got that sorted, I need a lighting rig, a water pump, and a generator. Oh, and we'll need a security team we can trust.'

'Security? Are you diggin' fae diamonds?'

'Tell the security guys to be on standby. If I'm right, we'll need them either later today or tomorrow.'

Mhairi stood with her thumb poised over her phone, ready to take notes. Gill moved closer and took her aside. 'Can we talk about the gold coin?'

'Of course.'

'I need you to go back to the office. Get on your computer and find me an explanation why there might be several hundred or even thousands of those coins buried below this grave.'

Mhairi stood open-mouthed. 'I don't understand. You haven't hit the bottom yet, so how could you possibly know that?'

Gill smiled. 'Maybe I'll be wrong, but I've got a really good feeling about this one.'

Chapter 12

I t's nice to have a bagman again,' said Wiley while he parked his car outside Glasgow's Stewart Street Police Station. 'Just like old times.'

Lillico accepted the implied instruction and grabbed Wiley's laptop bag from the back seat. 'Just for a couple of weeks, George. Then you'll be on your ownsome again.'

'Up and down the country, slaving away on my own,' Wiley continued, ignoring Lillico's pessimism. 'Just a hardworking Detective Chief Inspector, striving to solve the crimes our regular divisions won't touch with a barge pole.'

'And apart from the untimely demise of Harry Sinclair, what else were you working on?'

'It's top level, son.' Wiley gave one shake of his head. 'I could tell you, but then I'd have to …'

'Kill me?'

'Have you transferred to Fort William.'

'I like Fort William. It's got great views.'

'Views? When I worked in Fort William we thought sunshine was a conspiracy theory.'

'Okay, if you're still being so coy, can you at least tell me why we're in Glasgow?'

Wiley paused and seemed to choose his words carefully. 'Let's just say it's part of some ongoing investigations.'

'For Chief Super Macfarlane?'

'No. Come inside, and I'll explain who we're meeting and why.'

Sitting across from Freya Swanson half an hour later, Lillico studied her body language. She was a small woman, with straight, shoulder-length blonde hair, brown eyes and a slim, athletic build. He sat quietly while she explained her contract work for the *Glasgow Tribune*. In turn, Wiley reminded her this was an active case and that he'd not look kindly on any details appearing in the media. With that groundwork done, he asked her to recall her conversation with Houston.

'Let me recap,' said Wiley, a few minutes later. 'Mr Houston claimed someone was tampering with the software used to predict earth tremors in Scotland. And he didn't say who or why?'

Swanson's eyes darted between them. 'No, but looking back I think he was suspicious of the person who replaced him in the role.'

'He went on sick leave' Wiley said, looking at his notes. 'Then Agnes Fairbank stepped in. Who's she?'

'I've looked her up. She's a former head of the SGS. She'd resigned from the role following political fallout after the Great Glen Disaster.'

'Aye, they've had their share of scandal,' said Wiley, flashing Lillico a look. Investigating Fairbank would be on his follow-up list.

'Did he mention any worries he had, or reference someone who might try to hurt him?'

'It wasn't an intimate conversation, Chief Inspector. And he was entirely focused on the failure of his predictive software.'

'I see.'

'Can I ask how he died?' Swanson probed.

'We can't divulge …' Lillico began.

'Car accident,' said Wiley cutting across him. 'Crashed into the central reservation on the M8 after a mechanical malfunction.'

Lillico glared at his boss. 'Which is information being withheld from the public realm.'

She nodded. 'And of course, I'll respect that.'

'Phone records show Houston called you on a Tuesday evening, and yet your meeting with him wasn't set until the Friday,' said Wiley. 'What was the reason for the delay?'

'It was my next working day in Glasgow. I live up by Loch Lomond, you see, and I didn't want to spend a day travelling in and out of the city for what I believed was hysteria. When he didn't show up that day, I felt vindicated.'

'Has anyone else from the SGS reached out to you?'

'No.'

'Have you approached them or conducted any investigations of your own?'

'I haven't.'

'Why not?' Lillico asked. 'I'd have thought there's just enough intrigue in Houston's story to appeal to someone cutting their teeth in journalism.'

'I didn't think he was credible. Besides, I'm busy on another story.'

'What's that?' asked Wiley, fiddling with his pen as if it was an unlit cigarette.

Swanson turned to look at him. 'A light-hearted piece set in the Hebrides.'

Wiley nodded and passed her a business card. 'Thank you for your time, Miss Swanson. If you do recall any further details, please contact me on this number.'

When Lillico returned to the interview room from escorting Freya back to the reception area he found Wiley scowling at his phone. 'What's up, boss?'

Wiley dropped his phone on the table and used his left hand to stroke the skin above his receding hairline. 'That minging old bastard!'

'Which particular old bastard, boss?'

'Macfarlane. He's dumped us in a petty corruption case. And when I say, "dump" I mean he's literally just buried us under paperwork.' Wiley flexed and unflexed the fingers of his left hand. 'It's to be our top priority. All our other cases are to go on the back burner or be surrendered to other divisions.'

Lillico lifted his shoulders and dropped them. 'Petty corruption doesn't exactly reek of *Special Investigations*.'

'He's using the thin disguise of deploying us as impartial outsiders.'

Lillico picked up the discarded phone and after a nod from Wiley, scanned the contents of Macfarlane's email. 'Edinburgh City Council Procurement Division, and misuse of public funds.' He slid the phone back onto the table with a disgusted grunt. 'Am I going to spend my last two weeks as a police officer tracking down pilfered paperclips?'

'He's demanding a preliminary report the day before your dismissal hearing,' spat Wiley. 'It's an obvious ruse to keep us away from the things I've been working on.'

'And are you ever gonna tell me what you have been working on?'

'I took you to Brodie's Close, didn't I?'

'Yeah. That's a single murder investigation. I've seen you carry three separate investigations without oozing the kind of stress you were showing while I was in Wigtownshire.'

Wiley nodded. 'Yeah, well, Houston's death is just the latest in a string of things keeping me awake at night.'

'So, tell me about it! Let me help you, George.'

Wiley rubbed his fingertips together and studied Lillico's face with an intensity he'd never experienced before. 'Okay. Maybe it is time we talked. But not in here.'

'Why not here?'

'Never know who to trust,' Wiley grunted, pocketing his phone. 'Besides, after that little missive, I need a drink. Let's find a busy city centre bar where we can talk in peace. After that, you can drive me home.'

They left the station and crossed the main road into the theatre district. Wiley had a place in mind, so they walked across several city blocks to Hope Street and slid into a pub themed on an old-style bookstore. In the furthest recesses they found a booth with a horseshoe-shaped bench, then ordered drinks and talked quietly.

'Six months ago, I was handed a file on this man.' Wiley paused to call up the image of a tall, lean man with pushed-back dark hair and thick stubble masking his pointed chin. 'This is Robert Beggs, "Beggsy" to his associates. After Lillian Galloway went to prison, this is the lucky guy who inherited the smoking ruins of the Drumchapel crew.'

'What's he done?'

'Nothing criminal, so far. But he came to our attention after he'd been detected on CCTV testing the perimeters at a dozen sites in Scotland.'

'Places important enough to deploy facial recognition software?'

'Exactly. Food depots, fuel distribution hubs and most worryingly, the three main military sites in Scotland, housing some of Britain's biggest assets.'

Lillico snapped to attention, immediately recalling Roddy Canmore's USB stick passed to him by Lorna, via Adina. 'These sites, do you have a list?'

Wiley dug into the emails on his phone, and after a minute of huffing and muttering, he found what Lillico wanted to see. From what Lillico could recall of the locations mentioned in Canmore's files, there was extensive overlap.

'Did Beggs commit any crimes, or was this just surveillance?'

'Taking photos, Alex. Lots and lots of photos. And while that isn't illegal outside a big food depot in the Central Belt, it's certainly prohibited outside military bases.'

'Was he challenged?'

'Once, outside Faslane. The fella spent twenty minutes being entertained by Military Police while they deleted images from his camera.'

'Then they what, just let him go?'

'He claimed it was an innocent mistake, that he was bird watching.'

Lillico couldn't quite suppress a smile. 'Bird watchers get a tough rap in this country.'

'Aye, well, lingering near the UK's primary submarine base dressed in camo gear while clutching a long lens camera isn't a great look.'

'Can you speculate on Beggsy's intentions?'

'I couldn't at first. I mean, middle-aged men spot trains, so maybe they derive some perverse pleasure from watching submarines, or noting the numberplates of military lorries. But then I had another file passed to me. A lady in Whitburn saw some worrying correspondence on her grown-up son's computer. An email conversation discussing a plan to take control of a regional distribution hub a few miles from their house.'

Lillico nodded and wondered if he should have anticipated this moment. 'Then we had the Wigtownshire gun cache.'

'Exactly. Suddenly, a lot of random weirdness became more menacing the longer I looked at it. And at the end of all that, we had our little run-in with Macfarlane suggesting we're not all playing on the same team.' Wiley sat back a little and took a sip from his pint. 'The challenge ahead of us, Alex, is to figure out what's going on.'

Lillico glanced around to check they weren't being overheard. 'For once, George, I might be ahead of you.'

'What?'

'You're not going to like this one, boss.'

'Pity's sake, Lillico.'

Lillico took a deep breath, then spoke quietly. 'I've seen files suggesting our illustrious First Minister is planning a coup.'

Wiley just blinked at him. 'You're having me on, son.'

'Those sites Beggs was visiting are part of a longer list of facilities Canmore plans to control using an armed militia.'

'That's a weighty accusation, DI Lillico.' Wiley's face started to redden. 'How could you possibly know this?'

'I've got a source, and before you ask, I won't divulge their name. Suffice to say, it fits the behaviour you've observed, and I have files to prove it.'

'What kind of files?'

'Planning documents. Most likely early drafts for current events. They came to me on a USB stick stolen from Canmore's private vault.'

Wiley sat back and folded his arms. 'Is my imagination running away from me or am I detecting the stealthy footsteps of the amazing disappearing woman?'

'You can ask, boss, but I won't tell.'

'And was this USB stick ever entered into evidence?'

Lillico looked down at his hands. 'No. It's been circulating privately.'

Wiley erupted with an irritable snort. 'Meaning, it's inadmissible in court as the data therein could have been tampered with or forged.'

'I agree, and for what it's worth, I would have handled it differently. But it might explain the behaviour you've been investigating, and it points the finger at the man I believe is responsible.'

'Are you certain, Alex? I have to ask you, is there any chance you're being manipulated?' Wiley stroked the table. 'Consider who gave you this information. Who are they? What might they achieve by giving you this?'

'It came from someone I trust.'

'Cheyne?'

Lillico shook his head. 'Someone else who was keeping it for a rainy day.'

'Or maybe some enemy of our First Minister just concocted them?'

'I'll get you the files, boss. Let you make up your own mind.'

'And they're proof-positive that Canmore is planning an act of treason?'

Lillico shook his head. 'They're planning scenarios. What might happen if X does Y, and that kind of thing. Nowhere does he mention his name or the names of others in his inner circle.'

Wiley peered down into his glass for a long time before lifting it to his mouth and laying it down again without taking a sip. 'Damnit, Alex, what would he gain?'

'Control?' Lillico speculated.

'He's already First Minister. He's got control.'

'Okay, something else then. You mentioned you have concerns about Houston's death.'

Wiley stared down into his drink. 'Let's say for a moment, Canmore is buggering about with the SGS and finds a way to sabotage their predictive software. Then, when Houston threatens to uncover this malfeasance, Canmore has him killed.' Wiley finally took a sip, pausing to wipe beer foam from his ragged moustache. 'Even if that's what happened, I don't see how Canmore gains.'

Lillico nodded. He'd been having the same thoughts since Freya Swanson's interview. 'Earth tremors have become a regular thing since the Great Glen Disaster, and Houston told Swanson a bigger quake is likely. If that's true, I can't imagine any scenario where Canmore benefits by degrading Scotland's only predictive tool.'

'Do you have any ideas how we can take this forward?'

'I thought we'd been transferred to paperclip counting for Edinburgh Council?'

'I'm talking theoretically,' Wiley huffed. 'What would you do if we were still working this case?'

'I'd look closer at Beggsy and that young man in Whitburn. See who they're working for. Gather any evidence that conclusively links these actions back to Canmore.'

'Agreed. What else?'

'The plans on the data stick. I'd look for evidence they're reaching the implementation phase.'

'At the same time as running a petty corruption investigation throughout Edinburgh City Council? We're gonna be busy.'

'These might be my last days in Police Scotland, George, so I don't mind being busy.'

'Yeah. Sleeping is for wimps.'

'What about you? How do you want to move forward?'

Wiley looked worried. 'Canmore is almost untouchable. We'll have to be so careful. We'll need to look at every crime with fresh eyes. Every time someone steals a van, or beats up a geezer outside a pub, or breaks into a machinery yard, we'll have to map it all together and see if it ties to Canmore.'

'I agree, boss. But the complexity will be horrendous, so we'll need some help.'

'We could pull in Eliza to help us handle the data side of things. If you're certain we can trust her?'

Lillico drained the last of his diet cola. 'She's the best, George. Solid as a rock.'

Chapter 13

Freya left Stewart Street Station and wandered vaguely in the direction of the city centre. She needed to think, so rather than head back to the newspaper office with its endless noise and interruptions, she dropped down onto Sauchiehall Street and towards the Mitchell Library. Finding a quiet booth on the third floor, she fought to clear her brain. She had two major stories competing for her attention and she needed to figure out if either was a runner. Pulling out her notebook she started to create two lists. Firstly, Ailsa McIver and the waterhorses. What information could she glean on the *Treaty of Finlaggan*? What were the exact treaty conditions that could cleave the Western Isles away from Scotland? And finally, who was the laird with this potential power?

The second list felt more nebulous. Who was John Houston and what did he want? Was there any other data to corroborate his claim someone was sabotaging the SGS earthquake prediction software? Who would benefit if Houston turned up dead?

She sat staring at her notebook for a few moments. She'd never had a decent scoop during her short career, and now, she potentially had two. She rubbed her temples with her fingertips to dispel mental overload. What had her mentor said? Start with the easy stuff. Uncover the facts you can prove, then let them guide you. The Finlaggan Lairdship was considered a minor British title, so there were records for this kind of thing. She'd start there and see where it took her.

Two hours later, Howard's shoulders visibly drooped when she tapped on his door and walked in. 'I've got a parents' evening at the kids' school tonight, Freya. My wife was insistent, so whatever you've got will need to wait.'

'You asked me to check who holds the Lairdship of Finlaggan,' said Freya, taking a seat. 'And now I've got a name for you.'

Howard got to his feet and started to pack his bag. 'If you think you've time for a long drum roll, please, don't.'

'On the twenty-sixth of June this year, the title passed to a guy called Gill McArdle.'

'And who's he?' asked Howard, continuing to pack.

Freya pulled the "don't you know anything?" posture she'd perfected from the age of twelve. 'The very same archaeologist who found the waterhorse bones.'

Howard glanced at the ceiling. 'Sorry, Freya, long day. Join the dots for me.'

'We have an ancient treaty with enough legal clout to carve a chunk out of Scotland. To permit this, a certain laird needs to walk a full circle of Callanish riding the right type of horse.'

'Right type horse?' Howard grumbled.

'Yes. The same damn waterhorse you won't let me go to Lewis to investigate.'

'And the guy who discovered the waterhorse bones is now connected to the species by what? A five-hundred-year-old treaty?'

'Yes!'

Howard paused. 'Sounds like a set-up.'

'What?'

'Come on, Freya. A guy finds waterhorse bones, then five years later, he's suddenly the laird? Sounds like a hell of a coincidence.'

'Hear you, but that's what the facts are saying.'

'Have you tried speaking to McArdle?'

'I phoned his office a bunch of times. Apparently, he's working on a dig and is declining calls until he's back in the office.'

'Okay, let's backtrack a bit here and not leap to conclusions. How did you make the link between your waterhorse story and this treaty?'

'I interviewed a woman called Ailsa McIver. She was also involved in the waterhorse dig and suggested I read the treaty.'

'Question we've got to ask ourselves, Freya, does Miss McIver gain anything by giving you this information?'

Freya tucked her palms between her knees. 'She seemed genuine, but based on what you said before, I've been asking myself the same question all afternoon.'

Howard switched off his computer 'Go and talk to her again. Ask her why she felt minded to mention the treaty. And while you're at it, dig into the backgrounds of McIver and McArdle.'

'Are you going to pay me for that?'

'I'm paying you for the first story idea you brought in here. And now you're trying to pitch me another?' Howard gave her a furtive glance. 'You know how tight my budgets are.'

'Howard, if there's even the slimmest chance that horse is real and that McArdle could end up on its back, then Scotland needs to know.'

Howard gave his tabletop an irritable tap with his knuckles. 'Yeah, maybe. But I'm concerned McIver and McArdle are leading you a merry dance.'

'Meaning?'

'Meaning, that in a really quiet week for news, I'd consider slipping this Finlaggan stuff into our online pages and seeing how it ran. But right now, with what you've got … I'm not touching it.'

'But boss …'

'Do your research, Freya, if you're that excited. But it's at your own expense. If the horse actually exists, and your lucky laird shows up on Lewis, we might speak again. Right now, if I turn up late for school, I'll be as extinct as McArdle's waterhorse.'

Hurrying between the *Tribune* offices and the Finnieston hostel, Freya wished she'd asked for Ailsa's phone number. Mentioning the Finlaggan treaty had been a clear tip-off and implied she'd permission to talk to Ailsa again. Uppermost on her mind was her discovery that Gill McArdle was the laird and consequently, a man with the power to take a wrecking ball to Scotland's geographic integrity. Now Freya needed to understand Ailsa's motive. Did she support McArdle – the two were friends after all - or was she raising a red flag? Was McArdle, in fact, a danger to Scotland and was Ailsa asking Freya to alert the sleeping public to the threat?

She was warm and a little flustered when she arrived at the hostel, but at least the walk had given her time to decide a line of questioning. Stepping up to the reception desk, a young man was working where Ailsa had stood five days before.

'Hi, I'm looking for Ailsa McIver.'

The man nodded and smiled. 'She's not in today. Can I help?'

'Do you have any idea when she'll be back?' Noticing a reticence on his face, she added, 'It's really important.'

'Are you a friend of Ailsa?'

It would be so easy to lie, but Freya decided to play it straight. 'No, I'm a journalist. Ailsa has been helping me with a story.'

'Look, I'm not sure when she'll be back. She's had to take a leave of absence.'

'Oh, I'm sorry. What's wrong? Is she okay?'

'She's fine, but there's been a serious fire back at her family home in Tarbert. She had to leave quite suddenly, and really, that's all I know.'

Freya nodded urgently. 'Do you mind me asking, which Tarbert? I know there are a bunch.'

The man smiled at another customer who'd started fidgeting behind Freya. 'She's on the Isle of Harris.'

'Damnit, Howard,' spat Freya, two minutes later, while she walked back towards the city centre. Ailsa McIver was out of reach, and on Harris of all places. If only her boss had sent her to the island. And now she was a million miles from the action. Apart from scraping social media posts, how could she track the waterhorse? And if McArdle wasn't answering her calls, how the hell was she going to find out if he ever travelled to Harris? On the plus side, as Howard had ditched her story she wasn't working for the *Tribune* on this. That made her a free agent. Angry, and a little defeated, she wracked her mind for any way to access this data.

'Damn you again, Howard,' she shouted. She could only think of one way to pursue the unicorn story and that involved leveraging the power of social media to channel information to her mailbox. But it was a tonne of work as it meant contacting everyone making a waterhorse sighting and condensing the resulting mash of data into a blog. She'd need to spend hours every day, corresponding with her contacts, establishing herself as the authority on all things "waterhorse." She grimaced. She was about to take on the mantle of something she detested. Freya Swanson was about to become an "influencer."

Chapter 14

At the same moment Freya was seeking her in Glasgow, Ailsa was stepping off a bus at the ferry terminal. Uig was an unremarkable cluster of low buildings, nestled in a bay protected by Skye's most northerly peninsula. She bought a ticket and tried to find a warm spot in the draughty passenger lounge. When her phone rang, she checked the caller before picking up.

'Ailsa, it's Gill. Just got your message. Where are you?'

'On Skye, waiting for a ferry.'

'How are things at home?'

'Gran suffered smoke inhalation. They wanted to send her to hospital in Inverness, but she refused, so she's with my mum.'

'What a terrible thing for her to endure.'

'Aye. And apparently, the guest house is wrecked.'

'I'm so sorry.'

'It's okay. Mum and gran are safe and that's all that matters.'

'Okay. Give them my best regards. Is there anything I can do to help?'

Ailsa said nothing.

'Hello, are you still there?'

'I'm just thinking. Joining the dots.'

'What do you see?'

'Just sensing the hand of Roddy Canmore in this.'

Gill sighed. 'If it's his intention to lure you away from Glasgow, you need to take extra care.'

'If this was him, Gill, he's made this personal. I don't mind turning the other cheek, but, attacking my family, that's another matter.'

In the background, Gill heard a tannoy announcement that Ailsa's ferry was about to begin boarding. 'I'll let you go. Be vigilant.'

'I will. And you too.'

'And Ailsa?'

'Yes?'

'As you're going to be on Harris for a while, can you keep your eyes and ears open for a horse I'm particularly fond of?'

After sharing his suspicions about Ailsa's house fire, Gill and Salina agreed some extra precautions they'd add to their daily routines. There was no proof Canmore was behind the Tarbert fire, and yet, the Armour Group looked vulnerable. Setting these concerns aside for a few minutes, Gill threw himself into the family's evening routine. In the days before Josh arrived, he would have stayed late at the Fisher Street dig, pushing himself and his team to keep working while there was still daylight. But his attendance at Josh's bedtimes had been erratic this week and he'd decided to be home promptly to put in a "dad-shift." So far, Salina had only made a partial return to work. Temporarily confined to a desk job, she was super-excited to be offered the chance to start skippering DSVs again early in the new year. So, like many new fathers, he wanted to prove he'd cope when the time came he'd be managing their young son on his own.

A little later that Wednesday evening, he passed through the front room with an armful of damp Joshua. Bathtime was no sooner done and the child half-dried when Josh had spotted the absence of a favourite toy. Keen to avoid tears before bedtime, Gill was making a game out of finding the thing.

'Look at this,' called Salina to Gill when he returned from the kitchen with the desired toy now safely in Josh's clutches. With a meagre expectation the housefire on Harris would make the evening news, Salina was half-watching the TV, while sitting with a laptop on her knees responding to emails. When Gill turned to see what had caught her eye, he was unsettled to see a close-up of Roddy Canmore's face. Behind the man, the unmistakable ribbon of Loch Ness stretched into the far distance.

'Obviously, I'm concerned,' said Canmore, addressing an interviewer who was out of shot. *'Yesterday evening produced the latest in a recent sequence of tremors and I've spent today speaking to citizens from Fort William to Inverness. They're deeply anxious about the situation and the implications a bigger quake could have on their lives.'*

'What needs to happen?' asked the interviewer.

'Our greatest need is for information. Like many Scots, I suspect the British Government knows more about the seismic activity along the Great Glen than it's letting on. I'm calling on them to release that data so we can make informed decisions about how to proceed.'

'How might we proceed, First Minister?'

'If there's a significant risk of a major incident, we'll need to create evacuation plans for vulnerable areas. In the longer term, we'll need to survey buildings and assess what can be done to strengthen or replace them.'

'Which will obviously cost money.'

'Indeed, and as this risk predates Scottish devolution, I'd expect the British exchequer to look favourably on any requests we make.'

'How urgently do we need to address this?'

'Last night was just the latest tremor. This seismic activity began five years ago, and I'd say a response by the British government is already long overdue.'

'So, you'd like to see action taken in months rather than years?'

Canmore nodded vigorously. *'I've written to London today demanding the immediate creation of a working group to assess and respond to the downstream risks of geological upheaval. I'll let you know how they respond.'*

'In the meantime, First Minister, do you have any words for concerned local residents?'

Canmore broke eye contact with the interviewer and cast a fretful gaze across the water. *'Even if London drags its feet on this, I will do everything in my power to protect Scottish citizens and the lives of everyone living in the shadow of this great glen.'*

Salina flicked the TV back onto mute and turned to Gill. 'What do you make of that?'

Gill shook his head. 'It's absolute BS. All responsibilities for seismic monitoring are devolved to the Scottish Geological Survey. They hold the data and are responsible for risk assessment north of the border.'

'Sure, but the man in the street doesn't know that.'

Gill grimaced. 'I expect by this time tomorrow, the British Government will be falling over itself to fact-check Canmore's bluster.'

Cassy and Mhairi were at their desks when Gill made a reluctant visit to the office the following afternoon. He'd worked hard since Craig and Larry had joined his dig team the previous day and they'd exposed another two metres of the strange sandstone chimney that had once been the visible portion of the box grave. The thing now towered from the base of the pit and was a big red flag telling Gill this site was unusual. Rushing through his messages, he sensed today could be significant and fretted that his team might make a breakthrough while he was stuck in the office doing admin. He engaged in a hurried exchange with Cassy on issue 63 and was considering a late dash back to the dig site when Mhairi came over.

'Update on the big gold hoard you haven't actually found,' she began.

'Yeah, well, I'm beginning to doubt it myself,' moaned Gill. 'But it's worth asking the question if any local record exists of someone losing a bunch of those coins.'

'There are a few. If we go back three or four hundred years, Dundee was a walled city and regarded as very secure. Even the City of Edinburgh stored its gold reserves here. Over the years there were wars and raids when relatively modest sums were lost.'

'Were there any big ones?'

'There's one, Gill. And I'm being guided by the date on the coin you found. Clearly, if it was minted in 1601, then it was lost in subsequent years, which points to one particular cataclysm. What do you know of the English Civil War and its impact upon Scotland?'

Gill thought for a moment. 'I've got a schoolboy's grasp of the basics. It was half a century before the Act of Union, so when Cromwell marched an army into Scotland in 1650, they were foreign invaders. One sovereign nation attacking another just because Scotland supported Charles the Second in his bid for the united throne.'

Mhairi nodded. 'Cromwell's English Parliament had abolished the monarchy and established a republic. Meanwhile, the Scots wanted to enforce Presbyterianism throughout the British Isles. Supporting Charles seemed the best way to achieve this, with the downside it made Scotland a threat to Cromwell.'

'Where does the gold come in?' asked Gill.

'Cromwell's generals laid siege to Dundee in August 1651. They slaughtered the inhabitants and a few weeks later gathered all the city's loot onto ships. In some form of divine irony, Cromwell's fleet was wrecked off Broughty Ferry Castle before it reached the open sea.'

Gill nodded. 'Now you mention it, I've heard this story. A specialist dive company went looking for treasure in the summer of 2004, I think.'

'2003,' Mhairi corrected. 'And aside from a few cannonballs, they didn't find a thing.'

'But it was evidence they'd found the wreck site?'

'Yes, but despite extensive scans and multiple dives, the search didn't find any of the gold or silver reputed to be on that boat. And that led to a whole new line of thought.'

'That the gold was never on the ship in the first place,' said Gill. 'That it was either transported to London another way or …'

'Or the Dundonians hid their treasure before the city was overrun,' Mhairi concluded. 'And hence the possibility it's buried in the Fisher Street graveyard.'

'The dates work, Mhairi. The date on the coin, and the age of the oldest graves.'

Mhairi lifted her laptop. 'I'll leave you to keep digging.'

'Fancy joining us to watch history being made?'

Mhairi scrunched up her nose. 'Nah, the only digging I do is in the digital world. But if you do find those coins and need help getting them organised, I'll be down in a flash.'

Gill glanced at his watch. There was no way he'd be back at the dig site before Fiona locked things up for the day, so his cause would be better served by reviewing Mhairi's sources. Opening the file she'd sent him, he started to read.

He'd almost finished Mhairi's research when his phone rang. 'Gill, it's Adina.'

'Hi there. Glad to hear your voice. Alex says you're getting hassled.'

'Nothing I can't handle.'

'You sure?'

'Absolutely. These guys are persistent, but so far, they've resisted my efforts to reach out to them.' She released a little sigh and Gill thought she sounded tired. 'And if things go south, you and I have our emergency protocols.'

'Indeed, but don't take any risks you can avoid.'

'I hear you, Gill. In the meantime, I need to alert you to another emerging threat.'

'What's up?'

'Do you recall the Google alert system I use?'

Gill thought for a second. 'Sure,' he lied.

'I'm watching for keywords, like *Waterhorse*, *Armour Group*, and *Treaty of Finlaggan*. Thing is Gill, there's a young journalist based in Glasgow called Freya Swanson who's started blogging about your waterhorse.'

'Okay.'

'And Freya has linked you to the treaty and identified you as the laird.'

'Bummer,' said Gill, realising that if the treaty became public knowledge, then the government could act to strike it down. 'Okay, nothing we can do about that. Does this kid have many followers?'

'Just a few hundred. But it's being reposted, Gill, so this thing could grow.'

'Thanks, Adina. Can you keep an eye on it?'

'You mean, take time out of my regular day job so you're still free to do yours?'

Gill sighed. 'Something like that.'

Adina laughed at his embarrassment. 'I'll circulate a link to Freya's blog to the whole Armour Group. That way, we can all keep an eye on her.'

'Thank you.'

'You're welcome. But just remember; the moment someone in authority sees this blog and realises its implications, the treaty and the *Torn Isle*, are toast.

Chapter 15

With his meetings finished, Gill was packing up his laptop for the day. Chatting with Cassy, he noticed a crowd gathering in the conference room. It was 6 pm and the editorial meeting for *Game and Gun* had just ended and suddenly everyone's attention seemed captured by the early evening news bulletin. Tony waved to catch his eye and Gill wandered over to investigate the source of the excitement. On the screen, vivid, fast-moving camera shots of Loch Ness dominated the display.

'What's happening?' he asked. 'Is Canmore getting his arse handed to him?'

'News earlier in the day focused on a rather junior minister trying to explain the technicalities of why Scotland was responsible for its own seismic data,' said Tony. 'Basically, London has fluffed its response, and Canmore has called a news conference at Fort Augustus.'

'He's doubling down on a bad play?' asked Gill.

'Either that or he's got something new,' said Tony, enigmatically. 'And I've got a nasty feeling you and I might know what that is.'

Gill thought for a moment, then quietly mouthed an expletive, before turning and waving at Cassy to join them.

'What?' demanded Cassy, joining the rear of the scrum, while Gill just pointed at the screen.

At precisely 6.01 pm, Canmore stood in front of the cameras. He looked around the gathered news crews and nodded at them with an expression of regal apprehension. *'I stood on the banks of this great loch only yesterday expressing my concern about London and its reluctance to share local seismic data with the Scottish people. This morning, I passed the colonial government in London a note stating that unless it released the information it holds on increased seismic activity on the Great Glen Fault, then I would hold them accountable for their actions. I must tell you that no such information has been received, and consequently, I must expose their bad faith in this area.'*

Canmore paused for effect and his unhappy face grew even more sober. *'I must now reveal that in the 1950s the British government undertook to build a submarine base beneath the waters of Loch Ness. Part of the plans included routes to the sea, excavated in the already stressed rocks that exist along a natural boundary known as the Great Glen Fault.'*

Canmore paused and raised a hand to halt the flood of questions erupting from the news teams. *'You will have questions, I'm sure. And the foremost of these will be for me to prove this serious accusation. To that end, historical documents that only recently came to light have just been published on the Scottish government's website. Under the title "Project Leviathan," they include the detailed schematics of the proposed base.'*

'First Minister, what precisely are your concerns?' came one strident question. Everyone else fell silent while Canmore ruminated on his answer.

'At this stage, London is still denying plans for a submarine base ever existed. That is categorically a lie, so I don't find myself assured by their claim that no base was ever constructed.' He paused to shake his head. *'Again, the citizens of this country find themselves caught in an information gap created by our friends south of the border. And the evident question is this. If the base was built, or even if construction*

began and was halted … did that work provoke the seismic crisis that now hangs like a Sword of Damocles over northern Scotland?'

Gill stood open mouthed while Canmore started to field questions from the gathered reporters.

Tony leaned in close. 'That base was never built, right?'

Gill turned to him. 'How can you even ask that question? Salina went down in a DSV and looked. There is no base, and Steven Ackerson told me face-to-face, nothing was attempted. The geology was bad, so they went to Faslane.'

'Do you think Ackerson is Canmore's source?'

Gill shook his head. 'There are a million ways the Scottish government could legitimately know about *Project Leviathan*. And it was just military brainstorming. There was no need for it to be in the public eye.'

'Well, it is now. And Canmore's going to keep London on the back foot with this.'

'I agree, boss. But why now?'

'What do you mean?'

'Canmore was outrageous yesterday and now he's doubling down,' said Gill. 'He must know that these accusations won't withstand a week of sensible scrutiny so what's his game plan?'

'You spoke to the SGS when we did the Loch Ness story. Do you still have contacts there?'

'It's four years ago, boss, but there's a guy I can call.' Gill grimaced. 'That's if he's prepared to speak to the press.'

'Do it, Gill. *Mys.Scot* is intimately linked to the Great Glen Disaster. I need to know if any of the shit Canmore is tossing in the air is about to blow back on us.'

Agnes Fairbank had anticipated the evening intervention by the First Minister would provoke questions, so she'd lingered at her desk with a list of prepared responses. As long as she remained calm and didn't deviate from her script, she'd get through this. She fielded calls as best she could then before turning to the long list of telephone messages collected by the SGS receptionists. Reviewing the call log, she saw The *Daily Record* had called six times, the *Glasgow Tribune* eight times and the BBC had phoned twice. She shivered, wondering how she'd fair against these bigger media outlets. She needed to start lower down the pecking order with someone less challenging. Looking at the list, she recognised the name of one reporter she recalled meeting. Someone from a magazine with dubious scientific credentials who'd come calling in the days before the Great Glen Disaster. She'd phone him back on the basis they'd met. Afterwards, she'd call the BBC, and that would have to do.

'*Mysterious Scotland*, Gill McArdle speaking.'

'Agnes Fairbank at SGS. I'm returning your call.'

As she'd hoped, the voice at the other end of the line was hesitant. 'Thanks. I was trying to reach John Houston. Is he around at all?'

'He's been under a great deal of stress lately, so he was granted an extended period of sick leave.' Technically, that was still true despite her colleague's demise, so Agnes decided to leave her answer there.

'Ah, the poor fella.' Gill paused. 'Listen, I've been watching our First Minister on TV and I'm trying to get my head around an information disconnect.'

'What are you referring to?' Fairbank sniffed.

'The fact that devolution means the SGS has responsibility for Scottish seismic safety, while Roddy Canmore seems to think this information gap he's referring to is all London's fault.'

'Those are murky waters,' she sniffed. 'Are we on the record?'

'Yes, please.'

'In which case, you're asking about political manners, Mr McArdle. I get up in the morning, and come here to do my work, then I go home again. How we're represented in the public sphere doesn't particularly concern me.'

'It seems the First Minister wants the whole country writhing in uncertainty about a potential earthquake. But he could settle the matter by talking to you and asking about the whizzy predictive software John Houston was developing.'

'Perhaps, but I don't manage the First Minister's diary.'

'Or you could clear things up by going on the record with *Mysterious Scotland* and say whether or not there's likely to be a significant quake.'

'I provide data and quantified probabilities,' Fairbank replied. 'It isn't my role to campaign.'

'So, you do have data on this threat he's so concerned about?'

'We have data, but the algorithm isn't as reliable as we'd hoped. During his time here John tinkered a lot, and we've had to resurrect an earlier version of the software.' Fairbank paused when a member of her staff appeared at her doorway with a frown on his face. She held up a hand and motioned for her lab-tech to wait while she finished her call.

'Are you seeing anything in the seismic data to suggest a quake is imminent?' asked McArdle.

'Absolutely none.'

'Like, if I said I was taking my young family on a camping trip this weekend to Fort Augustus, you wouldn't try to dissuade me?'

Fairbank stroked her right eyebrow with the long finger of her left hand. 'I think you're repeating yourself. As I said, I perceive no increased threat from the Great Glen, so unless the First Minister knows something I don't, then an earthquake is definitely not imminent.'

'What about …'

'I'm sorry, but I've other calls to make and need to press on. Thank you for reaching out to the SGS.'

She hung up and closed her eyes. That hadn't gone as well as she'd hoped.

Chapter 16

Gill was still thinking about Canmore's stunt on Loch Ness when he left his house the following morning. The First Minister's rhetoric was starting to look like a violent first strike in a PR war with the British government. What Gill couldn't get his head around was how he'd maintain his advantage once the media unpicked his misrepresentations. And it was a pity Agnes Fairbank hadn't been more forthcoming. He understood her reluctance to step into the media spotlight, but if her data demonstrated no earthquake was imminent, then why didn't she come out and say so? Canmore's pronouncements had worried folk living along the Great Glen, and Fairbank could have lifted that burden with a single, carefully worded news release.

Back at the Fisher Street dig, it had been an intriguing though fruitless week. Even so, Gill was certain the coin discovered near the box grave wouldn't be the last. Finding the streets busier than usual, he arrived at the gate and found his way blocked by a crowd of several dozen. Squeezing through the mob, he found Fiona standing with hands on hips, daring anyone to even try stepping inside her dig site.

'What's going on?' he asked.

'This lot started turning up a few minutes ago,' she said, pointing full in the face to a nearby individual. 'And I've been carefully explaining the cemetery is closed to visitors.'

'Right,' said Gill, turning to speak to the crowd. 'What's the issue here?'

'We're here to volunteer,' shouted one guy while the men around him laughed.

'Here to pay my respects to grandpa,' called another, to similar derision.

'I want to find some of that gold,' yelled one wild-haired older man.

'Look,' said Gill, over the noise. 'I don't know what you've heard, but a single coin doesn't mean there's more under every damp stone. And even if there was, the law states that any precious item discovered must be declared "Treasure" and belongs to the nation.'

He had to pause when grumbles amongst the crowd drowned him out.

'And I have to say, this dig is at a critical juncture. It isn't safe to go tramping around in there, and for that reason, we're closed to the public.'

More catcalls from the crowd.

'Brilliant,' said Fiona. 'You've got them all fired up.'

'I'm calling the police,' said Gill. 'And once they've told this lot to disperse, I'm bringing in private security, ASAP.'

Turning his back on the crowd, he nodded to Fiona, then made good on his calls to the police and the security crew Larry had put on standby. With that issue in hand, he turned at last to the dig. Craig was taking a turn in the pit while Becka and Zack operated a pulley, and transported soil to a heap, a safe distance away.

'You guys don't know anything about the baying mob?' he asked while he pulled on overalls and prepared to replace Craig.

'Which baying mob, boss?' echoed Craig's voice from inside the chimney.

'The one alerted to the possibility of a gold find on this site.'

'Bloody morons, the lot of them,' said Zack. Beside him, Becka stayed silent and diligently avoided Gill's gaze.

Later that morning while the others took a coffee break, Gill and Fiona stood side by side on separate ladders, studying the smooth sandstone walls inside the vertical shaft. The confined space meant they could talk in low voices while they considered its construction.

'Are we absolutely sure it's not a well?' asked Fiona.

'Not below a graveyard. You couldn't have drunk the water.'

'A mine shaft then, or a priest hole?'

'No mining in this area. Nor do I think it was designed for regular use because there are no handholds. You'd have needed a ladder, just like us.'

'The slabs are all the same size,' Fiona murmured. 'My theory is they are quarried slabs.'

'I get it,' said Gill. 'Blank slabs intended to be carved into gravestones. I guess that would explain why so many were close to hand when this place was built.'

'And based on the thickness, it's double-skinned. That allowed the builders to overlap these stones and keep the whole thing strong.'

'The quality is incredible,' said Gill, running his hands down the wall. 'No sign of deterioration.'

'Which means we can keep on digging. However, the core samples we took outside suggest we're close to a base clay level. If I'd been building this in a hurry four hundred years ago, I'd have stopped there.'

'Do you think it would be safer to just demolish it?'

Fiona shook her head. 'We risk damaging whatever might be lying at the bottom. Besides, if we leave it like this, hopefully, our twenty-first-century architects will incorporate the feature within the new building.'

The bottom of the shaft finally appeared at 3 pm that afternoon. Reaching a slab, fractionally smaller than the dimensions of the channel, they found crude metal rings embedded at each end. Despite some evidence of corrosion, Fiona judged the metal would still hold the weight of the stone. Repositioning the earthmoving equipment, she attached a metal cable to the vehicle's winch. After checking the scaffold could handle the horizontal forces at play, they hooked up the slab to the pulley and started to lift.

The group stood in silence while the slab inched skyward, its modest weight being less of an incumbrance than the narrowness of the space. When finally, it was clear of the top, Gill, Fiona and Craig levered it to one side and laid it carefully onto the ground. Then after a nod from Gill, they clambered over the scaffold and peered down into the dark.

'Bloody hell,' whispered Fiona.

Gill felt Craig give him a congratulatory slap on the shoulders. There below them, reflecting what little daylight could penetrate the cavern was the glowing image Gill had seen in his dream.

Photographing the gold hoard pressed into a space not much bigger than a chest freezer took less than an hour. With the curious crowd still milling around at the gate, Gill was minded to proceed with immediate extraction, but before he did anything, he called Claire Vaughan and was fortunate to catch her at her desk. As the Director of Scottish History at the National Museum, she was the ultimate authority on what should happen to a find of this significance.

'You've got how many?' she asked, shakily.

'I'll send you some initial images,' said Gill. 'But I'm estimating in the tens of thousands.'

'And from what era?'

'I've just looked at a few. They're all early seventeenth century.'

'Meaning they'll be wafer thin like other coins of their era.'

'One millimetre, maybe two at most. I daren't put my weight on them so we'll have to lift them out a few at a time.'

'The way you describe it, Gill, it could take days.'

'We'll think of a way to do it quicker. But the shaft itself is historically significant, so demolishing it is out of the question.'

'Okay. It's late now but I'll fire out some emails and get the ball rolling in Edinburgh. It'll probably be Saturday morning before I talk to my colleagues. I'm sure you're aware that recovering a rich archaeological trove is especially complicated in an urban area, so can we talk logistics for a second?'

Gill mumbled his agreement. The belligerent crowd at the front gate had waxed and waned all day.

'You'll need to take extra precautions,' Claire continued. 'Assuming I can get a team to you mid-morning tomorrow, do you have somewhere you can store the coins for the next few hours?'

'Our private security firm arrived on site a few minutes ago. They'll guard everything we recover in an old lifeboat shed just around the corner from here. We should be fine until you arrive.'

'Sounds good.' She left a pause. 'The size of this hoard is far beyond the means of even a wealthy seventeenth-century

Dundonian. Do you have any insights on what we might be dealing with?'

Gill cleared his throat. 'My researcher has identified one theory, but really, it's too early to say.'

'Hit me, Gill. Just so I can start thinking on this.'

'Okay. You know your history, so you'll be aware that Dundee was Scotland's bullion town in the early seventeenth century.'

'Aye,' said Claire. 'Back then, it was a walled city and believed to be the best defended in the whole country.'

'We're thinking about the siege of the summer of 1651. Cromwell sent in an army under the leadership of a general called Monck. He slaughtered the inhabitants and plundered the city's treasuries.'

'But weren't those valuables lost in the Tay?'

'That was the story at the time. Cromwell's general looted Dundee, then loaded his ships with a big chunk of Scotland's national wealth. But as soon as they left the harbour, his ships hit a sand bar and were destroyed by a storm.' Gill left a dramatic pause. 'An alternative narrative says the city fathers at the time hid away the gold in a pre-prepared shaft in the middle of a graveyard.'

'Oh, my goodness,' gasped Claire.

'My researcher tells me it's rumoured to be two hundred thousand gold coins.'

Claire thought for a moment. 'Could that theory have any veracity? I mean, if it was the city's treasury, why didn't they go back for it?'

'I'd guess there was only a small inner circle who knew its location. Maybe they didn't survive the war. And we're aware of at least two high-tech surveys in recent years. Although they found wreckage in the spot where Monck's fleet was lost, not a single coin was ever found.'

'And you think it was buried in a specially constructed tomb before the siege began?'

'I'd say the tomb represents a high degree of planning by an enlightened individual or committee. I'll be looking for evidence this vault was built before these coins were even minted.'

'And if that's true, what did Cromwell's people load onto ships?'

'Who knows? Maybe his general fabricated the story so he could justify returning home without the coins.'

'A question for another day.' Claire paused. 'Right, give me until tomorrow morning and I'll be in touch.'

Gill hung up, triumphant that against the odds, the Fisher Street dig was producing something remarkable.

'What now?' asked Craig, his eyes gleaming.

Gill clapped his shoulder. 'If you're up for it, we're going to very carefully extract millions of pounds worth of gold coins. Where's Larry?'

'He's taken our security guys to show them the lifeboat shed. They'll be back shortly.'

They worked through the night in short shifts, with the teams rotating frequently so no one got so tired they injured themselves. With the private security team manning the gates and patrolling the perimeter, Gill was released to focus on emptying the coin vault. And it emerged that Larry's pals drove armoured vans on behalf of a bank. After a few phone calls, they were able to supply a vehicle to move batches of coins from the dig site to the old lifeboat shed. Mhairi made good on her promise to help, and by 10 am on Saturday, she was laying out the coins on trestle tables. The whole process started to tick like clockwork so that by midday, they'd recovered at least half of the hoard. Meanwhile, yesterday's crowd of curious onlookers was back again and seemed to know a significant discovery had been made. Seeing the time, and feeling the pressure of the mob, Gill worked on, fretting why Claire Vaughan wasn't on site yet. His phone rang and he was disappointed when it was only Mhairi.

'Gill, are you far away?'

'Still at the dig waiting for Claire to show up. Don't suppose she's with you?'

'She isn't. Listen, could you come down to the shed? I think we might have a problem.'

'What kind of problem?'

Mhairi's phone was muffled for a few moments, then it cut off.

Gill didn't exactly sprint the few hundred metres to the old stone shed, but it only took him three minutes. He feared the onlookers pestering his site for the past few days were alerted to the armoured transfer shuttling back and forth. They might even be attempting to storm his improvised strongroom. And when he arrived to find three police cars, splashed across the approach roads, he wasn't sure if he was unsettled or relieved. Reaching the door, he found his path blocked by an armed officer.

'I'm Gill McArdle,' he panted. 'I'm the guy running this dig.'

'Don't care if you're the king's aunty, pal. This hall is out of bounds.'

'Listen, I just need to check on a …'

'Did you not hear me?' the officer insisted. 'Move along if you don't want to face a charge.'

'I don't think you understand …'

'Let him through, Ewan,' said a calm voice behind the officer. 'Mr McArdle and I need to talk.'

Unsure whether to thank the officer or not, Gill manoeuvred around the stoic policeman into the porch, then stumbled on the threshold into the main hall. Finding his balance, he saw Mhairi standing dumbfounded while she watched four uniformed officers bundling the coins into bags.

'Hey! You should be using gloves,' yelled Gill. 'And don't just dump them on top of each other. You'll damage them.'

'Don't fret, Gill. We'll take good care of them.'

Gill turned to find a slim man, dressed in black jeans and an understated black leather jacket. He was clean shaven, with close cut hair to his temples, topped off with a thin covering of dark brown hair. In an unusual contrast, Gill noticed the man had pale blue eyes, the colour of ice. Athletic and a little older than him, Gill immediately felt wary.

'How's it going in the shaft?' the man continued. 'Need any extra manpower?'

'We're fine thanks. Where are you taking the coins?'

'Securing them for the nation.'

'That's the museum's job.'

'Oh, and they'll get their share.' The man looked amused. 'I'll make sure they get the half dozen they need, or whatever. Something to display alongside your waterhorse bones.'

'Look, I don't know who you are, but there's an official process with a find like this.'

The man threw out his arms and grinned. 'You see, we agree. I knew we would.'

'If we agree, get Claire Vaughan and her team in here. Then get these cowboys to stop touching the coins.'

'Ever been to the British Museum, Mr McArdle?'

'Of course.'

'Then maybe you'll understand my concerns. If Miss Vaughan gets her hand on your impressive find, then this precious piece of Scottish history could be whisked off to London.'

Gill shook his head. 'The two institutions have no formal link, so that's a ridiculous suggestion.'

'The Rosetta Stone, the Elgin Marbles, the Benin Bronzes, I mean at one level, I get it. Places like Egypt, Nigeria, or even Greece, could go up in a puff of smoke, but Scotland is different. We wouldn't want to see our cultural heritage raided, would we?'

Gill's fingertips bit into his palms. 'Spew out whatever weasel words you want to justify your actions, but be assured, you're not getting away with this.'

The man chuckled for a moment, then jerked his chin at the officer guarding the door. 'Did you see that, Ewan? Mr McArdle just tried to punch me.'

'I did, sir,' the officer replied, mimicking the man's mocking tone. 'And I think you should watch out. It looks like he's got a knife.'

'What?' spluttered Gill.

The man flicked his wrist at Gill. 'Yes, or a trowel or something. I definitely saw the flash of a blade.'

'Will you want to press charges, sir?'

'Absolutely, Ewan. Hit him with the full extent of the law.'

Gill felt his arms being twisted behind his back and moments later, the click of handcuffs being applied. 'Who the hell are you?' he hissed.

His adversary stepped closer. 'My name doesn't matter, but what's important, unicorn-man, is that going forward, I could be your friend or your very worst enemy.' He leaned in close and tugged at the tails of Gill's waistcoat. 'You wouldn't want us to be enemies, would you, Gill?'

Gill didn't get a chance to reply. Under Mhari's horrified gaze, and just a few steps from his front door, he was marched to a police car and driven away.

Chapter 17

It was Sunday morning, and Lillico stared along the length of St Andrews West Sands where a thousand acres of damp sand shone brilliantly under a clearing sky.

'Welcome to your second therapy session,' said Cassy, giving him a gentle push. 'How've you been?'

He smiled and tried to put his worries behind him. 'Much better, thank you, doctor. Or at least, I am when I'm around you.'

Cassy blushed a little but ignored the compliment. 'And what would you like to talk about today?'

'My love life,' Lillico shot back.

'You have a love life, detective? I honestly didn't think you had time.'

'Yeah, well maybe I should do something about that.'

'A tolerably good-looking man like you,' said Cassy. 'I imagine you get women's attention from time to time.'

'Well, here's the thing.' Lillico shot her a guarded look. 'At the moment, I'm interested in two women. I'm caught between the pair of them, and I don't know what to do.'

If this rattled Cassy, she didn't show it. 'Describe them to me.'

Lillico hooked his thumbs in his belt. 'One is the polar opposite to me in temperament. She's fiery, smart, ambitious. The other is calm, considered, playful.'

'Both sound cool, but I gotta say, I'm swinging for the fiery one.'

Lillico laughed. 'If you were doing this right, doctor, you'd be impartial. You'd let me speak my hopes and fears, and by being an excellent listener, you'd help me see the way ahead.'

Cassy looked away. 'I can't be impartial, Alex.'

'Really? I've never been sure you were interested.'

'Always interested. Just a little too messed up to deal with the intimacy. All that getting to know another person and needing to take their concerns on board.'

'And now?'

Cassy glanced up at him. 'I'm coming to the conclusion I have a Lillico-shaped hole in my life.'

He absorbed this new reality but said nothing.

'So, the question becomes, are you still interested?'

'How would Zack deal with it?'

'Zack is his own man, Alex. Apart from his genetically inherited suspicion of authority, I think he'd be okay.' Cassy laughed. 'And he likes you, even though you're a cop.'

Lillico smiled but didn't speak.

'The other girl. Tell me about her.'

'She's a good person, Cass.'

'If she's your friend, then I know she must be.' She took his hand. 'Tell me how you met.'

In amongst the madness of the past few weeks, the time with Cassy was healing for Lillico. The traumas that had plagued the last year of Cassy's life seemed to have eased, and although her wit remained razor sharp, she wasn't as abrasive as the person he'd first met three years before. Reaching the end of West Sands beach, she produced a packet of chocolate biscuits from her bag, and nibbling slowly, they talked and munched their way through most of the packet. Deeply peaceful in her company, Lillico was about to ask her something when his phone buzzed. He knew he shouldn't, but he glanced down at the screen out of force of habit.

'Work?' asked Cassy, while Lillico lingered over the text.

'Kinda. It's Gill. He wants me to pick him up from Bell Street Police Station.'

'Beg your pardon?'

'Didn't Mhairi tell you? He was remanded in custody overnight.'

'Haven't spoken to her. Was there trouble at the dig?'

'You could say that. A civilian claims Gill took a swing at him.'

Cassy seemed surprised. 'That doesn't sound like Gill.'

'I'd agree. But there was a fair bit of tension around yesterday morning. I've not heard Gill's side of the story yet, but I do know the police took the gold coins for safekeeping.'

'So, he might have punched someone? Maybe in self-defence.'

'I'll reserve judgement.' He jerked his thumb back in the direction they'd come. 'Look, I really feel I should go see him. Wanna tag along?'

Cassy shook her head. 'Too much like work. I'll walk you back to your car, then I'll leave you and take a stroll around St Andrews.'

'Sorry,' he said, glumly.

'For what?'

'Cutting short our time together.'

Cassy walked away from him and twirled her fingers in the air. 'Maybe I'll have to get used to that.'

Chapter 18

Gill had watched a lot of cop dramas over the years. In his mind he could picture the scene where an accused man, whether guilty or innocent, is marched to a cell with his hands cuffed behind his back. There he spends an uncomfortable night with thin bedding and inadequate toilet facilities. His only human contact is a surly voice behind the cuff port asking him to make a breakfast selection from two miserable choices, which the captive ignores because the jailer will ultimately spit in his food. In reality, he found his own experience far more humane. The bench was firm, and the pillow seemed quite adequate, and after the background noise died down a bit, he slept soundly after his extended shift on the dig site. And after a better breakfast than he'd had at many budget hotels, he was feeling quite refreshed when an officer came by to say that he would now be released.

When the Duty Sergeant passed Gill his belongings and pointed him towards the exit, he phoned Salina first. They spoke long enough to reassure each other they were all okay and that they'd talk at length once Josh was in bed. Then he called Lillico to beg for a lift and sound out how much trouble might be coming his way. Finally, with an hour to kill, he made one speculative call he doubted would be answered on a Sunday morning. The Holyrood switchboard kept Gill on hold for twenty minutes. Quite reasonably, they said it was unlikely the First Minister would be available to speak to him. But, if he wanted to hold, they'd see what they could do. And so, he was more than a little surprised when the line clicked, and he heard a familiar voice.

'Rodderick Canmore.'

'Gill McArdle. Thank you for speaking to me. You might recall we've met.'

'I remember you, Gill.' Canmore sounded like he was smiling. 'The man with the fake stone.'

'That was yesterday's battle. Today, I'm more concerned with the Fisher Street hoard.'

'Indeed, and on behalf of the nation, I'll thank you for recovering that asset at such an important moment in our history.'

'Can I remind you, the rules state that any valuable hoard should be declared as treasure and saved for the nation?'

'And that's exactly what we've done. Saved it for the nation.'

'To do what? Melt it down to fund some nefarious scheme?'

'If that's how you view my aspiration to see Scotland reclaiming its sovereignty, then yes, guilty as charged.' He laughed gently. 'What were you going to do with it, Gill? Display a fortune of gold coins in an old lifeboat shed?'

'You know very well I was in the process of handing them to the National Museum of Scotland until your rottweiler came barging in.'

'And being the levelheaded professional you are, you took a swing at him.'

'I did no such thing, though I guess you know that.'

'Anyway, I gather the man you attacked has magnanimously agreed not to press charges. And this might surprise you, Gill, but after seeing your passion for the Fisher

Street hoard, I'm wondering if I might find a role for you in my administration.'

Briefly, Gill was wrongfooted. 'You what?'

'When eventually we move into new constitutional arrangements with England, I'll need a man like you to help us identify and recover other assets from our erstwhile colonial masters. Yes, I could see how someone with your skills could expect a job for life in the new Scotland we're about to forge. A well-paid job too.'

Gill laughed. 'You honestly think I'd accept your patronage?'

'You have a wife and a young son, Gill. You want to provide for them, don't you? Keep them safe from the troubles that can bedevil a man's life.'

'Is that a threat?'

'I don't make threats, Gill. But I'm not a man to be toyed with.' Canmore left a brief pause while he continued to breathe heavily into the phone. 'Some of your friends are about to discover that for themselves. Adina Mofaz, for example.'

'You know Adina?'

'Not personally. Her name crossed my desk in a matter relating to national security.'

Gill swallowed. 'Honestly, Roddy. If you do anything to hurt her …'

'It very much sounds like you're about to threaten me,' Canmore interrupted. 'Please don't because all my calls are recorded, and I would hate to see your freedom curtailed for a second time in as many days.'

'Your man broke the law by having me unfairly detained. And you're breaking the law too by grabbing the Fisher Street hoard.'

Canmore laughed aloud this time. 'I think you'll find the law serves those who make it. Now, it's been lovely to chat,

Gill, and let me encourage you to think about my offer. In the meantime, I must go as I've got a radio interview to do. Tune in - you might enjoy it.'

Gill listened to Canmore hanging up. He didn't know exactly what game they were playing, but he had a sinking sense that Canmore held most of the cards.

Lillico collected Gill from Bell Street Police Station. Almost twenty-four hours had passed since his arrest, and before Lillico could make discreet enquiries about what happened in Broughty Ferry, charges against Gill were suddenly dropped.

'The guy in the lifeboat shed,' said Gill. 'Any idea who he is?'

'According to your charge sheet, the man you attacked was Steven Blaine.'

'I didn't attack anybody.'

'But you know who he is?'

'One of Canmore's lackeys, obviously.'

'Steven Blaine runs personal security for Roddy Canmore. Been doing that since Canmore's earliest days as a politician. Apparently, in retrospect, Mr Blaine understands why you were upset. On reflection, he thinks you were just lashing out rather than targeting him personally.'

'He entirely fabricated it. You do understand that, right?'

'I do. But you're up against a civilian plus two officers who claim differently. I think you're fortunate this didn't run and run.'

'Pity old lifeboat sheds don't have CCTV,' said Gill. 'That would sort things out.'

Lillico shook his head. 'Canmore's people are risk-takers, and that makes them dangerous.'

The pair drove in silence, until at Gill's request, they put on the radio to catch the lunchtime news bulletin. The program opened by reminding listeners of the debate concerning seismic data and Canmore's shocking claim that crucial information had been withheld by London. Quite fairly, it questioned the legitimacy of Canmore's recent claims while reflecting there couldn't be smoke without fire.

'First Minister,' said the interviewer. *'In a moment, I'd like to ask you about your reaction to the colossal gold discovery in a Dundonian graveyard, but first, how do you respond to accusations the devolved government has known about research into a possible submarine base on Loch Ness for the last twenty-five years?'*

'That's an excellent question and I'd like to answer it in full,' Canmore responded brightly. *'And of course, I'm not surprised that the Westminster news machine is weaponised against us. It seems these days that a minister from any of the devolved governments can't raise legitimate questions about public safety without facing a tirade of doublespeak from our colonial masters.'*

'You don't feel Westminster has the right to push back on comments you made they believe are misleading?'

'Oh, I expect it. It's their automatic response when someone asks a grown-up question that implies the UK government should have to put its hands in its pockets to save Scottish lives.'

'But, First Minister, it now appears the Scottish Geological Society has always had full access to UK seismic data.'

'That's a matter for debate. I'd suggest you only need to look at the body language of certain UK government ministers to know that Scotland was never given the full picture. Instead, why don't we examine the move to grab the Fisher Street gold for London rather than respect the due process for this kind of discovery?'

For a moment, the commentator seemed stuck for words, so Canmore continued. *'Before the gold was even out of the ground, Police Scotland was made aware of a network of English museums and universities planning to swoop on the archaeological dig and carry off what is clearly Scotland's gold.'*

'Scotland's gold?'

'Absolutely! You have to understand the history of this hoard. Preliminary investigations suggest this gold was part of Scotland's national reserve back in the days before the union. It was stored in Dundee to protect it from English invaders in 1651. To spare the civilian population the city fathers surrendered to Cromwell's army. As a precaution, it appears they hid our national treasure in a prepared plot in the Fisher Street graveyard. Unfortunately, the population wasn't spared as the invaders killed women and children as well as soldiers, including the officers who knew of the gold's location.' Canmore chuckled. *'I think it's quite ironic that the ground should spew up this gold right at the moment when our colonial masters are launching an information war against us.'*

Gill reached out and turned off the radio. 'Sorry, I can't bear to hear him twist history to justify his take on today's situation. That man is a snake.'

'He might be a snake,' whispered Lillico, 'But he's bloody good at it.'

'Yeah,' said Gill. 'He's offering Scotland a hate-filled apple, and if we're not careful, we're all about to take a great big bite.'

A few minutes later, after a nudge from Gill, Lillico pulled up outside the Fisher Street dig site. Finding the gates locked and chained, Gill paced up and down a few times in frustration.

'Just want to check on the state of play,' he said, grunting while he jumped up on the wall.

'You going in?' asked Lillico. 'Cause then I can arrest you for trespassing.'

Gill hung from the top of the wall long enough to cast his eyes over the acre of muddy ground. 'Nah. It's all quiet. They grabbed the loot and ran. The dig is basically finished.'

Lillico offered a hand and helped Gill down. 'Maybe you should get out of town for a few days? Get away before Canmore and his rottweiler have another crack at you.'

'Maybe,' said Gill, dusting himself down. He pointed down the street. 'Fancy coming round ours for a bite? Sal and Josh would love to see you.'

Lillico stared at his feet. 'Best if I don't. My career is hanging by its fingernails so this whole fraternising with delinquent archaeologists isn't a good look for me right now.'

'You sure? Josh and I can rope you into a game of lions and tigers.'

'Sounds great, but I need to have an out-of-office meeting with Wiley this afternoon, so I need to go.'

'Really? On a Sunday?'

'Our Chief Superintendent has burdened our day jobs with a tonne of petty corruption paperwork. Weekends and evenings are the only time we can work our main case.'

'And what's that if you don't mind me asking?'

Lillico looked away. 'Another corruption case, but this one's at the highest level.'

Gill nodded. 'I'm curious to ask you about it, but I know you won't tell me anything.'

'You're right,' said Lillico, glancing around. 'And I'll make that seem even more unfair by asking you to help me with something.'

'Sure.'

'You've mentioned you've dealt with the Scottish Geological Survey.'

'I have. Had a call with their Head of Operations just last week.'

'Ever heard of a guy called John Houston?'

'Spoke to him a few years back. According to his boss, he's on extended sick leave.'

'Very extended, Gill. He's dead, possibly murdered.'

Gill recoiled. 'What? Are you sure?'

'Died in a car accident and our CSIs suspect vehicle tampering. Wiley and I were working on his case before our Chief Super shifted it to another team.'

Gill wrestled with this unsettling news. 'Agnes Fairbank never mentioned he'd died, even when I asked about him. Do you think she might be in Canmore's pocket? Might he be controlling her somehow?'

'Wiley and I had the same thought. Fairbank isn't on record for displaying any political views, and an authorised review of her bank accounts didn't suggest she's being bribed.'

'There are other ways a man like Canmore can influence people like Fairbank,' said Gill. 'And we know he's going after Adina. He virtually admitted as much to me.'

'Adina and I speak regularly. Whenever she challenges her watchers, they just drive off.'

'If what happened to Houston is anything to go by, Adina should be careful.'

'She's a professional, Gill. But it's another reason you should get out of town for a few days.'

'I hear you, Alex. And thanks for the lift.'

'Think about what I just said, Gill. Canmore is tightening the noose, and if this whole thing escalates, the first thing you'll want is for your family to be somewhere safe.'

Gill nodded to confirm he understood.

'And Gill.'

'Yes?'

'If you decide to drop off the radar for a few days, be sensible and stop at a garage somewhere to buy a bunch of prepaid sim cards. That way, the only people who have your number, and consequently your location, will be the people you choose to tell.'

'Adina's definitely having an effect on you,' Gill smiled. 'But I hear you. Say hi to Wiley for me and take care driving back.'

Chapter 19

Mummy, who are those men?'

Douglas was clearing up after lunch while Adina prepared some drinks and snacks the family planned to take to Edinburgh's Meadows. It was Sunday afternoon, and he was looking forward to catching some sunshine and getting away from the house with all its undeclared tensions. Hearing their youngest, Sarah, calling from near the window, Adina abandoned her task and went to join her. From their living room on the upper floor of their modern townhouse, they'd be able to see the same drab saloon car that had shadowed Adina off and on all week.

'Don't worry, darling. They're probably just waiting for someone.'

'But they keep looking at our house!'

Yes, and they'll probably be lurking around The Meadows and spying on us all afternoon, Douglas thought. Adina turned around and rejoined him in the kitchen. 'My friends are back.'

Doug's shoulders sagged a little. 'You're sure they're nobody you know?'

'Probably regular police. There are too many of them to be an investigative team.' She paused to flick on the kettle. 'And are you certain they're not with your previous employers?'

Doug laughed. 'If MI5 has become that sloppy then Britain really is going down the tubes. What are you going to do?'

She shrugged. 'Enact *Operation Tea Bag*. That usually chases them away.'

He kissed her cheek. 'Try not to kill anyone. Not unless it's really, really necessary.'

'Douglas Baird!' she protested. 'I've never killed a soul in my life!'

He used the kettle to fill up the teapot and smiled at her. 'You know what I mean.'

Adina made up a tray and added a few wrapped biscuits. 'While I'm out, can you find Shira's favourite sun hat? Oh, and the big tartan picnic rug.'

He held the door for her as she headed downstairs and judged he had enough time to pop into his eldest daughter's bedroom. Finding she was already wearing her "Swifty" baseball cap, he alerted her they'd be leaving in a few minutes. Downstairs, and crossing the living room, he glanced into the street to see Adina approaching the silver-coloured car with her tray. Watching her slow, careful steps, designed to communicate an inoffensive meekness he knew she'd soon have the watchers eating out of her hand. In the meantime, the picnic rug! He opened a cupboard door and rummaged for what he needed. He'd only been looking for a few seconds when he heard Sarah scream. Without pausing to look out the window, Douglas dashed down two flights of stairs, across the tiny front garden and out into the street. Ahead of him, the silver car was already speeding away, and where it had parked, he found a broken teapot and the scattered contents of the tray.

Lillico pulled up in the Ratho Bridge car park, gripping his steering wheel while he waited for the rest of the Armour Group, minus Charlie and Lorna, to join a group call.

'Guys, we have some news,' Gill said. 'A few minutes ago, Adina's husband rang to report her abduction from outside their house.'

'Has he alerted the police?' asked Lillico.

'He hasn't,' said Gill. 'Apparently, Adina has always insisted he wait twenty-four hours before alerting the authorities.'

'Heavens, Gill,' said Solomon. 'Why?'

'It's a stipulation she made in the event she was ever lifted by her own people. She didn't want to raise suspicions by having false alarms.'

'But this is unquestionably Canmore. She could be in danger.'

'Agreed. But based on my overnight detention in a Dundee jail, they might just rattle her cage and release her again.'

'Is that it?' asked Ailsa. 'They're just trying to scare us?'

'We'd be fools not to be scared,' said Solomon. 'And Gill, you should protect Sal and Josh.'

Gill didn't respond right away. 'If things ramp up, Sal and Josh will go to her parents.'

'Alex, what do you think?'

'I'm working a case,' he said discreetly. 'I can't tell you much, but if we're successful, we might take Canmore down before he launches his coup.'

'Well, I'm nervous,' said Solomon. 'Everyone, please take extra care. And as soon as anyone hears from Adina, please let us all know.'

Lillico hung up the call and tapped his mouth with his left hand. Canmore was circling like a shark, and if they weren't careful, they'd be snatched, one by one. Glancing at his watch, he realised he was going to be late for his case conference with Wiley and Eliza. And as much as he'd like to go looking for Adina, this meeting was his most tangible step towards resisting their common foe. Finding his game face, he locked his car and strode into the old pub.

'Ah, here he is,' called Wiley a few minutes later when Lillico found them in a distant part of the beer garden. 'Comes wandering in when it suits him.'

'Took a minute to find you,' muttered Lillico, laying down their drinks. 'Feel like I've walked halfway to Glasgow.'

'It's far from the eyes and ears of the office,' said Wiley, accepting the pint. 'And of course … it serves beer. '

'You like canals, George?'

Wiley seemed to consider this while he glanced down at the slow-moving channel. It was still churning slightly from the narrow boat that passed several minutes before, and now the dragonflies were reasserting themselves on the gentle waterway. 'Not especially. I've never enjoyed boats, and I've had an almost pathological distrust of ducks ever since I was a laddie.'

'What about you, Eliza?'

She smiled a "thank you" when she accepted her drink. 'I like it here. It's peaceful.'

Lillico pulled gently on his half-pint of Guinness and tried to focus on the task at hand. 'Yeah, it is.'

'You two can come back later and take a stroll,' muttered Wiley. 'In the meantime, can we do what we came here to do and make a plan?'

'Food and fuel distribution centres keep popping up on the incident logs,' said Eliza, pulling an iPad from her bag. 'As we suspected, we're seeing a spike in confrontations

142

between security staff and groups of youths testing the perimeters.'

'Break-ins?'

'Attempted. Young guys checking the fences and chucking stones at the cameras in the middle of the night. In a few cases, I have images and a couple of names. I'll run them through the system and see if they've had their mucky hands on anything else.'

'That's all very well,' said Wiley. 'But it's petty criminality. We're gonna need a lot more than that if we're going to accuse Canmore. Is there any way at all we can link him to the Wigtownshire cache?'

Lillico shook his head. 'Been over this, boss. We can't touch him for that.'

'Billy Whyte was Canmore's lackey, and he's the one who ordered the guns.'

'Yes, but unless Whyte gives him up, he's no good to us.'

Wiley shook his head. 'If Whyte won't give Canmore up, what about the Drumchapel crew?'

'What about them?' asked Eliza.

'We have circumstantial evidence to suggest they carried out a bunch of hits for Canmore over the years. They're all serving long prison terms, so maybe we could turn one and blow this wide open.'

Lillico pulled a face. 'Those people follow a code. They'll never work with the police.'

'Lorna Cheyne,' said Eliza. 'Assuming she's the person who secured the USB stick, maybe she can get something else to use against him?'

'Lorna confirmed that Sinclair was one of the people she burgled,' said Lillico. 'She thinks Sinclair and Canmore joined forces to send Malkie Bell after the stolen USB stick and Sinclair's assets.'

'But it's her word against Canmore's,' growled Wiley. 'Apart from the low-hanging fruit we found on Canmore, is there anything else on Sinclair's laptop?'

Eliza winced. 'Lots of dross on Scottish politicians and celebrities. Nothing that illuminates Canmore's ultimate goal.'

Wiley fell silent. After a minute, he started tapping a cigarette on the table, but out of consideration for his health-conscious colleagues, he didn't light up. 'If I was planning a coup,' he said, thoughtfully, 'I'd order in a bunch of sandwiches.'

Eliza looked puzzled. 'Sorry, boss?'

'Crates of soft drinks. Maybe a few baseball bats.'

Lillico glanced at Eliza but said nothing.

'The point I'm making is if Canmore really does kick over the apple cart, there'll be a lot of stuff he'll need in a hurry. Food, drink, and clothing for his militia. I imagine there'll be lorry loads of materials he'd want to prep in advance before disrupting the supply network.'

Eliza caught Wiley's intent. 'You're thinking of using Chief Super Macfarlane's anti-corruption case to detect irregular purchasing patterns? Stuff being stored in central Edinburgh that's way and above normal consumption?'

Wiley indulged in a slow mischievous nod.

Eliza sagged. 'Oh goody. More gigabytes to trawl through.'

Lillico gave her a gentle nudge. 'It's actually quite a good idea.'

'This is good,' said Wiley, finally surrendering to his craving and lighting up. 'What else can we do?'

Lillico waved the smoke away and frowned at his boss. 'I've discovered how Murray McGovern accessed Harry Sinclair's flat.'

Wiley's face warmed a little. 'You're thinking it's time for a little chat?'

'We'll incur the wrath of our Chief Super, but yes, I'd like to see if we get a rise out of McGovern.'

'You pull him in first thing tomorrow and leave me to deal with MacFarlane.'

Later that evening, Gill was on the floor with Josh. They'd missed each other during his brief incarceration and now an elaborate game using pieces of wooden train track and a selection of tiny finger puppets was gradually escalating into a playfight. Gill was earnestly losing at this game of rough and tumble while Salina worked beside them at the kitchen table. She was eyeing him suspiciously, and he realised his exaggerated happiness around Josh was revealing how anxious he'd become. For the sake of his family, he was trying to have a normal evening, though he couldn't push the news about Adina from his mind.

And Gill had other concerns. He hadn't had a chance to sit with Salina and explain the events that led to him spending a day in a police cell. Nor had he shared his growing conviction the whole family should get out of town for a few days. Both conversations or were they one conversation, he wasn't sure, would happen as soon as Josh was in bed. There was tension in the household, and he was alert to every tiny signal in her voice.

'Gill,' she said quietly.

'I know, love. So much to talk about.'

'Yeah, but this is something else.'

Gill flipped over onto his back and swung his son in the air, pretending he was a tiny aeroplane. 'What's up?'

Salina pointed at her screen. 'I'm keeping in touch with the various chapters of the *Vigil* via Facebook. Stornoway just posted.'

'Cool. Anybody we know?'

'Don't think so, but listen, I think you should see this.'

Hearing the alarm in her voice, he scooped Josh into his arms and twisted around to look at her screen. It was a video feed where the only sounds were the wind and the muffled gasps of the cameraman's breathing. In the midst of a swaying camera angle, the only thing his senses could absorb was a misty, damp Scottish moor, with a single white cottage.

'Where is that?' asked Salina.

'Could be anywhere on Harris or Lewis,' said Gill, breathlessly.

'But that thing? Is that a …'

'Horsey,' squealed Josh, pointing happily at the screen.

Chapter 20

They left immediately. Driving through the night in Salina's car, stopping briefly at a service station at Pitlochry, where they paid cash for fuel and sim cards. Then it was onwards to Skye, where another cash transaction secured ferry tickets at Uig for the first boat to Tarbert. Arriving at the tiny port town in the early hours, Gill was tempted to turn north towards Callanish and the new sighting of Bru. But he'd more important business to attend to first. Pulling over in the car park of the gin distillery, he and Salina swapped out their sim cards and anonymised their phones. Then Gill made a short call to secure the family a bolt hole. The conversation that followed was brisk and businesslike. This would either work or it wouldn't, and it involved trusting a man Gill hadn't seen in years. Once his outrageous proposal was accepted, they were back on the road. Gill turned south, weaving his way down the main highway until the junction for the *Golden Road*.

'This is gorgeous,' murmured Salina sleepily beside him as the road dipped and dived among the headlands and bays of the isle's east coast.

'Even nicer when we don't have to share it with campervans.'

Salina shielded her eyes from the rising sun. 'Your time out here was your first job with *Mys.Scot*, right?'

'Aye. This is where it all began.'

They drove quietly into the village of Scadinish and parked up in front of cottage number four. Leaving Sal and the still-sleeping Josh in the car, Gill walked up the path and knocked on the door. The old man who answered was an older version of the Cormac McKellar he remembered. A little more wizened, a little stoop taking the edge off the man's impressive height. But looking into his friend's eyes, Gill saw the same grave determination he'd encountered all those years before.

Despite the early hour, Cormac was already dressed. He looked Gill up and down before stepping forward and embracing him. 'Wasn't sure I'd ever see you again,' he mumbled.

'I'm sorry,' said Gill. 'I'm a lousy correspondent.'

'You've been busy. Ended up subscribing to your magazine. Made it easier to keep an eye on you.' Cormac glanced back onto the road and the indistinct outline of Salina, sitting in the passenger seat. 'Listen, are you aware of rumours about a new waterhorse on Lewis?'

'Yeah, I saw it on Facebook last night and was surprised not to see a news crew on the ferry.'

Cormac waved a hand. 'That shaky bit of video isn't going to convince mainstream media, but you and I know better, Gill. It's size, the way it moved. I strongly suspect it's the real deal.'

'On the plus side, that might give us a day or two to find the horse ourselves.'

'Well, if you're planning to hunt this thing, we'll need a crew.'

'We're not going to kill it, Cormac. Or at least, I hope not.'

'What colour is it?' Cormac demanded. 'And do we know where it came from?'

'We don't know what colour he is,' Gill admitted. 'As for where he came from, I can tell you we've met him once before.'

Cormac scowled for a few seconds until comprehension flooded his face. 'That wee horse at the aluminium smelter?'

'That's the fella.'

'And despite the risk it poses, you've brought your young family to these islands?'

Gill followed Cormac's gaze to the car. 'We're being threatened, Cormac. They'd be in more danger if I left them in Dundee or placed them with family.'

'Who's threatening you?'

'Listen, old friend. There's a lot of stuff I need to catch you up on. And when that's done, and if you're still game, I'm going to ask you the biggest favour I've ever asked anyone in my life.'

The walk up the hill behind Cormac's house normally took a leisurely half hour or twenty minutes if you were pushing it. Gill and Cormac managed it in eighteen.

'You're certain our First Minister plans to exploit this quake if it ever happens?'

'If not that, then it'll be some other crisis.'

'If only Canmore would realise an independent Scotland would make so much more sense if he fixed public services instead of handing out sweeties to the faithful. And now the eejit wants to try bombs and bullets?'

'Not sure about violence, but it appears he's planning a cloud of opportunistic confusion.'

'And this horse over by Stornoway, you clearly don't think its arrival is a coincidence?'

'I don't, and that's why I need to find him.'

'Will you let me help you, Gill?'

149

'The very best way you can help is by keeping my family safe. Do you still have access to the old stables?'

'It's a riding school these days, but there are a dozen wee crofts around here I could use if we felt threatened.'

'Okay. I'm not going to tell a soul they're here. And I'll be back for them as soon as this is over.'

Cormac nodded. 'And in return, can you do something for me?'

'Anything.'

'Ailsa's all I've got in the world. Promise me you'll do everything in your power to help her survive this.'

Gill clasped Cormac's hands in his own. 'I promise.'

At the same moment when Gill and Cormac were climbing the hillside on Harris, Adina sat alone in a brightly lit room. The anger she felt at her illegal detention was only mildly less than her annoyance with herself. The rest of the Armour Group had warned her this moment was coming, and arrogantly, she'd walked right into Canmore's snare. Rather than call for backup, or apply her training to safely confront her assailants, she'd blithely walked into the lion's mouth. And now she was trapped, waiting to hear her captor's demands, if she was offered terms at all.

Trying to rest on a hard bench, she sat with her head in her hands and her elbows leaning on a table. But this gesture wasn't one of despair. Instead, keeping her palms pressed lightly against her eyes and fingertips against her ears, she minimised the shouts, screams and sounds of rattled doors coming from outside her prison. These noises were probably just a recording, but this auditory assault, plus the lack of human contact, were all in the interrogator's playbook. The twenty-four hours without water was a test, and the bright white light in the room, undiminished since her arrival, was the driving force behind a headache that would probably take days to shift.

The door burst open without warning and an athletic man in black jeans and sculpted black tee shirt hurried in. Up his biceps, tattoos of intertwined serpents, disappeared under his sleeves.

'Sorry to have kept you,' he muttered, sitting down and sliding a bottle of water across to her. 'Lots going on this morning.'

Adina caught it, and set it upright, but didn't break the seal. 'Clearly. Are you and the rest of Canmore's lackeys busy moping up the enemies of the state?'

The man smiled and opened a file on his phone. 'Is that an admission, Miss Mofaz, that you're an enemy of the state?'

'I love this country. It's my adopted home.'

The man nodded earnestly. 'It's just that you love certain other countries even more.'

'I don't know what you mean.'

The man shook his head with a wry smile. 'No time for games, Adina. Suffice to say your sojourn in Scotland is at an end. While your sleeper agent status has been energetically denied by your home government, we did get a tip-off from MI5 a few years back, so there's no point in denying it.' He looked up and grinned. 'Your own dear hubby was watching you.'

Adina gave a casual shrug. 'I knew that already.'

'Fortunately, you haven't done anything too treasonous, so we're prepared to let you claim diplomatic immunity as long as you leave the country immediately.' He met her gaze for the first time. 'Is that understood?'

'This is my home. My work is here. My girls are happy. Why should I leave?'

The man ignored her question. 'Aside from guaranteeing your immediate departure, the only other condition for your release is to reveal the location of this man.'

Her captor tapped his phone causing one of the white walls of her prison to become a screen. The image displayed an unsmiling Gill McArdle. 'This photo was taken two days ago when McArdle was booked in at Bell Street station after being charged with assault. Since then, he's managed to evade our surveillance, and I need to know where he is.'

'Most likely at home.'

'Tried there. He's not.'

'No idea why you think I would know.'

He glanced at his watch. 'Four and a half minutes, Adina. You'd better start remembering.'

'He darts around. Orkney, Wigtownshire, the Western Isles. Hard to know where he is on any given day.'

'I need his location, and because I don't trust you, you'll need to be able to prove it.' He swung an open palm in her direction. 'Four minutes.'

'Try his office. He was working some dig, so I haven't heard from him.'

'Let me jog your memory.' He tapped his phone a few times and a second wall illuminated, this time with a moving image. In contravention of her training, Adina swallowed.

'This is drone footage,' the man said in a conversational tone. 'It's lovely, isn't it? Douglas is such a devoted dad to his girls. Walking hand in hand like that, chatting away without a care in the world.'

'Leave my family out of this.'

He gesticulated vaguely at the screen. 'In a little over three minutes now, they'll be turning down Morningside. It's a busy old street, isn't it? Dangerous at times.'

Adina watched in horrified silence as Douglas paused to sort out one of the girl's shoes. Then he pointed in the direction of a bakery the girls loved. They didn't normally buy treats during the week, though she knew he sometimes broke the rules when she was "away on business."

'Your phone,' he said, sliding it across the table to her. 'Don't try calling Douglas. I just need you to give me McArdle.'

'Or what?'

'Or the big white van delivering parcels in Morningside on this lovely Monday morning won't be taking as much care as usual. I'm estimating he'll collide with your family at 42 miles per hour, roundabout … here.' A third screen opened up, showing a street map of the area. The drone location marked the slowly moving position of her family. A much faster dot was powering towards them.

'If you hurt my family, I swear I will kill you.'

He laughed. 'How very forgiving of you. I'll be honest and say I expected better from a follower of the Nazarene. Two minutes, Miss Mofaz.'

Adina snatched her phone from the table, unlocked it and let her finger hover over the screen. She didn't have any options here. She did, however, have the clarity of mind to know when she was beaten.

'Time's a wasting, Adina. While I don't normally compliment a traitor, I've heard you are a very clear thinker, so think quickly and do the right thing.'

With her head running faster than her heart, Adina urgently tabbed her way to an app. Then she held it up for him before sliding it in his direction.

He smiled. 'You have a geolocator on McArdle's phone?'

'With his permission,' Adina admitted. 'Gill has a habit of getting lost.'

'That data point. It shows he arrived at Tarbert an hour ago. Where is he now?'

Adina turned the screen to face her. 'Looks like he's switched his phone off, or maybe he's in a spot without signal.'

'And what would he be doing on the Isle of Harris?'

'Who knows? He's got friends out there, so maybe he's having a late summer break. I've done what you asked, now call off your goons.'

With another theatrical glance at his watch, he pushed her device back towards her. 'One minute and fifteen seconds. Plenty of time.'

'For what?' she hissed.

'For you to launch your emergency extraction protocol.'

'Why would I do that?'

'I'll be honest. I told my boss I'd be happier dumping your battered corpse in the River Clyde. But he reckons there are international considerations, so on this occasion, and this time only, you're allowed a one-way pass out of trouble.'

Adina did a quick calculation in her head, then watched her fingers dart around the screen.

'Wait,' he said. 'Show me what you're doing?'

'You're aware of the Tor Browser?'

'The dark web? Sure.'

'This is my home screen, for use only in emergencies.'

'Like when you're committing treason against your adopted home?'

'Like when I'm afraid for my life.' She pulled up a screen. 'When I enter my password in here, the process becomes irrevocable. Are you sure there's no other way to do this?'

'Unless you're willing to join me to subvert McArdle and his friends, then I need you either dead or gone.'

She tapped furiously for three seconds. 'There,' she said, holding up her phone. 'It's done.'

'What's your exit point?'

'Gimme a second.' She paused to look at the response now spilling onto her screen. 'A small airfield in Fife. I'll need to be there in six hours.'

He considered this briefly before dialling a number. 'Change of plan,' he said. 'Collect the targets and hold them. I'll be sending you an address in Fife.' He listened while his would-be assassin asked clarifying questions. 'Just linger nearby. I'll get her to phone her husband now.'

Adina glanced at the screens. The fast-moving dot had paused, and in the drone footage, she could see the white van shadowing her family. On her interrogator's instruction, she took her phone in her shaking hands and dialled her husband. Initially, Douglas was delighted to hear from her. But, then she needed to explain the situation, and found herself saying something she'd prayed she'd never have to say. He was confused. Then he was angry. And when finally, she raised her voice to him, he was scared. When she'd smothered his protests she gave him one clear instruction. 'There's a van behind you, Doug. You and the girls are to get in. Don't talk to the driver, and don't try to go back for anything. Follow their instructions and I'll see you at the exit point.' She waited for his acknowledgement, then whispered, 'I'm so sorry, my love,' before hanging up the call.

'I'll say farewell,' said the man. 'I took the liberty of checking, and the weather in Tel Aviv is to be beautiful this evening.'

Adina looked down at her hands. Never in her life had she felt this defeated.

'Just to make you aware,' he jeered. 'The First Minister, at some moment that suits his purposes, will break the story of an Israeli spy and a British Intelligence agent, working in lockstep to undermine this country.' He got to his feet and moved to the door. 'Don't ever come back to Scotland, Miss Mofaz. You're not welcome here.'

'Who are you?' spat Adina, not expecting an answer.

He manufactured a theatrical look of surprise. 'Didn't I say? You can call me Billy Whyte.' Then he laughed at some private joke and left the room.

Chapter 21

Mhairi hit her desk at 9 am on that Monday morning, determined to discover what had happened to the Fisher Street hoard. Scanning the weekend news, there was nothing official being said, other than a lot of BS about the gold being "saved for the nation." But somewhere amongst her research, she spotted a Facebook post mentioning unusual movements at Edinburgh Castle during Saturday evening and into Sunday. Picking up the theme, she tightened her search parameters and found an online group dedicated to the comings and goings at the castle. And without mentioning the Fisher Street gold explicitly, the consensus amongst the castle watchers was that two dozen large vans had entered the fortress. That sounded like overkill to Mhairi, for what was essentially three beer crates of gold coins, but then, maybe they'd split the load on security grounds. And Edinburgh Castle? It all sounded a bit medieval, but it was information that she needed to share with her boss.

'Where's Gill this morning?' she asked.

'Prison,' said Craig, matter-of-factly.

'South America,' chimed Larry. 'Searchin' fer Eldorado.'

Mhairi shook her head. 'Cass, do you know?'

Cassy's voice sounded strange like she was fuming and worried at the same time, the two emotions warring against each other so Mhairi couldn't know if her friend wanted to thump Gill McArdle or hug him. 'He's announced he's taking a holiday. No notice. No consultation, just a text this morning saying, "Sorry, Cass. Decided to take a few days off. I'll be in touch."'

Larry turned to glare at Craig's back. 'Okay, Craig wuz right. Oor boss is still in the clink.'

'Don't think so,' said Cassy. 'But it's bloody inconsiderate of him.'

'We've got three weeks to close issue 63,' said Mhairi. 'We'll be fine.'

'Yeah, but it's disruptive. I can't stand it when he goes on walkabout. Especially if he's on holiday because he won't bring me anything I can print.'

'We have Fisher Street,' said Mhairi. 'We can build the issue around that.'

Cassy sighed deeply. 'Already on it, my friend. Already on it.'

Freya was at home that Monday morning, working on her blog. Without any promise of financial payback, it was tedious work monitoring Facebook postings and gradually establishing regular direct contact with people who claimed to have seen the waterhorse. The sightings were always fleeting, always at a distance, but she was accruing enough data to say beyond reasonable doubt there was a living, breathing waterhorse on the Harris & Lewis mainland. Any thought she had of discrediting these people was gone. Now they were her collaborators in a giant digital game of cat and mouse. She was plotting the latest locations in some mapping software when her phone rang.

'I was watching your numbers over the weekend,' said Howard without a greeting. 'I think I became your ten-thousandth follower.'

'Thanks,' said Freya, flatly. It was already mid-morning, and she was too busy for what might turn out to be a social call.

'You seem to be posting the waterhorse's location every couple of hours. How are you doing that?'

'Yeah, I've got a good fix on where it's been, just not where it is right now. My blog went viral on Harris and Lewis almost immediately and now I've got a barnful of people sharing their sightings because the authorities don't want to listen.'

'And now your posts have got a bunch of islanders with nothing better to worry about, fretting that McArdle might be about to tear up Scotland.'

'This isn't a conspiracy theory, Howard. There's a clear danger.'

'Look, I know you're upset I didn't run with your waterhorse material. When the political storm around Canmore's seismic claims blew up, you've got to realise I had to focus on the big story.'

'Sure,' she said, tartly.

'But look, Freya, your blog taps into the Hebridean zeitgeist in a way the mainstream media can't. Your numbers just blow me away and …' He stopped to clear his throat. 'And I'm phoning to ask if we could work together on this?'

'What are you proposing?'

'Nothing in the print editions, for now. But I'd like to pull your blog into our online content.'

'You want me to be a good girl and slide my blog back in at the *Tribune*?'

'We'll pay you, Freya. Pay you well. It's too short notice to offer you an employment contract, and frankly, you'd be mad to accept one, but I'd like you to work for us on this waterhorse thing for as long as it runs.'

'I dunno, Howard.'

'Keep your blog,' he insisted. 'Run it whatever way you want and monetise it any way you can. But work with us, Freya. Summarise your daily findings and let me leverage them on the *Tribune's* website.'

'Can I have an hour to think about this?'

'Absolutely, but in the meantime, pack a bag and come see me this afternoon. You can keep your freelance status, but if you let me, I want to give you every help I can on this.'

'And then?'

'Then, if you're still willing, I'll put you on the first available flight to Stornoway.'

Almost two weeks had passed since Wiley's excursion to Brodie's Close. Following that discussion, it took Lillico three days to secure the CCTV images from around the murder scene. The work of trudging through hours of footage, from multiple locations, had devoured Lillico's mornings and evenings when he should have been resting. He'd experienced a surge of relief when all this hard work paid off and finally, the fruit of his labour was sitting, angrily, in front of him.

DCI Wiley looked up from his notes and smiled. 'Says here you hurt your leg in Wigtownshire, Murray. How's that doing?'

'Irrelevant question,' whispered the man's solicitor. 'You don't have to answer that.'

McGovern shrugged off the advice. 'Healing slowly, thanks for asking.'

'Still, it's a long walk down into the bowels of Bathgate Station. I notice you still walk with a limp.'

'I do, thanks to police negligence on the day I was injured.' He stopped to glower at Lillico. 'I've detailed that in my compensation claim. The same one where I accuse your bag man of deliberately withholding medical care.'

'Would you say you're good with technology?' asked Wiley, ignoring the accusation. 'I only ask as I'm a bit of a dolt when it comes to that kind of thing.'

McGovern shrugged. 'I work in very demanding environments. Dangerous caves, that kind of thing, so yeah, I keep my skills up to date.'

Lillico spun his laptop around. 'Do you own a camera system like this?'

McGovern stared at the screen. 'You know I do. You probably found this in my gear.'

'So, a miniature camera mounted on the end of a flexible proboscis.'

'Yeah. It's what surgeons use when they wanna take a look at your insides and stick a camera up where the sun doesn't shine.' McGovern lifted a hand to stop his solicitor's silent protests. 'And I own one because it's a useful way to explore tight spaces in caves.'

'Or, if you wanted to take discreet photos of someone entering or leaving their house.'

'Please,' said the solicitor, 'if you have evidence for that implied activity, present it now because I think you gentlemen are just shaking the tree to see what falls.'

'We'll leave the camera for now,' said Lillico. 'Let's move on to another piece of kit. Do you own a 3D printer, Murray?'

'Got one somewhere.'

'Owning a printer isn't a crime, Inspector. Please move on.' He turned to glower at McGovern. 'And given the line of questioning, I'll advise my client again that he doesn't need to respond to any of your questions.'

'Ever seen this before?' asked Wiley, laying an ancient key on the table.

Lillico's training allowed him to spot McGovern's eyes widen just a fraction.

McGovern shook his head.

Wiley leaned in closer to handle the key. 'It's plastic, just like the one you made. 3D printed, using images captured from a tiny camera. It's my belief you installed your proboscis camera outside Sinclair's door. That gave you multiple photos of this antique key, ensuring you printed it just right.'

McGovern's composure recovered quickly. 'Fascinating tale, guys. But I wasn't there.'

'I'll show you a photo,' said Lillico, displaying a different image on his laptop. 'This is you, isn't it?'

McGovern squinted at the image. 'Might be. Bit hard to say.'

'How about in this image?'

This time, McGovern swallowed. 'Nah, doesn't look like me at all.'

'Those images are from the Victoria Street area on the day Harry Sinclair was murdered,' Lillico withdrew his laptop. 'What can you tell us about that?'

McGovern swept away the suggestion. 'Nice part of town. Maybe I go for a wander from time to time. Grab a pint in the Grassmarket.'

Lillico looked down at his hands and smiled while Wiley recovered the key. 'Of course, you're absolutely right, Murray. We can't prove a word of it. But we suspect it's true, so we'll keep trying. In the meantime, thank you for your cooperation. You are free to go.' He paused. 'For the time being.'

Grumbling and muttering, McGovern and his solicitor left the room, leaving the two officers sitting by themselves. When the door closed behind them, Wiley turned to Lillico. 'Good work, son. I think that went rather well.'

Chapter 22

Six hours after Adina's capitulation, Roddy sat privately in his office, jotting notes for a speech. Meanwhile, on a Fife airfield, one of Stevie's boys was fiddling with the live video feed. The sound was muffled and the camera shot careened wildly while the operator positioned the equipment on the roof of a car.

'Right, here it comes,' said a voice, commenting on the incoming aircraft.

'You lot, out of the car,' commanded a second voice. Adina Mofaz appeared on Roddy's screen, followed by her husband and two little girls. She looked scared, diminished, and above all, she looked beaten. When she turned to help one of her girls, she noticed the camera.

'What's that for?' she asked, pointing straight into the lens.

'None of your damn business. Now shut up and stand by the car.'

The noise of the approaching aircraft started to dominate the feed, and Roddy caught a glimpse of a sleek business jet as it rushed past on the patched tarmac. There was a two-minute delay while the plane slowed, then taxied back to their position. Roddy squinted at the machine. He was curious to see who the Israelis had sent. The doors opened and two pilots got out to stand by the aircraft. To Roddy's disappointment, they were just two ancient white guys. Probably hired at short notice. White shirts, with black ties and trousers, plus long neatly trimmed beards, they looked like something out of a ZZ Top tribute band. Unsmiling, the two men guided Mofaz and her people onto the plane. Then, with a curt nod to Stevie's boys, they got back in the craft and taxied away.

Someone unclipped the camera from its stand and followed the aircraft as it made a final turn at the end of the runway before accelerating and lifting off into the early evening sky. The plane remained as a diminishing dot on the screen until Roddy tired of it and flicked off his screen. He smiled to himself, delighted he'd never see Adina Mofaz again.

The scene inside the aircraft was an unhappy one as it flew over the Firth of Forth and banked to the east. Adina clutched Shira to her chest and turned to look at Douglas. Since she silenced his protests back in Edinburgh he still hadn't spoken to her, and although he refused to meet her gaze, his normally kind eyes blazed with anger. The cockpit door lay open, and she heard the two pilots bickering about the flight plan and whether or not they might be shot down or arrested.

'Where are we going?' she called out.

One of the pilots half-turned to her, his eyes hidden behind dark glasses. 'Morocco, my darlin'. We'll be needin' a wee drop o' fuel.'

'And after?'

'Ye ken we cannae talk about that.'

She nodded and turned to Shira. 'Did you hear that? We're going to Morocco tonight. It'll be lovely and warm. Maybe we can go swimming?'

The pilot turned again. 'Would yous mind if Barley and I put on a little music? Help us calm our nerves.'

Adina turned to Douglas who just scowled and shrugged in a single miserable gesture.

'Just go for it, guys. Whatever makes you happy.'

The copilot fiddled with a dial and suddenly a long, powerful violin riff filled the confined space. As drums and vocals timed in, the two pilots nodded approvingly and started singing along.

Chapter 23

While Josh slept in his car seat, Gill and Salina stepped out of Cormac's house and strolled hand in hand across the short stretch of grass and out to the rock edge where they could look over the sea. They were weary after the long drive the night before and anxious about what the coming days might bring.

'Incredible sky,' said Salina. 'I don't think I've ever seen it bluer than this.'

Gill shook his head. 'Something about the Western Isles when August gives way to September. It's like the monsoon season is reserved for the tourists, and as soon as they all go home, you get this wonderful ridge of high pressure that turns the weather glorious for a month.'

Salina tugged his hand. 'We're tourists, aren't we?'

'Fugitives, my love,' he said, before kissing her. 'Doesn't mean we can't enjoy it.'

She sighed. 'I just wish we could spend more of it together.'

'I'll pop back when I can.'

She turned to nibble his ear. 'Yes, please.'

'Look, Sal. I know you understand the logic of hiding ourselves away, but are you going to be okay sheltering with an old man you only know by reputation?'

Salina bobbed her head. 'It'll have its challenges, but Cormac and I will find common ground. We can share stories about Glasgow and our experiences on the sea. We'll be okay.'

'And Josh?'

Salina laughed. 'He's a toddler, Gill. Every day is a new adventure. I already know he's going to have a ball.'

'If you've any concerns, call me.'

'Gill, go and do what you came here to do. Josh and I will be waiting for you.'

'You sure?'

'A big part of me would like to see you rested before you leave, but I can feel your need to be where the action is. Just take care of yourself and try to stay in touch.'

'Okay, my love.' He gave her a ragged smile. 'You tak' the high road an a'l tak the low. And all that.'

'Just, come back safe, Gill McArdle.'

He hugged her, and kissed the still sleeping Josh, and then he left.

Gill didn't go straight to Rani and Graham's croft. Instead, he stopped off at Catriona's house in Tarbert where Ailsa answered the door.

'Hey, jailbird,' she teased.

'You heard about that?' groaned Gill.

'Alex told us. About how you assaulted a police officer.'

'I didn't assault anybody!'

'I bet that's what they all say,' she teased.

'They were illegally confiscating an archaeological treasure,' said Gill, scratching the back of his head. 'Maybe I *should* have thumped somebody.'

Ailsa held the door open for him. 'After what happened here, we're all feeling the same.'

'Your dad is worried about you. He's already suspicious the fire was deliberate.'

'Don't tell him too much about Canmore,' Ailsa moaned. 'I won't be able to bear his fussing.'

Gill shook his head. 'I've only told him the basics.'

'Thank you. We can catch him up later.'

'Assuming the arsonist was Canmore's man, does your gran have any information about him?'

'A name and contact details, but that's probably faked. And he paid in cash.'

'Any sign of anyone watching you? Following, when you go out?'

Ailsa tapped her breastplate which flickered into the visible spectrum for a fraction of a second. 'Nope, but I'm ready for anything.'

'Even so, if you'd feel safer switching off your phone and staying with your dad until this blows over, no one will blame you.'

'What? And miss the firework display?'

Gill cleared his throat. 'I'm still hoping there won't be anything like that.'

'I'll pop and see Salina tomorrow and have a wee play with Josh. But, in the evenings I need to stay with mum and gran for a couple more days.'

'Thank you. Sal will be glad for your support.'

After tea and a chat with Ailsa's family, Gill left Tarbert and travelled alone to Callanish. It was his second visit to the monument since the day five years ago when he'd found the first waterhorse bones. A sprawling complex compared to most neolithic sites; he was surprised when the place felt a little smaller than he remembered. Wandering amongst the stones for an hour, he tried to imagine what it would be like to encounter his waterhorse then walk the beast in a single circuit around the stones. Would there be a crowd present or might he do it alone? Would people understand what he'd done, or would he have to explain the minutiae to a perplexed policeman? He shook his head – all this speculation was pointless. And really? All he wanted was to wrap his arms around his family until Canmore's plan had run its course. That instinct battled with another, urging him to rush to Adina's aid, even though he didn't know where to find her. Meanwhile, the rest of the Armour Group seemed weakened and exposed.

Walking around the monument helped counter the exhaustion brought on by a night without sleep. And of course, there was always the possible bonus of making a significant encounter. But even while he walked with all his senses alert there was no sign of Bru, nor Raphael, nor gentle guiding words from Aura. Instead, the old stones stood like petrified giants, and all around, everything was quiet, as if nature itself was holding its breath in anticipation of what might happen here.

Switching on his phone he discovered a decent mobile signal, so he decided to risk a quick call to Solomon.

'Where are you?' she asked.

'On Lewis. Callanish to be exact.'

'And is there any sign of "Scotland's royal horse of old renown?"'

Gill glanced around. 'Absolutely none. Though I sense he's not far away.'

'And if he appears, what are you going to do?'

'Canmore is full of BS, Solie. And while I can accuse him of plotting against Scotland's constitutional arrangements, I can't prove it. There's no way I'd declare *The Torn Isle* under present circumstances.'

'Still, we should be ready.' Solomon paused. 'How's the family?'

'Ensconced in a safe house, and hoping this is over soon.'

'And Ailsa?'

'Helping her gran recover from the fire and gagging to take the fight to Canmore.'

'I'm concerned we still haven't heard from Adina,' said Solomon. 'As much as I respect her husband's wishes, I'm wondering if we should involve the authorities?'

'But who would we speak to? Adina's priority is keeping her family safe, but let's not give up on her. She's incredibly resourceful.'

'Charlie is escorting me to Edinburgh tomorrow to make final prep for the Read*Scot* conference. We'll swing by Adina's house once we're finished at the conference venue and see if there's any sign of life.'

'Solie, the conference, are you sure it's right to go ahead with it?'

'I'll be surrounded by hundreds of delegates for two days. I imagine it's the safest place I could be.'

'Okay, look, about my speech …'

'We'll see you if we see you, Gill. As much as I'd love your support, it's more important you do what you're doing.'

They finished their call and Gill wearily got back in the car. Still holding his phone, he tried Douglas Baird. To his alarm, the number wasn't recognised. When he dialled the family's landline the result was the same. More than a little worried, he tried Adina with the same result. Swearing unhappily, under his breath, he recognised Adina and Lorna's freedoms were compromised, and as such, they were the opening casualties of Canmore's war.

After driving the few miles to Dalbeg, he parked at the back of Rani's croft and tapped the kitchen door before walking in. Inside, he found Rani on the phone while Graham pushed a pin into a wall-mounted map.

Amy saw Gill first, dashing to hug his legs. 'Thank you for coming back.'

Gill stroked her hair. 'I promised, didn't I?'

'Lots of people are seeing Bru,' she announced. 'I think it means he's coming home.'

Graham made eye contact with Gill before turning back to the board. 'You look exhausted, pal. When was the last time you slept?'

Gill rubbed his face and tried to focus. 'Uh, a couple of nights ago. How's the search for Bru?'

Graham turned back to his board. 'We've had sightings near Marybank, Rannish and Kintarvie. All in the last forty-eight hours.'

'If it really is Bru,' muttered Rani.

Gill was puzzled unless Rani was suggesting a second waterhorse was lurking on the island moors. 'What do you mean?'

'Aside from the tusk, his appearance has changed.' She glanced at him. 'Especially his colour.'

Gill stumbled against some furniture when he felt his heart jump. 'He's not a grey anymore?'

Rani watched his unsteady fumbling for a moment before she responded. 'He's white, Gill. A vivid, brilliant white.'

'Oh, thank God,' said Gill, letting Amy hug him again, even though the little girl couldn't know the implications of Bru becoming black or white.

'And he's changing his behaviour,' Graham added, while Gill shrank down into a seat with relief. 'Up until now, the only sightings were in gulleys and glens where he avoided human contact. Now Bru is taking the high ground, standing for five to ten minutes in plain sight before moving on.'

'He's EVERYWHERE on social media,' enthused Amy.

'Meaning the mainstream news will pick up on this story soon,' observed Gill. 'Is there any pattern to Bru's journey?'

'At the moment, it looks like he's heading for the remote uplands north of Tarbert.'

'Okay,' said Gill. 'Do you want to go looking for him?'

'Based on these reports, he's moving fast.' Graham looked Gill up and down. 'But honestly, pal, let us get you a sandwich, then please go get some sleep. We'll go out tomorrow once you're rested.'

Gill obeyed, noticing again that his body didn't carry a sleepless night the way it used to. He thanked his hosts and trudged up to the guest bedroom. Determined to finish his day on a high, he texted the Armour Group before sending the same message to Salina. 'Bru is a White! Repeat, White! Checks one more box on our journey to *The Torn Isle*.'

Chapter 24

It was after hours in the greasy café off Edinburgh's Cockburn Street where Roddy organised his little get-togethers. They were gathering at McGovern's insistence while Stevie Blaine made a song and dance about meeting in person.

'We should be doing this over an encrypted App,' fussed Blaine. 'We're too exposed like this.'

'Don't trust 'em,' said McGovern. 'And I'm not sure I trust you either, Stevie-boy.'

Blaine waved his hand dismissively at McGovern and received a forceful two-fingered flick in response.

'Enough!' Roddy signalled his irritation at their bickering and called the meeting to business. 'How are things at your end, Murray?'

McGovern dragged his glare away from Blaine. 'My teams are ready to go.'

'You've done all the necessary groundwork?'

He nodded slowly. 'We know how many we need and where. When you give the word, boss, I'll start locking down the key facilities in a matter of hours. Unless we meet unexpected opposition, we'll control all the major distribution centres within three days.'

'No problems?'

McGovern shrugged lazily. 'Beggsy got yanked in by Military Police at Faslane the other day. Then my eyes and ears inside Bathgate mentioned he'd become a person of interest, so I've had to let him go.'

'You fired him?' spat Roddy, fretting about another potential leak in his organisation.

'When I say, "let him go," I mean from the top of a tower block in Springburn.'

Blaine sniggered. 'A sad end.'

'Aye. I hear they're being demolished next year.'

'I mean of the Drumchapel crew. Beggsy was their last man standing.'

'Well, he got sloppy so he's not standing anymore.'

'Talking of being a person of interest, Murray,' said Blaine, mischievously, 'I hear you've been out to Bathgate yourself.'

McGovern ignored the taunt and turned to face Roddy. 'Yeah. That's something I wanted to mention, boss. Somehow my name came up in connection to Harry Sinclair.'

'The cops had you in?' growled Roddy. 'When?'

'This morning.'

'Bloody hell, Murray. You're meant to be the best of the best.'

'They don't have proof, obviously, or else I wouldn't be sitting here. But they seem to have pieced it together all right.'

'Do they realise why you might have done Sinclair?'

'Motive never came into it. They were too busy figuring how I might have entered the building.'

Blaine shook his head. 'Sloppy work, Murray.'

'Oh yeah? You wanna meet in Springburn? Maybe we can take a rooftop walk and chat about this some more?'

Roddy lifted his hands. 'We don't have time for this chest-thumping. Let's get back to our loose ends.'

Blaine turned to McGovern. 'Mofaz fled the country after confirming McArdle is on Harris.'

Roddy found this surprising. 'What the hell is he doing way out there?'

'He arrived in Tarbert this morning and switched off his phone. I think he went to help Ailsa McIver.'

'Help her, how?'

'Ailsa's granny had a wee housefire,' said McGovern. 'Nobody hurt, not that I give a shit, but as it's pulled her out of Glasgow for the next few weeks, it met the brief.'

Roddy grunted an acknowledgement. 'If you're happy to drop people like Beggsy off a tower block, maybe we should do the same with McArdle and his pals?'

'Aye,' said McGovern. 'I'd be up for that.'

Blaine rubbed his face. 'Seriously, Murray? A detective inspector, a journalist and the head of a local charity – do you think those deaths would pass unnoticed?'

Murray pushed back. 'What about McIver? Or Cheyne?'

Blaine disagreed. 'Great! You want to kill Ailsa McIver within a few miles of where she helped discover the waterhorse bones? Or Lorna Cheyne, who's safely in police custody? Listen, we'll keep tabs on their whereabouts, but right now, we have them contained.'

'Reluctantly, I have to agree,' said Roddy. 'Let's keep an eye on them. If anyone makes a move, we'll review.'

Blaine, again. 'Did MacFarlane find ways to contain the others in McArdle's circle?'

'DI Lillico is wrestling a tonne of paperwork in the vain hope he keeps his job,' McGovern reported. 'Charlie McKay is receiving goodwill gifts from his local dealer. See if we can lure him back to his unfortunate habits.'

'Bit of a lowlife?' asked Blaine.

'He's a hardman who basically, runs security for Rosemary Solomon.'

'Is she a threat to us?' asked Roddy.

Blaine seemed to think about this. 'Runs a big charity, so yeah, she's a strategic thinker. I suspect she's the brains in their operation, so I think we should hit her sooner rather than later.'

'Yeah, but you've got to get past McKay first.'

'How about we leave her in play until D-Day, then target her and her minder?' Blaine nodded across the table at McGovern in a conciliarity gesture. 'What do you think, Murray?'

McGovern puffed himself up. 'Let's not tip our hand until the big day, so yeah, you should target her in the opening salvo.'

'Agreed' said Roddy. 'Stevie, can you set that up?'

Blaine nodded.

Roddy flicked his chin at Blaine 'And you're on top of the Agnes Fairbank situation?'

'She's in position and ready to roll.'

'You sure? She's the person sitting with their hand hovering over the big green button. I need to know she's watching this around the clock.'

Blaine grinned. 'She's ready, boss. I paid her another visit last week. Never seen a person so scared in all my life.'

'Well, keep her like that. And keep her on her toes. Timing is everything.' He glanced around to confirm their agreement. 'Alba gu bràth, gentlemen.'

Lillico laid down the long-lens camera he was holding and rubbed his hands. It was cold sitting inside Wiley's car, and he'd not had the sense to bring a jacket. They'd been on location for fifty minutes and would be here for another thirty, sixty, he didn't know.

'Interesting,' said Wiley, scrolling on his phone.

'What?' said Lillico, keeping his eyes on the vennel across the street.

'I'm trawling through crime reports. To save my thumbs, Eliza set up a filter based on the criteria we set. I've just spotted an unexplained death in Springburn.'

'Someone we know?'

'Robert Beggs, the Faslane photographer. Remember him? Fell to an untimely demise after a night on the whisky, apparently.'

Lillico picked up the camera again. 'You're thinking he's another loose end being tidied away?'

'Sounds like it. Makes me think …' Wiley was interrupted when his phone rang, and Lillico saw the man's shoulders sag a little. He recognised the number and wasn't in a rush to pick up. 'Chief Super. It's a wee bit late for a social call. I was just about to pour myself a nightcap and kiss Mrs Wiley goodnight.'

'Don't you Chief Super me, DCI Wiley. What the hell were you doing interviewing Murray McGovern this morning?'

'DI Lillico had done some excellent work explaining how the perpetrator might have entered Harry Sinclair's property. We gather Murray McGovern has some expertise in the relevant technology, so we just wanted to run it by him and see what he thought.'

'Do you or do you not recall that I ordered you to pass on your current caseload to the Major Investigation Team?'

'Absolutely, but you know what these MIT guys are like, sir. Unless it's all tied up with ribbons and bows, they're slow off the mark on transferred cases like these. DI Lillico and I were doing them a favour.'

'And the Edinburgh City Council corruption case is going to solve itself?' Macfarlane snarled.

'We'll make up the time, sir. In fact, I can assure you that, despite the late hour, DI Lillico is working at this very moment to gain momentum on the corruption case.'

'Your intervention is still uncalled for. If you value your pension, you'll not make this mistake again.'

'I can assure you, sir …' Wiley was interrupted by Lillico, raising the camera in the direction of a taxi pulling up outside the vennel. 'I'm so sorry, sir. Mrs Wiley has just appeared with a cup of hot cocoa. I'm going to have to go.' Then, while Macfarlane started to utter more threats, Wiley hung up.

'Looks like we've dispensed with the ministerial car tonight,' Wiley observed.

Lillico fired off another burst of shots. 'Let's check it's him before we get excited.'

'Well, there's our friend Murray for starters,' Wiley muttered as McGovern turned left down The Mound towards the city centre.

'Tell me, George,' asked Lillico, firing off another burst to capture McGovern while he walked away. 'Is there a Mrs Wiley?'

'You impudent whelp,' Wiley replied evenly. 'We barely know each other, and just because we're doing some evening surveillance together, that gives you the right to …' He stopped as two more figures emerged from the vennel. They had a hasty conversation, and then the bulky and unmistakable figure of Roddy Canmore got into the back seat of the taxi before it quickly drove away. Lillico hadn't met the other man, though he'd seen his mugshots. For an uncanny second, Steven Blaine turned in their direction and seemed to look right at them. Then, furtive as a city fox, he dug his hands in his pockets, crossed the street, and slunk away in the direction of Waverley Station.

After the morning's conciliatory call from Howard, Freya's afternoon became a whirlwind. First, there was form-filling to formalise her working relationship with the *Glasgow Tribune*. The work would last until the story ran out or until Howard called it a day. Then there were tickets, and car hire, and accommodation vouchers for a holiday let within sight of the Callanish stones. Finally, Howard propelled her into a conference room to meet two of his most trusted older hands. For the next two hours they'd war-gamed the story together until she'd conceived every way the next few days might play out. In short, she'd learned more about journalism in those four hours than during three years at university. And now she was at Glasgow airport, waiting for the very last flight of the day to Stornoway on the Isle of Lewis. Even sitting in the sparsely populated departure lounge, her heart was pounding. She was excited and terrified at the same time.

She never did get around to telling Howard about John Houston. On reflection, the two detectives she'd met had seemed untroubled by his untimely end. The older, bald one, Wiley, had been polite but disinterested. The other, Lillico, had a faraway look on his face, as if he'd more important things he'd rather be doing. And the likelihood was Houston's death was an unfortunate accident. The man's paranoia had been unsettling. After all, the odds of a major earthquake in Scotland were millions to one. Sure, the very suggestion would have made Howard laugh.

As if in response to her musings, the ground beneath her feet gave a tiny tremor, like the Earth itself was giggling at the thought of a quake. Had she imagined it? No, she felt it again. This time the lights flickered and a few of the other waiting passengers glanced around in concern. The shiver continued to escalate into a rumble, and somewhere in the passenger lounge, a glass bottle fell spectacularly to the floor. Then as suddenly as it had begun, the rumbling stopped. The lights flickered again and came back on. As Freya stared at the departure board, one after another, the flights ticked over to "cancelled."

Agnes Fairbank fetched another coffee and returned to her desk to stare at her screen. It was almost 11 pm and she was long past the point when she'd normally have gone home, enjoyed a single glass of red wine, and gone to bed with a book. But tonight was different. Pulses of seismic rumblings, too weak to be detected by human senses, were passing through the Highlands like birth pangs, each pulse more powerful than the last. "Foreshocks" they were called in the trade. Little indicators that spoke of the stresses rising and falling in the Earth's crust below our feet. And of course, the SGS predictive software should be explaining all this. Sucking in fresh data in real-time and running the numbers on the expected risk. Yes, it should be doing this, though it wasn't. She closed her eyes and laid her hands flat on the desk.

'Boss?' inquired a man hovering in her doorway.

She lifted her eyes to his. 'What is it, Gary?'

'Another kink in the electromagnetic field, boss. Inverness end this time.'

Her tongue flitted across her dry lips. This was another "hot" indicator of an imminent quake, and she had to cling to her mask of indifference. 'Kink, Gary? Forgive me, but that doesn't sound very technical.'

'It's faint, boss, but I'd say it's statistically significant.'

'Okay. Noted, thank you.' She opened her eyes and glanced at her watch. 'You're late tonight. Isn't it time you were away home?'

He blinked twice before speaking. 'Boss, this is the most significant bout of seismic activity we've had since I've worked here. Honestly, I'm concerned about this one.'

'What's the predictive algorithm saying?'

182

'Flat as a pancake. I've no idea why it hasn't seen this coming.'

'Okay, Gary. I need to make a call. Let me just do that and I'll be right out.'

Watching Gary nod, then turn away from her door, she was surprised how calm she sounded. He wouldn't have noticed how she'd tucked her hands away as soon as he'd walked in. Now they were shaking so much she could barely hold her phone. Trapped between the terror of the man who'd been stalking her and the consequences of what he'd compelled her to do, she realised the time was upon her. A number, written in faint pencil and loosely taped below her desk, was one she'd never contacted before. With one eye on the open doorway, she retrieved it and typed in the agreed text message. 'It's beginning.'

The reply when it came was brief. 'Stick to the plan.'

She tore up the scrap of paper, tossing half of it in the bin before stuffing the other half in her pocket. Then she dropped her elbows on the table and waited. A few minutes later, the ground perceptibly trembled beneath her feet, and she heard Gary screaming her name.

Chapter 25

In her dreams, Sandy Brightman was on the water. She'd
gone to bed early in preparation for taking tourists on a
dawn cruise at 4 am. Since the closure of the *Ness
Explorer Visitor Centre*, she spent most of her working hours
on the loch, and tonight while she rested, a dreamed
adventure slid into her subconscious. In her sleeping reverie,
she was at the helm of the *Ness Explorer* - she was dreaming
about the old boat, the one lost in the Great Glen disaster,
not the ponderous old river cruiser they'd bought to replace
her. And in her dream, the *Explorer* was at top speed,
aquaplaning down the loch at a rate she'd never attempt in
real life. The wind threw her ponytail around her head, so she
plucked away its restraints and let her hair flow free. Glancing
left and right, she knew it wouldn't be long before he
appeared, because, you know, this was her favourite dream
and magic could happen here.

Two hundred metres to her left, a splash erupted from the
surface. She laughed. He was taking air, and now the game
was afoot. She coaxed the throttle and magically found a few
more revs. But a great bow wave was building to her left, and
try as she might, he was gaining on her.

Breaking all the rules of the loch, she swung right into
Invermoriston Bay and let the boat's wash crash amongst the
birch trees growing down to the waterside. She'd try to block
him now, swinging hard across his path. But he knew her

ruses, and after another explosive gulp of air, she glimpsed his tiny dorsal fin breaking the surface while he fled to deeper water. Moments later, the mighty creature roared under her boat like a huge grey torpedo. He had the advantage now, his sights set on the finishing line set vaguely below Allt na Criche. She watched him snatch another breath and imagined his powerful tail pushing him into a new burst of acceleration. She swung the boat into his wake. Win or lose this race, she was happy to be here with him, exulting in his company.

She didn't see the log in the water, which was weird as there were normally no surface hazards in her dream version of Loch Ness. But in this dream, the boat stopped dead, smacking her head on the console, then lurching under her as she slithered to the floor. The boat's klaxon began to sound, which again was strange as the *Explorer* had no such device. And now the vessel rose up, as if the Leviathan had hoisted the damaged boat upon his back before dropping it again, throwing her sideways.

Sandy woke in the middle of her bedroom floor with her shoulder and face hurting. Rushing a hand to her forehead, it came back bloody. Around her, her room was in chaos, and she wondered if there'd been a gas explosion. That made sense as all she could hear was the fire alarm in the old house, wailing for her attention. Staggering to her feet, she realised her windows had shattered. Peering through the jagged glass, she witnessed pandemonium unleashed.

Leone Miller was working late. Months ago, she agreed to review a PhD thesis for the daughter of a friend. The paper, a treatise on the latest archaeological finds in Argyll, had appealed to her. But the summer months had prompted a peak in her Iona workload, and now, as the year drifted into September, she was under pressure to get the girl meaningful feedback in the time available. Making herself another coffee, she took it upstairs to the first-floor living room of her sensible little cottage on Oban's Duncraggan Road. Apart from her bedroom and bathroom, the room took up the whole of the first floor. Taking her drink to the front window, she stared down at the harbour, where the comings and goings of the island ferries were finished for the day. Behind her, a tiny window looked over her pocket garden and up towards the brooding presence of McKaig's Folly. This Romanesque tower with its ninety-four arches was a far less impressive place when you lived under its mossy shadow. Leone preferred to view it from the town where this shrunk-down Colosseum added a classy touch to Scotland's busiest port town. Over the last year, Oban had grown on her, and though the house wasn't perfect, it was a homely bolt hole after a lifetime of city living. From here, she could reach anywhere in the highlands or islands in a matter of hours.

Leone glanced at her watch. It was after 11 pm, and she decided she'd read one more chapter before heading for bed. She laid her drink down on the coffee table, picked up her glasses, and started to read. She was midway through an article describing the discovery of an important burial mound in Kilmartin Glen when she noticed rings forming on the surface of her drink. Something was vibrating, and for a second, she wondered if she'd left her washing machine running. But the shaking was getting more noticeable, and she yelped in terror when the rear window behind her buckled under pressure, sending glass spraying into the room. And still, the vibration was building, rising to a rumble until the whole house began to shake beneath her feet. Through the broken window, she heard the growl of tumbling stones and watched in horror as the rear of McKaig's Folly collapsed, slewing masonry across the street behind her house.

Gradually, the shaking ebbed and died and finally stopped. Leone swallowed and tiptoed down her stairs and out into the garden. Apart from a few broken windows, her house seemed unperturbed compared to many nearby dwellings. Moving to the middle of the street, she peered out over the town. Smoke and dust rose in the still evening air. A cacophony of alarms of all descriptions rang into the night and everywhere, everywhere, the sound of human voices in distress.

In the first light of the new morning, Sandy Brightman stepped carefully onto the jetty at Drumnadrochit and filled her lungs with fresh air. The sun had finally risen to put an end to a ghastly night, and before her, Loch Ness was extraordinarily calm. The cloudless dawn was casting a golden glow on the water to the north, while above her, a dark blue sky was turning paler. After the Great Glen disaster, it took two years for the loch to recover sufficient water volume to return to normal. In contrast, this morning, it looked pristine. The waves that danced here two hours before were tame compared to the tsunami set off by the collapsing silt columns four years ago. However, the quake damage back then, aside from that caused by the torrent, had been minimal. Not so today.

She turned and looked again at the former hotel that had housed the *Ness Explorer* Exhibition. Damaged in the original disaster, her trustees had submitted plans three years ago to upgrade the old building before reopening it to the public. But permission never came. "Too much red tape," her architect complained. And after today, she doubted the facility would ever reopen. The quake, although small on an international scale, had crashed the gable wall of the old building, sending a deluge of rubble to crush the cafeteria kitchen. The resulting fire had gutted the entire structure. Would it have changed the outcome if a fire engine had reached them in time? Probably not. And besides, the emergency crews were needed elsewhere. Anecdotal reports suggested the older parts of Inverness were badly hit. The news coming out of Fort William and Oban was even worse. And behind her, Drumnadrochit licked its wounds. She imagined it would be like that in lots of places; old Scottish houses built so long ago the only thing holding the stones together was gravity. And last night, gravity hadn't played fair.

She reached up and touched her bandaged forehead. A neighbour had done a good job, but the dressing was loosening, and she'd need to get it attended to. She shivered to think how much worse it could have been.

All in all, it was a beautiful morning, though there'd be no boat trip today. Looking up and down the loch, she caught glimpses of flashing blue lights and heard the overlapping sounds of distant sirens. Feeling a tear roll down her cheek, she glanced down at her feet and noticed something rather strange. Loch Ness was barely tidal, and yet, a slick of slimy rocks revealed the water level had dropped a little. Not dramatically, but it was as if somewhere, someone had pulled the plug on the mighty beast that had once been, Loch Ness.

Chapter 26

In the same moment as Sandy Brightman was counting her blessings on the shore of Loch Ness, Gill was waking in Rani's guest bedroom. He'd been exhausted the previous evening after the long drive north with Salina and Josh. Consequently, he'd slept like the dead. Waking late and quite refreshed, he shaved and showered before making his way down for breakfast, feeling self-conscious as after all, he didn't know Rani's family all that well. Arriving downstairs, he found them clustered around a TV screen in the kitchen.

'Morning,' he announced, just to let them know he was there.

Rani turned. 'We were about to come and find you. There's been a big quake.'

Alarm chasing away the last vestige of sleep, Gill joined their anxious huddle. 'Where?'

'Fort William to Inverness. They're saying there are hundreds dead.'

Gill pulled a hand to his forehead, watching as the newsreel spun from one tumbled building to another. And a dreadful feeling began to creep up his skin. 'Can't believe I slept through it.'

'So did we. Apparently, we're well outside the shock zone.'

Gill pointed at the screen. It looked like an off-the-cuff news conference was happening outside the Scottish Parliament building. 'What's happening?'

'Canmore is blaming London,' said Graham. 'Claims the submarine base reawakened the Faultline.'

'I've looked into this,' muttered Gill. 'All they did was dig a couple of test wells.'

'But that makes London look worse. They must have known there was a problem. That's why they abandoned the project.'

Gill conceded that with a nod. Who knew what would be important when the history of this day was written? But right now, miles from the action, all he could do was stare at the rolling TV images, helpless while he watched Scotland bleed.

'How are you doing?' Gill asked Salina on a call, later that morning.

'Oh, we're fine. It only rattled windows down here. How about you?'

'I slept through it all.'

'Do we know anyone who's affected?'

'Funny how it takes a crisis to put you back in touch with old friends,' said Gill. 'I exchanged texts with Sandy Brightman this morning. She suffered cuts and bruises, and one of her old staff at the exhibition was killed.'

'That's dreadful.'

'Sandy reported six fatalities in her town. And dozens injured.'

'Was her visitor centre okay?'

'Completely destroyed,' said Gill, flatly. 'It's safe to say some of the towns and villages we know well won't ever look the same again.'

'Everyone's in shock, Gill.'

'Getting angry too, if you believe the news.'

'I believe it. I hear there's going to be a big demo in Dundee this afternoon. Venting anger at London's handling of the seismic data.'

'I hope my guys keep well out of it.'

'They're grownups, Gill. They'll be fine.' She paused. 'Are you still going looking for Bru today?'

'We decided we couldn't face a helpless day in front of the TV, so Graham and I are going on the moors this morning. We'll come back for some lunch and see if there's any way we can join the relief effort on the mainland. If that isn't possible, we might stay out all night to see if we can catch our boy during twilight.'

'You take care.'

'I will.' Gill left a pause, then said what needed to be said in these uncertain times. 'I love you, Sal.'

He found Graham a short while later, grim-faced while he watched live footage of Canmore visiting a ruined street in Inverness. The politician paused to shake hands with survivors, then stood with a business owner while the man pointed to roof damage. When he eventually came to the microphone, Canmore seemed angry. The reporter asked him why.

'The physical damage we're seeing here today can be repaired,' Canmore began. *'But the lives lost? The businesses ruined? It didn't need to be like this.'*

'What are you suggesting, First Minister?'

'The British government had eighty years of seismic data they could have shared with us. Data specific to the Great Glen Fault, gathered to support their infernal submarine project. We could have used that to build robust prediction systems. The quake might still have happened, but at least we'd have been prepared.'

'The British government says it refutes your claim. They say the only data held outwith the Scottish Geological Survey was a single monitoring station, decommissioned four years ago.'

Canmore stepped closer to the mic and adopted a more conspiratorial tone. *'If we're going to talk about the British government, then let's ask, where are they?'*

'What do you mean, First Minister?'

Canmore pointed down the street and the camera angle followed his perspective. *'I want to ask, where are they? I've been in Inverness for two hours, watching brave Scots men and women continuing to rescue their neighbours from the rubble and restore order to this great town. Where are our colonial masters? I'll tell you; tucked up in London when they should be here, bringing the resources of our so-called shared nation to bear on the biggest natural disaster in a generation.'*

Graham flicked the TV off. 'That's bollocks.'

'Which particular bit?' asked Gill.

'My brother is a GP in Inverness. He's been helping with triage at the Raigmore Hospital. He says that within hours of the quake, there were English accents everywhere. And a fleet of ambulances from Birmingham, and an army of nurses from the English Midlands.'

'I've met Canmore,' said Gill. 'He's got a flexible arrangement with truth. Listen, Graham, do you think we should still be looking for Bru? Maybe we should make another attempt to join a rescue team on the mainland?'

'The ferries have been requisitioned for the relief effort, Gill. No way we can get across.' He jerked his head at the TV. 'The best thing we can do right now is find our missing horse.'

'Mysterious Scotland, Cassy Tullen speaking.'

194

'Ah, darlin'. Ev'ry time I hear your name, I get a shiver doon ma spine.'

Cassy glanced around to make sure she wasn't being overheard. 'Och, Corrie, you old flirt! How are you?'

'I'm braw, lass. Barley and I took a run down tae Casablanca in the hours afore the earthquake hit. Now we're squirreled away at a beach resort for a couple o' days until the airports reopen.'

'All that way, just for a boys' day out?'

'Aye. We rented a private jet from a firm in Dundee.' He paused. 'Barley and I flew it ourselves. Did you know we've both got our pilot's license?'

'I didn't.'

'Blame it on Tom Petty. He got us all learnin' tae fly.'

'Sounds brill, Corrie. Can't wait until I'm rich and famous.'

'And while we're sunbathing and hangin' aroon, we're gettin' some quality time tae listen tae your new album.'

'Oh, that's so sweet.'

'And while we've got a bunch of production notes fer ye, I need to say straight up, the song writin' is first class.'

'Oh, Corrie, you don't need to say that.'

'Well, ah do, cause if the music wuz shite, ah'd need to tell you that an' all.'

'Well thank you. A big part of me is relieved to hear you say it.'

'And how are things back home in poor old Scotland?'

Cassy rubbed her forehead. 'Getting a bit crazy to be honest. People are angry there wasn't any warning about the quake. The police seem too stretched to deal with all the big demonstrations and meanwhile, Roddy Canmore looks like the hero of the hour.'

'Am sorry tae hear all that. And whit aboot Gill? Is he still countin' his gold?'

'Gill has been relieved of his gold, which annoyed him. And to make matters worse, he skipped off to the Hebrides a few days before the quake. Goodness knows when we'll see him back.'

'Whit's he doin' out there?'

'I'm not sure,' Cassy mused, remembering a conversation she'd once had with Ailsa. 'Maybe something to do with a horse.'

'Whit kind o' horse?'

'Never mind, Corrie. It's probably nothing.'

'Cass. Is there any way you could get a message tae Gill?'

'Sure. The phones were dodgy straight after the quake but they're fine today. I hope to speak to him this week.'

'It's just a phone number I need tae pass on. And I need him tae ring it at his earliest convenience.'

Gill and Graham were trudging back to the car after a second unsuccessful day looking for Bru. They were getting first-hand reports of his whereabouts and supplementing these from Freya Swanson's blog. But wherever Bru appeared, he was long gone by the time they reached the location. Adding to this irritation were facts Freya's blog revealed about Gill's deeper connection to their runaway.

'This treaty,' Graham began, suspiciously. 'You found out about it, when?'

'About three years ago.'

'And the lairdship?'

'Technically, that passed to me a few months before I read the treaty.'

Graham fell silent. 'And are you really planning to tear up Scotland?'

'I wasn't,' said Gill. 'But then all this nonsense from Canmore kicked off and I'm beginning to wonder if enacting the treaty might be the way to stop him.'

'Just so you know,' said Graham, grasping Gill's wrist. 'I'm looking for Bru for the sake of my little girl and not so you can cover yourself in glory.'

Gill stopped abruptly when he felt the anger in Graham's voice. 'Listen, you don't know me very well, and you've every right to be suspicious. But there's more going on here than two men trying to protect the welfare of a horned horse. Tell me, did Rani ever explain how it went down that day?'

'What day?'

'The day the Black waterhorse came for us. And how a White appeared and saved us. Three men and both horses died, and then all the bodies were tidied away by some kind of supernatural clean-up crew. Did Rani tell you, Graham?'

'I … I heard how the Black became dangerous. All of the rest …' he stopped and shook his head.

Gill ripped away Graham's grip on him. 'If I get on that horse and fulfil the obligations of the treaty, there won't be any glory. Instead, let me tell you what I think will happen. I will be opposed, and people will die. And quite possibly the horse. So, be completely assured that it's not on my agenda unless frankly, the consequences of not doing it are even worse.'

Face to face the two men glared at each other. 'I'll need to talk to Rani about this,' muttered Graham.

'Do, but don't be hard on her for keeping the secret. It's what we all agreed to do.'

'Doesn't sound like you've managed to keep it private.'

'Circumstances forced my hand.'

Graham inhaled the cooling evening air. 'Well, I don't know enough about the rights and wrongs of this, but I can tell you one damn thing for sure.'

'What?' Gill demanded.

Graham started to walk away. 'You'll be a dead man if you ever try to get on that horse.'

Chapter 27

Hey, Cass. How's it going?' It was 5 pm on Wednesday, three days since the quake. Three days in which Gill and Graham had sullenly scoured Harris and Lewis for any sign of their missing horse.

'Nerve-wracking,' said Cassy. 'Today's demo is a lot bigger than yesterday. Apparently, Glasgow is even worse.'

In the background, Gill could hear chanting and drums banging. 'They sound angry.'

'If half of what Canmore says is true, they've every right.'

Gill doubted if Canmore's complaints had merit but decided to let that pass. 'Are you safe?'

'We are right now. But Tony has told everyone in the building to work from home for the rest of the week or as long as this takes to blow over.'

'The police will keep a lid on it.'

'Will they, Gill? There were three police vans outside Zack's school this morning and three more at the county buildings, but I haven't seen a single cop in the city centre.'

'They're probably up north,' said Gill, barely believing his own answer.

'What about you? Any sign of your waterhorse?'

Gill swallowed. 'You know about that?'

'When I was getting to know Ailsa, she told me what really happened five years ago during your time on Harris. And how one of those things almost killed you.'

'Yeah, sorry,' Gill stumbled. 'There's never been a good moment to talk about this.'

'And instead of bones, this time you're looking for a living animal?'

'Well, to answer your question, we've seen nothing so far.'

'You sure someone's imagination hasn't run away with them?'

Gill winced. 'People have seen it, Cass.'

'Salina must be worried sick.'

'Sal doesn't scare easily. And besides, she'd already taken Josh out of town for a few days.'

'Good plan. Listen, when you're back, take me out for a drink and catch me up on all this unicorn stuff?'

'Will do.'

'In the meantime, there's not much work to talk about today, so I'll top and tail the main things, then email the rest. Is that okay?'

'Seems almost an irrelevance to be talking about work with all that's going on, but yeah, hit me.'

'Oh, and I almost forgot. Corrie McCann was in touch. He passed me a telephone number and needs you to ring it ASAP.'

On that same Wednesday afternoon, Roddy had the wind in his sails. He was standing on the balcony of Edinburgh's Mercat Cross, beneath a centuries-old stone tower capped with the gilded sculpture of a unicorn. Grasping the edge of his improvised pulpit, he looked down on the massed crowd filling the area around St Giles Cathedral. And though he wouldn't have admitted it publicly, he was enjoying himself.

'Do you ever read the poetry of Robert Burns?' he bawled at the crowd.

He nodded at their yelled responses and clasped the microphone. 'I do too, and my favourite is *A Parcel o' Rogues. Do ye ken it?*'

Around the throng, a hundred voices bayed their satisfaction.

'If you don't, let me gie you a wee history lesson. For Burns is harking back to the year 1695 when a group o' wealthy investors launched the *Darien Scheme*. These rich men were Scots, but only notionally as they mostly lived in London. They aped England's colonial prowess by developing Scotland's first overseas colony, raising a large sum o' cash to send colonists to South America. Unfortunately, the enterprise failed. The few survivors returned home in shame, and the investors, who hadnae pulled up their breeks to assist the new colony, lost their money. They sat in their London clubs and grumbled about their losses. Meanwhile, the squandered wealth, extracted from Scotland to fund this madness, starved investment in this wonderful land we call home. Jobs became scarce and hunger became the norm.'

Around him, the crowd booed and hissed at this historic outrage.

'That might have been the end o' it had not representatives frae the English parliament discreetly approached these investors, this parcel o' rogues, in Burns' words, and offered them a deal. "Sign an Act of Union with England," they said, "And you'll be compensated for your losses in the *Darien Scheme*." This they duly did, convincing the rest of the Scottish parliament to sign the 1707 Act of Union that saw Scotland absorbed into the United Kingdom.' Roddy glowered at his audience while he was drowned out by screams of indignation. 'That disgusts me, and I can see it disgusts you. And it disgusted Burns when he used his poem to compare the treachery o' these men to the heroism of

Robert the Bruce and William Wallace. Burns says he'd rather hae died with heroes than share in blood money gained from the treacherous sale of Scotland.' Roddy pointed at his audience, 'What about you?' He hoisted a clear plastic bag containing coins from Gill's dig. 'If I offered you a mess o' gold in exchange for your country, would you take it?'

The crowd yelled back at him that they wouldn't.

'Well mind your back, Scotland, because if our southern neighbour comes whispering with another get-rich-quick-scheme, you'll need to choose between their money or your life free o' chains.'

Roddy stood with his legs apart and nodded in appreciation when twelve thousand people started chanting his name.

Gill had been walking alone, among the hills and lochs of Lewis during Canmore's *Rogues* speech, so he missed the excitement. On Solomon's advice, he decided to watch it the next day, plus the analysis that followed. In some media reports, commentators marvelled that British forces hadn't arrested Canmore for treason and speculated wildly about the headwinds facing this nascent Celtic nation. Gill found it all rather depressing, so it was a mercy then when he heard a tap on the door and was a little surprised to see Graham.

'Look, I want to apologise,' he said.

'Don't apologise,' said Gill. 'I came into your house and enjoyed your hospitality without being completely open about my motivation for being here. You've every right to keep me at arm's length; to send me away if you want.'

'Yeah, well. It's all out in the open now.'

'I gather Rani filled you in?'

Graham winced. 'Don't pretend you didn't hear us arguing.'

'Yeah, sorry about that. I feel it's my fault.'

'We're grownups, Gill. I think everything has been said that needs to be said. And for what it's worth, you might be right about Canmore.' He stopped and started to pick nervously at the door frame. 'Bloody hell, Gill. You might even be right to do your *Torn Isle* thing.'

Gill stood and soberly shook his friend's hand. 'What makes you say that?'

'You remember how Canmore was moaning London hadn't sent us any help?'

Gill nodded.

Graham shook his head. 'Well, it's just been on the news. The British Army has dispatched two massive aid convoys, and now Canmore says we're being invaded.'

Chapter 28

In Bathgate the following morning, Wiley came and rapped Lillico's desk with his knuckles and jerked his head towards his office. Lillico glanced around and wondered why Wiley was being so secretive. It was a Friday morning, and the only team not in the field policing angry demonstrations was *Special Investigations*. But dutifully, he followed and closed the glass door behind him. 'What's up?'

Wiley pointed at his laptop screen where he'd opened a mainstream news website. 'Take a look. That's where the A1 highway joins the Edinburgh bypass.'

'Glad I'm not trying to commute through that.'

Wiley tabbed to a different camera. 'And here's the scenario over in the west on the northbound M74.'

Lillico peered at the screen with its snaking column of khaki-green vehicles. 'Trucks, ambulances and heavy equipment,' he mused. 'And they're all static.'

'And the reason is this,' said Wiley, using his mouse to tab to a traffic camera.'

Lillico studied a grainier image showing a cluster of civilian vehicles stuck at the head of the queue, where two police cars were blocking the carriageway. Zooming in a little, it was possible to see uniformed soldiers remonstrating with the cops who'd created the block. Looking at the body language, Lillico was glad the video didn't have sound.

'Canmore bleats he isn't getting enough earthquake assistance from London, even though anecdotal reports from around the country contradict him,' Wiley surmised. 'Then when London sends in two very visible relief columns, he treats it like an invasion.'

'Oh, this just gets worse,' muttered Lillico.

'And we have these,' said Wiley, pointing to a screen reporting ongoing incidents. Reading the list, Lillico scanned reports of demonstrators swarming across four food distribution centres and the country's main fuel depot at Grangemouth. 'Do these look like the scenarios we saw on Canmore's data stick?'

'Something's kicking off,' Lillico nodded. 'And if there's anything we can do to stop this, boss, then I'm up for it.'

'There just might be,' said Wiley, abruptly standing and yanking his jacket from off the back of his chair. 'Come on.'

'Where are we going?'

'Just had a message from the little bird in Glasgow,' he growled. 'And if we're very lucky, he might sing us a useful little song.'

Lillico knew George Wiley wasn't a stranger to Barlinnie Jail. Dropping in on a snitch, or visiting some old con, he'd find himself bargaining for a sentence reduction in exchange for "a little information." So, the man appeared nonchalant while he subjected himself to the searches and the signing-in protocols. Except Lillico knew Wiley. Perhaps it was the extra redness about the man's collar, or little fidgets highlighting his stress. Here they were doing regular police work while across towns and cities, Scotland burned. But this was their job; more than their job, because their patient case-building might eventually defuse the current crisis.

After yet another deep sigh, plus an inevitable delay, Wiley and Lillico were finally shown into a private room to await the prisoner. A few minutes later, Billy Whyte lingered in the doorway with uncertainty spilling across his face.

'Are you going in or not?' grumbled the guard behind him.

Billy mumbled an apology and shuffled into the room. He lingered in a standing position until the guard ordered him to sit. And once Billy was secured, the man finally withdrew.

'Signing my own death warrant just seeing you guys,' Billy grumbled.

Wiley slouched in his chair. 'You asked for this meeting. If you've reconsidered we can stop right now.'

Billy glanced at Lillico. 'Don't like that copper. I'd prefer to talk to DCI Wiley alone.'

'DI Lillico and I are a team,' Wiled drawled. He glanced down at the bandage on Whyte's hand. 'What happened to you?'

Billy checked no one could overhear; bodily turning around to put his back to the CCTV camera covering his end of the room. 'They tried to kill me.'

'Who?' asked Lillico.

'The Drumchapel crew. Monty Galloway,' he hissed.

Wiley grimaced and looked away. 'Sorry for your trouble, Billy, but if Monty Galloway wanted you dead, your sorry arse would be laying on a stone slab right now.'

'He was interrupted,' Whyte protested. 'But he'll try again. I know he will, and next time I might not be so lucky.'

'Did you complain about his actions?' Lillico probed. 'Do you have any witnesses?'

Whyte's laugh was pure exasperation. 'Yeah, like anybody's gonna cross Monty Galloway. Listen, Wiley, you need to get me protection.'

Wiley dropped his hands in his lap. 'And why would I do that, Billy?'

'Because … because … you people put me in here. A place you knew I'd be in danger.'

Lillico edged towards the sweating figure. 'You attacked a defenceless girl without provocation. And when you plead guilty, the court handed you a just punishment. Violent offenders normally get sent down to Barlinnie, so I don't see what you're complaining about.'

'Aren't you listening? I'm alerting you to a crime.'

Evidently tiring of Billy, Wiley stood and buttoned his jacket. 'Without witnesses or proof, it's just your word against his.'

'They're gonna kill me.'

'I'll be sure to say a wee prayer for you. Now, if you'll excuse …'

'I can give you information.' Billy blinked twice. 'I can give you proof.'

'Of what?'

'Of who ordered me to capture the girl, Lorna Cheyne. My attack on Corrie McCann four years ago outside some caves. And other stuff.'

In their preparations, Wiley had anticipated this play for leverage and made certain he didn't look interested. 'All details, Billy. Water under the bridge. So, you'd have to do better than that.'

Whyte stared at him, then back at Lillico, his face frozen somewhere between arrogance and terror.

Wiley made for the door, then looked back and winked. 'Righto. You take care, Billy. Best if you sleep with the light on.'

'I can tell you who ordered the Wigtownshire guns. I can explain where they came from and where they were going. And I can tell you about something else they ordered that's far worse.'

'To be fair, Billy, you look like a man who'd tell me lies just to get what you want.'

'I can get you proof.'

'What kind of proof?'

Billy clenched his fists and slowly pushed his knuckles together. 'My guvnor didn't use email. And every text came from a different burner phone. But once or twice we spoke by voice call.' Whyte's throat bobbed up and down in terror. 'I recorded those. I've them backed up in the cloud. You can have them if you get me out of here.'

Wiley sank his hands in his pockets and ambled back to the table. 'They'd better be good, Billy. If you set a lot of hares running and even one of them turns out to be a dud, then your next cellmate will be one of the Galloway brothers.'

'It's real, and it's yours if you help me.'

'We know you've done a few odd jobs for Roddy Canmore,' said Lillico. 'You obviously recall we had a chat when we linked you to the Wigtownshire gun stash?'

Billy nodded furiously. 'We can talk some more about that.'

'And we've detected some unusual activity at the Scottish Geological Society,' said Wiley. 'I'll need everything you know about Canmore's plans.'

'I don't know much about that. Different department. But I'll give you what I have. So long as you get me moved somewhere safe.'

At a leafy address in Edinburgh's Marchmont district, Lillico took a deep breath. Billy Whyte's confession had produced a slew of new leads. Most were confirmations of things they already suspected, but there was one juicy titbit that might just become the key to it all. It had been one thing hearing Billy's story, but it was quite another proving it. He and Eliza had worked through the night on Friday, and somewhere around 4 am, they'd had a breakthrough. They'd gone home for a few hours' sleep, then reconvened to double-check their findings. If Eliza hadn't been on the civilian staff, it would have been her joining him to interview a female suspect. But for now, Lillico was staring at the solid blue door of a lovely stone townhouse and nodding to a different female colleague to take the lead. She rapped on the door and waited until a woman in her mid-fifties came to open it. He recognised her face from the SGS website though she'd aged since that photo.

'Agnes Fairbank? I'm DC Prentice, and this is DI Lillico. May we ask you some questions?'

The woman clutched the door and peered at them. 'About what?'

'In relation to your work at the Scottish Geological Society.'

Fairbank tugged at a lock of hair, falling against her face. 'I'm … I'm trying to enjoy my weekend, officers. If this is about work, can't you visit my office on Monday?'

'It's very important, Agnes. Can we come in?'

Her head shake was more in confusion than in denial. 'Will I need a solicitor present?'

'That's really up to you, Agnes. Do you feel you'll need a legal representative?'

Her hand moved from her hair to her chin. 'Look, I'm not sure I want to talk to you … what's the problem?'

'It concerns the death of John Houston and the …'

'I'd nothing to do with that. At least, I heard it was an unfortunate accident.'

'We'll get to that in due course,' said Lillico in his calmest voice. 'Of greater urgency is the sabotage of SGS seismological prediction software.'

'Sabotage?'

'Yes. It really might be best if we discussed this inside.'

'Let's just chat here.' Fairbank seemed to recover her composure and folded her arms. 'How could you people even suggest our software has been compromised? Is this Westminster's attempt to shift the blame from London onto the SGS?'

'I work with a digital analyst who has reviewed the code in your model. It appears that key parts of the algorithm were neutered to kill its predictive potential.'

'That's a very serious accusation,' Fairbank spat.

Lillico calmly pressed on. 'The saboteur tried to hide their identity by using a variety of logins. Those details are only known to the most senior members of your organisation.'

'Well … that could have been Houston …'

'Indeed. But they gave themselves away by their coding tics.'

Fairbank's head twitched. 'I don't understand.'

'When people write code, they tend to have certain habitual tics. The arrangement of certain phrases or instructions. Little things the coder does subconsciously. It's like a fingerprint or a sample of someone's unique handwriting style.'

'Great, if you think someone was tinkering with the software, go catch them.'

Lillico and Prentice held their ground.

Fairbank laughed and pointed at her chest. 'You think it was me?'

'Our analysis clearly demonstrates your digital fingerprints are all over it.'

Prentice took a step closer and lowered her voice. 'What's it to be, Agnes? Shall we discuss this inside, or alternatively, we can arrest you and take you down to the station?'

A little colour drained from Fairbank's face. 'Yes, very well, come in … would … would you like some tea?'

Chapter 29

One week on from the quake, Salina and Josh
endured an unsettled night. Something he'd eaten,
or licked, or sucked had bothered him, causing the
limited hours of darkness to pass with him clinging to her
while she stroked his head. Sometime around 7 am, he settled
again and fell into a deep slumber. Salina would have joined
him if she hadn't been so self-conscious about sleeping away
the morning in Cormac's house. Instead, she went to make
herself a coffee and was surprised to see Cormac in his front
room, grimly watching a morning news program.

'What's going on?' she asked.

'More madness,' said Cormac, quietly. 'The British Army
has established exclusion zones around three big military
bases.'

Salina stepped into the room and sat down beside him. On
the screen, two large military helicopters were sweeping low
over a sea loch towards an unknown destination. 'Is that
Faslane?'

'Aye. I can see why they'd protect their nuclear
submarines, and perhaps the Lossiemouth air base, but
Leuchars in Fife was a surprise.'

'It's got a massive airstrip,' said Salina. 'Tactically, it's
important.'

Cormac shook his head. 'Canmore's going to feast on this. He said we were being occupied and now these eejits have made that accusation look legitimate.'

'But they're just protecting dangerous military assets, Cormac. With all the unrest, you have to agree it looks prudent?'

'I do, but it's the optics of this that'll be important. They'll be like Gibraltar.'

'I don't follow.'

'Think about it. Three territorial incursions, made for tactical reasons, are held against the will of the host nation.' Cormac plucked a used mug from the table beside him and stood up. 'There's one man in Edinburgh playing a dangerous tune, and instead of us asking him to stop, most folks seem to be dancing.'

At about the same time as Salina was watching the news with Cormac, Gill was staring glumly at Rani's TV. After a dawn excursion looking for Bru, he was back for a late breakfast to give Graham time to attend to his veterinary work. Later, they'd be going back on the hills, so with a little time to kill, he tabbed to a BBC message alerting him to a live broadcast in Edinburgh. Tuning in, Gill watched Canmore, back in his improvised pulpit from which he'd delivered his now famous *Parcel of Rogues* speech. This time, he was berating the "British" for their "land grab" at various military sites. Back in London, the Prime Minister would appear shortly, no doubt to refute Canmore's claims. But the direction of travel was becoming clearer, and the rhetoric was rising. Although the gap between these British nations was narrow, it ran as deep as the Great Glen fault.

Graham appeared and sat down beside him to watch the broadcast. 'I've got to pop in on a client for an hour. Foot rot amongst his Blackface ewes,' he said.

'Sounds lovely,' said Gill. 'Can't wait.'

'You can hold the woolly buggers while I inject them.'

'The life of a Hebridean vet can't be all glamour.'

'Beats having a city practice,' he grumbled. 'Treating yappy wee dugs the size of handbags.'

Graham managed to endure another five minutes of the televised conflict before he got to his feet again. 'Let's go and fix those sheep. Then we can go find our living, breathing unicorn, Gill. See if we can knock Canmore off the news for two minutes.'

Eliza tapped Lillico's shoulder, rousing him from near slumber. It was Sunday afternoon, and he still hadn't slept. 'You look exhausted, detective.'

Lillico lifted his eyes. 'Not too fresh yourself, Miss Hemmings.'

'How's it going with Fairbank?'

'Touch and go. So far, she hasn't alerted Canmore, but she's pushing us for immunity, and because we can't take this to Chief Super Macfarlane, we're treading softly.'

'Whatever happens, please tell me she'll pay for what she did?'

'That is definitely the plan, however, we've other fish to catch first.'

Eliza flashed him a smile. 'I might be able to help with that.'

'What have you got?'

'To save me repeating myself, is it okay if we go see the boss?'

215

Moments later, they were hovering in Wiley's doorway. The man himself was hunched over his laptop, typing furiously until Eliza tapped the glass. 'DCI Wiley. I have the first results on those purchase order irregularities you asked me to look at.'

Wiley looked up. 'The what?'

'Central Edinburgh, sir. A clerk in Holyrood who's been ordering excessive quantities of bottled water and that kind of thing.'

'Sorry, Eliza, I'm really not …'

'Too many sandwiches, George,' added Lillico over Eliza's shoulder.

'Yes, yes, that. Come in the pair of you and close the door.'

Wiley rubbed his face. 'Sorry, I was miles away. What have you got?'

'I've only scratched the surface of this thing, but I suspect a proper investigation would uncover a host of invoice irregularities.' She waved her hand. 'It's city wide. Low-level fiddling and boxes falling off the backs of lorries. Point is, I'm detecting some weird purchasing behaviour, everywhere from Holyrood to Edinburgh Castle.'

Wiley sat back in his chair. 'And are we seeing accumulations of excess stock?'

'We are. Of just the kinds of materials we talked about.'

'Though I doubt the First Minister's signature is on any of the paperwork?'

'It's not. But I did find something peculiar.'

'Go on.'

'Late last year, the city placed an order for three thousand drones.'

Wiley coughed. 'Maybe you don't watch the New Year celebrations, Eliza, but they've announced the annual fireworks display will be replaced with a drone swarm.'

'Yes, but I've now traced five identical orders, each from a different department of government.' Eliza lifted her hands. 'Either that's gross incompetence, or it's something else entirely.'

Wiley rubbed his face. 'Hang on. Billy Whyte mentioned drones.'

Lillico folded his arms. 'Maybe he's planning a huge celebration.'

Eliza shook her head. 'In that case, why order them from a bunch of different cost centres? Something about this feels weird.'

'Boss, did Whyte even hint what the drones were for?' asked Lillico.

'It was just a throwaway comment,' said Wiley. 'I'm not sure he even knows their purpose.'

'What then?' said Eliza. 'What would Canmore possibly do with fifteen thousand drones?'

'It's the tool of choice in modern warfare,' Lillico observed. 'Take out the lights and the cameras and retool the device to carry munitions instead.'

'But, why?

Wiley shrugged. 'Maybe Canmore is thinking of fighting a war.'

After another fruitless afternoon on the hills, Gill and Graham decided they were getting nowhere. Salina was missing Gill, and Graham needed to get back to his veterinary business so reluctantly they agreed it was time to halt their searches. Turning their backs on the rugged peak of *An Cliseam*, they began the long walk back to the car.

'Amy will be devastated,' Graham reflected.

Gill patted his new friend's shoulder. 'It's not like you're giving him up for dead. The sightings tell us he's out there, but he's just running us in circles. We'll try again once the great lump decides to stay still for five minutes.'

Graham shot him a look. 'You'd not call him a lump if you'd seen him in the flesh. Honestly, Gill, I cannot fathom how he did it. Almost doubled in size. Grew this big tusk.' Graham shook his head. 'I'd understand if you didn't believe me, but then, of course, you and Rani have seen this before.'

'Personally, I haven't seen the transformation process, but it sounds incredible.'

'Very traumatic for the horse. Bloody and painful.'

'And Amy saw all that?'

'More than I would have liked. I don't think Rani really admitted to herself what was happening until it was too late.' He winced. 'Then all hell broke loose.'

'That's why he ran off. I bet one of these days he'll come wandering back, tusk and all, wondering what the fuss was about.'

'If he does, I've told Rani that she and Amy must stay inside. Until we know what we're dealing with.' Graham paused to check an incoming message on his phone. 'Speak of the devil,' he muttered. 'Just a sec 'til I see what she's saying.'

'Everything okay?' asked Gill. 'I'll be so pissed off if this is the day Bru decides to saunter in on his own.'

'No. Rani says Canmore is going to make a big announcement at six. She says it sounds serious.'

Gill glanced at his watch, fighting a sense of nausea sweeping over him. That's just a couple of minutes away. Why don't we sit? They looked around for a flat rock and sat down. Gill used his phone to tune in to a national radio station and waited. He wasn't sure, but the blank space before Canmore spoke seemed to crackle with the fake static of an old radio.

'*I am speaking to you today from the ramparts of Edinburgh Castle,*' Canmore's voice began.

'Bloody good acoustics for a windy battlement,' muttered Graham. 'Why does that man have to lie about everything?'

'*One week after the earthquake that rocked our nation I need to speak to you with the utmost urgency.*' Canmore left a pause. '*Today I've become alarmed by the British Government's attempt to militarise our society under the guise of bringing much-needed earthquake relief. Instead of being our friends, south of the border, they are using this opportunity to bring us to heel. At this very moment, reinforcements are pouring into British military bases by air, land and sea. And their intention is clear. From these bases, at Faslane, Leuchars and Lossiemouth, they plan to reach out and snatch back control of this country. They will attempt this by declaring an emergency. An emergency, friends, that all evidence suggests was of their own making. Nature has knocked Scotland to her knees, and now our neighbour wants to place his heel upon our neck.*'

'Did I fall and bang my head today?' Graham spluttered. 'Because none of this is making any sense.'

'*In response to this treachery, Scottish citizens have spontaneously been rising up and seizing key assets to secure them against this invader. They're not soldiers, or tacticians, just Scotsmen in the mould of William Wallace, whose words remind me I have a choice today, "to do or die."*' Canmore left a moment's silence. '*And those very same Bravehearts have asked me, Rodderick Canmore, will I act, even if that means I risk my life? And I tell you today, Scotland, I will.*' Somewhere in the background Gill and Graham heard distant roars of approval. '*And for this reason, I have recalled our members of parliament from London, because it is clear to me that we must travel a different road. On behalf of Scotsmen and women, everywhere, I announce tonight, a historic realignment of our nations. Tonight, Scotland is making a unilateral declaration of independence, severing our ties with the United Kingdom. It is finished,*' he shouted. '*Our broken marriage with England is at an end.*'

'Don't believe I'm hearing this,' gasped Graham.

'Today I announce that the Scottish parliament will abandon its existing business and will meet in emergency session for the next seven days to begin the work of reorganising our constitutional affairs. At the end of that time, Parliament will vote to ratify my decision and formalise our withdrawal from the United Kingdom.' He took a deep, theatrical breath. *'People of Scotland, I won't disguise the challenges we'll face over the next few weeks. They will be costly. But tonight, I urge you, to find some friends and celebrate, because one week from today, Scotland will be free once again.'*

As the radio mic seemed to pick up rapturous applause, it appeared Canmore's announcement had finished.

'Can he do that?' Graham asked. 'I don't think he can do that.' He shook Gill's arm. 'That man is trying to tear up my country!'

Gill's sudden desire to bellow with rage battled with a shocking wave of nausea that threatened to make him retch. 'No, no,' he spluttered. 'You can't just declare something like that. You have to … you have to …'

'Come on,' said Graham, dragging Gill to his feet. 'We need to get back to the house.'

Chapter 30

133 Hours until the Scottish Parliamentary vote on independence

Freya stayed at home the day after Canmore's announcement, watching the news and hugging a pillow. The interviews on broadcast media reflected the sentiments she saw amongst her social cohort. Excitement about new beginnings. Terror at being cut adrift amidst a sea of bigger nations. Puzzlement at the legal basis Canmore had employed to make his declaration. Opinions on every topic were as diverse as her friendship circle. Only one question united them all; "Why didn't I get a say?"

The government in London appeared just as shocked. This scenario had clearly not been subject to contingency planning, meaning the Westminster establishment seemed lost at sea. Amidst speeches demanding Canmore be tried for treason, and refusals to abandon strategic military assets, the only clear message coming out of London was, "This isn't over yet." And in every speech, Canmore harried them, skipping past the technical issues that would prevent naval bases from being redeployed in decades, never mind days. "A land grab," claimed Canmore, referring to the bases. "Expropriation by the retreating colonial power." The British government explained it had no plans to leave, while in every news bulletin, Canmore remained victorious in the battle of words.

The international reaction was incredulous. Domestic commentators were flabbergasted, while on social media, those with opposing opinions rained down vitriol on each other until it seemed the whole of Britain might be swallowed by a sea of hatred. As the clock approached 6 pm on Scotland's first day after Canmore's declaration, it was announced that he would be speaking to the nation again. At this point, Freya began to feel unwell, fearful of what terrors might be unleashed within her homeland. And while she waited, a message pinged it from Howard, saying, 'As if there wasn't enough going on … can you call me?' She clicked on a link he'd sent to the lead story on the *Tribune's* website. Front and centre was a crystal-clear image lifted from her own blog. He'd fairly credited the image to her, plus the regular correspondent on Lewis who'd advised Freya to distribute it as widely as possible. Standing on a road junction, with moorland in the background, stood a great, white waterhorse.

'Sorry I've been quiet for a few days,' said Howard, when he picked up. 'And sorry we haven't got you to Harris yet. Booking a plane or ferry up north has been impossible since the quake.'

'No worries. Earthquakes, both real and political, have kept you busy.'

'You're right there. I'd heard rumblings about Canmore pulling some kind of stunt, but his unilateral declaration; never saw that coming.'

'So, if you can't push forward with my waterhorse story right now, I get it.'

'We can talk again about the Hebrides once things calm down.'

'Actually, Howard. My correspondents tell me the horse keeps moving around. I could spend a month out there and never see it in person.'

'I hear you, but on the other hand …' Howard paused, and she could hear him tapping his keyboard. 'I've been thinking about the *Treaty of Finlaggan*. I see you've reported it in your blog.'

'I didn't at first, then I decided I would. A living, breathing waterhorse pitching up at the same moment Scotland endures its biggest crisis in a generation. I think people should know.'

'Aye, and so far the high-heidyin in Edinburgh hasn't seemed to notice the threat.'

'Maybe it's best if he doesn't.'

'You think we should let McArdle declare his *Torn Isle* and add his own dose of chaos to an already toxic mix?'

Freya laughed. 'Says the political journalist looking for his next big story.'

'Guilty as charged,' said Howard, flatly. 'If you're not about to commandeer a rowing boat to get to Harris, what are you going to do?'

Freya thought for a moment. 'I'll keep blogging. And in the meantime, if that horse is ever sighted within a mile of Callanish, I'll let you know.'

Sandy Brightman and her skipper looked down on the surface of the loch. It was more than a week since the quake, and Loch Ness had changed. Hell, everything had changed, though what concerned her most was the long body of water close to her front door. 'Dear heavens, Johnny. Look at this place,' she said. The loch was still there, but now a deep rim of black rocks cradled the sparkling water.

'Like the water's just draining away,' he said.

'Aye, I'd say we're down fifty feet. Where's it all going?'

'It's the same all along the Great Glen. Robert Dias says Loch Lochy is down one hundred feet.'

'Help me collect another water sample. We need to find out what's going on.'

'If we can reach it without breaking our necks,' he grumbled.

They walked along the loch's high bank until they reached an outcrop of rocks acting as a vantage point. From this promontory, they studied the changing topography. The former beach areas were now high and dry, forming a ribbon around the loch that gave way to precipitous drops along the length of the shore. Johnny spotted a bay where the drop in water levels had exposed an area of flat rock they could stand on. 'Let's try reaching the loch from there.'

He'd concocted a simple arrangement, comprising a small bucket on a very long cord. Sandy waited while he launched it out, watching it fall until it hit the surface of the water with a gentle splash. Then he carefully retrieved the cord, trying to keep the bucket from scraping the bank.

Sandy reached into her bag for her testing kit, dropping a little of the water into each tube. Like the last three times they'd done this, the water showed no change, except in one notable respect. She tapped the salinity meter. 'It's increased again. The water's getting saltier.'

'Meaning what?'

'Meaning, we've got sea water penetrating the Great Glen lochs.'

'That'll bugger the trout fishing.'

'Aye, though it might help the salmon.' She looked up at him. 'But you see what this means?'

He shook his head.

'If the Great Glen is now a continuous sea loch stretching from Fort William to Inverness …'

Johnny tipped the remaining water on the grass. 'Then everything north of the glen is now an island.'

Chapter 31

114 Hours until the Scottish Parliamentary vote on independence

Roddy was in the driving seat. The TV interview had opened with tough questions about riots in Scottish cities, and dismal predictions from major local employers. But he'd deftly handled them all, explaining these troubles were simply the birth pangs of a great nation. They'd pass, he explained, and then Scotland would stride towards a brighter future. When the interviewer had tried to rattle him, alluding to a possible arrest warrant, Roddy had just swelled out his chest. 'Just let them try!'

'First Minister, people seem confused why you've called a vote in the Scottish parliament rather than put your plans to the wider public via a referendum?'

'Simply, the urgency of our situation. London's scurrilous handling of the earthquake relief underlines the pressing need for this nation to fend for itself.'

'Are there any plans to put these dramatic constitutional changes to the wider electorate?'

'We're legally required to hold the next election to the Scottish Parliament by 2031, and of course, parties will be free to campaign as they like.'

'By which time, it would be hard to reverse your move to independence?'

'Scotland will be free. There'll be no appetite to reverse anything.'

'Talking of legal obligations, how do you respond to the story in today's Glasgow Tribune that a security team, acting on your orders, invaded an archaeological site in Dundee and seized a large quantity of gold?'

'I recall the incident.' Roddy nodded gravely. *'This cache was a significant portion of Scotland's wealth when it was hidden from English invaders in 1651. And while I'm glad we were able to save it for the nation, let us not forget the thousands of innocent Dundonians who were slaughtered by Cromwell's invading army.'*

'Where is the gold now?'

'In safe keeping. The invaders didn't successfully grab this gold in 1651 and they're sure as hell not going to take it now.'

'First Minister, can I ask you about last night's news confirming a live waterhorse has been seen on the Isle of Lewis? What do you make of that?'

'Well, clearly that is momentous news. Every scientific opinion has suggested this animal was extinct, so lots of people will be excited.'

'Coming just a day after your unilateral declaration of independence, what do you make of the timing?'

'It's like a sign from God.'

'You're on record as identifying yourself as an atheist, First Minister. In the light of the waterhorse discovery, are you reconsidering that?'

Roddy shook his head. *'I'm using a figure of speech so let me clarify. The waterhorse, or unicorn, is Scotland's national animal, and this fresh appearance feels like nature itself is stamping its blessing on the freedom of this great country.'*

'You feel it's an omen?'

'I do, and an encouraging one at a time when our national militias are peacefully containing British forces in their military bases while we negotiate for their withdrawal. And in the meantime, the cleanup process continues in the areas damaged by Westminster's earthquake.'

'London has repeated its assertion that no submarine base was ever constructed. They've challenged you to produce facts to the contrary.'

'Aye, and that'll come. I'm sorry to report that the water level in the Great Glen lochs has dropped considerably since the quake. My scientific advisors believe the loch gates joining the submarine base to the sea must have shattered, causing the water to drain away. That's clearly an environmental catastrophe, the reparations for which I'll be requesting from London.'

'First Minister, thank you for your time.'

Chapter 32

Freed from the daily grind of searching for their missing waterhorse, Graham went back to work, and Gill was left to make his own plans. And while he could have continued to search alone, he knew he was needed elsewhere. Salina was putting a brave face on things, but Josh was increasingly out of sorts in the unfamiliar environment, and Gill's continuing absence gave her little time to herself. On top of that, she was finding Cormac's frugal larder a struggle. So, he got a list of the things she needed and began his day in a Stornoway supermarket, where he picked up a load of groceries and a few treats. The shopping trip would bless them with bagfuls of fresh food, plus an excuse for some precious family time. After loading a trolley, he paid in cash, then took the long road south to Scadinish, checking regularly he wasn't being followed.

Cormac helped them pack away the shopping, then announced he was heading out for a few hours, using the opportunity to run a few errands of his own. And for a short time, they were a family again. After hugs and more hugs, Salina led them off to a small patch of sand she'd discovered amongst the rocks below Cormac's croft. She and Gill chatted while Josh roamed, exploring this new habitat, and returning every few minutes with a beachcombed treasure for them to admire. Salina spoke at length about how kind

Cormac was being, and how he managed to be persistently infuriating at the same time. Gill cradled her, happy just to let her talk and to forget about waterhorses and political turmoil for a while. But all too soon it was time to take Josh back for a nap. While they gathered themselves, Gill convinced himself that he would stay here for a couple of days now they'd abandoned their relentless hunt for Bru. So, he was alarmed when he crested the hill and found that Cormac's battered Land Rover was back, and Ailsa was waiting for him.

'Your phone's off,' she called.

'Security,' he replied. 'How's your gran?'

'Feeling better. Furious with whoever burnt down her house.'

'Have the police officially confirmed that?'

'I think, Gill, with all the riots on the mainland, my gran's case is no longer a priority. How's your holiday going?'

'You know, nice, when I actually get to see my family.' He drew to a halt beside her and twisted around so Josh could see Ailsa's face. 'Spent too much time trying to find that blasted horse.'

Ailsa cleared her throat. 'I might be able to help you with that.'

'You've seen him?'

'No, but I've seen this,' she said, opening a web browser on her phone and tabbing to the *Glasgow Tribune's* web page.

Gill and Salina scanned her screen before flashing looks at each other. Under a headline declaring, "New constitutional threat rocks Scotland," there was a clear image of a large horned horse.

'They know about the Treaty,' observed Gill.

'Confession time,' said Ailsa, tapping the article. 'This journalist came sniffing around three weeks ago and Aura prompted me to mention the treaty.'

Gill studied the byline. 'Freya Swanson. Adina mentioned her before she went AWOL.'

'Sweet kid,' said Ailsa. 'All of this madness will probably make her famous.'

Salina's voice was frosty. 'You never thought to mention this?'

'Gill wouldn't have agreed because he hates attracting attention.' Ailsa looked down at her feet. 'But that's all about to change.'

'Why would it change?' asked Salina. 'I thought we were keeping our heads down.'

'I've been watching her blog. She rumbled along last week with just a few hundred followers then it took off after the latest sightings of your horse. As of this morning, she's got eleven thousand.' She pocketed the phone. 'This could go ballistic.'

'But it's more than that,' said Salina. 'I have this rising dread in my spirit …'

Gill shook his head. 'I can feel it too. Pieces falling into place.'

'So, Gill,' whispered Ailsa. 'What are we going to do?'

Gill hugged Sal and Josh close to his face. 'I think it's time I took another stroll around the *Temple of the Isles*.'

While Gill and Ailsa drove towards Callanish, the lunchtime news was playing on the radio, and the presenter was quizzing a legal historian.

'Well, Freya Swanson's blog has sent us all scrabbling for the Treaty of Finlaggan,' said the historian. *'And despite its great age, it's still on the statute books with the full force of law behind it.'*

'But the archaic requirements for enforcing this law are very peculiar. On top of all the recent turmoil in Scotland, surely this is just a sideshow?'

'You say that, but the fulfilment of these bizarre conditions would effectively abolish the power of the Scottish state to rule as a single entity. By carving off a sizeable portion of the Scottish landmass, it would drive a coach and horses through Roddy Canmore's plans for Scotland to secede.'

'You're talking about the Western Isles?'

'It's more than that. The reactivation of the Great Glen Fault has seen sea water penetrate the deepest lochs. Effectively, everything north of the glen is now technically an island and therefore vulnerable to this treaty.'

'But the age of this treaty; surely there's little chance it will be invoked?'

'It's a complex consequence of the UK not having a formal constitution. Basically, any law or treaty sits on the statute books until it is either repealed or replaced with contemporary legislation. The Treaty of Finlaggan laid obligations on the Scottish parliament, and when it was dissolved in 1707, those obligations passed to the United Kingdom.'

'Meaning what exactly?'

'Ultimately, this is a Scottish matter, though the initiative lies with London. Westminster could treat Scotland as a rogue state and let this ancient treaty split the Scottish nation in half. Or it could ignore the current constitutional crisis and pass a quick bill incorporating the treaty's obligations into the remit of Scotland's devolved government.'

'Which would hand this headache back to Holyrood,' concluded the presenter. 'But thinking of the clause in question, surely the conditions are so bizarre there's no chance they'd be fulfilled?'

'Well, this is the other thing. Social media is awash with images of a horned horse, and the Tribune printed the latest of these in this morning's issue.'

'And this mysterious laird? Is there any indication he's a willing party to this extraordinary set of events?'

'Mysterious, indeed,' the historian tittered. 'Ha! That's very good. Swanson revealed a week ago the laird is none other than Gillan McArdle, the original discoverer of waterhorse bones. But no one seems *to know his present location. And I'll finish by saying that if he does have any aspiration to implement this treaty, he needs to act quickly.'*

'Why is that?'

'Simply that the UK and Scottish governments will not tolerate a law like this for very long. I'm aware emergency debates have been scheduled in both parliaments for this afternoon. If I were a betting man, I'd wager that by the time the sun goes down, the Treaty of Finlaggan will be consigned to the dustbin of history.'

Ailsa turned off the radio. 'Sounds like a dodgy geezer.'

'Who?'

'This Finlaggan laddie.'

Gill glanced left and right before exiting The *Golden Road* onto the main highway. 'Why am I doing this, Ailsa? I should be collecting Sal and Josh and getting the hell outta here.'

Ailsa reached across, and in a rather maternal gesture, she stroked his head. 'Sometimes it hurts.'

'What does?'

'Doing the right thing.'

'And what is the right thing, Ailsa? Because at this moment, I'm no clearer than I've ever been.'

Ailsa pulled back her hand. 'You'll know when the time comes.'

Gill growled in response. He was driving the main highway back to Stornoway and multiple exit routes off this island. And shortly, if he held his nerve, he'd be turning onto the narrow approach road to Callanish and towards the croft of another old friend.

John McInnis owned the land where the waterhorse bones had been discovered and when they knocked on his door, he invited them in. He spoke politely to Gill, and affectionately to Ailsa for a few minutes, then it was time for Gill to walk on alone, across the fields and into the heart of the stone circle.

'What are you going to do?' Gill asked Ailsa.

Ailsa thumbed over her shoulder. 'John has the kettle on. We're going to sit in his front room with binoculars and tell each other funny stories until the show starts.'

Gill flexed his back like an uncomfortable child. 'Maybe I should hang with you guys and see how this plays out?'

'Imagine you're Roddy Canmore,' said Ailsa evenly. 'You've just become aware of Freya Swanson's blog and have seen the remote possibility that a guy on a horse might demolish your carefully laid plans.'

Gill nodded reluctantly. 'He might block my access to the stones.'

'That would be my guess. And then he'll …'

Gill spun around when Ailsa stopped mid-sentence. He followed her gaze across five hundred metres of moorland towards the ancient monument. And while he stared, a great, white waterhorse crested the hill. Bru had beaten him to the stones.

Ailsa gripped the tails of Gill's waistcoat. 'Time we were moving.'

'We? I promised Cormac I'd look after you.'

'Oh, I'm not going near your precious horse; you're on your own there.' She flashed him a beautiful smile. 'See me more as your public relations assistant.'

'What?'

Ailsa pointed at a column of police cars rushing down the Callanish approach road and converging near the stones. 'While you're doing whatever it is you're going to do, I'll be trying to persuade the cops not to shoot you.'

Gill bit his lower lip. He could see the merit in what she was saying.

'Let's go!' she urged. 'And make sure your phone is on. I'll need to stay in touch with you.'

They held a hasty exchange with John to gauge the best route to Callanish that would keep them off the roads. Then, following the meagre cover offered by a fence line, they dashed for the stone circle.

One hundred metres shy of the stones, they paused. As soon as they pressed beyond this point, they'd be visible to the gathering crowd of official-looking vehicles. Ailsa indicated she would turn towards them and present herself to whoever was in charge. Meanwhile, Gill would step into … the unknown. She clutched his chin and hastily kissed his cheek. 'Try not to die,' she whispered, and then she was off, walking tall and purposefully, with her dark red hair flowing behind her. Given the opportunity, Gill would have swapped a pocketful of gold coins for just a glimmer of her courage. Facing forward, feeling like an infantryman about to step out of a trench, Gill breathed a quick prayer and started to run.

Immediately, there were shouted protests as he approached the stones. Passing an area of camouflage netting, he took the precaution of making eye contact with a police marksman setting up his rifle. 'Just don't,' Gill barked at the man while he slowed to walking pace. He could hear someone running up behind him, but they stopped the moment the horse detected his approach. With its ears up and its tusk silhouetted against the sky, Gill felt a surge of panic. The animal was fifty metres away, facing him, with limbs poised. Everything in him wanted to start stepping backwards. But by now, he was too close to outrun the waterhorse. And if he drew Bru out from the stones, he risked making the horse an easier target to the marksmen scattered around the perimeter. So, with no logical alternative, he kept walking forward.

'Hey, Bru. How're you doing?' he called. 'Do you remember me?'

The horse cantered a few steps closer and stopped again, eyeing Gill.

'You've changed since I saw you last,' cooed Gill, knowing that he wasn't being understood, but hoping that somehow, Bru would find his voice reassuring.

'For what it's worth, big man, I'm sorry about what happened to you. It must have been terrifying enduring all that on your own.'

Bru tossed his head from side to side. If he was scared, angry, or just confused, Gill couldn't tell.

'Wherever you fell in the water, it must have been a very lonely baptism, my friend.'

Bru snorted, then raised his nose to sniff the air.

'But now you're a waterhorse, and that changes things.' Gill swallowed. 'I'm hoping you're one of the good guys because sometime in the next few minutes, I need to climb up on your back.'

With its head high, the waterhorse cantered another dozen steps towards him, then stopped again. Gill had witnessed this behaviour before on this very same moor the morning the black waterhorse had stalked them. Flashing its head left and right – grasping the size and distance of its prey. And Gill knew what was coming next. With a degree of inevitability that made him want to retch with terror, he stopped and planted his feet. He watched as Bru lowered his head and tusk towards him. Then the horse pushed his leading leg forward, and charged.

Chapter 33

97 Hours until the Scottish Parliamentary vote on independence

When Ailsa approached the clutch of cars and police vans, she felt strong hands grab her from behind. Feeling her breastplate glow, the weapon emitted an energy burst that flung her assailants away. Turning to check she hadn't physically hurt anyone, she pointed at one of the officers. 'Tell me who's in charge here?'

'DI Lundy,' said the shocked officer. 'With overall command falling to Chief Super McLeod.'

'Take me to them.'

'No, miss. You need to be …'

'I'll find them myself,' called Ailsa, heading for the biggest of the vans. Two more officers quickly got in her way.

'I have information,' she said, holding up her phone. 'And I'm in direct contact with the man trying to calm the horse.'

'No matter,' said one of the officers, pointing at a car at the rear of the cluster. 'Step back this way and we'll get some details from you.'

Ailsa shook her head and with a burst of unnatural strength, she forced the men aside. Reaching the van, she took a deep breath and tore the door open. 'Officers Lundy and McLeod?' she demanded. 'You need to speak to me.'

'Who the hell are you?' asked Lundy without looking up from a screen displaying close-up footage of the action among the stones.

'Ailsa McIver. I'm a friend of the guy talking to the horse.'

'And who's he exactly?'

'That, gentlemen, is the Laird of Finlaggan.'

'Well, whoever he is, he's getting his arse kicked.'

'Clear line of sight,' yelled a voice over a radio link. 'I repeat, clear line.'

Lundy glanced at McLeod, who nodded once. 'Firearms authorised. Take the shot.'

As Bru's charge bore down on him, Gill gritted his teeth while he felt his armour manifest around his body. With seconds to deploy, he grabbed his shield from where it rested on his right shoulder and swung it in front of him. Tucking his face behind the shield, the animal struck Gill with the force of a speeding car. As Bru hurtled through the space where Gill had crouched, he felt himself spin through the air and crash against the turf. Waiting for pain to flood his body, he was pleasantly surprised when it didn't come. The shield didn't stop the impact of the blow but somehow had protected him from injury, and that was good enough.

The horse had reached the end of its run and now turned to face him again. Its ears were up, and Gill could predict what would happen next. Running to cut the distance between himself and the horse, he saw Bru steady his feet to charge again. Then to Gill's horror, four shots rang out. The horse flinched backwards, rearing his head to reach something stinging in his rump. And to Gill's dismay, Bru sank to his knees. Gill rushed to his side and found four tranquilliser darts embedded in his back. Instinctively, he plucked these out and moved around to his head.

'Hey, Bru,' he murmured. 'You and I never seem to get off to a good start.'

The horse peered dizzily at him and rested his muzzle on the turf, and Gill took a moment to look around him. Several armed officers were closing on his position with their weapons raised. Over amongst the vans, he could see several officers pushing Ailsa out of the command post, followed by two older men. Gill watched the distinctive shape of DI Lundy raise a megaphone to his mouth.

'McArdle. Step away from the horse and get back here.'

Bru looked sleepy, and Gill grasped his tusk and gave it a vigorous shake. 'Hey. No dozing!'

'Final warning, McArdle. If my officers need to fire again, they'll be using live ammunition.'

Gill repositioned, placing himself between the marksmen and Bru's head. He shook his shield, watching it extend a little, though not enough to fully enclose the collapsed horse in its shadow. Charlie was better at deploying this style of defence, and Gill made a mental note to get lessons. Meanwhile, back at the command post, he saw Rani's car pull up. He watched Rani and Graham spill out and join Ailsa in her storm of arm-waving and shouted protests. Immediately, they were intercepted and grabbed by two officers. No doubt aware of weapons pointing at the horse, they kept yelling at Lundy. They were too far away for Gill to hear anything of what was being said, but the body language wasn't pretty. Back in the car, Amy's head bobbed from side to side as she struggled to see the action.

He noticed Ailsa extricate herself and raise her phone to her ear. Then, from somewhere under his armour, he heard his phone ring. He groaned. 'How the heck am I meant to …' he managed to squeeze his right hand under the breastplate and access his waistcoat pocket. Extracting the device, he saw the caller was Ailsa.

'Can see your armour,' she announced. 'Looks shiny at this distance.'

'That armour just saved my life,' he wheezed.

'You okay?'

'So far. Even from this distance, Lundy doesn't look happy. Who's the other guy?'

'A more senior officer called McLeod. My reading of the situation is that Lundy is in charge of tactics, and McLeod is in continuous contact with someone more senior in Edinburgh.'

'Ask them not to shoot me. Bru and I are making a connection. If they leave us alone for a few minutes, I think I can bring him under control.'

'Look, Gill, I don't want to rush you, but Westminster just kicked the *Treaty of Finlaggan* back to Edinburgh.'

'Meaning anything we do here is futile?'

'Not quite. Now the Scottish government has to strike it down too before you're out of time.'

'How long?' asked Gill.

'I dunno. An hour, tops? The unionist parties at Holyrood are delaying the debate so it's impossible to tell. But it sounds like Canmore has the votes. One way or another, the treaty will be off the statute books this afternoon.'

Behind him, Gill heard the horse struggling to its feet. 'Thanks, so it's decision time?'

'*The Torn Isle*, Gill. Yes or no?'

Where Gill crouched, he felt hot, horsey breath on the back of his neck. 'That might depend on my friend here.'

Out across the moor, he watched Lundy ignore the protests around him and raise the megaphone to his mouth. 'That creature doesn't get to kill anybody, McArdle. This is your final, final warning.'

With all the fussing and shouting, Rani, Ailsa and Graham had overlooked one tiny detail. While he listened to Ailsa outlining the merits of *The Torn Isle*, Gill noticed Amy sprinting along the road towards him. 'Sorry, Ailsa. Gotta go.'

Some unquantifiable part of a mother's instinct provoked Rani to break away from the melee where she and the others were resisting arrest and caused her to glance towards the stones. She shrieked when she realised Amy was halfway between the car and Gill. Dashing after her child, she was immediately intercepted by an officer throwing his arms around her waist. 'Amy!' she shrieked.

'No way, missus. Too dangerous,' said the officer.

'I can reach her …'

'You can't. Not at the rate that thing can move. Stay here. We'll work something out.'

Shouting and screaming, Rani tried to fight off her constraints. Beside her, Graham and even Ailsa were being overpowered, even while they shouted at the police to do something. Turning back to her child, Rani saw Amy had almost reached Gill. The horse meanwhile was back on its feet and fretting with his head. She knew that look and realised what would happen next.

'Clear line of sight,' yelled one of the marksmen. 'Live ammunition ready to fire.'

'What?' spluttered Lundy. 'No. Absolutely, no. Not with the child where she is.'

Chapter 34

In the First Minister's office at parliament, Roddy's busy in-tray lay spilt across his desk. At one level, the implementation phase of his lifetime's ambition was going well. Keeping Westminster on the back foot was a dawdle, and his militia had locked down key resources without a shot fired. But there was so much complexity! And many downstream issues from his sudden declaration of independence had never found their way onto his planning board. This afternoon, a forecast crash in financial liquidity, plus a series of dark announcements from major employers were two fires he was fighting to extinguish. So intractable were some of the problems he began to wonder privately if he hadn't decapitated Britain so much as cut Scotland off at the knees. He was pressing his fingers into his temples when Stevie Blaine dashed into his room with no more than a hasty knock.

'Have you seen what's going on?' Blaine shouted.

Before Roddy could stop him, the man had grabbed the TV remote and was tabbing across to a 24-hour news channel. On the screen, he saw a distant circle of old stones, and a bunch of cops milling around looking out of their depth. One of them waved the camera away and the scene changed to a grainy image of an out-of-control horse making agitated forays amongst the stones. Roddy glanced at the screen and away. 'Stevie, as curious as this unicorn business is, I don't have time for a nature program.'

'Boss …'

'I mean it's a handy distraction for the masses, but seriously, I've got a country to run.'

Blaine leaned in close to the TV screen and pointed at a diminutive male figure, darting between the stones and only narrowly avoiding the waterhorse's tusk. 'If Gill McArdle and his horse manage to kiss and make up, your problems are gonna get a hell-of-a-lot bigger.'

'You talking about this old treaty?'

'Yes, boss. The treaty that could crash everything we've worked for.'

Roddy glanced at his watch. 'It's on the docket for this afternoon. Our parliamentary colleagues will have it tidied away by teatime.'

'Boss, this isn't a wee procedural niggle. The next hour could see this blow up in our faces.'

Roddy waved a hand at him and kept one eye on the email he was crafting. 'If it's just an ancient law, can't we ignore it?'

Blaine disagreed. 'If this was UK law, I'd agree with you. But this is an ancient Scottish treaty and if we just turn a blind eye, you'll undermine your legitimacy amongst our people.'

Roddy still wasn't convinced. 'It's a guy on a horse! What's the worst that can happen?'

Blaine now looked exasperated. 'Breaking out of the UK is hard enough, but if the Scottish regions fragment, we'll never keep a lid on this.'

'And what if northern Scotland hives itself off? It's just sheep country.'

'Those regions could make a legitimate claim to our entire energy sector, boss. Scotland wouldn't work without them.'

Roddy abandoned his email and turned to face Blaine. 'What do you recommend? Do we have assets on the island? Or can we get Macfarlane's men to shoot either McArdle or the horse?'

'We're on live TV, boss so there's nothing we can do to stop this. We need to watch and react accordingly. But first things first. You need to get down to the debating chamber and accelerate that emergency bill. One way or another, we've got to kill that damn treaty.'

Bru's head seemed to be clearing, but this was clearly not a happy waterhorse and he started to pace in a circle, snorting, and with one eye on Gill. For his part, Gill reciprocated this wary body language, flinching into a defensive posture and raising his shield each time the animal braced to attack. But Bru delayed his charge and moments later, something else hit Gill from behind.

'Gill!' cried Amy happily as she flung herself around his legs. 'You found Bru.'

'Amy, you shouldn't be here. I need you to run back to your mum.'

'No. I'm here to help with Bru,' she said, tearing herself away from him and moving towards the horse. Gill leapt after her, just as Bru exploded into motion. He caught Amy who yelped in pain as Gill planted his shield in front of her. Then, he listened in terror while the horse's hooves bit into the ground in a drunken burst of acceleration. Moments later, Bru hit Gill's shield with a glancing blow before he tore past them like an express train. Gill was trying to judge if the tranquilliser might buy them enough time to escape when Bru circled again. Planting his forefeet and lowering his head, the animal prepared for another charge. Amy whimpered beneath Gill while they braced for his next attack. But this time, the animal's approach was slow and deliberate. Peeking around his shield, Gill watched Bru's careful steps until they were a metre from the tusk tip that flashed down to meet them.

'Bru?' said Amy quietly as the first sound of doubt crept into her voice. 'It's me. Don't you remember?' With the girl's protection Gill's highest priority, he eased himself in front of Amy's crouched body, the curved tusk scraping off his armour as Bru pushed forward so his nostrils were close enough to sniff Amy's clothes. Gill held his station, ready to react if this investigation turned hostile. He watched as a tiny hand appeared and started to stroke Bru's nose. Then Amy started to giggle. 'It's okay. He's scared, but I think he can still smell the sweets.'

Gill swallowed. 'Sweets?'

'Yeah,' she said, popping her head around his body. 'I've got his favourites.' He waited while Amy took a painfully long time to unwrap a treat from a piece of waxed paper.

In this state of half war, half peace, Gill held his station while the great white unicorn crunched his way through the hard-boiled sweet. Compared to the horses Gill had ridden during his meagre practise sessions, Bru was built on an entirely different scale. And in this close proximity, the scientist in him flashed with curiosity while he studied the spot where the tusk budded from the skull. The blade seemed to be entirely of bone, but distinct from the skull, like the antler of a deer. And the skull was unlike any horse Gill had ever seen, the eye sockets deeper, and the nasal and frontal bones thicker than a regular horse. Confronted by the physicality of this beast, he wondered again how much pain Bru had endured during his transformation.

In the distance, Gill could hear Lundy's muffled voice bellowing into his megaphone, and he was shaken back into the present. He needed to find a way forward and that's when he had an idea.

'Amy, if we gave Bru another sweet, do you think he'd let us ride on his back?'

'Think so,' Amy murmured, stroking Bru's ears. 'If he stops being grumpy.'

'Shall we try?' he asked.

In response, she sprang free of him and fearlessly extended her palm to the horse. 'Bru. Kneel,' she demanded.

They watched while Bru ground Amy's latest offering in his molars and seemed to deliberate on her request. Then obediently, Bru lowered his front legs and knelt. Amy moved in and grabbed his mane, swinging up over his neck and wriggling back onto its withers before holding out an arm to Gill. 'Coming?'

'Gill, *bloody*, McArdle,' came Lundy's irate voice across the moor.

Gill retracted his armour and stood to swing his leg over the horse's back and tried to remember his meagre training. But he didn't have reins, or stirrups or any other control over this beast, so if Bru ran, he and Amy would be tossed aside like fallen leaves.

'He's bigger,' said Amy, matter of factly. 'You get a better view. Though the pointy thing is a bit in the way.'

'Pointy thing,' repeated Gill, uncertain if he was elated or terrified.

'Right. Where would you like to go?' asked Amy.

'How about …' Gill began. 'How about we just walk around the stones? And after that, I'd really like you to go back to your mum. I can see she's very worried about you.'

'Who'll look after Bru?' Amy protested.

'I will,' said Gill.

And so, it began. The laird of Finlaggan, plus his tiny groom, began a slow circuit of the *Temple of the Isles*. Realising what he was about to do, a terrible feeling descended on Gill. This was the moment he'd dreaded; pushing it away during all the years when tearing up Scotland had seemed like a bad idea. But Canmore's announcement had changed all that, plunging Scotland into crisis. Sitting unsteadily upon Bru's back, all he wanted to do was live in that moment, for this to go forever while he mulled the pros and cons of what was being asked of him. It was an irritation, therefore, when his phone rang.

'Gill. Why did you take that kid on the horse?' asked Ailsa.

'It was Amy's idea. Technically, Bru is her horse.'

'Bru?'

'Never mind. How goes it at Holyrood?'

'The speaker has just intervened. Once the next representative has finished speaking, we're going straight to a vote.'

'Not long then?'

'You've fifteen minutes, tops.'

Gill snorted. 'Fifteen minutes left to kill the country I love.'

'Don't get sentimental on me. Not if this is the only way to stop Roddy Canmore.'

'Is it, Ailsa? Is there not another way?'

'If you declare *The Torn Isle* before the treaty is eliminated, then the modern nation of Scotland ceases to exist. Holyrood will go into limbo and Canmore will effectively be out of a job.'

'And afterwards?'

'The constituent kingdoms of the old Scotland get around a table and talk. We work out the details without a despot at the helm.'

Gill felt the horse turn. Already, they'd completed a quarter circuit around the monument. 'Thanks, Ailsa. We'll talk again shortly.'

Sitting astride this magnificent animal, with Amy chattering away in front of him, the crushing magnitude of what he was about to do compressed his chest. Since the first day he'd heard about the treaty, he'd dreaded this moment. He'd pleaded it wouldn't come and yet, while pieces fell into place, he'd steadily walked towards it. Aghast that he, just one ordinary man could end Scotland.

He suddenly became aware Amy was looking up at him. 'Why are you crying?'

Gill wiped his face. 'Long story, Amy. Long, long story.'

'Do you want Bru to walk faster?'

'No, thank you. This is perfect.'

They turned again and Gill saw they were halfway from completing the circuit. Then he heard a horse gallop up behind him. His first thought was police, or some ill-judged intruder. But, turning around, he found Aura, dressed in gleaming silver armour, riding another great white waterhorse. She smiled a greeting and stroked her own animal's neck where a deep, dark scar was visible. The presence of this good-natured beast seemed to settle Bru, and for a minute, horses and riders fell into step alongside each other. The two animals seemed to acknowledge one another, before continuing their steady plod towards the finish line, and all the while, Amy chattered on, oblivious to the new arrivals.

'Is this it?' he asked Aura. 'The end of Scotland?'

Aura's patient face gave nothing away. 'In a few moments that choice will be in your power.'

'But should I do it? Is this the only way out of the mess we've created for ourselves?'

Aura smiled 'I gave you a brain, Gill McArdle. Not a shackle around your neck.'

'Always riddles with you.'

She laughed. 'Wisdom is like a lost coin, Gill. It shines so much brighter when you've had to dig for it.'

He nodded and wanted to tell her he was so much better at finding gold coins than exercising the power that was within his grasp. She seemed to see his burden, reaching across and grasping his arm. 'Be brave. I'll be waiting for you.'

'Aura, what, where?' But she had already turned her horse and sped away.

'Look,' cried Amy. 'We're back where we started.'

As if on cue, Bru stopped and lowered his head to graze. Using his neck as a slide, Amy slithered off him and following clumsily, Gill did the same. A text came in from Ailsa. The debate was over. A vote in the Scottish Parliament would happen in the next few minutes and the *Treaty of Finlaggan* would fall. Gill wrestled with this knowledge and the last words Aura had said to him. "I'll be waiting." And with a terrible, crushing conviction, Gill finally understood what he needed to do.

'Amy. I need you to run as fast as you can. I need you to find your mum and dad, and a policeman called Detective Inspector Lundy. And I need you to give them this message.'

The little girl swung her hips in a little gesture of embarrassment. 'Uh huh.'

'Amy, It's very, very important. I need you to say exactly these words.'

'Okay.'

'Exactly these words. I want you to repeat them back to me and then I want you to run like the wind.'

Rani shrieked as she watched Amy slide down off the waterhorse and safely onto the ground. Gill followed her and they had a short, intense conversation, then suddenly, Amy was running back, the little girl sprinting down the tarmac towards the cars. She felt the officer's grip on her shoulder

252

weaken just a fraction allowing her to finally tear free of him and run towards her child. The man seemed to pursue her until Lundy called out, 'Let her go.'

Scooping Amy up into her arms, Rani walked briskly back towards the safety of the cars. Amy burbled about how big Bru had got and how nice Gill was, though frankly, Rani herself was having second thoughts about that last piece. 'Who was he talking to as you walked along?'

'He talked to me,' said Amy

'I definitely saw him talking to someone.'

'He was on his phone a bit. And he gave me a message. For you and Daddy and the policeman.'

Graham met them and took Amy into his arms. Finally, they were together again. He went to strap her into their car, but Amy was insistent she had a message for the policeman. She noticed Ailsa glancing sharply at Graham and the joy on both their faces instantly disappeared.

Rani beckoned Lundy over. 'Firstly, Detective Inspector, thank you for not shooting my daughter or her horse. I think Gill has demonstrated the waterhorse poses no danger. Secondly, as you are the official "sheriff of the state" in this situation, Amy has a message for you from Gill. She witnessed the scowl on Lundy's face deepen and Superintendent McLeod stiffen.

'Gill says the message is very important,' said Amy solemnly.

'Go on darling,' Rani coaxed.

'And I've got to tell you *exactly* what he said.'

Lundy shot a worried glance at MacLeod. The senior officer gripped an earpiece before urgently shaking his head.

'Gill says …' she paused to remember the exact wording. 'Gill says … he and Bru are going to Edinburgh, and he needs to borrow a boat.'

Chapter 36

After watching Amy make it safely back to the cars, Gill turned to find Bru. The horse was still grazing amongst the standing stones without a care in the world. While Gill stood by his head, wondering how to proceed, the animal lazily lowered its front legs and allowed him to climb untidily upon its back. Delighted with this modest progress, he was even happier when, after a few nudges, Bru started to amble away from the monument in the vague direction of Stornoway. They'd been walking for less than a minute when his phone rang again.

'Gill, I've got Solie and Alex on the line,' said Ailsa. 'And I'm going to open with the obvious question. What happened to *The Torn Isle*? I thought we agreed it was the only way to defeat Canmore?'

'I take it they've struck down the treaty?' Gill clarified.

'It's gone,' said Ailsa, flatly. 'Consigned to the history books.'

Gill sighed. 'I couldn't do it, guys. Canmore created chaos by threatening to bust the UK into two without the backing of a democratic mandate. If all I'd done was break Scotland into smaller pieces, I'd be doubling down on the turmoil.'

'But you had the law on your side!' Ailsa protested. 'Or at least, you did until twenty minutes ago.'

'Having the backing of the law isn't the same as taking people with you. I'm troubled by all the unrest. What if *The Torn Isle* had tipped Scotland into civil war?'

'But it was right in your hands, Gill. A centuries-old invitation to call our self-appointed king to account.'

'Don't worry, Ailsa, that's still the plan. And if I can figure out the logistics, I'll do it before he holds his damn vote.'

'Okay,' rushed Ailsa. 'Next obvious question. Why go to Edinburgh? From your perspective, that's the lion's den.'

'It's something Aura told me just before I completed the circuit. She said, "I'll see you there."'

Solomon's voice. 'There being …?'

'A few years ago, she said I'd lead a donkey up Edinburgh's Royal Mile.'

'I see.' Solomon let silence hang for a few seconds. 'Sorry to split hairs, Gill, but that's a waterhorse you're riding, not a donkey.'

'I'm still working that bit out. Have a think about it. And please ask *The Vigil* for insight.'

'This one-man-and-his-donkey road trip; how long's it going to take?' asked Ailsa.

'I dunno. I've got four days until the vote to make an intervention, but a lot depends on how quickly I can get a ferry.'

Ailsa released an exasperated sigh. 'Haven't checked CalMac's terms and conditions, but I'm pretty sure they'll have rules about unicorns.'

Gill winced. 'I might beg them to make an exception. Are the ferries running again?'

'Essential travel only,' reported Lillico. 'How are things with the horse?'

'He was better while I had Amy around. So far, he's let me get up on his back again, so I think he'll be willing to walk with me, but honestly, this is all a game of chance. He might ditch me and disappear into the Hebridean mist at any moment.'

'I'll cut back to the coast road and try to meet you at the port,' said Ailsa. 'Give you any help I can.'

Solie again. 'Gill, the chances of you and Bru, safely reaching Edinburgh and arriving at some form of accommodation with Canmore, before you and a whole bunch of other people end up getting killed; they're vanishingly small.'

'I know, Solie. But this life we've been living … it's been building to today. I'm going to move forward until Aura says stop.'

Solomon's long silence underscored her discomfort. 'Okay. Apart from helping you find a vessel, is there anything else we can do?'

'Does anyone know how the cops will react if I start walking Bru towards Stornoway?'

'Your antics are going out on live TV,' said Lillico. 'Having brought Bru under control, I think it's very unlikely you'll meet violent opposition while you're still in view of the cameras.'

'That's good.'

'But I doubt the same rules will apply when you get closer to Edinburgh.'

'Could really do with Adina's help,' Gill grumbled. 'Especially her tech skills to help me find the best route.' He listened to the collective silence on the other end of the line. 'Hello? You guys still there?'

Solomon took the lead. 'I had a call from Douglas, Gill. He and the family are in Tel Aviv.'

'They're where?'

'I'm sorry, Gill. Canmore threatened her family. She sends her deepest apologies, but Adina has been forced to flee.'

When Gill and Bru walked calmly away from Callanish, the officers, plus the few news crews in attendance, watched in utter silence. After the brief call with the Armour Group, he struck out on the eighteen-mile walk along a narrow country lane that would take them to Stornoway. He didn't have a plan, just the conviction that he needed to challenge Canmore before the parliamentary vote. How that would happen was still a mystery to him, and the challenge would be harder without Adina. He understood why she needed to flee and trusted her to make the right decision. He patted his trousers to reassure himself he hadn't lost his phone in all the excitement. It was still safe in his pocket, and with it, the emergency number, delivered via Corrie, he'd saved to his contacts list.

On and on, they walked alone. Sure, there were police cars, but the vehicles kept their distance, and their orders seemed to be, "Do not engage." Bru walked consistently, occasionally breaking into a canter when he found a soft verge to run on. For the most part, Gill let him do what he wanted, stopping to drink when one of the many roadside burns ran clear, or grazing the verge when good green grass broke through the heather. When the road narrowed, their pace slowed when Bru was forced to walk on the hard, unfamiliar road surface. Consequently, the trek extended into the late afternoon while distant police cars moved far ahead of them to block the few intersections with other roads.

The land around constituted poor grazing, dotted with smatterings of small, grey cottages, which gradually became more numerous as they advanced on Stornoway. People stood watching from windows or came to the end of their gardens to say hello. As they approached the end of Marybank Road, three other horses and riders emerged from a field and onto the road ahead of them. Gill felt Bru stiffen under him while the horses whinnied and complained as their riders drew alongside.

'Edinburgh?' shouted Rani over the sound of the animals fussing.

'That's where I'm going,' Gill replied. 'The Scottish parliament building, to be exact.'

Rani blinked at him like he might as well be walking to Australia. 'Why?'

'Bru and I want a wee word with our First Minister.'

'Couldn't you call him? Drop him an email?'

Gill rubbed Bru's neck. 'I kinda like the imagery of taking the horse.'

'And do you have a plan? The remotest idea what you're doing?'

'Following my instincts here, Rani.'

'Do you even know your way to the port?' asked Graham.

Gill made a little show of casting his gaze around Bru's neck. 'These older models don't seem to have satnavs. We'll figure it out.'

'How do you know there'll be a boat? I mean, Amy insisted we put your message out on social media as soon as we got back to the house, but seriously, Gill, who's going to pitch up for that?'

'I think it'll be fun,' cried Amy. 'And you should cut across the golf course. It'll be quicker, and nicer for Bru.'

'Thank you,' said Gill, glancing up at a helicopter, circling far above their heads. 'Point the way to the harbour guys, then I'll see if I can beg a lift in somebody's boat.'

Rani nodded at Graham. 'You lead.'

Gill wasn't sure he'd heard her correctly. 'Hang on guys, this could get hairy.'

'You're sitting on Amy's horse, Gill. No way you're doing this on your own.'

'I thought you regarded Bru as a feral?'

'You know what I mean. And if we stand here much longer, we'll cause a traffic jam.'

Gill glanced at the empty road junction and the flashing blue lights in the far distance. 'Okay. If you're sure.'

Graham moved off, with Amy cantering up beside him, badgering her father about whether or not she'd be on TV that evening. Graham's response hung somewhere between a rebuke and a father's intense pride for his daughter. 'Amy, my love, for the rest of your life and forever, you will be the little girl who rode upon a unicorn.'

'I'm not that little,' Gill heard her huff.

Rani seemed nervous to be stationary, so Gill gave Bru a nudge and they crossed the road together. Following Graham and Amy down a narrow track through woodland, they emerged a few minutes later onto the golf course. Pushing through the last of the trees, Bru's ears flicked up as a player smacked a ball and sent it flying down a fairway. Turning irritably to investigate the source of the disturbance, the man's club froze at the top of his swing, then dropped silently from his hands.

'It's this way,' said Amy, pointing down the hill towards the port.

'I'm not sure we should be riding on a golf course,' said Graham.

'Extenuating circumstances,' muttered Rani. 'Now move it.'

Slipping into a canter, the four horses rode abreast, with Rani and Graham to Gill's left, upon Highland Ponies, and Amy to his right, on a dabbled grey cob, barely half the size of Bru.

'Down to the skatepark,' called Rani, then we can hang a right through those trees. There's a footbridge that will bring us out at the edge of the port. Graham cantered ahead of them, calling out warnings to bemused golfers and earning howls of protest from a greenskeeper. Everything was going fine until they reached the bridge. Gill dismounted first and guided Bru across, followed by Rani and Amy. His phone started to ring just about the moment when Graham's horse refused to cross. He took the call and watched while Graham coaxed and called, but nothing he could do would persuade his horse to step onto the narrow bridge. Meanwhile, nearby, a crowd was starting to build.

'Go ahead,' Graham shouted. 'I'll go around the long way and meet you at the port.'

Reluctantly, Rani led them off the path and onto tarmac, pointing her animal towards the sea. The police must have anticipated their move because Bayhead Road was devoid of traffic. Along the roadside and verges, groups of people were waiting for their strange little procession. Gill realised the word was out and the crowd was there to see Bru. But Bru didn't seem certain about all the attention. He lowered his head and pointed his tusk straight ahead of him, while on the roadside men took a step backwards, and women grabbed their children, hauling them out of reach.

Passing the marina on their right, and shops and pubs to their left, they trotted through the town centre to a mix of catcalls and cheers. The waterhorse was curious about this strange environment and threatened to lose momentum while he investigated the world around him. In response, Gill talked to him continuously, rubbing his neck and gently urging him forward.

Passing along Northbeach, they arrived at the industrial port. It was early evening by now and amidst a blizzard of small and large vessels, Rani pointed out the ferry terminal where a large crowd was being contained by a small knot of police.

'No way you'll get Bru on a Calmac,' called Rani. 'He needs to be outside.'

'No worries,' said Gill. 'I got a message from my office while we were waiting for Graham.'

'The ferries will let us on board?'

'No, but your shout-out on social media did the trick because our taxi is arriving shortly.'

Three abreast, they slow-trotted as far as the berthed ferry, then had to wait while the police pushed back the crowd so they could approach the adjacent berth. Gill could hear powerful diesel engines roaring as a vessel far smaller than the ferry drew up alongside. From an open window in the high wheelhouse, someone waved.

'You know these guys?' asked Rani.

'We've worked together,' said Gill, happily. 'Welcome aboard the Harlequinn.'

Chapter 37

92 Hours until the Scottish Parliamentary vote on independence

Once the horses had boarded and Jack had the gangplank stowed, Captain Quinn came to say hello. He took a long moment to marvel at the waterhorse, then turned to shake hands with Gill, then listened politely while he was introduced to Rani and Amy.

Rani waved a hand between Quinn and Gill. 'How do you guys know each other?'

'Had a little adventure with Gill around Corryvreckan a few years ago,' said Quinn. 'Which reminds me, did you ever see that good-looking lass again? You know, the DSV pilot.'

Gill pointed at his wedding band. 'Married with a kid. I'll be calling her as soon as we're moving, so I'll let you say hello.'

Rani broke away to answer her phone, while Amy rushed to tell Quinn about all her adventures over the last few hours.

'The police have blocked the town centre,' Rani reported. 'Graham can't get through.'

'Same with Ailsa,' said Gill, looking at his phone. 'What do you want to do?'

Quinn leaned in close. 'There's a portion of this crowd who love you guys, but there's a group who looks pretty ugly to me. If it's okay with you, I'd prefer not to hang around.'

'Let's go then,' said Rani. 'Graham is going back to the farm to get a horsebox. He can link up with Ailsa and they can catch us up whenever they find a ferry. In the meantime, Gill, can you help me settle the horses?'

The smaller horses quickly calmed, walking in circles a few times before seating themselves on the deck. Only Bru refused to sit or be tethered, walking the empty deck space to the bow and peering out over the water. Even as the Harlequinn gunned her engine and pulled away from the dock, the horse stood steadfast as if anticipating the start of a great adventure. He was still standing there, occasionally nodding his head while the little ship left the Isle of Lewis behind and powered out into The Minch.

'Right folks, where're we going?' asked Quinn.

'I'm hoping to go to Oban or Fort William and walk to Edinburgh from there.'

Quinn shook his head. 'Road and rail are still out, and the main west coast harbours are restricted to earthquake relief vessels. Try again.'

Gill looked at Rani. 'If they dropped us near Glasgow, we could walk along the motorway to Edinburgh.'

Rani's hands came sharply to her hips. 'You've not given this even the tiniest thought, have you?'

Gill bobbed his shoulders. 'It was a real spur-of-the-moment thing. I mean, either tear up Scotland or take a ridiculous road trip. Honestly, I was fifty-fifty for a few minutes.'

'Bru was like a cat on hot bricks in Stornoway. If you're planning to take him into a dense built-up area and not have him kill somebody, you need to acclimatise him to urban spaces.'

'Okay. What do you suggest?'

'Keep it rural. Small towns, and lots of grazing along the way. And places we can stay.' Her hands flew to her hair. 'What the hell are we doing, Gill? This could be a disaster.'

'The John Muir Way,' said Quinn, calmly.

'The what?'

'My girlfriend likes to do these long-distance trails. The John Muir links Helensburgh in the west with Muir's birthplace in Dunbar in the east.'

Gill nodded. 'And you could land us near there?'

'Helensburgh is just outside the Faslane exclusion zone. It doesn't have much of a pier, but the water's deep enough, and the Harlequinn has flexibility. We'll get you ashore one way or the other.'

'Okay,' said Gill. 'In the absence of another plan, let's do it.'

When the sun dipped in the west, and Bru finally relented from his sea-watch, he plodded over and settled beside the other horses. Rani had brought the simple leather bridle that Bru had worn in the days before his transformation, and in his sleepy state, he accepted it from her as she laid the soft material gently around his muzzle. Amy looked tired, so Rani left her to get acquainted with Jack while the pair took a turn watching the horses. The others retired to the ship's bridge to add details to their plan.

'The horses need to eat,' said Rani. 'We need to give them three or four hours grazing in the morning or they'll turn into a basket of weasels.'

Quinn tapped a digital map. 'We're making nineteen knots at the moment so by dawn tomorrow, we'll be about here, off the coast of Islay.' He glanced at Gill. 'According to the guy on the news, you've got connections there?'

Gill winced. 'I own a small island in the middle of a freshwater loch. I doubt that'll be much use to us.'

'Islay only has two deepwater ports, but they're used by the ferries,' said Quinn. 'If we berth without authorisation, we're asking for trouble.'

'Can you suggest anywhere else?'

'Let me have a think. There might be something connected to the whisky industry. Give me a minute to look at the charts.'

Gill felt Rani touch his elbow. 'I'm worried. We've no idea what Bru will do when we land him on an island. He was free-spirited enough when he was just a regular horse, and since he sprouted a tusk, he's developed some real attitude. You need to face it, Gill. He poses a threat to himself and anyone he meets.'

'I think ...' said Gill, battling to find confidence, 'Bru and I are building a working relationship.'

Rani didn't look convinced. 'Can I be really honest?'

'Go for it.'

'Passing through Stornoway today, you looked like a little boy sitting on top of a tank. Just because Bru has vaguely gone in the direction you want doesn't mean you're in control.'

'Look, he's brought me this far, and he's even started listening to my voice commands. And if he does decide to go wandering off, Islay has good habitat for him.'

'If he abandons you on Islay, he'll make you look like an idiot.'

Gill shrugged. 'I think I passed that point a long time ago, so Bru and I are just going to have to trust each other.'

'Got a suggestion for you,' said Quinn, calling Rani and Gill to join him at his Nav screen and pointing at a map of Islay. 'There's a small oil terminal here, in Lochindaal. From memory, they use it to land heating oil and petrol to serve the island. It's a well-serviced berth with plenty of depth for a boat the size of the Harlequinn.'

'What about grazing?' asked Rani.

'I called it up on satellite images. There's a long strip of uncultivated land on either side of the harbour. An all-you-can-eat buffet for hungry horses.'

'Will we attract attention?' asked Gill.

Quinn took a glance at his watch. 'By the time we get there, it'll be five in the morning. It's well away from the main settlements and we'll arrive unannounced. Chances are we'll be in and out before we attract much attention.'

Gill nodded. 'Rani?'

'So many things could go wrong.' She didn't look convinced. 'But yeah, I guess.'

'A couple of other things for you to consider,' Quinn added before touching a screen so that a screed of messages scrolled past faster than anyone could read. 'Try this list for starters.'

'What's that?' asked Gill.

'I'm being bombarded with information requests from police, marine traffic controllers and a host of media outlets. They all want to know our course and destination.'

'Tell them nothing,' Rani urged.

Quinn bobbed his head. 'They'll work it out eventually. As soon as we turn into the Firth of Clyde, they'll think we're heading for Glasgow. You might throw them off for an hour by landing at Helensburgh, but you need to plan ahead. What will you do if you find your route blocked.'

Gill shuddered. 'We'll figure that out as we go.'

'In the meantime, here's the other thing we need to bear in mind,' said Quinn, pointing to a coloured dot on the Nav screen.

'Is that a boat?'

'HMS Jura. She's a fisheries protection vessel, but for all intents and purposes, she's what passes for police around here once you step on a boat.'

'And she's headed in our direction?' asked Gill.

'Aye. She's coming from the southeast, closing on us at eighteen knots. She'll be right on top of us by the time the sun comes up.'

'What'll they do then?' asked Rani.

Quinn shrugged. 'I'd guess their orders will be to monitor your location. As for what they'll do next, that's anyone's guess.'

Chapter 38

80 Hours until the Scottish Parliamentary vote on independence
The Harlequinn made landfall on Islay at 5 am, under the shadow of the Bruichladdich Distillery. Quinn rigged the gangplank allowing the horses to come ashore, suggesting they walk south of the village so they could graze the lush summer verges. There was no traffic in this remote part of the island, and only the brooding presence of HMS Jura out in the bay suggested anything out of the ordinary was happening. The industrial shape of the Harlequinn didn't look out of place on the berth, and there was no one around to notice the great horned horse stepping out onto the machair to find the choicest grasses.

Wandering in his wake, always keeping Bru in sight, Gill felt dog-tired after a sleepless night. Sometime around ten, Rani had chased Amy off to find a bunk and hadn't returned herself, leaving Gill in sole charge of the animals. And now, for a short time at least, it was a pleasure to be off the boat. To Gill's relief, Bru just started to graze.

At 7 am, Gill watched an old tractor pull up on the harbourside and a man of an even greater vintage clambered down from the cab. It was too far away for him to hear the conversation between the driver and Quinn, but the tractor drove away and, a few minutes later, returned with two large hay bales spiked on the vehicle's front loader.

Shortly after that, a grey-haired lady arrived in a white van and pressed a box of supplies into Quinn's arms. Next, a car pulled up, and a young woman dashed across with what looked like a tray of hot drinks. Gill smiled. Even in these most unusual circumstances, island hospitality gleamed as brightly as the morning's sunlight reflecting off Lochindaal.

But the peace couldn't last. By eight, a small crowd was gathering, and two uniformed officers arrived. They didn't approach Gill, but lingered in front of the crowd, keeping them well back from the waterhorse.

'Come on, big fella,' said Gill, rubbing Bru's side. 'Time to go.'

Bru lifted his head and continued to chew. He seemed to notice the distant knot of people for the first time, though it didn't appear to disturb him. Instead, he sniffed the breeze, drawing in and expelling great lungfuls of air. And even in his tired state, Gill could smell it too. The distillery had begun the day's production, and now the sweet, faintly alcoholic aroma of raw spirit blew towards them on the wind. Lazily, Bru began to walk towards the smell.

'Hey, hey!' called Gill, taking the leather bridle and trying to coax Bru back towards the ship.

Bru snorted and shook his head, snatching the reins from Gill's hands.

'Come on now,' Gill called, sprinting around the animal until he was ahead of him.

Bru feigned a leftwards step, then ducked right and slid past Gill with ease. With his huge head lifted high, inhaling the wind, he broke into a trot and went in search of the smell. Helpless, Gill was left to trail in his wake. Ahead of them, a police officer blocking the road sprang to attention and urgently started talking into his mic. Spotting the fast-approaching horse, the crowd flinched backwards.

The distillery buildings were a sprawl of whitewashed warehouses fronting a section of taller structures that housed the manufacturing equipment. In an effort to make the Victorian-era architecture more contemporary, all the doors and window frames were painted an aquamarine green, achieving a vibrant if slightly synthetic symmetry to the colour of the sea in the sandy bay. But Gill doubted Bru was attracted by the decor as he tacked left and cantered into an enclosed concrete yard, sandwiched between the warehouses and the whisky stills. His hooves clattered on the hard surface while he trotted in a circle, pursuing the source of the enticing smell. Just as Gill caught up with him, a young woman emerged from a doorway clutching four bottles of spirit. Gasping at the sight of the vast horse, she abruptly halted, allowing one of the bottles to slip from her grasp. Smashing on the hard floor, the yard filled with the smell of old whisky.

'Don't move,' Gill called out to her. 'He's just curious.'

And Bru was curious, stepping towards the woman with his head bowed low. Gill watched terror spreading across her face as Bru's long, dark tusk swung in her direction. Easing alongside Bru, he tried to reassure the girl. 'It's okay. He won't hurt you.'

'How … how do you know that?' asked the girl.

Gill stepped closer to grasp the tip of Bru's horn and gave it a gentle shake. 'Because I've known him since he was little. He can be feisty, but fundamentally, he's good-natured.'

The girl's frightened face watched the bony tip swaying close to her abdomen as the horse continued to savour the smell on the ground. 'And he likes … whisky?'

'I didn't know that about him until today.' Gill gave her an embarrassed smile. 'I'm so sorry he made you drop the bottle.'

When Bru pressed deeper into her space, the girl stepped backwards two inches, then froze while Bru raised his head to snuffle her legs and pockets. 'It's … it's okay.'

Gill glanced over her shoulder. She'd obviously been carrying bottles to restock the tasting room. 'Say, what time does your gift shop open?'

'10 am,' rushed the girl. 'Licensing rules. We can't sell alcohol until then.'

'Ah, right. I was hoping to buy a couple of bottles for friends.' He laughed nervously. 'Maybe even one for the horse.'

A lump in the girl's throat bobbed up and down. 'I'm allowed to give you free samples.'

Gill shook his head. 'Really, I couldn't …' But the girl was already thrusting the first of the three bottles into his hands.

'Does he like peated or unpeated?' asked the girl in a shaky voice.

Gill tried to act like this was just a normal conversation. 'He's an islander, so probably peated.'

'This one then,' said the girl, offering him a bottle with a black label.

Gill slid the first two bottles into his jacket pockets and accepted the third. 'Honestly, this is so kind of you.'

'No problem,' she said, managing a petrified smile. 'Not every day a unicorn shakes you down on your way to work.'

Behind him, Gill heard the urgent crackle of a radio. He spun around to find the two police officers peeking into the yard. 'Right, Bru. Time to go.' But Bru just lowered his head and continued to inhale the peaty vapours.

'He'll prefer the one in your hand,' said the girl. 'Older. Richer. Wee bit more complexity.'

Gill could hear the creak of metal on metal as one of the officers tried to close the gate to the yard. In desperation, he tore the foil closure, uncorked the bottle and wafted it under

Bru's nose. Immediately, Bru lifted his head. 'Thank you,' was all he could say while Bru clattered on the concrete and swung to follow Gill. With the horse now coming towards them, the officers backed away. The gate was still half open, so holding the bottle aloft, Gill strode out of the yard and turned right towards the ship.

'You have got to realise the optics of this are worse than terrible,' Gill complained quietly to the following horse. 'Bad enough we have the mad scientist and his gigantic killer unicorn, but then they do a stop-over on Islay for what, a booze run?'

Bru just came alongside and breathed contentedly. 'And what was all that about, anyway? I thought you were a soft drinks guy. Are you considering a rebrand?'

There were a few shouts from the crowd behind them while ahead, a second police car sat silently with its blue lights flashing, blocking the road to Port Charlotte. Mercifully, Bru did not deviate, and a few minutes later, Gill led him along the gangplank and back onto the ship.

'Most people reward their horses with carrots,' Quinn jeered, playfully.

'Just don't,' muttered Gill.

'Is that how he got his name?' asked Jack while he nodded at the brand on the whisky bottle.

'What can I say? Bru and the distillery might negotiate a sponsorship deal.' Gill reached into his pockets. 'And as a thank you, he blagged you these.'

Quinn and Jack high-fived each other and looked ready for more banter until Rani's voice shrieked from the wheelhouse. 'Guys! Look behind you.'

'No, they bloody don't,' shouted Quinn, dashing to join her. 'Gill, secure the horses. Jack, throw off the lines.'

Gill dashed to the side to see the cause of the alarm. One hundred metres away, the green-grey bulk of HMS Jura was creeping towards them.

'They're trying to berth alongside,' yelled Jack. 'Trap us against the dock.'

There was no point trying to contain the now pacing Bru, so Gill tethered Rani and Amy's horses within a safe deck area, then felt the rumble of the boat's engines beneath his feet. With bow and stern lines free, the Harlequinn's engines growled as the boat began to drift away from the dock. In response, a tannoy voice from HMS Jura instructed them to stay exactly where they were, while up in the wheelhouse, the Harlequinn's equipment blared out a collision alert. Gill pitched forward slightly as Quinn threw the engines into reverse. Slowly, the boat began to move, the sides of HMS Jura towering above them as she tried to spring her trap. But Quinn was already pulling clear before he threw the boat into a one-hundred-and-eighty-degree turn. The Jura was also firing up her engines and was swinging away from the dock to give chase.

Quinn laughed aloud when his Nav system projected data showing they would be the victors in this sudden game of chicken. 'Raise the skull and crossbones, Jack. Disobeying His Majesty's navy means we're outlaws now.'

Jack laughed and recklessly sent up three long blasts from the ship's horn. Behind them, the Jura responded with a single long blast of her own. Carbon-dense smoke was billowing from her funnel, the vessel sprinting to gain its maximum speed. But the Harlequinn was faster, and a few minutes later, she steamed out of Lochindaal ahead of the warship and into the Irish Sea.

Chapter 39

64 Hours until the Scottish Parliamentary vote on independence

Gill was startled out of his doze by a blast on the ship's whistle. When the Harlequinn rounded the south shore of Aran late that afternoon, they'd discovered a small flotilla of boats waiting for them.

'Jack,' Quinn groaned. 'Cut our speed to two knots.'

'What's up?' asked Rani.

'Pleasure boats, sightseers and journalists,' Quinn replied. 'They have the water-sense of toddlers. It's ahead dead slow from here.'

'Maybe we should spend a second night on board,' said Gill, sleepily.

'We couldn't land you right now, even if we wanted to. Not with all these wee boats around. You guys get some sleep.' He nodded at Gill. 'Especially you.'

Gill turned to watch the boats criss-crossing their bow as people tried to get a glimpse of Bru. 'You sure? I hate to leave you to this.'

Quinn gesticulated at the water. 'This is madness, but I imagine it's just a foretaste of what you're going to get as you approach Edinburgh.'

Gill knew the captain was right, and for a few seconds, his mind tried to grasp the complexities of what lay ahead of them. But his brain yearned for sleep, and his body ached.

Lying down again on the bench in the rear of the wheelhouse, he fell straight back to sleep.

At 5 am the next morning, the Harlequinn's engines were idling while she held station between Gourock and Kilcreggan. While Gill had slept, the flotilla of onlookers had dwindled away, and now only HMS Jura was keeping them company through the short summer night. After a nudge from Jack, everyone assembled in the wheelhouse.

'You excited?' Jack asked Amy.

'Very,' she beamed. 'This is my best summer ever.'

Rani touched Amy's shoulder. 'We're only staying with Gill while people are kind to Bru. That's the deal we made, remember?'

Amy shrugged, then dashed over to hug Jack's legs. Gill, meanwhile, reached over them to grasp Quinn's shoulders. 'Thank you. For everything.'

Quinn nodded. 'Been my pleasure, pal. Come and visit me in prison.'

'You think?'

'Nah, we'll be fine. Worse than that, we'll be famous now we've transported the world's only waterhorse.'

Jack stepped in to give Rani a hug. 'You guys take care out there.'

Gill felt Rani's gaze hard upon him. 'We will. And listen, if any trouble comes out of this, blame it all on me.'

'Like it,' said Jack. 'We'll claim you threatened us with your whisky-impaired waterhorse and its big spikey-horn-thing.'

'More likely he'd lick you to death,' said Amy.

Quinn laughed. 'And now ladies and gentleman, to your stations, please.'

Under the cover of dawn-twilight, Gill, Amy and Rani went out on deck and stood by their horses, counting down the seconds until the Harlequinn surged forward. Whoever was watching aboard HMS Jura reacted slowly, with ninety seconds elapsing until the water boiled behind the warship. Gill remembered she could make 18 knots, then smiled. Very shortly, the Harlequinn would manage 22.

For fifteen minutes, Quinn followed a strict course for the port of Glasgow. Then, as Gare Loch opened up on their port side, he swung the boat through ninety degrees. Ten minutes later, they were on final approach for Helensburgh.

'Go,' yelled Jack as the gangplank found a sound footing on the dilapidated pier. In the background, the Harlequinn's engines roared, holding the vessel hard against the wall.

Gill went first, with Bru snorting and protesting against the stress in the atmosphere. 'Come on, big fella,' Gill soothed, his hand gripping the whisky bottle in his pocket. But Bru's ears were up, his attention focused on something Gill couldn't detect.

'Can you hear sirens?' asked Rani, pushing her mount to step up beside Bru.

'Didn't take them long,' moaned Gill.

Rani glanced back at Amy while she steadied her animal in preparation for mounting. 'This could go south very quickly, Gill. I just need you to know that the moment there's any danger to Amy, I'm going to remove her.'

'Totally agree,' said Gill. 'I didn't ask for your company, but I think it's been a massive help to Bru to have you guys around.'

He moved in front of Bru and grasped the creature's tusk with his left hand. Obediently, the animal lowered his head and allowed Gill to take a handful of Bru's long mane. Putting his left foot on the tusk base, Gill swung up onto Bru's shoulders and slithered backwards into a seated position. Immediately, Bru's head was back up, his ears twitching. And this time, Gill could hear it too. Six riders cantering to the far end of the access road. Pausing briefly, the lead rider left the others and trotted to their position.

'Good morning,' said the late middle-aged man dressed in hunting tweeds. 'Sorry we're late.' He stared at Bru for a long moment. 'My goodness, but what a fine animal.'

'Isn't he,' said Rani, coolly. 'And who may I ask are you?'

'David McKane,' said the man, before casting a wary glance at Gill. 'I'm with the Lomond *Vigil*. Aura sent us.'

'Aura?' said Rani.

'They're friends of a friend,' Gill explained.

Rani grasped Gill's arm. 'Hang on, we don't know these people. Why should we trust them?'

'They're *Vigil*,' said Gill, flatly.

'Which means?'

'Which means, I'll assume their intentions are good, and I'll ride with them up until the moment that changes.' Gill nodded at the new arrival. 'Let's move before the police block us on the pier. David, thank you, and please, lead on.'

Following their new guide, Gill, Rani and Amy exited the pier and joined the coast road. Following the other riders, they clattered towards the town centre, with flashing blue lights coming at them from the east. David took point, steering the party through the still-sleeping streets of Helensburgh, weaving down vennels and up lanes in a game of hide and seek with the police cars trying to block their way. Twenty minutes later, they were almost at the foot of the John Muir Way when emergency vehicles began converging on their location.

'I think the orders have definitely changed from "observe" to "contain" our waterhorse,' shouted Rani. 'Let's pull over before somebody gets hurt.'

'Don't give up,' called David, nodding to his party. 'We're going to create a little diversion. See if it gives you enough time to get away.'

Rani urged Amy to ride ahead of her before the pair led their horses around the gates and onto the long-distance trail. Meanwhile, David and his party had dismounted and tethered their horses to a roadside fence. Then they raised their hands and gingerly stepped into the paths of the approaching vehicles. As brakes squealed and officers piled out of the cars, David's group seemed to blunt the advance. But Bru wasn't happy with the burst of commotion. Snorting fiercely and swinging to face the nearest vehicle, Gill felt Bru's body tense beneath him, and moments later, the horse reared up. Powerless to stop him, Gill clung on in terror until he was almost in the vertical, digging in with his knees and holding Bru's mane with all his might. He felt a twinge of negative gravity as Bru dropped his front legs and leapt the four paces to the nearest police car, then reared again and plunged his front hooves into the bonnet of the car. When he sprang away to one side, Gill just had time to yell at one officer lying sprawled in the street.

'Tell your pals, don't ever crowd my horse.'

And without another glance at his pursuers, Bru was off and running. Gill had joked the horse didn't have satnav, but this waterhorse seemed to know exactly where he was going. Reaching the start of the John Muir long-distance trail, Bru coasted over the gate designed to restrict cars and sprinted down the track. He quickly overtook Rani and Amy and kept this pace for a mile until the spittle flying from the horse's mouth started to get in Gill's eyes.

'Come on,' called Gill, slapping Bru's neck and rubbing him. 'Slow down now.' Which he did, slowing to a canter, then finally stopping to graze the verge. With his heart pounding and adrenaline coursing through his body, Gill slid off and staggered to sit on a nearby wall. From his left, he could hear another party of riders approaching, while to his right, Rani and Amy were riding hard to catch up. Spotting a bloody gash on Bru's front right leg, Gill picked himself up and went to inspect the damage.

Amy was whooping when she arrived. 'That was AMAZING!' she yelled.

Rani didn't seem to agree while she struggled to catch her breath. 'We've less than two miles … under our belts, and now … we're officially fugitives from the law.' She glanced at Bru's leg. 'And you've hurt our horse.'

'It's just a scratch,' said Gill, 'And to be fair, attacking the police car was Bru's idea.'

'Not a great advert for taking a waterhorse into a city centre, Gill. I'm asking you again to reconsider.' Rani groaned and looked up at the second party of approaching riders. 'Oh, good grief, who's this lot?'

There were four riders in this new group. And aside from Bru, the lady at the front was riding the biggest horse Gill had ever seen.

'Amelia McKane,' she announced as the immense creature slithered to a halt. 'We're with David.'

'Have you heard from him?' asked Gill. 'Are his guys okay?'

'They've been arrested, or maybe not. Nobody seems too sure.'

'I'm sorry for their trouble.'

'All in a good cause. Look, let's get moving. In a couple of miles, the path splits. We can get under tree cover and attend to any injuries.'

Rani thumbed over her shoulder. 'What about the police?'

'Too narrow for a car, darling. Let's just find a steady pace, and that'll give you all a breather.'

'What breed is that?' asked Gill fifteen minutes later, nodding at Amelia's horse. The big stallion was only fractionally smaller than Bru and carried a similar amount of muscle.

'He's a Percheron. They're French, bred to pull heavy loads. David and I breed them on our Lomondside estate.'

'Fine animal.'

Amelia smiled her thanks, revealing a perfect set of even white teeth. 'I'll be honest, I wasn't sure how he and Bru would get on. Ardie can be quite fickle around other males.'

Gill looked down at the two great horses, matching each other for steps and stride. 'They seem perfectly paired.'

'Aura nudged me to bring him. My first choice for these paths would have been a trusty little cob, but now I see why Ardie was the horse for the job.'

A short forest layover gave the group room to breathe. Equipped with materials carried by the Lomond *Vigil*, Amy and Amelia treated Bru's damaged fetlock and wrapped it with protective tape. On Amelia's suggestion, they strapped Bru's other three legs. "To protect him during further incidents and retain balance in his visual appearance," Amelia explained in the face of Rani's disdain.

'Now he looks like a racehorse,' Amy giggled.

Afterwards, Rani retreated from the others and squatted on a log with the heel of her left hand pressed against her forehead. 'Racehorses don't have tusks,' she muttered, wearily.

Meanwhile, Gill and Amelia were studying a map. 'I know we've only just met, and I'm not going to tell you your business, but you have to anticipate little clashes with officialdom each time you dip into an urban area,' she said.

'And I just had a call from a friend in Balloch which is the next town on the trail. Apparently, there's quite a crowd building already.'

'What do you suggest?' asked Gill.

Amelia glanced at Bru. 'You're using the flimsiest set of reins I've ever seen. How are you controlling him?'

Gill patted the bulge in his pocket. 'I use whisky.'

'Sorry?'

'It's my last resort when he wanders, and kinda underlines the truth I'm not controlling him. So far, we're both operating on instinct. I mean, he listens to me when he feels like it, but that doesn't mean he's trained to obey my voice commands.'

She nodded. 'The waterhorse and the Percheron seem to have bonded. It means you can guide Bru by guiding me.'

'Okay. Sounds like you have an idea.'

'I do.' Amelia dipped her head. 'It's risky, and I mean threatening to life and limb risky, but here's what I think we should do.'

Chapter 40

Freya Swanson stood in the car park of the Balloch House Hotel and waited. She'd known something was up from the moment the commotion in the McKane's yard had woken her. The sky had still been pale when the reversing of vehicles and the clatter of hooves on the concrete surface signalled an unusual early-morning manoeuvre. Peeking out her window, she'd watched them load their big Equicruiser and leave in a hurry. Most noticeably, they'd included Ardie, the big Percheron. That beast was like a Lamborghini and only got rolled out on very special occasions. She'd been following the news reports, of course, and realised, in a wonderful twist of fate, McArdle and his waterhorse weren't far away. Somehow, through a connection she couldn't comprehend, she suspected the McKanes were also involved in this. Rushing to prepare her little mare, she'd loaded her horsebox and warmed up the battered 4x4, a pale comparison to the McKane's kit, and made ready to leave. Tuning into a news report of an incident at Helensburgh, she'd dropped a quick blog post on the waterhorse's location, then looked at a map. Judging they were riding the John Muir Way, she'd a pretty good idea where McArdle would go next.

Now, as she prepared to execute her hastily made plan, she was nervous and consequently, Poppy, her dappled mare, seemed edgy. Freya knew she was taking a risk here and if she misjudged this, the consequences could hit her in unforeseen ways. People were milling around on the road bridge, killing time by peering down into the marina below. This narrow neck of Loch Lomond where it spilled into the River Leven would normally be dead at this time of the morning. But replies to her blog post confirmed the waterhorse had landed at Helensburgh and was coming in this direction.

There were two places where the waterhorse could cross the river. She knew the main road bridge through town was wider and already bursting with people. The marina bridge was an older, flimsier affair but it was closer to the John Muir Way and so this is where she waited.

A commotion at the far end of the bridge caught her attention. Something was happening. 'Let's not mess this up,' she told Poppy, giving the old girl a neck rub. And then she was up into the saddle, guiding her horse to begin a slow step towards the road. Soon, they were mired in onlookers and could only move at the pace of the people around her. Only when they heard the sound of fast-approaching hooves did people start to pull back. Four riders rushed past her in single file, shouting warnings to the crowd to stand clear. Next came the big horses. Freya felt her jaw drop a fraction as the two gigantic beasts thundered over the bridge and passed her position. The waterhorse, brilliant white fading to grey down his legs, with the metre-long tusk thrusting high from its forehead alongside Ardie, the chestnut-coloured Percheron she knew from her duties on the McKane's estate. And in their wake came more riders. A small, Asian lady alongside a child who couldn't have been older than ten. And behind them six, a dozen, no, two dozen other riders. Far behind and mired in pedestrians spilling out into the road, two police cars sat with their blue lights flashing irritably. Freya swallowed, and spurring Poppy, she joined the cavalcade at the rear.

An hour later, the convoy pulled off the road to rest in the shade of a conifer forest. There was a small reservoir, and after a brief inspection, they allowed the horses to drink.

'So far so good,' said Gill when Rani came over to check on Bru.

'Meaning nobody's died yet,' said Rani, eyeing Amelia suspiciously.

Amelia's smile was confident and reassuring. 'We carry along this path for another three miles, but after that, it gets quite steep. David and I hack around here, so I'd like to suggest a diversion that gets us down to Strathblane, avoiding roads and high ground.'

'Sounds good to me,' said Gill. 'And somewhere along the line, we need to eat.'

'I've got friends at Balagan,' said Amelia. 'We can stay there overnight, and I'll arrange food for the troops.'

Gill winced at the military analogy. 'Thanks, but you and David have done so much already.'

'We want to help. After tomorrow, you're off our patch and become somebody else's responsibility.'

'You'll be leaving us?'

'No, we'll support you until you reach your goal, or we're all arrested. But our friends in the next county know the land better than us.'

'Okay then, thank you.'

'Sorry to interrupt,' said Rani, curtly. 'But I need to make you aware we have an infiltrator.'

Amelia arched her eyebrows. 'A what, darling?'

'There's a journalist amongst the riders called Freya Swanson. She says she knows the McKanes and wants a word with Gill.'

'Oh, yes, I know Freya. She's a dear. Works as a journalist and moonlights as our stable girl. The poor thing barely earns a penny.'

'Not sure we need extra publicity right now,' said Rani.

Amelia disagreed. 'If I can be so bold, you need to grasp the public relations challenge, and Freya could be just the person to help you.'

Gill felt all eyes fall on him. 'Actually, I've heard of her. Kind of a friend of a friend. She broke the *Treaty of Finlaggan* story.'

'I'll tell her to come see you, shall I?' said Rani.

'Yes, but not until we're moving again,' said Gill. 'I'm going to call Salina while we're stopped. And sometime today, I need to speak to Ailsa. She's still stuck on Harris, and I want her to join me in Edinburgh.'

'She'll have a job. Graham says public transport on and off the island is still restricted.'

'Ailsa will find a way,' he said. 'In the meantime, shall I send her your regards?'

'Aye, tell her we're all grand,' said Rani, sarcastically, while she walked away.

If Gill McArdle was the leader of this rabble, then Rani Kumar was his first lieutenant. 'Gill is prepared to meet you,' she said. 'Move up to the front of the column and stay as long as he lets you.'

Freya swung in behind Rani and coaxed her little horse around the other animals in the caravan. Their numbers had doubled since they passed through Balloch, and she wondered where they were all coming from. As she approached the waterhorse from the rear, the great Percheron cantered forward a few steps to make space for her. Poppy seemed reluctant to come alongside the waterhorse, and

Freya had to push her a little harder than she liked. Perhaps like herself, Poppy was unsettled by the waterhorse's great tusk bobbing up and down as they walked up a gentle gradient. After a little skittering and bickering, she finally coaxed her little horse alongside.

'Freya Swanson,' she said nervously. '*Glasgow Tribune*.'

'Gillan McArdle,' he replied with a mischievous smile. '*Mysterious Scotland* magazine. How're you enjoying the road trip?'

'In the last two hours, I've spoken to people from the Borders, Perthshire and The Highlands. I'm trying to work out why they're all here.'

'A few sightseers. Others who feel called to this,' said McArdle, before asking suddenly, 'Do you know the Nazarene?'

Freya shook her head. 'Is that a bar? A restaurant?'

'Never mind,' he said. 'A conversation for another day.'

They fell into silence for a few steps, and she wondered if she'd failed some kind of test, but he just smiled and asked, 'Where would you like to begin?'

She took a deep breath. 'Are we on the record?'

His shoulders sagged a little. 'I'm a man with a dubious reputation, coaxing a semi-mythical animal halfway across Scotland. I think people have a right to know why.'

'Can we start with Bru? When you discovered Waterhorse bones on the Isle of Lewis five years ago, did it ever occur to you that a living example might be discovered in Scotland?'

He nodded over his shoulder. 'Rani identified the genetic strain that separates these beasts from their kin. The process that allows this latent ability to manifest isn't properly understood, but yes, let's just say we saw the theoretical potential.'

'For such a dangerous animal, you seem very comfortable in each other's company.'

'Bru and I have history.'

This news surprised her. 'You knew him before his transformation?'

'Yes. And before you ask, we never intended to throw him into the public spotlight. He kinda forced that on us.'

'Us?'

'Rani and her daughter are Bru's custodians.'

'They own him?'

McArdle turned to stare at her. 'You don't own a waterhorse. They trust who they trust ... and God help the rest.'

'Take me back to Callanish,' she said, recovering from his mild rebuke. 'What drew you there?'

'I wanted to make sure Bru was kept safe.'

'Any other reasons?'

McArdle rubbed Bru's flank and mustered his response. 'Obviously, you know about the treaty.'

'Yes. I've written about Finlaggan in the *Tribune*. Ailsa McIver put me on to it.'

McArdle didn't seem surprised by this news. 'Well, as you've had time to ponder it, you'll have realised its potential power.'

'And now, Westminster and Holyrood have struck it off the statute books.'

McArdle smiled. 'The treaty might be gone, but the truth it underscored doesn't go away.'

'What do you mean?'

'Do you remember the opening clause? "*Should the Laird of Finlaggan, upon hearing a supremacy of our citizens voice displeasure at Scotland's ruler ...*" Let's just say, I think plenty of Scots are unhappy with our First Minister's secession plan, and I'd like to have a word with him about that.'

'Let's come back to that in a second. What was going through your mind when you circled the stones?'

He looked sober for a second. 'Right at that moment, not being gored by Bru or being shot by a marksman were high on my list.'

'And yet, there you were. In a remarkable set of coincidences, you, the recently acknowledged Laird of Finlaggan, found yourself on Lewis, at the very moment the first living waterhorse in generations walked on Scottish soil.'

'Coincidences,' he repeated. 'No such thing.'

'I'm sorry, I don't follow.'

'The fact that the universe exists; that it what, puffed out of nothing? And that the Earth exists and that it isn't too hot or too cold, too toxic or too irradiated. I could go on, but do you get my drift? Every time you look in a mirror you are looking at a unique human who has the privilege of existence.' He shook his head. Please don't talk about coincidences, Freya, because I no longer believe in them.'

'If not that, then what? A calling? A mission?'

McArdle shrugged and turned his eyes back on the path. 'I think there are jobs to be done in life. And the grubbiest jobs just lie there until someone with enough curiosity picks them up.'

'As you did at Callanish a few days ago. For a few brief minutes, you held the legal authority to dissolve the Scottish nation. Why didn't you?'

'Why didn't I declare *The Torn Isle?*'

'Yes. For a few moments, it was in your power.'

He leaned forward to whisper some encouraging words to the waterhorse. 'I realised something.'

When he didn't elaborate, she pressed him to continue.

'For years, I fretted about tearing up Scotland. But, when I completed the circuit of Callanish, I realised, in so many different ways, Scotland is already torn. If you think about it, Canmore's plan is a reflection of our divisions. For a few minutes, amidst those ancient stones, I had the legal right to rip Scotland apart, without recourse to a democratic mandate. By implication, I could have styled myself as the new *Lord of the Isles*, though I chose not to. Meanwhile, our First Minister is trying to force Scotland out of its union with Britain without preparation or consultation. He has no democratic mandate, nor does he have an arcane law allowing him to do whatever the hell he wants. I did have the law, but I don't have the mandate, so I would have been a hypocrite to ape him.'

'Invoking the treaty could have worsened those divisions?'

'Yes, and when I stopped to think about it, I saw a better way.'

'Which is?'

'Implementation of the treaty would have forced Scotland to reimagine itself. Shorn of the highlands and islands we would have faced constitutional chaos while still having the opportunity for a massive reset where everyone got to have their say about the future. I didn't invoke the treaty because I believe we can still have the reset but without the chaos.'

'May I ask where you're going now?'

'The Scottish parliament,' he said flatly. 'Although if it's okay with you, I'd prefer you didn't put that in your blog.'

'Parliament?' she foolishly repeated.

'Aye well, depending on the horse, we might only get as far as the Irn Bru factory in Cumbernauld.'

She blinked at him. 'I thought his name was Brùth, as in the Gaelic word for *press for breakthrough,* but you're telling me he's named after a soft drink?'

'I like your version better,' McArdle shot back. 'Yes, you can publish that. Let's name him after the Celtic god of bashing into stuff. Honestly, you should see what he did to Rani's stable block.'

'But why go to Holyrood?' she asked, trying to get the conversation back on track.

He sighed and raised his gaze heavenward before replying. 'We're going to meet our First Minister and tell him we're unhappy with the way he's running things.'

'We?'

The horse snorted as McArdle gave him an encouraging rub. 'Me and the one-horned-Celtic-god of bashing into stuff.'

'You're against nationalism?'

'No. There are many aspects of it I find attractive. But there are many ways to conceive a new Scotland, and Canmore's illegal declaration is just about the worst version of it I can imagine.'

'There are people who say you're grand-standing. That in effect, what you're doing borders on terrorism.'

Gill smiled. 'If we were talking about Ireland or the US capitol riots, I'd be forced to observe that one person's terrorist is another person's freedom fighter.'

'You're siding with terrorists?'

'I'm not. I'm simply saying that in today's lazy politics, we don't work hard enough to understand the other guy's point of view. We snap towards vitriolic language and divisive dogma.'

'And if Canmore refuses to meet you, what will you do?

McArdle smiled ruefully. 'Wait and see.' At that point, Bru took it upon himself to catch up with the Percheron. Freya found herself falling behind and wondering if his tactics were indeed a secret or if he just hadn't worked them out yet.

Chapter 41

48 Hours until the Scottish Parliamentary vote on independence

Ailsa stood in the terminal building of Stornoway Airport and waited for her taxi. Soon after Gill had departed Callanish on his waterhorse, she'd planned to board a ferry. But before she could leave, she'd been detained by police. Not arrested as such, but "invited" to assist them with their enquiries. In practical terms, this had meant spending two evenings at her mother's home followed by two long days having protracted conversations with DI Lundy. The man was trying to find some illegality he could pin on Gill, but as Friday afternoon wore on, he tired of the exercise and dismissed her.

By then, Gill was progressing across the Central Belt and she felt far from the action. Public transport was still locked down, and somehow, she needed to get to Edinburgh. And like many things in life, the answer when it came was fortuitous. A call from a friend in Dundee, anxious about her welfare and wondering if there was any way she could help. 'Yeah,' Ailsa had said. 'I can think of something.'

Out on the tarmac, the sleek business jet came to a standstill and powered down its engines. When the gate controller gave her the all-clear, she hoisted a small bag on her shoulder and strode out to join the aircraft.

'Thanks for sorting this,' she called to her friend.

'No problem,' Cassy smiled. 'It's a chance of a lifetime for me. Never been in one of these things.'

'Thanks, Corrie,' Ailsa shouted to the pilot, who raised a hand in greeting. 'Hey, Zack,' she added, spotting the copilot, before whispering to Cassy, 'Zack can fly?'

'Gracious, no!' Cassy snorted. 'But Corrie has glued his hands to the seat so we should be fine.'

The pair settled back in luxurious leather seats and exchanged their news while Corrie waited for permission to join the runway. By the time they were fully airborne, Ailsa was hearing Cassy's worries about the trouble escalating across the Scottish lowlands. Then it was Ailsa's turn to tell the others about their adventures at Callanish and Gill's unanticipated road trip. Pressed on what the plan was from here, Ailsa had to confess she wasn't sure.

'Get him on the line and ask him,' Cassy scolded.

'Who?'

'Gill. There's a phone in your armrest.'

Ailsa lifted the leather-coated padding to reveal the device. 'Corrie. Is it okay if I make a call?'

'Help yousel', lass. Does conference calls an' everything.'

Ailsa stared down at the complex device, then flashed a pleading smile at Cassy.

'No problem,' she sighed. 'Just gimme the numbers and I'll set you up.'

When Amelia announced she'd secured a campsite for the night, Gill couldn't hide his relief. In another twenty minutes, he'd be able to slide off Bru's wide girth and rub some feeling back into his thighs. Only twenty minutes and yet it felt like an age, so it was a welcome distraction when his phone rang.

'Gill, it's Ailsa. And with Cassy's help, I've got Solie, Lillico and Charlie.'

Gill didn't hide his pleasure while he rattled around the group, sharing a few words with everybody, including Zack and Corrie McCann who were there in the background for reasons Ailsa didn't explain.

'Right,' said Ailsa. 'We've only got a few minutes. Gill, what's the plan and how can we help?'

'Still working on the details,' said Gill. 'Basically, I'm taking Bru to parliament. At the very least, I plan to create a photo opp to highlight the fundamental injustice of Canmore's actions. Based on the current rate of progress, we'll be there by the morning after tomorrow. If anyone can join me, I'll have tasks for you all.'

'I'll be there,' said Ailsa. 'And Alex, you said you can round up Lorna?'

'Yes. She and I agreed a safe place for me to leave her messages. I'll let her know when we're ready for her to skip prison and meet us. Can anyone suggest where we can rendezvous?'

'Ask her to jump to my location at 6 am,' said Ailsa. 'And I'll make sure I'm somewhere she can arrive without being observed.'

'Got that,' said Lillico.

'Apart from mounting a very public stunt,' said Solomon, evenly. 'Is there anything we can do to bring Canmore to justice?'

Lillico cleared his throat. 'I can't give you specifics, but there's a good chance there'll be a case brought against Canmore.'

'I thought the police were on his side?'

'A portion, certainly,' said Lillico. 'But a number of senior officers seem to be gearing up to challenge the legality of what he's done.'

'Okay, I wish you well with that one because Canmore is a weasel,' said Gill. 'They'll need to be careful he doesn't misrepresent their actions to strengthen his own position.'

'Which brings us to an important point,' said Solomon. 'At the moment, the media coverage of your antics is pretty fifty/fifty, for and against. Meanwhile, you're saying nothing, and frankly, I think you need to be smarter than that.'

'I'm on the road all day, Solie. What do you expect me to do?'

'You need to talk to the media or start posting online. Something to reassure the watching public your intentions in Edinburgh are peaceful.'

'Freya Swanson, the journalist pal of Ailsa's,' mused Gill. 'She's travelling with us. She seems genuine.'

'That's good. I've read her blogs, and she seems quite fair.'

'Solie, talking of acting smarter, please tell me you're postponing the Read*Scot* conference?'

Solomon laughed. 'The conference is this weekend, Gill. Around the same time, the Laird of Finlaggan will be walking his horse into the City of Edinburgh. Do you sense Aura's hand in that, or shall we write it off as a coincidence?'

'But Solie, we'll be busy with Canmore. We won't be able to protect you,' Gill pleaded.

But Soloman wasn't budging. 'Remember the conference centre is in the Grassmarket. Charlie and I will be well away from the demonstrations centring around Holyrood, but close enough to assist if you need us.'

'Ah'll look after her, ken,' said Charlie. 'Mak sure she disnae git intae any trouble.'

'I take it there's still no word from Adina?' asked Solomon.

In the background, Gill heard Corrie having a protracted coughing fit, so it was a few seconds before he could jump back in. 'I know Adina will be with us in spirit.'

'With us in spirit,' mused Ailsa, 'As in, lying by a pool, drinking cocktails and hoping we don't die? Or as in, commanding a Tel Aviv operations centre, ready to bring all that sexy high tech to our aid?'

'You're breaking up,' Gill lied. 'Can't hear you very well. Hope to see you in Edinburgh the day after tomorrow.'

Chapter 42

45 Hours until the Scottish Parliamentary vote on independence

Weary after a long first day in the saddle, the riders and horses camped near Strathblane using facilities generously provided by friends of the McKanes. Gill didn't plan to let Bru out of his sight until all this was over, but after thirty miles riding a saddleless waterhorse, he desperately needed a break. So, after a nod to Rani, he left her in charge and went in search of a shower. He returned twenty minutes later to find Rani nearby, tending to Amy's little horse while Freya was using a textured curry comb to tackle the mud embedded in Bru's white coat.

'You're brave,' he observed.

Freya smiled but didn't turn around. 'I don't think there's a horse alive who doesn't like this if it's done right.'

'Still, I'm glad he trusts you.'

'Well, I think he's a bit of a show-off. He wants to look his best before you parade him in Edinburgh.'

'You know a lot about horses?'

'Since I was a kid. These days, living on the McKane's estate, I help out in their stables in exchange for cheap rent.'

'I noticed you chatting with Amelia,' Gill nodded. 'They seem like good people.'

Freya paused. 'They are. Decent. Very honest.'

'I'm detecting a "but" at the end of that statement.'

'No, seriously, they're great.'

299

'I've just met them,' said Gill. 'If there's anything I should know?'

'They're a tiny bit eccentric,' rushed Freya. 'I mean, running a big country farm would do that to you. Having old buildings to maintain and complicated families. They come across as dead posh, but financially, I hear they just about get by.'

'How do they earn their money?'

'A mix. There's a big arable farm. A farm shop. And they subsidise all that by managing horses for stud.'

'They're good with horses. Outside of Bru, that Ardie is the biggest horse I've ever seen.'

Freya smiled her agreement but said nothing.

'So, how are they eccentric?'

Freya glanced to ensure she wasn't being overheard. 'They're a bit religious.'

'No harm in that.'

'They used to go to a church, but that closed a while back, and now they have this group that meets in their house.'

'I see.'

'They get all types coming, so I suppose they must be quite brave. It was small-scale at first, but lately, there are loads of cars coming and going a couple of evenings a week. I just hope they're not exploiting anyone, or being exploited themselves.'

'I hear your concerns,' said Gill, with a mischievous smile. 'And does this group have a name?'

Freya cast another furtive glance behind her. 'It's called *The Vigil*. Sounds creepy, yeah?'

'Very,' said Gill.

'I mean, "vigil" implies waiting for something. Who wants to waste their life waiting for something that might never happen? Something that might not even be real?'

'I guess Amelia and David have considered that and are living in the light of whatever they've experienced.'

'Yeah, well, they'll not be recruiting me for their weird little get-togethers.'

Gill laughed.

'What?'

'Nothing. It's just you remind me of somebody else. Somebody a long time ago.'

Chapter 43

The following morning, the caravan was up and moving not long after first light. In a deep green glen, hidden from any buildings and far from any roads, the convoy of Lomond horses made fast progress along the John Muir Way. This part of the trail was so straight, Gill imagined its origins must have been an old railway line.

An hour into their ride, they arrived at a node scattered with picnic tables and found their way blocked by a dozen riders on horses and around sixty on bikes. Leaving their mounts, Gill, Rani and Amelia moved forward to meet the new arrivals.

'Oh, look,' said Amelia, waving at familiar faces. 'I was wondering when these chaps would show up.'

'You know these guys?' asked Gill.

'They call themselves the Stirlingshire *Vigil,* but they're not a big group. Last I heard, they were pulling people from Falkirk to Kirkintilloch.'

'I see.'

'Not so rural,' Amelia explained. 'Fewer horses.'

'Not as posh as the last lot,' muttered Rani. 'No bad thing.'

'What are you suggesting, darling?' asked Amelia, basking in Rani's discomfort.

303

Rani ignored her. 'Gill, when we next reach civilization, Amy and I are dropping out. My advice would be to keep Bru in the company of the horses he knows. Don't let the bikes get too close or he'll freak out.'

'I think you and Amy are doing splendidly,' said Amelia. 'Why would you leave now?'

'My horse is lame, and there's no way Amy is carrying on without me.'

'Where will you go?' asked Gill.

Rani shrugged. 'Graham still can't get across to the mainland, so until he does, we'll hunker down somewhere.'

'You could take Ardie and stay with the convoy,' said Amelia. 'Do him good to have a different rider for a few days.'

'What?' Rani spluttered. 'That Percheron must be worth high five figures. There's no way I …'

'Mid-six figures, actually,' Amelia replied. 'But I've watched you these past few days. Your compassion for these animals is outstanding. I can't think of anyone better to take him forward in this little adventure.'

'Are you thinking of leaving us too?' asked Gill.

'I need a few hours off the road. I'll go and retrieve David, then we'll rejoin you tonight.'

Rani looked at Gill, who just shrugged. 'If Ardie turns around, Bru might follow. We need him, Rani. And we need you too.'

'David is bringing in our Equicruiser. Let me take your mare and I'll get her rested.'

Rani seemed struck by this generosity. 'If you're absolutely sure?'

'I am,' Amelia announced. 'And for what it's worth, I think Gill needs you more than he's letting on. You're a natural sceptic. I think you keep some of his wilder notions in check.'

Rani nodded her thanks. 'It was all these hard paths that did for my animal. 'I'm wondering if we should have a farrier look at Bru?'

'I'll make some calls,' said Amelia. 'And Rani …'

'Yes?'

'Make sure Bru doesn't lead Ardie into any mischief.'

Led by an ever-growing herd of cyclists, with horses joining the convoy at the rear, Gill imagined their fast progress would continue. Moving like an express train, they'd slice through town and country, covering perhaps another thirty miles and reaching Falkirk by nightfall. Instead, by mid-morning, the whole caravan staggered to a halt west of Lennoxtown. The town centre was blocked by sightseers wanting a glimpse of Bru, and not all of them were friendly.

Gill and the others dismounted and let their animals graze the verge for an hour, but eventually, Bru became agitated. The lack of forward motion and the uninvited claustrophobia of the caravan was stressing him. Gill was feeling it too, glancing at his watch and seeing the hours tick down towards tomorrow's vote. Needing an escape route, he phoned Amelia who immediately passed him to David.

'Head for Lennox castle,' David advised. 'I'll guide you through a mess of wee roads to the south that will allow you to bypass the urban areas. And I recommend you avoid Kirkintilloch town centre. There's some kind of demonstration there.'

Gill caught a glimmer of the trouble rumbling across Scotland. 'Is it bad?'

'Some injuries, yes. A group of your supporters is being pelted with Irn Bru cans. I think your detractors are trying to be ironic.'

'These "detractors" don't even know me,' Gill spluttered.

305

'Actually, Gill, from the waterhorse bones to the Great Glen Disaster and your reporting on the *Fated Stone*, they do know you. And now you're a laird and some folks with a reversed sense of snobbery are offended by that.'

Gill looked down at his mount and wondered again how Bru would respond if confronted with violence. 'Yeah, let's give the towns a miss.'

'I mean, I'm sure Bru could sort them out, but that's not the point, is it?' He laughed nervously. 'No pun intended.'

'It's not.'

'Stay on the line, Gill. I'll navigate you to the point where the John Muir Way intersects with the Forth & Clyde Canal. After that, one of the Stirlingshire people has a farm near Auchinstarry. I suggest you stop there for the night.'

'Thanks, David. This is a huge help.'

'Look, Gill, I don't mean to be a pain, but have you considered how you'll reach Edinburgh city centre without instigating a deadly clash?'

Gill rubbed his face. Between one thing and another, he wasn't getting enough sleep. 'If you have suggestions, I'm all ears.'

'I was hoping you would say that. When I see you this evening, let me grab a map, and I'll show you what I'm thinking.'

That evening, while they camped near Kilsyth, and the sun was setting behind the Kilpatrick hills, Gill picked up his phone and tabbed to Freya's blog. Looking at her stats, he saw she'd posted forty-eight times in the two weeks since starting her online diary. If he wanted an insight into this woman's opinions, there was plenty of scope by just looking at her writing.

The first thing he noticed was her numbers. Starting with barely one hundred followers, her stats had grown slowly for a few days while she'd set out the *Treaty of Finlaggan* and its threat to Scotland's geographic integrity. She'd also revealed Gill as the laird and reminded her readers that he'd been instrumental in proving the waterhorse was more than a myth. Patiently laying the groundwork and answering her reader's questions, it was four days before Freya announced with certainty there was a waterhorse stalking the Hebridean moors. And a couple of days later, she had a breakthrough when the clearest image on her blog was reprinted by the *Glasgow Tribune*. As a fellow journalist, Gill decided he liked her style. She'd worked her contacts to gather data and built a network of island eyes and ears. Six days in, her numbers jumped when dozens of people started reporting sightings of Bru, or simply became excited by the possibility of his existence.

The only time Freya skipped writing a blog post was the day of Canmore's declaration of independence. She returned the following morning full of concern for Scottish democracy and the potential impact of independence on the rural regions. Her blog still focused on the Hebridean waterhorse, but her analysis of the Finlaggan treaty now gave her reporting a political undertone.

She was just shy of eighteen thousand followers the day after the quake when Canmore escalated his war of words with the British government. And that day marked a change in her writing tone. While consistently critical of Westminster's usual ham-fisted response to any crisis in the regions, she systematically deconstructed Canmore's accusations and displayed him as a merciless opportunist. Her numbers wavered for a while, perhaps as some people tuned out of yet another political discourse. And then came Bru.

On the day she joined the caravan, she wrote of her uncertainty about McArdle and his motives. Keeping her promise to protect Gill's secrets, she refused to speculate what might happen when they reached Edinburgh. Nor did she bait her readers with "an inside track" on what this "insurgence" had in mind. But the reality was this, as the only journalist openly travelling with Bru's caravan, her numbers skyrocketed. This wasn't just about politics anymore – this was about a mystical horse and his master on their journey towards Edinburgh and some unknown destiny. She reported fairly on her conversations with Gill, and with many others of their fellow travellers. And he laughed out loud when he read that amongst her diverse followers, were those who thought Gill would cement the move to independence, while others believed he would ride to the top of Calton Hill and wave a Union Jack. And yet … and yet… Freya saw a deeper nuance, that this wasn't about being on one side or the other. She called out the slander and manipulated truths coming from both camps and challenged her readers to consider what they really valued about their nation. She didn't care if they were for independence or union because her strongest instinct, pounding like a heartbeat through every post, was that any change without a democratic mandate was essentially an injustice. Her last blog had been posted two hours ago. She'd speculated about what might happen next and pleaded with her countrymen to refrain from violence.

Closing his phone, Gill arrived at a decision. Getting to his feet, he set out to find Freya Swanson.

He found her with Amelia, working amongst the horses. The McKanes had returned with supplies, and now they were strapping the knees of an elderly little cob who was struggling after two days on the road. After a nod from Gill, Amelia excused herself to fetch something from their support vehicle while Freya leaned back against a fence, ready for a rest.

'How's it going?' he asked.

'Just helping Amelia do some first aid amongst our herd.'

'They've got problems?'

'Nothing serious. Cuts and bruises. A few that are weary from walking on hard surfaces and will probably need to drop out.'

'Amazing to think our forbears relied on these animals for so many things.' He paused to stroke the animal's neck. 'Transport, heavy-lifting, war.'

'And now we keep them as pets. And the poor things are a bit knackered because they're not used to working so hard.'

'Well, I appreciate what you're doing.'

'No problem. I have the skills and the time. Seems the right thing to do.'

'I've been catching up on your blog.'

Freya's pale cheeks immediately flushed. 'What do you think?'

'Half a million followers, Freya. You must be proud.'

'Pride doesn't come into it, Gill. I've had the good fortune to be here on the ground with you. If there's an upside to my career, I hope you won't mind.'

'I don't mind. For what it's worth, I think you've been very fair.'

Freya flashed him with a shy smile. 'Made the front page again today. *Glasgow Tribune's* inside girl embedded in the first army to march on Edinburgh in three hundred years.'

'We're not an army. I hope you're not calling us that.'

'My editor,' she said, looking away. 'He's milking this, and seriously, if I ever make you uncomfortable, please just send me away.'

'Listen, Freya. Things are going to get edgy as we approach Edinburgh. There'll be lots of risk. I'm only taking a few folks into the city centre.' He paused and studied her face. 'I wanted to ask if you'd be one of them?'

Freya's eyes narrowed. 'Even though my editor might misreport you?'

Gill looked away. 'Your blog stands on its own. Maybe it's time to tell the *Tribune* to either print what you give them or risk the possibility you'll start reporting for somebody else.'

Freya nodded slowly. 'I could do that.'

Gill glanced around to make sure no one was listening. 'David's come up with a plan. If we pull it off, we'll sneak into the centre of Edinburgh without anyone knowing we're there. I don't know what'll happen, and there's every chance it'll be dangerous. But somebody impartial needs to report this, and I'd like that person to be you.'

Chapter 44

16 Hours until the Scottish Parliamentary vote on independence

Gill stood with Amelia and David, going over the details of the plan one more time. It was risky in so many unquantifiable ways, and if Canmore had a spy in their camp, and detected what was happening, they'd forfeit the element of surprise. They stopped talking when they saw Rani and Amy walking slowly towards them. They were hand in hand, and noticing her red eyes, Gill observed he'd never seen Amy cry before. Seeing him staring at her, she broke away from Rani and ran up to Gill.

'I want to be with Bru,' she demanded.

Gill got down on his knees and folded his arms. 'You and I have a deal, remember?'

'But he's my horse!'

'He's a wild animal, Amy. But you're the person he trusts the most. You demonstrated that when you calmed him down at Callanish.'

'That just proves you need me.'

'We do need you, Amy. Bru is about to do a very brave thing. And I don't get to force him, you know that. But I think he'll do it, and afterwards, he needs you to be safe.'

Amy wiped her nose and seemed uncertain how to press her case.

'How old are you?' asked Amelia.

'Eight,' sniffed Amy.

'My goodness,' said Amelia, shaking her head. 'Eight years old, and you're having the biggest adventure, ever. You must be so pleased.'

Amy gave a non-committal shrug.

'And that wee cob you've been riding. How old is she?'

'She's seven.'

'Which makes you older,' said Amelia. 'And I'll tell you something; I can see she's scared.'

'It's all these people. And there are so many horses. It stresses her.'

'You're a good horsewoman,' Amelia announced with a nod. 'You know your animal, and really, Amy, I think you already know what needs to happen here.'

Amy looked down at her feet. 'I guess she needs to drop out.'

'Mine did too. She likes the company, but all these hard paths have hurt her feet. So, what I think we should do is go back to my house near Loch Lomond and set up a base.'

'A base?' queried Amy.

'Yes. A place to rest our horses and tend to their injuries. And get a special paddock ready for Bru and Ardie for when they get back from Edinburgh.'

Amy nodded, then bursting into tears again she hugged Gill's legs. 'It's your job to look after him now.'

'I promise,' said Gill. He hugged her, then cleared his throat to stop emotion choking his voice. 'You got any more of those special sweets?'

Amy nodded silently.

'Then come with me. Before you go, I want you to give Bru one of those sweets and tell him to be a very, very well-behaved waterhorse until you see him again.'

Late that night, under complete darkness, only a few people were awake to witness a slight disturbance in their encampment south of Kilsyth. Roused from their tents, those same few people observed five masked figures untethering a great, horned horse, poorly disguised under a night blanket, and leading him out of the camp. A few of them couldn't resist this secret endeavour and followed at a distance while the animal was led down to the canal. A few even helped as they coaxed and pushed the muscle-laden beast to step on board a seventy-foot narrow boat, its huge weight rocking the "Songbird" against her berth in the Forth & Clyde Canal. When he was finally on board, he whickered, nervously, while Rani spent the next twenty minutes stroking his face and whispering to him. When, at last, he finally bowed his head sufficiently, she pushed his tusk lower and led him into the hollowed-out shell of the old boat. The watchers dared to approach as the diesel engine thrummed, with a few stepping forward to cast off its lines before the vessel discreetly turned for Edinburgh.

Chapter 45

6 Hours until the Scottish Parliamentary vote on independence

Early on Sunday morning, Roddy looked out over the Holyrood Palace from his office in the Scottish Parliament and found himself fretting about the day ahead. This was meant to be the culmination of his plans – the moment when everything fell into place. This was the day he would secure his legacy as the first leader of a newly independent Scotland. The William Wallace of the modern age! And in the Scottish Parliament, he had the votes. Opposition parties would oppose him, of course, but his coalition partners would back him, and his motion would pass. Alas, it wasn't the same story out in the regional councils where his dominance was being challenged.

Roddy swore under his breath and despite the early hour, had to resist an urge to refresh his whisky glass. He was still winning the media battle, but out in the real world, fires were burning. The demonstrations that had flamed for Scotland's declaration of independence were now being met with even bigger crowds demanding the venture be subject to a democratic mandate. The two sides had clashed violently in Jedburgh the previous evening. In a bad-tempered and thinly policed confrontation, the militia had been too eager to deploy their guns and casualties on both sides had died. This bloodshed in the Borders seemed to spur resentment further north. Abhorring the violence, Shetland announced they wouldn't recognise parliament's decision. Instead, the island's council informed the Scottish Government that a referendum would be held in six weeks' time, requesting Shetlanders' support for a transfer of sovereignty to Norway. On hearing the news, Roddy had immediately phoned the island council, trying to persuade them of the merits of Scotland's unilateral independence. He'd argued, pleaded, and threatened the grey-haired men and women, but finished by getting his own logic thrown back in his face. If Scotland could pursue its own self-interest by just walking away from the UK, then Shetland could follow the same rationale.

Next came rumours that Orkney was considering its own vote. In their case, the local council was seeking a mandate to open discussions with Denmark. Meanwhile, the landmass north of the Great Glen was celebrating its cultural affinity with the Western Isles and had begun a dialogue around forming an independent territory. Rushing to defend his strategy, Roddy spoke to the Highlands and Islands Council, arguing the same clear logic about the wealth that would accrue to an independent Scotland. He'd expected a more sympathetic hearing, but instead, he had to endure a thirty-minute beating, condemning Holyrood's centralisation of services and the hollowing out of rural communities. When yet another person started complaining about the ferries, Roddy just hung up the call.

And none of this worked for Roddy. The Central Belt had finance and commerce and was well onboard for independence. But Stevie Blaine was right about one thing. The isles dominated Scotland's energy sector, and without the forests of wind turbines and the legacy fossil-fuel industry, Scotland's economy didn't add up.

Roddy knew there were debates to be had and olive branches to be offered, and behind closed doors, a few heads needed banging together. But with good diplomacy and sound politicking, it could all be fixed. And he already knew he should have been better prepared. Somewhere, back at the earliest conception of this great project, he'd planned to hire a bevvy of advisors, parcelling off each of these problems and assembling a strong playbook of responses. But the loss of Glenure Gold had severed his money supply, and instead, he'd focused on delivering the break with Britain, parking the downstream problems until another day. That "day" was fast approaching, and while these challenges bayed for his attention, he honestly believed, given enough time, he'd figure them out. But the clock was ticking down until McArdle's circus arrived in town, hogging the media focus and delivering an almighty distraction to the tense crowds already arriving in Edinburgh for today's vote.

Blaine texted him to say that McArdle had tipped his hand by loading the waterhorse onto a canal boat and cruising east. During the night, their craft had boarded the Falkirk Wheel, a complex piece of mechanics that lifted boats out of the Clyde Basin and raised them to the level of the Union Canal. If McArdle didn't delay, he and his horse would emerge at Fountainbridge, close to Edinburgh Castle, around 10 am. Then, whatever this pain-in-the-arse had planned would swing into motion.

Roddy returned to his desk and considered his options. Macfarlane's attempts to slow McArdle's progress had been woeful. It was possible the police would suppress McArdle and his horse at Fountainbridge, but based on the scrambles at Balloch and Helensburgh, containment seemed unlikely. Searching for an alternative strategy, he'd phoned his key allies to ask for options and wasn't surprised when McGovern argued for deadly force. 'Find a quiet stretch of the canal and take them out,' he contended. Roddy was more mindful of the prying eyes of a digital world and fully aware that the opportunity to cull these irritants had already passed.

Blaine, on the other hand, advocated greeting McArdle with open arms, celebrating his unusual horse, before taking him aside. By fair means or foul, they needed to persuade McArdle to join them at the independence celebrations.

Arriving at a decision, Roddy snatched up his phone again. 'Stevie, we're going with your plan. We'll intercept McArdle outside the city and make one last attempt to bring him on board. And spell out the consequences if he doesn't play ball.'

At the same moment as Canmore was pacing his rooms at Holyrood that morning, Lillico was in the Bathgate office, trying to concentrate. They'd pulled an all-nighter, and George Wiley was still on the phone with the Chief Constable. Whatever plan of attack they'd agreed, they still hadn't shared it with Lillico. An update was desperately required from Gill too, but Lillico had to wait until the raiding party phoned him. It was a relief, therefore, when his phone screen illuminated with Gill's number.

'How's it going?' he demanded.

Gill's voice, when it came, echoed in a confined space. 'We're good. I'm reluctant to use military parlance, but we're getting ready to deploy.'

'And how's Bru?'

'Not excited by his continuing confinement. When he gets restless, I let him smell the whisky he blagged on Islay.'

Lillico shook his head but said nothing.

'How are things in the city?'

Lillico glanced at the citywide CCTV he'd routed to his laptop. 'People are pouring into the old town already. Looks like we're going to see big demonstrations for and against independence in advance of the midday vote. The suits upstairs are worried.'

'I get that. And the rest of the Armour Group?'

'I've just had a message from Ailsa. Lorna jumped in a few minutes ago and now they're moving into position at the bottom end of the Royal Mile.'

'Has Solomon had second thoughts about her conference?'

'Sorry. Takes more than a little constitutional chaos to deter that lady from her task. But Charlie's with her, and on the plus side, they're both near to hand if we need them.'

'And Wiley?'

Lillico looked up at his boss, just visible through a smoked glass screen separating his private workspace from the rest of the office. His expression was deadly serious while he finished his call and carefully replaced the handset. 'He looks like a lieutenant who's just been told it'll be his privilege to lead his men over the top and into the teeth of enemy fire.'

Gill released a dry laugh. 'Okay. If everything goes to plan, I'll see you at Holyrood in a couple of hours.'

The raiding party comprised Gill McArdle, Freya Swanson and David McKane. As soon as Rani's diversionary group had walked off towards the canal boat, they'd loaded three horses into the McKane's Equicruiser and driven south on Edinburgh's ring road. Arriving at a modest equestrian centre belonging to friends of Amelia, they'd unloaded the horses under a dawn sky and joined a footpath that would take them north. While they cantered paths bordered by gorse bushes, Gill let his hand drift along the tops of the branches. The silky yellow flowers enveloped him with the sweet coconut and vanilla fragrance, even while the dark green thorns prickled his skin. Beauty and barbs in one dense thicket, like a metaphor for life itself.

An hour later, the sun was rising when they climbed a grassy knoll under the shadow of Arthur's Seat, the highest hill in the city. He'd given up trying to lead Bru, the great horse choosing his own path since they'd set out from a field near Dalkeith and wound their way north through green spaces and towards the city centre. This continuous green corridor was the inspiration for David's plan, and when he'd demonstrated the route on a map, Gill wondered why he hadn't thought of it himself. And he'd always admired that about Edinburgh. So many European cities would have carved their way into the face of the volcanic peak and peppered it with flats and offices, but Edinburgh protected not only the peak but the vista around it. It brought a tiny bit of Scotland's wilderness to the door of its parliament building and was the perfect cover for anyone smuggling a waterhorse into the heart of government. Below him, despite the early hour, he could hear the raucous chants of opposing demonstrations.

His phone rang and as expected, it was Rani. 'How's it going?' he whispered.

'We've stopped at a place called Wester Hailes. There are kids on a bridge up ahead trying to pelt us with bottles.'

'Any sign of police?'

'Loads, but they're wrapped up trying to contain one bunch of people who want to confer a sainthood on you and another who wants to burn you at the stake.'

'You've done enough, Rani. Retreat to Ratho and evacuate that boat before someone does you real harm.'

'Is that okay? I have to say, the Percheron has a gorgeous temperament, but he can sense the stress in the air. I need to release him from this confined space.'

'Yeah, definitely. How's his tusk?'

'It was straw and cardboard, Gill. He's amused himself these last few hours by systematically shredding it.' The phone muffled for a second as Rani updated her skipper on the plan. 'How about you? How far did you get?'

'I can see the parliament building below us so we're half a mile away.' Gill paused to wave lazily at an early morning runner, skidding to a halt when he found a waterhorse dominating the path. 'We've been spotted so I've no idea how much opposition we'll face.'

'Just take care, Gill. Nobody needs to die today. And that includes Bru.'

Chapter 46

Stevie arrived at Roddy's office around the same moment Gill's party crested Arthur's seat. Roddy had used the intervening time to shave and find a fresh shirt, plus a navy blue suit that looked rather well on him. He shook out the tension from his tingling fingers and launched into the new day.

'McArdle's narrow boat has crossed the aqueduct over the city ring road,' Blaine reported. 'I sent Murray to contain him at Wester Hailes.'

Roddy rubbed his eyes. 'How did McArdle react?'

'He and the horse are still on the boat. Maybe he thinks he can still bluff this out and make his way undetected to Fountainbridge.'

'You've told Murray not to do anything stupid?'

'Aye, he'll not start swinging his fists. But he's got a big crowd with him to make sure McArdle knows he's not welcome.'

'Maybe McArdle will have second thoughts. After all, if his horse dies, that will be on him.'

'Yes, but there's a big showing from people opposing us. Things could get ugly.'

Roddy pictured a messy confrontation in a distant suburb and imagined nothing but adverse headlines. 'What do you think I should do?'

'This is an opportunity, boss. Show those country crofters the real steel of Rodderick Canmore.'

Roddy flexed his right fist. 'I could take McArdle aside for a wee chat.'

'How about you take back the initiative by welcoming him, boss? Ask him what he's trying to achieve. Talk to him about your vision and how much you have in common. One way or another, you've got to bring him on side or at least allow Roddy Canmore to be seen as the man extending an olive branch.'

Roddy couldn't help but laugh. 'He's a stubborn red-haired bastard, Stevie.'

'But this is different. It'll be like the moments before a battle. Imagine, two great armies, ready to tear each other to shreds, but then the commander of one army asks to confer with his opposite number. Next thing you know, they've taken the first steps towards peace. They enter the city arm in arm, ready to celebrate the rebirth of the nation.'

'Me and McArdle? Arm in arm?'

'Think about it, boss. Let McArdle lead his damn horse into Edinburgh if he wants, but on the condition Rodderick Canmore sits upon its back!'

Roddy added this image to his mental calculation, and suddenly, the headlines looked more promising. 'Aye, man. If you think we have enough time, let's do it.'

Twenty minutes later, Roddy was sitting in the back of his ministerial car as it sped through the West Port towards his date with destiny. He was using the time to conjure up some words he'd address to the gathered masses. Something magnanimous, celebrating this new alliance, assuming they got McArdle to agree to terms. His train of thought crashed when Blaine emitted a string of filthy expletives.

'What now?' barked Roddy. 'I'm trying to write a sodding speech!'

Blaine leaned forward and banged on the privacy screen. 'Turn this car around, right now.'

'Stevie, what the hell?'

But Blaine was holding up his phone to display an image. 'McArdle's not at Wester Hailes, and he's not on that boat.'

Roddy felt his mouth gape. 'Is that Holyrood?'

Gill stared at the narrow entrance to the Holyrood parliament. 'They've changed the doors since I was here last' he moaned, ignoring the cluster of armed officers anxiously guarding the building's main entrance. 'How're we going to get Bru through a revolving door?'

'There'll be a back entry,' said David. 'Maybe a big door for catering lorries.'

'I'll ask,' Freya murmured while she dismounted and passed her reins to David before stepping towards the officers and saying a few words Gill didn't hear. In response, the men glanced nervously at Bru before vigorously shaking their heads.

Gill felt Bru move under him as if the horse was looking for a route inside the building. Or perhaps he was spotting his own reflection in the thick sheets of glass protected by what looked like mishappen bamboo rods. Gill just let Bru walk while he tried to work the problem. But it was hard to concentrate while his mount shuffled from left to right, taking in the sounds and smells of the urban environment.

'That's better,' Gill told the horse when he abruptly halted. His head was up, and Gill followed his gaze to where Bru was studying his unclutterered reflection in a long sheet of unprotected glass. When Bru started shuffling his feet as if assessing the distance to the window, Gill got a nasty feeling about what was going to happen next.

'Bru, no,' Gill shouted as the horse lowered his head and suddenly sprang at the huge window. Gill just had time to duck his face into the horse's neck before a cascade of glass erupted around him.

Lizzie McBride hadn't wanted to work that day. Trouble growled in Edinburgh's streets, and her partner had pleaded with her to stay home. But Lizzie was the Senior Supervisor in the Scottish Parliament's Gift Shop, and today, her entire crew had phoned in with one excuse after another until she was the last-woman-standing. Trotting off to work she reflected that with all the unrest in the city, parliament was unlikely to be busy. Everything would be fine if the police kept the opposing sides apart, and well away from her. As expected, the landscaped area at the front of the building was largely free of visitors and she imagined the armed policemen guarding the entrance would deter many more. Satisfied she'd made the right decision, and that her loyalty would be rewarded with a quiet day on the tills, she loaded up a juicy murder mystery on her Kindle and held it discreetly below the counter.

She was on the cusp of finishing chapter three when the glazed fire escape door facing Holyrood Palace suddenly exploded. The glass blew inwards under the power of what she hastily reasoned must be a bomb. Instinctively, she ducked below the counter and covered her face for protection against the flying shards. She held this position until she heard the clip-clop, clip-clop, foot treads of a horse coming towards her, followed by the sound of a man clearing his throat. Peering around the counter, she saw someone she didn't recognise riding the great big unicorn she'd seen on TV. The animal seemed good-natured, though blood oozed from a dozen cuts.

'Gill McArdle,' said the man, brushing glass from his clothes. 'Plus Bru, the Celtic-god-of-bashing-into-stuff. Is the First Minister in today?'

Lizzie swallowed. 'He was earlier, sir. I believe he went out.'

The horse started walking again. 'No problem. We're happy to wait.'

From the doorway, she heard two of the guards yelling, though they seemed reluctant to follow the horse on his steady plod through the building. And it was in Lizzie's mouth to tell McArdle that he couldn't go any further without either booking a ticket or proving he had official business in parliament offices. But then she remembered the rules of this building didn't specifically proscribe unicorns, so perhaps they had official business after all. She dug out the phone list for the First Minister and his aides and considered how she was going to word this request.

'McArdle duped us. He just rode his damn horse into parliament's debating chamber,' yelled Stevie

Roddy gripped his seat, and the car swung hard into a hasty three-point turn. 'What the hell do we do now?'

'Change of plan, boss. Take our video team into the chamber. Confront the invader while he tries to usurp parliament.'

'Stevie, that damn thing might kill me!'

'Doubt it, boss. Not unless both horse and rider want to end up dead.'

'What do I say to him?'

Roddy felt Blaine grip his hands. 'Give him a more assertive version of what you would have said at Wester Hailes. Get him to come on-side for the good of Scotland or face the consequences of being against us.' He paused to wrap the screen. 'Stop here. I'm getting out.'

Roddy looked aghast. 'You're abandoning me?'

Blaine shook his head. 'I'm going to the castle. I'm organising a fallback position in case things go badly at Holyrood.'

'Fallback! What are you saying, man?'

'For starters, I need to make sure the castle is horse-proof, as clearly, Holyrood isn't. After that, I need to make some calls.'

'Stevie, you're my personal security. Your place is by my side.'

'I hear you, boss. Chances are, you'll swing McArdle behind us. But if that doesn't work, we need to retrench at the castle and play the part of plucky defenders making our last stand. Maybe it's time to break out the weapons, Roddy? Command our militias to come to our aid and show Scotland who's boss.'

'But … did you see what happened in Jedburgh? Look, Stevie, I don't mind the lads waving their guns in the air for a bit of a show, but I never intended this to become a bloodbath!'

Blaine looked surprised. 'Can you think of another time when Scotland asserted its independence without spilling a little blood?'

The car stopped in the Grassmarket and Blaine jumped out. 'Do your best, sir.' Then the door slammed, and Roddy's bodyguard disappeared up a stone staircase towards the castle.

Chapter 47

3 Hours until the Scottish Parliamentary vote on independence

At the same moment as the First Minister's car was hurtling up Victoria Terrace, George Wiley's was idling at traffic lights somewhere on Dalkeith Road.

'You're not planning to blue-light it, sir?' asked Lillico.

'Justice won't be rushed, Alex. We don't need to take extra risks.'

Lillico pointed out the window at a right-facing junction. 'Nip past the Commonwealth pool. Then we can join Queen's Drive and be there in half the time.'

Wiley patted the breast pocket of his suit. 'Need to stop for some ciggies, so I'll nip up onto Clerk Street if it's all the same to you.'

Lillico lifted his elbow up against the doorframe and pressed his face against his palm. He was stressed. His police career hung by a thread, and there would be many in the force who'd never forgive him and Wiley for what they were about to do today. Even worse was the knowledge the Armour Group was still scattered. While most were converging on the parliament building, all remained vulnerable to anything Canmore might have up his sleeve. And Lillico was worried about what might be asked of him. The last time he'd faced down enemies of the state, he'd had to kill a man, and today, the stakes were so much higher.

'Feeling a bit peckish,' said Wiley, halting the car on double yellow lines outside a small general store. 'Fancy some chocolate?'

Lillico shook his head and tried not to retch. The car quivered a little while Wiley clambered out of the driver's side and slammed the door. He wanted to yell after his boss to hurry up but was distracted when a text pinged onto his phone. It was from Gill.

We're in. Waiting for Canmore.

Entering the parliament building, Roddy dashed through the lobby, pointing at glass and blood on the floor. 'How many did the horse kill?' he demanded.

'No one's dead as far as I know,' said Lizzie McBride from the door of the gift shop. 'The blood belongs to the horse, and maybe a bit from the guy riding him.'

'And they're where exactly?'

'Blood trail leads to the debating chamber. We've not followed them any further.'

'And you people just let them walk in?'

'The security guys bottled it,' said Lizzie, turning on her heel. 'And I couldn't exactly stop him on my own.'

Turning to five police officers who'd shadowed him since his arrival, Roddy beckoned them to follow him deeper into the building. Calling on a few of his staff, he assembled a small team in the Garden Lobby and found a few words to rally his troops against the invader. Beside the police officers stood his principal parliamentary aide, plus a cameraman and a sound engineer who all looked as scared as he felt. But the difference between them was this, he was Roddy Canmore. A leader and the man destined to lead Scotland into a new age.

'Would you all pull yourselves together,' he muttered, before straightening his jacket and climbing the steps up onto the Black & White corridor that served as an anteroom for the debating chamber. There were muddy hoof prints on the floor tiles, and a scratch where the animal had slid on the hard surface. Here and there, the ceiling seemed scuffed, caused perhaps by the animal's horn. When they paused at the door to the chamber, he turned to the officers and glanced at their weapons. 'If the animal threatens us, you know how to use those things?'

The men looked at each other and nodded.

'Okay, then,' said Roddy before pushing the door open and striding into the debating chamber. McArdle, he discovered, was standing in the centre of the large room with the waterhorse and a girl. She was spilling what looked like whisky onto paper towels and dabbing lacerations on the animal's neck. At the sound of Roddy's firm footsteps on the wooden floor, everyone, including the horse, looked up.

They were still treating Bru's lacerations when Canmore burst into the chamber. 'Mr McArdle, have you brought your horse to crap on the floor of Scotland's parliament?'

Gill was tired but not so exhausted he couldn't laugh and turn to his horse. 'Did you hear that, Bru? What do you reckon?' He nodded twice as if listening to a muted exchange, then turned back to Canmore. 'Bru would like to remind you that you're the one disrupting this parliament without democratic consent, so right back at you, First Minister.'

'Who's this?' asked Canmore, glaring at the girl.

'Freya Swanson,' she replied. '*Glasgow Tribune*, plus some freelance work.'

'Oh, I've heard of you,' Canmore snarled, pointing at the door. 'Out!'

Gill shook his head. 'Bru likes her. She stays.'

Canmore turned to one of the officers. 'Get Chief Superintendent MacFarlane in here, immediately.' The man nodded urgently and seemed happy to scuttle away.

'What are we doing here, McArdle? And why did you bring that thing?'

'On behalf of many Scottish people, I wanted to tell you we're unhappy with the direction you're taking this country.'

Canmore grunted. 'If you're referring to the treaty, you're too late.'

'No treaty required, First Minister. On behalf of many of my countrymen, I'm just a citizen making representation.'

'Really? Polling data suggests most people support me.'

'Do they? Then why don't you retract your declarations and subject your plans to democratic scrutiny? And if that gets approved, then we can ask the rest of our shared nation what they think.'

Canmore shook his head. 'Those are procedural minutiae stopping a great country standing on its own two feet.'

Gill tilted his head. 'I think those "procedural minutiae" are called "democracy." Meanwhile, you've harnessed a natural disaster to manufacture a crisis.'

'In the run-up to the earthquake,' Canmore declared. 'Scots believed Westminster had let them down. That they'd been lied to. And the reason they found this so plausible is it's happened so many times before.'

'You're basically admitting you lied?'

Canmore folded his arms and sneered. 'I could walk you through the reasons I did what I did, but I've no time for people like you who're afeard to break away from London.'

Gill laughed gently and gripped Bru's horn. 'I have many faults, Mr Canmore, but being a coward isn't one of them.'

Bru stopped chewing on a whisky-soaked bandage and took this moment to slowly, heavily step towards Canmore. The First Minister, to his credit, held his ground. Bru examined the man, his tusk waving perilously close to Canmore's vital organs. Behind him, the remaining officers in the room raised their firearms.

'Don't,' snapped Canmore, raising a fist. 'Not yet.'

Gill laughed wearily. 'What a contrast. On one side, we have a truly noble beast that personifies strength and nobility. He's as mythical as the image of a Scotsman painted on the front of a porridge box, and he's forged at the remote extremes of Scotland. And then we have the politician, happy to lie and cheat and throw his own people on the fires of a natural disaster if it gets him closer to want he wants.'

'Really?' Canmore protested. 'I've devoted my life to the cause and the country I love, and you have the audacity to criticise me?'

'Well, if we're speaking personally, then I recall you're the one that sent the Drumchapel crew to kill me on the Isle of May. You gave Lillian the same task at Glenure and again in Wigtownshire when Murray McGovern was ready to do me harm. You've scorned my work, mocking the *Fated Stone* and sequestering the Fisher Street hoard.' Gill flicked his chin at Canmore. 'Suffice to say, you and I don't see eye to eye.'

'It will take more than that pile of horse crap before I give way to you, McArdle.'

'And for what, Roddy? Do you really think, running a small independent country on the fringe of Europe will be an easy gig? People might've bought your song and dance two weeks ago, but the truth is coming out. Put it this way, I don't think we're about to build you a palace.'

'Scotland is my palace, McArdle. The mountains and glens. The rivers and the sea.'

Gill raised a quizzical eyebrow. 'Oh yeah? When was the last time you climbed a Munro? Or hiked in a glen? Or walked a coastal path?'

Canmore folded his arms. 'Actually, about four weeks ago. I attended a function at Doune Castle and took some time outside to spot a couple of red kites.'

Gill gave a slow clap. 'Okay, score one to the First Minister.'

'I'm driven by my passionate desire for this to be the independent country it used to be.'

'I hear you. And truly, there are days when I find the idea appealing,' said Gill. 'But like most reasonable people, I'd prefer to be persuaded by decades of sound government, not tossed into some ill-considered abyss on the back of politicised mayhem.'

'I politicised nothing!'

'Your usual strategy is to politicise everything! You use technical discussions as an excuse for militant differences of opinion between us and our southern neighbour. That's not leadership, First Minister, that's bigotry.'

'Underscoring the material and attitudinal differences between ourselves and our southern neighbour is the very definition of my job. Meanwhile, you're the one turning a crack in the planet into an excuse to tear up one of the oldest nations on Earth.'

Gill spread out his arms. 'Am I? The treaty was never enacted. I had the power but chose not to use it. Instead, I've come here, with my horse, to tell you in person this afternoon's vote is unacceptable.'

Canmore theatrically lifted a hand to his ear. In the distance, they could hear a large crowd baying Canmore's name. 'Sounds like you're in a minority.'

'I've no doubt many Scots agree with you. But your actions demonstrate that if the Highlands and Islands are no longer ruled from London, they might as well be shot of Edinburgh too.'

'Your treaty was struck down. Those regions have no legal right to secede.'

'Oh, listen to yourself then consider this. Citizens of Edinburgh and Glasgow have more in common with your average Londoner than an Orcadian or a Hebridean crofter. I could give you a dozen comparisons, but the point is simply this. You don't know the Highlanders. You have no clue about their lives, and honestly, I doubt you've earned the right to speak for them.'

'What, and you do?'

'I'm a lowlander like you.' Gill nodded at Bru. 'But I think he does.'

Canmore looked incredulous. 'He's just an animal.'

'An animal foretold by the last *Lord of the Isles*. A little check and balance in the turning of history that reminds the Highlands that maybe, they'd be better off running their own affairs.'

'Well, that's not going to happen.'

Gill shook his head. 'Who knows? In the meantime, you've unleashed a whirlwind.'

They were distracted by a tap at the door. Canmore's hasty glance revealed another cluster of armed officers and one man in a suit. 'Macfarlane,' he called. 'About bloody time.'

The man in the suit, a rather shabby suit, cleared his throat. 'Actually, sir, my name is DCI Wiley. I'm here to make an arrest.'

Canmore gesticulated at Gill. 'Help yourself, assuming you can pry him free from his horse.'

'Actually, sir. It's you I need to talk to.'

'What?' spat Canmore as Wiley and his group approached. Canmore's own guards pivoted to defend against this new threat, and for a few terrible seconds, four officers on each side faced each other with weapons primed.

'Call Macfarlane,' Canmore yelled. 'He'll sort this out.'

'Chief Super Macfarlane is unavailable,' said Wiley, calmly. 'He's been detained for attempting to pervert the course of justice. Amongst other things.'

Canmore's defenders glanced urgently at each other.

'With the utmost esteem for the loyalty of your security team, First Minister, I'm forced to observe the situation here has changed.'

Canmore thrust a hand at Wiley and his officers. 'Disarm them, immediately.'

Wiley shook his head. 'With Macfarlane's arrest, all his orders have been rescinded. Respectfully, I'd like to ask my fellow officers to shoulder their weapons and return to their stations at the front of this beleaguered building.'

The standoff lasted several more seconds until finally, the sergeant commanding Canmore's detachment relaxed his posture. 'Come on, lads.'

Canmore started protesting immediately and kept up the performance until his entire team had vacated the room. Then Wiley took a deep breath. 'Rodderick Canmore. You are now under arrest for conspiracy to murder John Houston and Harry Sinclair, and for attempted murders of Billy Whyte and Lorna Cheyne. You do not have to say anything. But it may harm your defence if you do not mention when questioned, something which you later rely on in court.'

'You may not have noticed, detective, but I'm trying to fix a country here.'

Wiley nodded thoughtfully. 'And in that regard, you'll likely face further charges.'

Canmore finally turned to face his accuser. 'Ach, away hame ye stupid little man.'

Wiley stood aside and jerked his head at his team. They moved on Canmore, and amidst shouts and kicks and struggles, they cuffed his hands and dragged him out of the chamber.

Chapter 48

2 Hours until the Scottish Parliamentary vote on independence

Georgy Wiley seemed to hold his breath while the sounds of Canmore's protests faded into the background. The shouts were replaced by the sound of Bru's heavy footsteps walking towards him. Then the horse paused, turning to notice Gill's pocket where a little whisky had leached out. Wiley surveyed the mess on the floor and decided he'd add his own by striking a match and taking a first long drag on a cigarette.

'What happened to Lillico?' asked Gill.

'Left him outside,' Wiley sniffed. 'No need for us both to risk censure should this manoeuvre go south.'

'Ah,' said Gill. 'Meaning, if Canmore comes out on top today, you take the hit, and Lillico is left to carry on the good fight?'

'Something like that, and at the end of the day, there's only so much glory to go around.' He wagged a smoky hand at Bru. 'So, these things do exist after all?'

'Aye,' said Gill, stretching his back. 'Who would've believed it.'

Wiley jerked his head at the door. 'Any chance you and your pal could, you know, vacate the building?'

'Certainly, Inspector,' said Gill, plucking the whisky bottle from his pocket and waving it under Bru's tusk. 'Can I assume this afternoon's vote is cancelled?'

337

'Way above my pay grade. But it's hard to see it happening today.'

Gill nodded before giving Bru's rein a tug and leading towards the door. 'By the way, DCI Wiley.'

'What, McArdle?' he barked.

'That was a brave thing you did. When the history of this day is written, it'll remember you as a very courageous man.'

'You are finished,' spat Roddy Canmore at Wiley when he joined his uniformed officers in a parliamentary conference room. 'I'll make it my personal mission to make sure every last one of you never works in public service, ever again.'

Wiley gave a thin smile and pointed at the wide pine table. 'Take a seat, sir. While we wait for transport, I'll be explaining some of the additional charges you'll be facing.' Around him, the armed officers took up defensive positions, two outside the small conference room and two inside, guarding Canmore.

'What's the meaning of this? Who's behind it?'

'The charges against you are complicated and far-reaching, sir. In a few minutes, we'll travel from here to my office in Bathgate where you will meet the Chief Constable and face further charges. You can arrange legal representation, then we'll present our evidence against you.' Wiley folded his hands in front of him. 'At that point, you'll have the choice of admitting to some or all the charges. Or you can contest them. Now, is that clear?'

'You've got nothing on me!'

Wiley looked down at his hands. 'I assure you, sir, we would not be sitting here unless my case against you had passed the most rigorous cross-examination.'

Without free use of his hands, Canmore struggled to his feet and heeled back his chair. 'Listen to me, you idiotic little cop. We're in the middle of a national crisis here. Now, release me so I can get back to work.' Canmore moved to walk away, but strong hands pushed him down into another seat.

'I know you're a busy man, sir, so I'll be brief. For starters, aside from the murder charges, we'll need to talk to you about Glenure Gold.'

Canmore shook off the hand gripping his shoulder. 'Never heard of it.'

'Ah, well, I have a senior member of what was known as the Drumchapel Crew who begs to differ with you. Lillian Galloway, do you remember her?'

Canmore's lunge at Wiley was blocked by the officers restraining him. 'Don't believe a word she says.'

'Well, that's a pity because it appears she has a lot to say. For example, the small-town assassinations were, for many years, the Drumchapel's bread and butter. Your name came up in connection to several murders.'

'More lies. Probably from Westminster.'

Wiley's smile was genuine this time. 'I hear you. Blame the Tories, shall we?'

Canmore said nothing.

'Getting a bit closer to home, we have a Mrs Agnes Fairbank under police protection at an undisclosed location. She provided the means for you to time your earthquake charade. We'll need to go over the details, though I'd anticipate your sabotage of the SGS early warning system means you'll both face manslaughter charges for the six hundred people who died.'

'She's the expert on Scottish Seismology. I wouldn't know anything about that.'

'Well, I'll demonstrate our evidence trail and give you the opportunity to reconsider.'

Canmore started to laugh. 'Do you know the funny thing here?'

Wiley cocked his head. 'Do enlighten me.'

'I'm ripping the United Kingdom in two, and you're trying to convict me of a wee gold scam.'

'Well, that's the thing about justice,' Wiley observed. 'Sometimes you start with the small stuff and build your case from there. Your political motives may attract more scrutiny once I've demonstrated your callous disregard for human life.'

Canmore seemed amused, and in response to Wiley's logic, he spat on the table.

'Okay, we're wasting time here,' said Wiley to the lead officer. 'Let's get him up to Bathgate. Then we can all get cosy for as long as this takes.'

Gill was sitting in the foyer while Bru explored the visitor's lobby and made friends with the gift shop manageress. She seemed to have overcome her initial fear and developed a soft spot for waterhorses. Beside him, Freya's fingers flew over her phone screen while she rushed to record what she'd witnessed in the chamber.

'Thanks for being here,' said Gill.

Freya flashed a smile. 'Second only to wee Amy McGregor, I'm the happiest girl in Scotland right now.'

'Scotland isn't out of the woods on this. Canmore's actions laid bare a lot of deep divisions in this country.'

'I know. And people are baying for information.' She looked up at him. 'If you think we're done here, may I slip away? I'm getting a dozen requests a minute to do news interviews.'

'We're done,' said Gill, with a smile. 'Go and tell our story, and I'll ask David to take Poppy back to the Equicruiser.' He glanced at the doors where the police were struggling to contain Canmore's supporters at the foot of the Royal Mile. 'Hope you're not going out there?'

Freya shook her head. 'There are journalist facilities deeper in the building. I'll see if I can grab a booth.'

Gill stood and offered her his hand. She ignored it and gave him a swift hug. 'Thank you, Gill.'

His face reddened a little. 'Glad to help a fellow journo.'

She laughed and with a smile and a nod, turned away into the building. Gill watched her go, then, hearing the crash of a collapsing display stand, he found the tusked culprit snuffling the debris and pretending it had nothing to do with him.

'Right, Bru,' he called. 'Time to go home.'

Gill and Bru stepped out of the parliament into bright sunlight where Canmore's supporters, unaware of their hero's detention, were hurling abuse at the riot police containing them at the end of the Canongate. A thinner uniformed cordon, near the entrance to Calton Road, restrained the opposing crowd. Gill wasn't sure, but he thought some of them were cheering. Close by, three police cars were pulling in, along the aptly named Horse Wynd.

Ailsa, Lillico and Lorna were waiting for them, and when he emerged, they crowded around.

'You did it,' said Lorna, kissing his cheek.

'I was expecting more fireworks to be honest. Wiley just wandered in and arrested him.' Gill nodded at Lillico. 'Where are they now?'

'Wiley has taken Canmore to a committee room for orientation. Then, once we're sure the roads to the south are clear, we'll transfer him to Bathgate.'

'You're in for a long shift?'

'Aye, so I imagine. It'll be bluff and bluster and truckloads of BS until the wee small hours. What about you?'

Gill nodded at Bru. 'I've got a waterhorse to return to the isles.'

'You planning to walk?'

'I'm hoping we can borrow an Equicruiser from some new friends.'

'A what?'

'Think limo for horses. It transported us last night after we slipped camp. Bru loved it.'

Just then, Wiley exited the parliament, with Canmore being propelled by four officers. Lillico bid farewell and went to join them.

When Lillico wandered over, Wiley was explaining his requirements to the driver. 'Queen's Drive, then out the Dalkeith Road. We're to be the middle car in a convoy of three.'

'Want me in with you, or shall I travel in one of the other vehicles?' asked Lillico.

Wiley pulled back and took Lillico a few paces from the car. 'Official channels still have no sign of McGovern or Blaine. You heard anything?'

'I heard McGovern was at Wester Hailes, and Blaine was with Canmore about the same time. You sure he's not in the parliament?'

'It's a big place, Alex. I'm sorry to say it, but one of us needs to go back inside and look for them.'

Lillico's shoulders sagged. 'I can do that.'

'When you're done in there, stay in the city and be my eyes and ears. Canmore is bound to throw up dust that I won't be able to confirm or deny. I'll probably have tonnes of questions for you later in the day.'

'And who's going to be your bag man while you interview Canmore?' asked Lillico with mock offence.

Wiley instinctively straightened his tie. 'The Chief Constable, of course.'

Lillico nodded his understanding, for once enjoying Wiley's pride.

'By the way, Alex,' said Wiley, glancing at his watch. 'Your disciplinary meeting was scheduled for tomorrow. In the light of extenuating circumstances, Chief Super Macfarlane sends his apologies.'

'Thank you, sir,' Lillico replied, with a grin. 'Looks like you'll have to put up with me for a while longer.'

After they watched Canmore being bundled into the back seat, Lillico gave Wiley a deferential nod. 'Go get him, boss.'

Wiley winked, jumped in the front passenger seat, and after a word to the driver, the small convoy sped away. While Lillico stood watching, Gill, Ailsa and Lorna came and stood beside him.

'Change of plan?'

Lillico nodded at the Parliament building. 'I'm going back in there to sweep that for Blaine and McGovern.'

'I thought George was excellent today,' said Gill. 'I doubt there'll be many detectives who'd have done what he did.'

'Say what you want about George Wiley …' Lillico began, while the little convoy braked in preparation for joining Queen's Drive. But he paused, catching sight of something falling from the sky, just before the middle car exploded in a ball of orange flame.

Chapter 49

As the enormous detonation ebbed away, Gill uncovered his head. The occupants of the first and third cars were fleeing from the fire engulfing the wrecked remains of Wiley's vehicle. And while he stared in disbelief, he heard other detonations echo across the city. Beside him, Lillico was starting to stumble towards Wiley's car. Gill sprang after him and grabbed his shoulder. Angrily, Lillico shook him off. 'I need to help!'

'Alex, look at that thing,' Gill yelled over the roar of the fire. 'It's an inferno. No one can help George Wiley.'

Lillico started moving again. 'I need to try.' But Gill was too fast for him, launching himself at Lillico's legs and dragging him to the ground. They scrambled in the dust for a few seconds until the fight ebbed from Lillico's body.

'I'm sorry, Alex. He was a good man.'

Lillico had pulled a hand over his eyes to mask his tears. 'He was a pain in the arse!'

'Aye,' gasped Gill. 'That too.'

Keeping a hand on Lillico, Gill started to look around him. People were screaming, some running towards the wreckage and others away. Behind him, Gill could hear Bru's agitated hoof steps while he trotted in circles outside the gift shop. Gill was surprised to see the horse hadn't bolted. Instead, with his head bobbing, the animal twisted and turned, studying the sky. Gill followed Bru's gaze and noticed a large black box descending steadily towards them.

'Inside,' he yelled to anyone who would listen. 'Find cover.'

He hauled Lillico to his feet, beckoning Lorna and Ailsa to help. Together, they dashed back through the ruptured window into the parliament building, with Bru clattering in behind them. They'd barely reached the main concourse when the glass lobby behind them erupted with an ear-splitting explosion.

'Someone's attacking us with drones,' yelled Gill over the sound of screaming.

'Who?' shouted Ailsa, staggering towards him through a cloud of dust.

'No idea.' He swung an arm around Ailsa. 'Come on, guys. Get away from the doors.'

'Where's Bru?' Ailsa screamed.

Gill shook himself and glanced around. He couldn't see the horse, but he could hear his agitated hooves, clattering on a hard floor. 'Back this way. He's run through to the Garden Lobby.'

Between them, Gill and Ailsa started dragging Lillico further away from the glass. 'Hang on, where's Lorna?' yelled Gill. He started searching for her, stepping over debris in the poor light.

'There,' shouted Ailsa, pointing at Lorna's crouched form, with her back pressed against a concrete pillar. As Gill ran towards her, he could see she was ashen-faced.

'Are you hurt?' he asked, patting Lorna's arms and shoulders.

Lorna shook her head. 'Text message from Solie. There's been an explosion in the Grassmarket.' Tears sprang to her eyes. 'They got Charlie.'

Gill grabbed his phone and felt part of his world shake when he saw the message from Solomon. Her message was characteristically terse and didn't say if Charlie was dead or alive. While he was tapping out a response, a bulletin dropped in from the National Emergency Alert system. It said simply, "View this," followed by a URL. Gill tapped the link, and it took him to a video of a wooden desk, flanked on either side by the blue and white of Scotland's national flag. At the desk sat a familiar male figure with close-cropped hair and dressed in a black polo shirt.

"My name is Steven Blaine, and I'm the national security adviser to Scotland's Independent Government.' He left a slight pause for this information to sink in. *Regretfully, it is my duty to announce that, a few minutes ago, First Minister, Rodderick Canmore, was assassinated by forces opposed to the independence of this great country. Furthermore, I need to alert you that an attack has been launched against government buildings throughout our capital. No details are available at present, but I regret to inform you that there are casualties at multiple locations. Consequently, all citizens are urged to seek shelter indoors and remain in place until the all-clear is given. I'm ordering all uniformed staff of the Scottish Government, plus anyone registered with volunteer militias to immediately report to their stations and await orders. Thank you, that is all."*

'Blaine,' yelled Lillico wiping dust and tears from his face. 'Since when did he earn a seat at the big table?'

Gill pulled all four of them into a huddle. 'Were drones mentioned in Canmore's files?'

'You're asking us?' growled Ailsa. 'I thought you'd read them?'

'Some of them,' Gill shot back.

'I read all the files,' said Lillico before clenching his eyes shut. 'Oh, dear God.'

'What?' snapped Ailsa.

Lillico shivered and opened his eyes. 'Wiley and I saw invoices suggesting the city recently bought thousands of aerial display drones.'

'Alex, you're not making sense,' said Gill. 'I think you're going into shock.'

'What if they're military-grade and Blaine deploys them against the city?'

'To kill their own people?'

'Who knows? But it fits the bill. Create mayhem, then blame it on the opposition.'

'Yes. But if Blaine is tasking the drones, why kill Canmore?'

'Martyr figure,' said Lorna. 'Robert the Bruce, William Wallace, Rob Roy. You're not a famous Scot until you're a dead Scot.'

Lillico disagreed. 'Doesn't make sense. This has been Canmore's gig the whole way through. Unless the guy was dying of something nasty, I doubt he'd volunteer for self-sacrifice.'

The room reverberated with nervous whispers as another detonation sounded in the city.

Then, Gill remembered something. 'I ... I think I might know what's going on,' he stumbled. 'On Macdui, where we faced Sariel and won *The Torn Isle*, the demon told me the opportunity to take dominion over Scotland had already been offered to another man.'

'Yeah,' said Ailsa. 'You've always said Sariel picked Canmore.'

'What if I was wrong? What if he actually meant Blaine?'

'Blaine is just security, Gill. A nasty wee man with a tendency to violence.'

Gill wasn't convinced. 'I first met Canmore when I researched the *Stone of Destiny*. He was arrogant, and resourceful, and when Sariel described a new "king" in

Scotland, Canmore so fitted the bill. But Blaine has been with Canmore since the beginning. Maybe Blaine is the master and Canmore was just the puppet?'

'All well and good,' said Ailsa. 'But if that's true, where is he now, and how do we stop him?'

Gill nodded. 'I think it's time we deployed our secret weapon.'

'We have a secret weapon?' Ailsa spluttered. 'Like an eighth member of the Armour Group?'

'Better than that,' Gill winked, putting his phone on speaker and waiting for his call to connect. 'Adina. It's turning pretty shitty out here. Please tell me you've got news.'

For a few seconds, the phone at the other end was muffled, before a familiar voice spoke. 'I've taken up a position in the National Museum and I'm ready to be your eyes and ears.'

'Wait, what?' spluttered Ailsa.

'Canmore threatened my Family,' Adina explained. 'I needed to get them to safety in North Africa, but now that's done, I'm with you guys until this is over.'

'Where's Blaine?' Gill demanded.

'That broadcast came from Edinburgh Castle. I've checked archive footage and confirmed the room he's using is deep within the castle's Government House.'

'Nice and easy then,' said Lorna. 'Straight up the Royal Mile. Ring the doorbell, then hey Mr Blaine, can we have our country back?'

'But you need to get moving,' Adina continued. 'Because I just checked a satellite image of Edinburgh Castle. There's an enclosed yard busy with people stacking plastic boxes on top of each other.'

'Meaning what?' asked Ailsa.

'Meaning that first wave of drones is going to be followed up with a far bigger swarm,' said Gill. 'Put it this way, I doubt Blaine is planning a light show.'

'If you're going straight up the Royal Mile, you'll have to hack your way through sixty thousand Canmore supporters,' said Adina. 'And news is spreading about his death. That mob will rip you apart if they think you'd anything to do with killing their chieftain.'

'We'll figure it out. Adina, I think your priority is to tackle the drone risk.'

Adina released a ragged sigh. 'I'm gonna be in so much trouble, but yeah, I'll find a way.'

Gill looked at each of them in turn. 'Okay. Anyone got anything else before we roll?' Those around the stone column blinked at each other, and Adina's voice came back. 'Once you've dealt with Blaine, you need to get to Solomon. She's holding it together down there but if the conference centre takes another hit, there's a serious threat to life.'

Gill shook his head. 'Why didn't she stay away?'

'Adina,' asked Lorna. 'Any idea what's happening with Charlie?'

'I've seen him on CCTV from within the building. Someone is administering first aid so he must be alive.'

'Another reason to get moving.'

'Okay,' said Gill, staring at Scotland's national flag, displayed serenely in a glass case. 'Alex, are you with us?'

Lillico still looked shell-shocked. 'What?'

'If you're up for it, I'm going to ask a brutal favour of you.'

Lillico wiped his face. 'Will it give me the chance to stop Blaine?'

Gill nodded. 'It's ugly, but I think I have a plan.'

Chapter 50

The angry mob facing the police at the foot of the Royal Mile was winning. They didn't know how he'd died, or by who's hands, but the news of Roddy Canmore's assassination had inflamed the crowd. Now, while bottles and other projectiles flew, the line of plastic shields was starting to crumble. Sensing victory and that the parliament was within their grasp, the crowd pushed forward. As the police defences finally shattered, the crowd surged, until cries of alarm halted the front of the column. Right before them, the unicorn emerged from the side of the parliament building. With its head bowed low, and its tusk hovering just above the street cobbles. Turning left towards the old city, it came towards them with slow, steady steps. Beside the horse, two figures were visible, a man and a woman, dressed in the most polished armour anyone in the crowd had ever seen. The man nodded a slow 'thank you' to the police officers, and also to the first ranks within the mob as they parted to let them pass. There were gasps from the crowd and a few sobs, for strapped across the creature's back was a body, trussed in a saltire.

There could be no doubting the identity of the shrouded figure, for among the crowd, a few started to shout, 'We love you, Roddy.'

Slowly, respectfully, the tiny procession started to make its way uphill. Passing the Museum of Edinburgh and walking with dignity onto the Canongate. Their pace was slow, almost regal, the majestic beast carrying a treasured load. Ten minutes later, they approached the main junction with the North Bridge. They paused, this man and woman with swords drawn and armour gleaming. Between them, the unicorn huffed impatiently, with its head bowed, until a way parted for them to move forward again. At St Giles Cathedral, a piper who'd been part of the demo, fell in behind the procession, the horse twisting sideways for a moment to identify the source of the noise. And all around them, some in the crowd began to gently sing, *Flowers of the Forest*, an old Scottish lament.

As the High Street gave way to the Lawnmarket, Ailsa stepped a little closer to Gill. 'I have never been so terrified in all my life as I am right now.'

'There wasn't an easy back street route, so there's no alternative to going through the front door.' Gill nodded soberly to an old man who was standing to attention. 'You should try excavating fairy caves. After that, nothing scares you.'

'You know these people could turn on us in an instant. Armour or no armour, they could literally tear us to shreds.'

'Then, let's hope our corpse doesn't sneeze.'

'How'd you even come up with this dumb idea?'

'It was Aura. Something she said to me years ago.'

'Which was?'

'She said, "Will you parade a royal mile with me or choose to lead a donkey?" I've pondered on it for years.'

Ailsa chanced a glance behind them. 'Sorry to alert you, pal, but that's some donkey.'

'Symbolism, Ailsa. Only the victors get to claim the city fortress by riding a warhorse.'

'What does that make us?'

'Humble peacemakers,' he said quietly. 'Carrying really big swords.'

Ailsa said nothing more, relieved her armour offered her anonymity as well as protection.

'Okay,' Gill whispered. 'I can see a first set of guards at the entrance to the esplanade. Park the chat and get your game face back on.'

Nodded to by one guard and saluted by another, they marched slowly up across the tarmac towards the castle. An area bigger than a football pitch, the esplanade had recently hosted the annual Military Tattoo. Walking through the central area, they paused on a stone bridge linking the esplanade to the castle over a grass moat. There was a temporary traffic barrier blocking their passage, but after a brief consultation, the two guards lifted it and allowed them to proceed.

They were within the castle walls now, walking up a narrow channel that in olden days would have allowed the castle's defenders to rain down hell from above. Ahead of them was another obstacle, built from stone and gated with steel. Gill's little procession halted at the Portcullis, which for now, remained firmly closed.

Lorna watched the crowds close behind the others while the waterhorse began its slow progression up the Royal Mile. The police line was re-established, but no one was pushing anymore because everybody's eyes were fixed on the flag-draped body slung over the horse. Poor Alex Lillico, she thought. They'd trussed him in a body bag salvaged from the back of a police car, then strapped him on Bru's back. So many things could go wrong with this plan, including how

Lillico's stomach muscles would fare over a journey lasting at least half an hour.

Her part in this plot involved utilising her gift to get into the castle just ahead of the others and opening any locked gates. To make her jump, she needed a clear image in her mind of her destination point. This was a challenge as she'd never visited Edinburgh Castle. But there was one spot she knew well because she'd seen it on TV once a year since her youth. It was risky because it was an open location, high on the battlements. But really, if someone saw her, what did it matter? Today was laced with risk, so when the agreed time came, she found a quiet spot in the shelter of the parliament building. She checked she wasn't being overlooked, then pictured her destination, and jumped.

She arrived in a crouching position beside a huge black metal tube mounted on a robust carriage. This was "Mons Meg," a fifteenth-century cannon and the largest piece of Scottish artillery ever built. With the ability to hurl rocks bigger than basketballs over two miles, the relic was one of those strange old things the Scots held dear. Lorna's mind could grasp its image because the thing was ceremonially fired every Hogmanay to signify the arrival of the new year. Glancing around to double-check she hadn't been observed, she got slowly to her feet. The portcullis was just below her, accessed by way of a long stone staircase. A short distance away, she could hear Bru's impatient sidesteps in the confines of the gulley. Needing to hurry, she put on a brave smile and prepared to be persuasive.

The guard room defending the portcullis was a wooden shed, normally reserved for handing out the castle's audio guides. Lorna rapped the door with her knuckles and burst in without waiting for an answer. A guy in the livery of Historic

Scotland, plus a uniformed cop, both looked up from their phones in surprise.

'Well,' she demanded. 'What are you waiting for?'

'You what, lass?' said one, studying Lorna's lithe figure dressed all in black.

'The boss says to open the gate.'

The two men glanced at each other. 'The boss said the gate was to remain closed under all circumstances,' said the officer.

'Yeah, he was pretty bloody clear about that,' huffed the other man.

Lorna pointed at the portcullis. 'There's a ceremonial guard outside. They have the waterhorse and a body. Let them in, then get the gate closed again.'

The officer got to his feet and fretted with his jacket buttons. 'How's it looking on the cameras, Bill?'

Bill was scrolling through CCTV angles. 'She's right. And there's nobody we don't know on the esplanade.'

'Hang on. Is that Roddy Canmore's body?'

'What do you think?' snapped Lorna.

The officer nodded urgently. 'Okay. Let's get them inside.'

Bill nodded and flicked several switches. Nearby, Lorna could hear two electric motors start to hum, and the grating of metal on metal as the ancient portcullis started to lift. Moments later, Bill appeared by her elbow. 'Relieved to see it's working. We haven't lowered that thing in years.'

The officer meanwhile was standing to attention while Gill and Ailsa, still in dazzling armour, walked beneath the raised steel teeth. He glanced at the waterhorse before saluting the flag-draped body upon its back. Behind the procession, the gate was already lowering again. He gaped when the two armoured figures shimmered a little and reappeared in normal clothes. When they dashed to release their flag-draped load, the officer seemed shocked when the body emitted a groan.

Chapter 51

Lorna stepped over to Bru and helped Ailsa steady him while Gill released Lillico from his confinement. 'Oh, you are beautiful,' cooed Lorna when the horse turned to examine her and puff air from his nostrils when she met his approval.

'He's been awesomely well-behaved,' said Ailsa.

'Especially through all those crowds,' Gill agreed. 'I'm worried it can't last.'

'Hang on a second,' said the watching officer. 'That's not a body! Who are you people?'

Ailsa helped Gill ease Lillico to the ground then strode over to her accuser and mustered her most winning smile. 'We just need a second to let our colleague recover, then we'd like a meeting with Steven Blaine. Please.'

'The hell you do,' he spat. 'The only appointment you clowns have today is with my Duty Sergeant.'

But the Saltire-draped body had other ideas. Lying on his back, he held up his warrant card. 'DI Alex Lillico,' he wheezed. 'And I demand to see Blaine.'

'That's not happening, buddy. You creep in here under the pretence …' but the man's words were drowned out by a deep rumble of thunder above their heads.

'Gill,' said Lorna, slowly.

'Hang on. Just helping Alex,' Gill muttered.

'No really, Gill. What's happening to the sky?'

They were all aware of it now, as the bright September day suddenly darkened. Lifting their heads to stare they saw a great mass of purple-grey clouds erupting from the highest reaches of the atmosphere. Centred far above the castle and shaped like a funnel with a wide lip extending above the entire city, the cloud started to swirl while localised lightning raged inside its impenetrable darkness. In response to the aching sky, the two guards scuttled back into their hut and closed the door.

'Oh, look,' said Ailsa, staring at the eerie cloud. 'We're gonna get a spot of rain.'

'Master of understatement,' groaned Lillico, getting to his feet. 'Lorna. What's happening higher up in the castle complex?'

Lorna plucked a visitor's map from a plastic dispenser. 'There's lots of activity around this building here.' She studied the sheet. 'The Great Hall. Does that sound right?'

'What's there?'

'Well, there's a war memorial and a …'

'I mean, describe the space.'

Lorna shook herself. 'Sorry. It's a stone courtyard surrounded by high buildings. Perfect for stacking drones ready for launch.'

'Lead on,' wheezed Lillico.

'What do we do with Bru?' asked Ailsa.

'This road carries on,' said Gill. 'It winds around and meets these stairs higher up. He'll come to us if he wants to.' But Bru was already walking, his tusk nodding with every step while his curiosity took him towards the ramparts looking out over the city.

Leading the way, Lorna dashed back up the stone staircase and ran along a castellated wall until they reached a half-moon-shaped battery overlooking the moat and bridge. Various people, in uniforms and plain clothes ran past, but all seemed more perplexed by the dramatic change in the weather than the sight of unidentified strangers roaming the castle grounds Above them, the sky darkened, and Ailsa suddenly doubled over in pain.

'Oh, can you feel that?' she gasped. 'An incredible blackness.'

Gill glanced at Lillico. While neither had Ailsa's ethereal sensitivity, they'd both encountered this feeling before.

'I've a nasty feeling we're about to be reacquainted with an old friend,' said Gill.

'Can you walk?' asked Lorna.

Ailsa nodded urgently. 'I'll manage. Where next?'

Lorna pointed towards an archway slung between an ancient barracks and a church. She was just about to dash for the arch when they were halted by the irritable buzzing of swarming metal insects. Moments later, the quadrangle in front of the Great Hall erupted with thousands of tiny machines rushing over their heads and into the sky like legions of manic bats.

'The drones,' gasped Lillico.

Ailsa staggered again, just catching herself as her legs crumpled under her. 'I sense, death. Lots and lots of death.'

Above them, the drones were pouring higher, creating an inverted grey cone that mirrored the cloud formation boiling above their heads. Gill stared at the great coordinated mass of metal and plastic, and for a terrible moment, it seemed quite beautiful. But while he watched, the drone vortex sub-divided into a dozen separate streams, each torrent tipped with arrowhead formations. After completing two more accelerating circuits, the black arrows broke away, each targeting a different part of the city. The Armour Group ducked as one of the arrow-shaped formations dipped low over the battlements and swept down towards the old town.

Gill scrambled for his phone, tabbing to Adina's number with shaking hands. It answered immediately. 'Something bad is happening. If you can do anything, please do it now.'

'I'm on it. I have to warn you …' And at that moment, the call cut off.

'Damnit,' he muttered. 'I've lost signal. Any of you guys still got reception?'

One by one, they answered him by shaking their heads, until Lorna pointed skywards. Slowly, perceptibly, the arrow above was losing some of its definition. Ailsa looked up, and her eyes flashed wide in alarm. She grabbed Lorna's hand and dragged her sideways, just as a drone not much bigger than a shoe box zipped through the space where Lorna had stood and smashed on the cobbles.

'Look,' cried Lillico, pointing at the sky, where the drone formations were being dulled as each drone started to hover or circle in a gentle orbit. In the crowded airspace, collisions were multiplying. With each small explosion, pieces of metal and smoking debris started raining down on the city.

'Adina killed the phone network,' Gill realised.

Lillico pointed at the darkened streets of Edinburgh below them. 'I think she did a lot more than that.'

At the same moment, as Adina triggered the destructive cascade amongst the castle drones, the lights throughout the National Museum went out. Then a warning on her laptop screen alerted her that her internet connection had dropped. She heaved a sigh. If she wasn't in enough trouble before, she definitely was now. On any average day in this dis-United Kingdom, knocking out a city's power grid could be considered an act of war.

Gathering her things, she headed for the stairs. Due to the tension in the city, the museum was quiet today. Now the few remaining visitors were wondering what happened to their phone connection and why the lights had suddenly gone out.

She did what she'd been trained to do in a situation like this. Walk calmly and slowly towards an exit with the air of an office worker whose day has been interrupted. But she didn't feel calm. Her cursory analysis of the drone that killed Canmore revealed it to have been the most dangerous type. Able to fly autonomously, it had employed the mobile phone network to locate him using his phone number. These bigger drones ran AI software that allowed them to wait for an opportunity to strike rather than waste themselves against walls and roofs. Canmore had been safe while he was inside the parliament building, but once outside, the drone had detected the opportunity and done its deadly work. The drones pouring off Edinburgh Castle weren't as big and unlikely to be as sophisticated. But the sim card-based targeting would make them effective assassins and she'd had to stop them no matter the cost. Knocking out the mobile network required time she didn't have, so she'd gone one better and hacked the power grid, cutting the electricity across the city. And she shuddered because people die in big cities during power cuts. If they caught her, Scotland would jail her, and when her past employers realised what she'd done, Tel Aviv would deny they ever knew her. She and her family were now stateless, but that was a problem for tomorrow. First, she had to survive today.

Reaching the first floor, she spotted Claire Vaughan waving at her in a gesture as if to say, "What's going on?" Adina shrugged, then tapped her wristwatch in a gesture meant to imply she had another meeting. She picked up the pace as she reached the main foyer. Pocketing her phone, she lightened her load by ditching her raincoat and day bag. Then, stepping outside, she paused to sense her surroundings. Traffic was already snarled, and the angry mob strewn along the nearby Royal Mile now sounded anxious. The cone-shaped cloud, high above the castle, had unnerved the crowd, but then they'd lost their phone signals and panic was spreading.

The National Museum was only a few blocks from the fortress, so after a quick glance to check for threats, she decided her route and started to run.

Chapter 52

Six minutes' running at her best speed carried Adina from the National Museum to Edinburgh Castle, while all around her drones dropped from the sky with the grace of frozen geese. After one narrowly missed her she was forced to keep one eye on the sky while navigating the debris-strewn streets.

Reaching the castle perimeter, she stopped to climb over a wrought iron fence. A crash beside her made her gasp when a drone impaled itself on the spiked railings while she was still at a vulnerable point in her manoeuver. Having survived that, she jogged up a triangular patch of grass pinched between the castle's outer defences and the mound of bare rock on which the castle was built. Her goal was the half-moon battery one hundred feet above her head. The wall here wasn't sheer. Instead, it moved up in steps, with a break in the vertical incline every twenty feet or so. She'd stood here with Douglas back in the days before they'd kids and still did some recreational rock climbing. They both reckoned it could be free-climbed, at a push, and today was just that kind of emergency. Stepping out of the path of a drone that came tumbling down the outer walls, she picked out a route offering reasonable handholds and started to climb.

Twenty minutes later, her sweating body ached as she finally grasped the castellated part of the wall and dragged herself into a horizontal resting position. Nearby, she could see smoke rising from two buildings within the castle interior and realised the damage caused by the collapsing drone swarm was worse here. From her horizontal position, she could see a dozen walking wounded and several more, lying on the ground and receiving medical attention. None of them paid any notice to her as she started to press deeper into the castle complex. She didn't know the Armour Group's location, nor had she any means to contact them, but the vortex of the unnatural cloud seemed to be descending into the centre of the castle grounds. Gitting her teeth, she plotted a route towards it and started to wish she'd stayed by the hotel pool in Morrocco.

By the time the Armour Group had run back to the battlements, the falling drones were raining down on the troubled city. Gill winced as the sporadic sound of gunshot-like explosions suggested at least a few were detonating. The other noise he could hear was Bru, whinnying. Whether it was anger or fear, he couldn't tell. Gill and the others ran towards him until they found the horse surrounded by men in uniform. Sensing danger, he was bucking and rearing, catching men with his hooves rather than his tusk. Alarmed that Bru would kill someone or injure himself, Gill led the others towards the scuffle. By the time he arrived with the others in his wake, Bru's molesters were retreating into the nearest building. He heard footsteps running behind them. Turning towards the sound, he discovered to his relief, it was Adina. Hastily, she embraced each of them in turn.

'Thought you'd walked out on us,' said Ailsa, with a hint of accusation.

'As we anticipated, Canmore threatened my family, so I had to capitulate. Or at least, that's the impression I gave.'

She turned and selected Lillico for a deeper hug. 'Thanks for linking me up with Corrie McCann. That worked brilliantly.'

'Actually, it was another friend who put us in touch,' said Lillico. 'But I'll pass on your thanks. Were he and Barley convincing as a Mossad extraction team?'

Adina jiggled her shoulders. 'They need to work on their patter, but yeah, they pulled it off.'

Nearby, they heard a door slam and Gill turned to see Steven Blaine standing on the steps of the Governor's House. Dressed in a black T-shirt and jeans, Gill recognised the ice-cold eyes from the day in the lifeboat shed. Beside him stood Murray McGovern, holding a handgun he'd trained on the Armour Group.

'Aw, man,' cried Blaine, sarcastically, while waving one forefinger at the sky. 'You messed up the light show!'

'Indiscriminate and deadly,' growled Lillico. 'You killed a good friend of mine when you assassinated Canmore.'

Holding out his arms in the pretence of good-natured protest, Blaine revealed his serpent tattoos. 'That wasn't me. You can blame the Brits for that.'

'Actually,' said Lillico, 'I've seen the invoices, so I don't believe you.'

'And mercifully, most drones need phone signals to navigate. And phone towers need electricity,' hissed Adina.

'Clever trick taking down the power grid. Though I've got something far more potent than drones.'

As Gill stepped forward to challenge Blaine, he felt his armour manifest. 'You seem very relaxed for someone who's going to spend the rest of their life in prison.'

Blaine laughed. 'I'm not going to prison. I'll be right here doing a very important job. A job that could have been yours, Gill McArdle.'

Blaine let his arms drop to his sides. 'Anyway, we're talking when you people should be dying.' He turned to McGovern. 'Keep McArdle for now. Kill the rest.'

McGovern nodded, then aimed at Ailsa.

'You might not want to do that,' shouted Lillico. But it was too late for Murray McGovern, his bullet ricocheting off Ailsa's breastplate, flew straight back into his chest. McGovern coughed twice, lifting his hand in a gesture of pained confusion, then slumped to the ground. Blaine made to reach for the weapon, but Lorna jumped to within inches of his hand, snatching McGovern's gun, and jumping away before Blaine could react.

'Another neat trick,' said Blaine, in amusement.

Gill glanced at Ailsa, making sure she was okay, and found her stooping into a winded posture. 'What's wrong? Are you hurt?'

Ailsa gasped in some air and shook her head. 'Gill, above us. Something's happening.'

Following her gaze, he could see the funnel cloud above their heads descending, the neck of the twisting vortex illuminated with flashes of lightning. Down, down, down it came until eventually, it touched the cobbles.

Ailsa doubled over again, reaching out to Gill for support while a large humanoid figure emerged from the cloud and started walking towards them. Muscular, with his sword drawn, he was dressed in armour similar to their own. A visor covered the visitor's face, and when he flicked it back, he revealed familiar eyes.

'Raphael,' breathed Ailsa before wincing in pain. Two more angels emerged from the pillar of cloud, dragging a wheeled cage. Inside this enclosure was another creature, who spat, and lunged, and cowered, leaping up again and again to throw curses at his captors.

'And that foul thing is Sariel,' said Gill.

Chapter 53

'Great to see you, Raphael, but why have you brought that?' said Gill, pointing at the hunched, grey-skinned creature in the cage. 'I thought Sariel was confined to The Lake?'

'Unfortunately, he's been invited,' said Raphael.

'Invited?' Gill echoed.

'Consider it a day pass. A legal loophole that allows him to appeal his sentence.'

'Yeah, but invited by whom?'

'Mr Blaine, in the first instance.' Raphael shrugged. 'And implicitly by Roddy Canmore and all others who knowingly collaborated with the dark realm.'

Inside the cage, Sariel had halted his ravings and now cackled with delight. 'And by you, Gill McArdle.'

Gill folded his arms. 'Really don't think so.'

'Like a rat running into a trap,' the demon continued. 'Boosted by the knowledge you'd secured the lairdship, I knew your pride would suck you forward.'

'I didn't ask to win your prize.'

Sariel cupped his hands together in an exaggerated cringe. 'Oh, how publicly you've fretted about not declaring *The Torn Isle*, and all the while, your curiosity, your infatuation, pulled you like a moth to a flame.'

'Maybe you weren't paying attention, but the treaty was never invoked.'

Sariel howled with delight. 'Regardless, the resulting chaos created by your actions has been the perfect cover for Steven's plans. Especially, when you chose to walk that silly horse all across Scotland to menace Edinburgh's good people. Shame on you, Gill McArdle.'

Gill had to pause to remind himself that Aura had foreseen these events. Sariel wasn't in control here, any more than he was. 'If your plan is going so well, Sariel, why are you the one sitting in a cage?'

Sariel grasped the bars and shook them violently. 'I'll win my freedom today when we overcome you, McArdle,' he wheezed. 'You and your pathetic confederates.'

'Then it will be our pleasure to send you back to prison,' said Lillico.

'Not so fast.' Blaine took a step towards Gill. 'Sariel is my lord, and last time I looked, I'm the one in charge here. I demand you grant Sariel his freedom, and afterwards, we can talk about what happens to the rest of you.'

'Says the man who's been destroying innocent lives throughout this city,' gasped Gill.

Blaine laughed. 'This isn't about one city. It's Scotland I want. I want folk to bow their heads when I pass them in the street. I want them to serve me and my master. And when my flesh wears out, I want them to venerate me.'

Ailsa laughed. 'Oh, you're a proper hero.'

'A hero? Then I should have a pretty costume, just like you,' Blaine laughed, planting his feet and holding out his tattooed arms to Sariel. The demon was mumbling inside his cage and whatever incantation he uttered caused Blaine's appearance to instantly change.

Gill watched in horror while a black, leatherlike coating spread quickly around Blaine's body. Moments later, weapons erupted from the surface of his dark armour, a dagger, bow and arrows, plus a clutch of throwing weapons.

'Let's make this simple,' said Blaine, leaning back his arm to draw a short, sharp blade from a scabbard slung behind his back. 'I challenge a member of the Armour Group to step forward. One-on-one armed combat, where the winner gets to choose what happens to Sariel. Oh, and as a bonus prize, the last man standing becomes King of Scotland.'

The Armour Group glanced at each other, but nobody moved.

'Come on, McArdle,' said Blaine, pointing. 'Or are you scared?'

'I don't recognise your authority,' said Gill.

'Oh, he has authority,' whined Sariel. 'My chosen representative on the surface of the Earth, from before the time I was unjustly incarcerated.'

Gill turned to his angel friend. 'Raph?'

Raphael nodded soberly. 'He has authority. And my role here is to contain Sariel. You, my friends, must deal with Blaine.'

Gill shook his head. 'I refuse to gamble with Scotland.'

'You might have the isles, McArdle, but right now, the mainland is all mine.' Blaine paused to examine the sharp edge of his weapon. 'What do you say? Winner takes all?'

'Even so, I choose not to fight.'

'Then choose to defend yourself,' spat Blaine, lunging at Gill with wild swings of his blade. Gill evaded easily, butting Blaine with his shield and forcing him sideways. Blaine responded by coming in hard and low, thrusting against Gill's shield, before sliding onto his back and hacking at Gill's ankles. Gill felt a sting in his shin and swung his blade down, catching Blaine's weapon and sending it spinning off across the cobbles.

Now defenceless, Blaine sprang away, and for a moment, Gill thought their clash had ended before it had barely begun. But Blaine was muttering some form of invocation, clasping his hands together and drawing them apart until a long black lance rested in his right hand. He seemed to feel its weight for a moment, then hurled it at Gill, forcing him back behind his shield as the black rod glanced off and away into the gloom. But Blaine was drawing another, and again, Gill had to crouch until he felt its passing blow, before charging at Blaine, crashing his adversary back against the battlements.

'Let me put this crudely,' said Gill. 'My guy is bigger than your guy, so this can only end one way.'

Blaine laughed, even as Gill's shield pressed his face against the stone. 'Two thousand years of human history since the Nazarene, and I gotta say, I don't think your guy's doing all that well.'

Gill winced in pain as Blaine's weapon morphed into a dagger, the man jabbing at Gill's shield arm. While he was distracted, Blaine sprang away, his dark arts swiftly conjuring a bow and quiver. Blaine plucked an arrow and launched it at Gill. Then, darting to a different angle he launched another. In a demonic blur, Blaine found position after position, and although Gill's shield caught most of them, his helmet and breastplate saved him more than once. Gill had endured his share of punches over the years, plus a slur of unkind words. He'd been incarcerated and begged for help during dark moments of his soul. None of that, however, had prepared him for the ferocity of Blaine's attack. He could sense the man's loathing for him, and that hatred came tipped with steel. Cut and thrust, lunge and parry, Gill fought with every fibre of his being. But while the battle raged on, he couldn't hide the fact he was tiring, and after a particularly dreadful fusillade, Gill had a flicker of doubt if he would survive this encounter. Instantly, his armour began to fade. Sensing victory, Blaine leapt up on the battlements so he could fire down on Gill, launching arrow after arrow and starting to penetrate his shield. Staring at a porcupine of deadly tips,

Gill's strength suddenly withered. Blaine's bow disappeared, and another javelin materialised in his right hand. Lining up the kill shot, he drew back his arm and hurled the projectile at Gill's chest.

The Armour Group cried out in alarm, but only Lorna acted. Gill clenched his eyes shut and gritted his teeth as the javelin, coming straight for his chest hit home. He heard the slash of flesh and the crunch of bones, and a tiny gasp of pain from Lorna as she took the full force of the blow.

'No, Lorna, no,' Gill yelled, realising she'd thrown herself in front of Blaine's weapon. Her eyes met his, and her golden hair swept against his face while Gill felt her weight gradually descend upon him. In this intimate death, he could feel her body shudder; Lorna panting while her crashing blood pressure begged her lungs for oxygen. Beyond his field of vision, he heard Blaine laugh.

'What a pity,' Blaine sneered. 'Might have kept that one as a pet. But hey ho, time's up, *Sword-Bearer*.'

He manifested and hurled another lance, but it ricochetted harmlessly away when three crystal shields sprang up to cover Gill and Lorna's fallen forms.

'Hey. Not fair,' yelled Blaine.

'Nothing in *The Book* obliges us to play by your rules,' Adina shouted, planting her shield again and forcing Blaine to take a sideways step.

'And since when does the father of lies ever get to set the terms of battle?' shouted Ailsa, forcing Blaine's feet to slide on the damp stonework.

'Justice wins in the long run,' growled Lillico, bruising Blaine's face with another thrust of his shield.

Gill, meanwhile, had rolled Lorna off him and was desperately trying to stem her bleeding. He held her gaze while ferocious metal-on-metal clattering told him the others had engaged Blaine.

'Hold on,' Gill shouted over the crashing battle. 'Help is coming.'

Lorna gave her head a tiny shake. 'Let … me … see … the fight.'

Gill realised there was nothing he could do for her, so he elevated Lorna's shoulders so they could watch the remaining three force Blaine back between the ornamental cannons and up onto the castellated wall. Launching sword thrusts, pushing him with their shields, dodging the blows he rained down upon them. But although they fought fiercely, they couldn't quite overpower him.

'My dagger,' whispered Lorna through bloodstained lips.

Gill grasped it from where it was strapped to her thigh, watching the crystal blade shine brighter than the fading light in Lorna's eyes. And when she had it firmly in her hand, Lorna disappeared.

Blaine staggered the moment Lorna materialised behind him, her blade reaching precisely between the folds in his black armour and striking his heart. The battle froze for a moment while everyone reacted to Lorna's daring tactic. Then they watched as Blaine lost his grip on his lance, hanging as if suspended, the colour draining from his face before, in synchronous death, the two bodies fell from the battlements and tumbled towards the rocks below.

The others stood in shocked silence until there came the clink of chains. Gill spun around to see Raphael and his colleagues starting to wheel the enraged Sariel back into the vortex. Gill dashed up to his protector and grasped the angel's arm. Pointing back to where Lorna had fallen, Gill demanded, 'Is there anything we can do?'

Raphael didn't respond straightaway, and Gill had to endure the angel's long rumination before he finally spoke.

'Yes, Gill. We can think of her every day and remember how brave she was.'

'Anything, Raphael. I know the Nazarene can restore life.'

Raphael arched his eyebrows. 'Do you sense that is his will?'

'I … I don't know,' Gill mumbled.

'Lorna gave up her life to preserve yours, Gill McArdle. Never feel guilt for the price she paid, but instead, resolve to live every precious day in a way that honours her sacrifice.'

He peered down to where Gill was gripping his arm until finally, Gill released him. Then, following his peers, Raphael strode into the vortex, and moments later the whole phenomenon softened and disappeared.

Gill stood, watching the place where Raphael had vanished, and felt the cost of victory burn him more painfully than the injuries he'd received to wrists and ankles. And while he stood, the three others gathered to Gill's side, their chests rising and falling at the end of the hard-won fight.

'Are we done?' asked Adina.

Ailsa nodded wearily. 'The blackness has gone.'

Gill grasped Lillico's shoulders. Looking into his friend's eyes, he could see the man was emotionally on the brink. 'I can't believe we lost her,' Lillico gasped. 'Wiley was bad enough, but Lorna …'

Clumsily, Gill embraced him, feeling the metallic touch of Ailsa and Adina when they added themselves to the squeeze. For a moment, they savoured a victory, snatched from their enemy at terrible cost. Then gradually, they sank to their knees in exhaustion, while piece by piece, their armour faded from sight. Around them, from all points of the compass they could hear vehicle sirens while the city rushed to recover its wounded. And above them, the sky shone with brightest blue.

'What now?' asked Adina, mindful that some of those sirens were heading for the castle.

Ailsa gasped and jumped to her feet. 'We need to get to Charlie!'

Chapter 54

Gill was the last to leave the castle for two practical reasons. He was injured, and he'd a wandering waterhorse to collect. Bru had found his way to the half-moon battery and seemed transfixed by the flashing blue lights below him in the Grassmarket. There was a slew of emergency vehicles, and Gill knew, somewhere in amongst that turmoil, Solomon and Charlie were injured or worse.

Bru was different now, perhaps because Gill was different. Yielding to Gill's command, he allowed his rider to mount and followed his direction as they clattered over the cobbles, sweeping down through the castle grounds and under the portcullis. They overtook the others on the esplanade, and at the top of the Royal Mile, they bore right into Victoria Terrace, where Gill urged Bru to gallop down the hill. Soon, they were outside the Zenith Hotel, where the Read*Scot* conference was being held. Scattering pedestrians and emergency personnel, he guided Bru to the front of the hotel and stared in horror at the ruined lobby strewn with glass. He slid off his mount and took several anxious strides inside the building.

'You missed my keynote,' said a voice behind him.

He spun around to find Solomon, bruised and tousled, though he judged most of the blood she was wearing wasn't her own. 'Solie,' was all he could say as he embraced her.

He knew, in that inexplicable way she always did, she'd already sensed what he was about to ask next. Tugging his hand, she led him to the open rear doors of an ambulance.

'Charlie?' Gill asked, looking at the recumbent figure. On either side of the patient, two faces he recognised were whispering words of encouragement to the injured man. One of them had a blood-filled tube connecting her arm to Charlie's.

'Aura got us through the initial attack,' said Solomon. 'But it was these girls who saved Charlie's life.'

Hearing Solomon's voice, Frankie and Judy turned to give Gill a little wave.

Solomon turned away. 'Judy's powers are growing, Gill. Turns out she can manifest a shield as well as a sword. And Frankie has the same blood type as Charlie, which was providential. Once they've got a couple of pints into him, we'll move him to a hospital.'

Gill nodded, at a loss for words. Behind him, Frankie shouted. 'Know what I want to be, Gill. I'm gonna become a paramedic!'

Gill smiled wearily. 'You go for it, girl.'

'Couldn't help but notice the atmospheric abnormality up on the castle mound,' said Solomon. 'I take it we won?'

'Yes,' said Gill.

'And did we all make it through?'

Gill turned to raise an arm towards Lillico, Ailsa and Adina as they crossed the road towards them.

'Ah,' said Solomon, studying their diminished ranks. Then, taking a deep breath, she pressed her forehead against Gill's shoulder and gently started to weep.

Chapter 55

Edinburgh - Two weeks later

DI Lillico stood on the battlements of Edinburgh Castle and stared out over the city. It was a Friday morning towards the end of September, and this was the first time he'd been here since the showdown with Blaine. The castle still hadn't reopened to visitors, however his warrant card, plus his familiar face, had opened the gates for him. To scaffold his emotions, he'd brought one special guest, and she gripped his hand in silence while Lillico placed a single white rose on the spot where Lorna fell.

'I'm sorry about the people you lost that day,' said Cassy, quietly.

Lillico shook his head. 'Don't be. If you could've seen what we were up against, it was a miracle any of us made it through.'

'But you must let yourself grieve for them. Otherwise, the loss will poison you.'

'I hear you, Cass, and of course, I miss them. But, when I grieve, I'll always remember George and Lorna died doing something they believed was important.'

'Wiley was a piece of work,' said Cassy. 'I'm gonna miss him.'

Lillico smiled, though he teetered on the brink of tears. 'Yes, and … yes.'

'And I never got to meet your friend Lorna. Ailsa says she was amazing.'

'She was.' Lillico gripped her hand. 'And in a strange way, she was the best friend you never had.'

Cassy looked puzzled. 'What makes you say that?'

'She was your advocate.'

'Nope, still not following.'

Lillico turned away from the city to face her. 'There was a time when I thought Lorna and I would become more than friends. And she was up for that until she realised my heart was stuck on you.'

'If she realised then … what about you?'

'I didn't know her long, but Lorna seemed to understand me better than I understood myself. Long and short of it is, I want to be with you.'

Cassy allowed her left hand to drift behind his back so she could lean her head against his shoulder. 'Was that you asking me on a date, DI Lillico?'

'I'd like to ask a lot more of you than that.'

'Have you carried out a thorough risk assessment?' whispered Cassy. 'Considered all the angles? Filled out the right paperwork?'

Lillico drew his hands around her waist. 'I love you, Cass.'

Cassy pulled away from him and stepped between the cannons to lay her hand on the battlements close to where Lorna had fallen. 'Not long ago, I would have jumped up on these walls if you'd said that. Danced with danger across these walls to fend off your friendship. I'm wondering, what's changed about us?'

He walked over to join her so they could look down on the old city. 'We get older. Surer of the things that are important to us. More certain of who we are and how we can share ourselves with another.'

'We'd make an odd couple, you and me. You with your big police job and strange armour, which you still need to explain to me, by the way.'

'I can do that.'

'And I have my work, because with my promotion and all, I'm desperately important.'

'Girl, stop blethering,' Lillico sighed.

'You didn't think I'd make this easy for you?'

'Cass, just shut up and let me hold you.'

Cassy cocked her head to one side and thought about this for a moment. 'Yeah. I think I'd like that.'

On that same Friday morning, Freya arrived at the Scottish Parliament building a few minutes behind schedule. A security guard quickly added her name to the register and if he recognised her, he didn't let on. That wasn't true of many other people, who seeing her face, gave a little smile, or nod of recognition as she moved through the campus. Her destination was a large conference room almost as big as the main chamber. It had spaces for a hundred delegates and even had its own press box, so when she looked for a seat, she discovered one reserved for her, right at the front. Glancing along the rows, she saw several faces she recognised. She waved to one or two, then paused to greet Howard, seated several rows back. Immediately, he stepped into the aisle to speak to her.

'Great to see you,' he said. 'What a meteoric rise you've had, my girl. I hope you won't forget who gave you your first break.'

She lightly gripped his upper arm. 'I'll always have a soft spot for the *Tribune*.'

'You're accepting my job offer then?'

Freya bobbed for head from side to side. 'I'll keep you on my ad hoc roster, Howard. But I've a few other irons in the fire I'm going to try first.'

Howards slumped a little. 'Has one of the Edinburgh dailies offered you more money? Or one of the big podcasters?'

Freya shook her head. 'A far loftier publication.'

'You're going to London,' he groaned. 'Or New York?'

An usher appeared at their elbows and chased them to their seats before Howard could press her again. She pushed away the distraction and sat down. Watching the faces and bodies milling around in the room below her, she shivered, but not because she was cold. Right before her, history was being made. She'd been present during the key moments that had brought Scotland to this place, and now it would be her honour and her duty to report on what happened next.

Below her, the delegates were taking their seats, and Freya found herself studying their body language. The Orcadians, she noticed, were laughing and joking with the Shetlanders. They'd travelled down together, she imagined. Might even be staying at the same hotel. Controlling the lion's share of Scotland's fossil and renewable energy sources, they held the strongest hand in the negotiations that would shortly begin. The Hebridean crew were less chatty, but they were men and women well used to adversity, so nothing about today scared them. And they were from the land of the waterhorses, so from their point of view, anything was possible.

Morayshire and representatives from what was becoming known as the "Glen Isle" were mingling and building metaphorical bridges in advance of the physical ones needed to join their two regions. She smiled as a crowd from the Scottish Borders came up and introduced themselves to the Morayshire crew. Both regions had good farmland she recalled, with strong regional identities. And the Borders had a firm offer to link with England if the Scottish negotiations didn't go well for them. In a seating arrangement that was far from random, the British delegation arrived last and sat quietly beside their Border cousins.

In a widely reported row, the Central Belt group had split in two before today's inaugural meeting. Below her position, they glowered at each other, with Glasgow tilting towards a federal realignment and Edinburgh fighting to retain the status quo.

A flurry of action near the door caught her attention, and the chairperson arrived. Puffing out her cheeks, Freya didn't envy this woman for the task she had in front of her. The urgent practicality of choosing someone to chair the constitutional negotiations had been herculean. Ex-politicians, judges, captains of industry and even religious figures had been proposed, examined, then cast aside by one delegation or another. The steering committee had gone back to the drawing board, pulling together a long list of people with lives spent in public service. Police officers, doctors and teachers were scrutinised until one person stood alone. Someone who'd been in Edinburgh on the day of the failed coup. Someone who had distinguished herself for bravery and tenacity when her volunteers came under fire.

Below Freya's position, Rosemary Solomon, a former teacher and co-founder of the Read*Scot* charity asked everyone in the room to rise.

'I wonder if we might take a moment,' Solomon began, her pause allowing her energetic gaze to dart around the faces. 'To remember the eight hundred and seventy-two people who died upon this *Torn Isle*. Victims of the disaster and of the violence that followed it.' She bowed her head and led the delegates in a minute's silence, during which time no one spoke or coughed.

'While we remain standing, let us make a promise to do our best for this nation. The challenge before us is to reconsider Scotland's constitution before arriving at a recommendation to go before a public referendum early next year. As part of these negotiations, we will consider our future relationship with the UK and evaluate the reorganisation of the Scottish regions along a federal model. And, Ladies and Gentlemen, if we fail in our duty and this land endures protracted division, then may history judge us harshly.' She gave the gathered throng a businesslike nod. 'This working party is now in session. Please take your seats.'

Chapter 56

As usual, Mhairi was first in the conference room for Monday's team meeting. Craig came next, followed by Larry and the smoky trail he dragged in his wake after grabbing a "quick one" in Slessor Gardens. Next came Cassy, and following meekly was their illustrious editor. Mhairi sat quietly while the rest of them finished conversations and got themselves organised.

'Right,' said Cassy. 'In a moment, we're firing the starting gun on issue 64. But firstly, how are we all doing?' She glanced around the faces while her question echoed around the silent room.

'It's been a lot to think about,' Craig said, eventually. 'We need to see how things settle down.'

'You have concerns?' Cassy asked.

'Not really. It's just everything is awash with change right now.'

Larry nodded. 'Mebbe I'm a bit slow but wid you go o'er the organisational changes wan mare time?'

'In Scotland, or just *Mys.Scot*?' Cassy shot back.

'Scotland's beyond me,' moaned Larry. 'How's about we stick tae the mag.'

Cassy pulled on her patient face, which looked as sincere as the Halloween masks that had started appearing in shops. 'I'm moving to a new role as "Publisher of New Titles," reporting directly to Tony. He'll hold on to all the legacy titles, apart from *Mys.Scot,* which is mine. Okay so far?'

Larry nodded.

'We've got a new launch starting in January, so I'll be splitting my time between that and our favourite crypto mag. In the meantime, I'll be training a new office manager to replace me.'

Craig fired a glance at the editor. 'But until January, you're running our mag, and what, the editor is just a wooden figurehead?'

'Absolutely,' said Cassy. 'No change from the last five years.'

'If I can intervene,' said Freya Swanson. 'I've never been anything other than a journalist, and I can assure you, I'm anything but wooden. Tony has employed me on a contract basis for one year. I'll be working three days a week for *Mys.Scot,* and two for my old employer at the *Tribune* so I can report on the continuing fallout of the last few weeks.'

'An whit aboot the year efter?' asked Larry.

'In the longer term, it remains to be seen if I step into a full-time editorial role. In the meantime, as your publisher, you'll have Cassy's continuing leadership.'

Cassy signalled her agreement before Larry raised further objections. 'We'll figure it out. In the meantime, this arrangement gives Freya time to get the lie of the land.'

'Aye,' Larry intervened. 'Ye need tae ken who the good guys are and who're the bad yins. Now, ye see yon cat mag …'

Freya smiled warmly when she cut across him. 'Why don't you leave me to arrive at my own conclusions.'

'I agree,' said Cassy, as she used the thumb on her left hand to spin a slim silver band mounted with a single large diamond.

Mhairi smiled, amused by how quickly this little mannerism had inserted itself into Cassy's personality. It was a "tell" that revealed when she was nervous. That meant, with Cassy on the back foot, it was time for Mhairi to spring her trap. 'And what about you, Cass?'

'Told you. I'm a publisher now. Get to hold my own meetings and everything.'

'I meant, personally.' She nodded at the ring. 'I mean, after your sudden announcement, will you even be staying in the area?'

Cassy's jaw dropped. 'You're my pal. You know all this already!'

Mhairi winked at Larry and Craig. 'But they don't.'

'And we put her up to asking you,' said Craig. 'Because deep down, we really care about you, Cass.'

'And we're nosey,' Larry added.

Cassy gave her head an irritable shake and stared at a distant point. 'Police Scotland has authorised DCI Lillico to move *Special Investigations* to Dundee.'

'Excellent,' said Mhairi. 'Meaning you'll have a workaholic, a Detective Chief Inspector and a petty criminal all living under one roof.'

Cassy threw Mhairi an air kiss. 'Gonna tell Zack you said that.'

'When's the weddin', Cass?' asked Larry.

'Soon. Our only problem is finding a decent ceilidh band. Obviously, *Calum's Road* isn't available that night.'

'Nah,' said Mhairi. 'We could give you a guest spot then me and the girls could do the rest of the gig without you.'

Freya cleared her throat. 'Look, all this chit-chat is lots of fun, but I wonder if anyone has had a chance to look at my story idea for issue 65?'

The rest of the team glanced at each other. They'd all read Freya's proposal for an investigative piece, and no one was rushing to support her.

'Tough place to start,' said Craig.

'You're settin' yourself up tae fail, lass.'

'I think it's a long shot, really.'

Freya turned to Cassy. 'What about you?'

Cassy stopped fiddling with her new ring. 'Honestly?'

'Yeah. Tell me straight.'

Cassy nodded and stared at the table. 'Look, Freya. I think your idea is tenuous at best. You will be ridiculed and opposed. The chance of you finding any data to substantiate your theory is vanishingly small. And if even you overcome all those hurdles, the rest of Scotland will probably end up laughing at you.'

'Meaning?'

Cassy chewed on a smile. 'Meaning, I think you're right on the money, girl. Let's do this.'

Chapter 57

At the same moment as Cassy was leading the meeting in Dundee, the newly promoted DCI Lillico was paying a second visit to Barlinnie in as many months. When he signed in, the guys on the desk assumed he was there to see Billy Whyte, but Lillico shook his head and asked for someone else. Following directions to the private meeting room, he was surprised to see Monty Galloway was already waiting for him. Lillico signalled the guard to confirm he was happy to meet Galloway alone, before taking a seat on a hard plastic chair.

'No DCI Wiley?' asked Monty.

Lillico shook his head. 'But you knew that already.'

'Aye, but I cannae believe it's true. Maybe they'll name a high school after him, or something.'

Lillico looked down at his hands and smiled. 'Do you know, that would really piss him off.'

'Maybe a bar? A scabby old place with lots of dark wood and even darker ales. He'd have liked that.'

'Yes, he would.'

'On the plus side, I'm glad he got Canmore.'

Lillico nodded once but said nothing.

'That man was a monster.'

Lillico picked at some graffiti scratched on the table in front of him. 'Says the man convicted of more murders than any other Scot in living memory.'

'You only got the Drumchapel crew for six,' Monty said, evenly. 'I confessed to the rest.'

'Yeah, that was unexpected. Why did you do that?'

'Spent the best twenty years of my life as a gun for hire,' said Monty, looking away. 'The victim's families deserved closure. It was the only thing I had to give them to say sorry.'

'Noble gesture of you. I bet you feel really good about yourself.'

'Park the sarcasm, DCI Lillico. A day came when it was just the right thing to do.'

Lillico's forefinger circled the graffiti. 'Talking of doing the right thing, tell me why you let Billy Whyte live?'

'Who says I did?'

'Your reputation, for one.'

Monty gave him a bitter smile but said nothing.

'On, come on, Monty. I'm curious, and it's probably the only reason I agreed to this meeting.'

Monty looked away and chewed a few times before he spoke. 'When we got Canmore's order to do Billy, I thought to myself, Roddy, you arrogant prick. For right or for wrong, Billy was Canmore's faithful foot soldier, loyal like a dog. And when his usefulness was gone, Canmore just wanted him put down.' He turned to peer earnestly at Lillico. 'That wasn't right. Even I knew that.'

'So, you carried out the hit but let Billy escape with just a scratch?'

Monty sat back and folded his arms as far as his chains would allow. 'Billy deserved better. A couple of years and he'll be out of here. And besides, I knew if I gave him a wee scare, it might loosen his tongue.'

'Thank you. That was very helpful.' Lillico finally found the courage to look this successful predator in the eye. 'Did you have to scare Lillian to make her confession?'

Monty looked away but said nothing.

'You realise her sworn evidence was crucial in charging Canmore. His backdoor ownership of Glenure Gold. Paying the Drumchapel crew to eliminate anyone standing in his way.'

'Lillian's still young. If she's played her cards right, she'll have negotiated a few years off her sentence.'

'I think the fiscal is considering her request. Maybe you should have done the same.'

Monty shook his chains and flicked a glance at the guard to signal he was done. When he was handcuffed and halfway to the door, he stopped. 'Helping your boss wasn't about me, Mister Lillico. I'll spend the rest of my life in here. I hope I live long enough to see Lillian walk free.'

'And, of course, it allowed you to take revenge on your old paymaster.'

'Not revenge. We were paid for our services. Our mistake was to rely too much on Oscar, and that got us caught.' He stopped to peer at his feet. 'Being fair by Billy and Lillian seemed the right thing to do.'

'Forgive me,' said Lillico 'But how does a man like Monty Galloway decide that doing the right thing is suddenly a good idea?'

After some urging from the guard, Monty moved forward a few steps. In the doorway, he turned and winked at Lillico. 'Maybe I got a wee nudge from my guardian angel.'

Chapter 58

Cormac was dreaming. In his mind was a picture, half-imagined, half-remembered, of a black waterhorse facing off against a white. Between them stood his daughter, Ailsa, plus his long-dead son, Callum. As the horses pawed the ground, he shouted a warning to them, but they didn't have time to react before the horses lowered their heads and charged. He yelled in alarm, waking himself so violently that he found himself sitting upright in bed. And beside him, his phone was ringing. He glanced at the clock. Just gone 4 am. Who the hell would be phoning at this hour? Remembering Ailsa's peril in the dream, he snatched up the receiver. 'Cormac McKellar.'

'Cormac. It's Rani.'

Cormac rubbed his face and guessed why Rani would be calling. 'You have him?'

'Not yet. But the Harlequinn kept him on radar until an hour ago, and now we think he's in amongst the skerries.'

'Where?'

'Beacravik. There's a single small beach set amongst low cliffs. If he makes landfall, that's where it'll be.'

Cormac snorted. 'He's got a hundred miles of coastline, and he comes almost to my front door?'

Rani ignored him. 'The Harlequinn is berthing at Tarbert as we speak. Will you be joining us or not?'

Cormac managed an ironic laugh. 'Wouldn't miss it for the world.' He slammed down the phone and double-checked the time. It would be a pity to wake his guests, even though they'd been anticipating this. Stepping to the back bedroom, he tapped the door and waited for a mumbled response. He pushed the door open a crack and was grateful to find that Salina and Josh had slept with their clothes on.

'They're coming,' was all he said.

The old Land Rover rattled and banged as Cormac navigated a short section of the *Golden Road* under a starlit sky promising a perfect autumn day. There was precious little parking to be had at this remote spot so he mounted the verge as best he could and turned off the engine. Salina passed Joshua into his arms while she clambered out of the car and stretched.

'Who are those people?' she asked.

'I recognise a couple of the cars, so I'd say you're looking at anyone in the Hebridean *Vigil* who can face being awake at this ungodly hour.'

'Did you call them?'

Cormac shook his head. 'You know how this works, my dear.'

'Daddy!' shrieked Josh, pointing towards a huddle of people standing close to the water.

'Well done, you,' whispered Salina, following his gaze. 'Shall we go and see him?'

They threaded their way down a grassy track, mumbling "good mornings" to a few who needed to step out of their way. When they arrived at the beach, Cormac felt a lump rise in his throat while he watched the McArdle family merge together in the morning twilight.

'Sorry to drag you out of bed, old man,' said a voice.

He turned to find Ailsa, beautiful Ailsa, hands in the pockets of a battered leather jacket and her rich auburn hair flowing gently in the light morning breeze. Unable to speak, he pressed his forehead against her shoulder and let her arms envelop him.

'Aw, did you miss me?'

Cormac wiped his eyes and pulled away. 'You, Miss, need to be more careful.'

Ailsa released him and did a little twirl. 'Look, barely a scratch.'

Cormac considered telling her she was an idiot and that he loved her and couldn't bear seeing her in danger ever again, but decided to make do with taking her outstretched hand, pulling it to his mouth to kiss. 'How was your journey back?'

'Och, ye know. Quiet.'

Cormac shook his head. Ailsa and her entourage had stoked a media storm for the past two weeks, trailing Bru while the waterhorse trekked ever northwards. Resisting capture, he had zigzagged across Scotland while he followed whatever genetic roadmap had led him and his kin back to the *Temple of the Isles.*

'Friends of mine put us up on Raasay for a couple of days, and oh man, was I ready for a rest.'

'Thought you'd never get Bru out of that distillery.'

Ailsa rubbed the back of her neck. 'Shit, was that on TV?'

'Drones, helicopters and media ambushes. You haven't exactly been keeping a low profile.'

Briefly, she looked embarrassed. 'Raasay was just R&R.'

'More like a load of PR.'

Ailsa laughed and noticed a familiar face down by the waterside. Dragging her father's arm, she nodded "hello" to Rani and glanced down at the little girl gripping her hand. The child looked extremely nervous, and Ailsa seemed drawn to her.

'Scuse me,' she said, kneeling beside the child. 'But aren't you the famous kid from the news?'

Amy turned to face her and gave Ailsa a shy smile.

'It is you!' gushed Ailsa. 'The waterhorse whisperer. I am so excited to meet you.'

Amy twisted a little in embarrassment. 'It was nothing.'

'Are you kidding? There isn't a person alive who could have done what you did that day. You probably saved my friend Gill's life and made history into the bargain.'

'Why isn't Bru here yet?' Amy fretted.

'He'll be along. I was with your mum, trailing him all the way back from Edinburgh. I'm sure he can't wait to see you.'

'Mummy says it's ninety miles to cross the sea. Bru might not be able to swim that far.'

Ailsa made eye contact with Rani for a second and turned back to Amy. 'He's a waterhorse, kid. He can swim like, forever.'

Just then, there was a ripple of hushes among the two-dozen people gathered around the beach. And when Cormac tuned his ears, he could hear it too. The sound of water being disturbed and the snorts of a horse as it forced seawater from its nostrils. At last, silhouetted against the first glimmer of dawn, they could see him.

Cormac glanced at McArdle, then at the creature, walking slowly from the water, its head low, its tusk pointing at the welcoming party.

'Stand back, love,' urged Rani to the little girl holding her hand. But the child broke away from her and ran to the water's edge. As the horse stumbled on the seaweed, he turned toward her, his great tusk pressing against Amy's body while he started to sniff her pockets.

'I know what you need,' she said, fearlessly, reaching into her jacket and unwrapping a boiled sweet. Offering it to the horse's mouth, Bru licked it from her hand and let the hard sugar fall between his molars before he started crunching. And when it was finished, he hung his head, looking

394

inconsolably weary, the last warrior coming off the battlefield and realising he was finally home. The crowd watched in silence as Bru simply stood for several long minutes and breathed in Amy's scent.

Cormac watched, transfixed, bewildered that a creature with the potential to be so cruel could also be so wonderfully kind. He was disturbed from this reverie by the man holding Rani's hand. 'Do you think he'll let us check him over? He looks exhausted.'

The waterhorse seemed to hear this, lifting its head and pricking its ears. Then, with a last sideways glance at Amy, he strode over the shingle and accelerated as his hooves hit the firm ground at the back of the beach. Bru battled up the gradient, briefly touching the road, before leaping over a fence and disappearing into the Harris hillside.

'Will I ever see him again?' Amy protested to anyone who was listening.

Ailsa took the little girl's hand. 'Are you kidding? You're his bestie. Bru swam a hundred miles to get back to you, so what do you think is going to happen the next time he fancies a highly caffeinated sugar hit?'

Amy smiled. 'But he might swim away again.'

Ailsa shook her head. 'No way, darlin'. This is unicorn country. He's home now.'

Amy flashed Ailsa a smile, then dashed to join her family, and they in turn, started to file up the hill towards the cars. Seeing Ailsa's hands were now unoccupied, Josh slid from his mother's arms and into Ailsa's.

'Are you going to introduce me to your friends?' asked Cormac.

'Sure. This is Adina. She's a retired secret agent from Israel via Iran and Edinburgh. And this is Alex from the Borders, who I think is quite cute but unfortunately, he's in love with a pal of mine. And finally, the one with his arm in a sling is Charlie from Dundee. He's a headcase.'

'Taks wan tae ken wan,' muttered Charlie.

'Well, you're all welcome at mine for breakfast, or whatever.'

'Great,' said Ailsa, taking Cormac by the arm. 'Did I mention we need to stay for six months to hide out from the media?'

Two hours later, after a hearty breakfast, and endless storytelling, the group started to flag. Salina and Josh went back to bed while Adina and Lillico passed out side by side on the sofa. Finally, Cormac and Charlie retired to the kitchen to tidy up and share stories of Glasgow.

Gill was desperately tired, having barely slept since their layover on Raasay. But before he could lie down, he needed some time alone. A brief text exchange with Solomon confirmed her early days in the political arena were going well. Meanwhile, preparations for Lorna's memorial were in hand, and it was agreed that four days from now, they would all meet at Portsoy. The Armour Group would be complete for one last time while they celebrated Lorna's life and said goodbye to her at the family's graveside.

And now, finally, for the first time in weeks, he was alone. Climbing the hill behind Cormac's house, he churned over the events of the past few days and pondered what he could have done better. When he reached the spot where he and Cormac had argued many years before. He sat down on the old flat rock and wept for Lorna, and rejoiced the cost hadn't been higher. But even though he was wrecked with emotion, he realised he wasn't alone after all.

'Can I ask you something?' he asked.

Aura gently pushed against his shoulders. 'Of course.'

'The day after the battle, the police recovered Blaine's body. However, they never found Lorna.' He paused to consider his question. 'Meaning that, in the moments before she died, she managed to jump away.'

'She did.'

'So, where is she?'

Aura sighed. 'She's safe, Gill.'

'But her body, is it …?'

'Hush, Gill. She's with me.'

Gill accepted her gentle rebuke and nodded, tucking away his private theory about where Lorna's body might lie. 'It should have been me that died.'

She stroked his head. 'Maybe I'm not finished with you yet.'

Gill stared at his feet while exhaustion and grief threatened to rob him of his composure. 'What would you have me do?'

'What would you like to do?'

'Not tearing up Scotland would be a great start.'

'Oh, Scotland, dear Scotland,' whispered Aura as she drew Gill's gaze up and out over the distant Isle of Skye. 'When you look at it, what do you see?'

Gill sighed. 'Beauty. Brokenness. And so much potential.'

'And if anything were possible, what would you do?'

'Anything?'

'Yes.'

'I'd celebrate the beauty and do everything in my power to mend the rest.'

'That's a good plan, Gill McArdle.' He felt Aura whisper close to his ear. 'Shall we begin?'

Chapter 59

Editor's comment, Mysterious Scotland, Issue 63

Back at my laptop after the surreal events of the last few weeks, I want to pause for a moment to take stock and remember. Like so many people who lost loved ones, the tumult in Edinburgh cost a dear friend of mine her life. The challenge for those of us who survived is to ensure their lives weren't lost for nothing.

My most recent dig seems ages ago now. We discovered an extraordinary amount of gold in a Dundonian cemetery, a hoard buried during an earlier bout of turmoil in Scottish history. As greedy men tried to take this valuable metal for their own ends, that gold became representative of Scotland herself – something precious to be coveted. And whether you agree with my personal politics or not, let the record show, I did what I thought was best, and I did it with all my might.

I have a few critics in the media, and from among the ruins of our political system. Most are people who seem to think I amplified the recent instability, and that perversely, I should seek high office to help sort out the mess. My response is simple - I'm not called to that, nor do I have the skills. But I do know what my passion is, so let me take responsibility for the bit of the mess I understand and can help to fix. With the retirement of Rosemary Solomon from the educational charity we ran together, I'll be stepping into the Executive role of ReadScot. We have a strong and growing team, dedicated to improving educational standards across this beautiful country, and if all goes to plan, I'll devote the remainder of my working life to that worthy cause.

As a consequence of that decision, it's with some sadness I write this, my last editorial for this magazine. But fear not. We have, within our team the person who has been the true powerhouse of Mysterious Scotland right from the start. I've watched her editorial prowess grow over the years until they've eclipsed my own, so I'm delighted to announce that Cassy Tullen will be publishing Mys.Scot from the next issue. I'll not wish her luck, as people like Cassy don't need luck. She works hard and does a great job, assisted by one of the best teams in the business. Alongside her as acting editor is a journalist who needs little introduction. Freya Swanson is as talented as she is fearless, and I know from spending time with her she has some amazing stories to tell.

A last thought for you before I go. In the days of tumult, I spent a lot of time in the company of a very special horse. Just an animal, who barely knew his own strength. Appearing at Callanish that fateful day, he seemed driven by an instinct so strong, that a human would have declared it a personal destiny. And when I steered him towards Edinburgh, he came willingly and bravely. When our work was done, and his "duty" fulfilled, he turned around and went home. Back to the wild lands and into the care of the people who love him. Permit me to suggest, Scotland needs to be like that. To rediscover ourselves, our history and our character. To look at our neighbourhood, be it our croft or our city scheme, and say, "This is my home, and it's worth defending." And if you don't have a waterhorse or another miraculous animal to accompany you, just look around. There are people within a hundred steps of your own front door who are even more miraculous than a waterhorse, and when you share your vision, they just might join you.

So, friends, until the next time I meet you amidst hilltops and glens, or we chance upon each other in a city street, let's revel together in this wonderful land that is, and always will be, Mysterious Scotland.

The End

An introduction to the Next Adventure …Coming later in 2025

Shadow Castles – Book 1

The Caledonia Regression

Connal Canmore tumbles towards his death from the walls of Stirling Castle. But instead of crashing onto rocks, he lands face down in the dirt. Bruised, but freed from the disease that was killing him, he sees a city he recognises. It is Stirling, but not the same city he left. For reasons he doesn't comprehend, this is a version of the place that existed long ago.

Connal picks up the threads of this new existence and exploits his futuristic knowledge to achieve material gain. And life is good until another brush with death sends him tumbling further back in time. As the years stretch to centuries Connal is on hand to witness the birth of Scotland, bloodily wrought through migration and war. Stripped of his riches and his dear ones with every fall, Connal recognises in himself the seeds of change. But how will it benefit him if his only destiny is to descend, further and further back in time? He is renewed, but at the same time unhinged, for Connal cannot keep his grip on history.

Back in the twenty-first century of another Scotland, terrorists target the leading prince of the realm. Seizing this latest assassination as a judicious moment to strike their enemies, powerful clans jostle for influence ahead of the coming fight. Alliances rise and fall in the Caledonian court while the old guard is convulsed by the coming succession. And when finally, the aggressor nation is revealed, only one obstacle restrains this nation from unleashing a shockwave of revenge. The old king is dying, and with his passing, Caledonia will choose a new sovereign and go to war.

Image credit: Cocoparisienne from Pixabay, licensed by Canva

Acknowledgements

My editors and beta-readers! Where would I be without you? Especially to Woodeene and Kath, rushing to give the book a final readthrough before we went to print. And to Audrey, for listening to me war-game the endless possibilities for this book.

My thanks to Ian Wallace for joining me for a day while we road-tested David McKane's green corridor. It was a long, wet walk from Edinburgh's ring road to the peak of Arthur's Seat, and afterwards, the security guys guarding the parliament building seemed in two minds about letting us in.

And thanks to James, for taking a weekend to hammer out the story arc for the new series. Under the working title, 'Shadow Castles,' I feel we're at the start of something special.

Acknowledging my inspiration for the Armour Group, I finish with some words from *The Book*, penned by an itinerant preacher writing to spiritual people everywhere, paraphrased by me, so I can get my head around its brilliance:

Dress yourself in the Creator's armour to withstand all the evil demon's strategies. For we're not fighting against flesh-and-blood enemies, but against malicious rulers of the unseen world, against mighty powers and evil spirits whose presence is tolerated, even in heavenly places. Let me challenge you to wear every piece of it so you will be able to resist the enemy and survive the coming battles. Stand your ground, putting on the belt of truth and the body armour of the Creator's right-mindedness. For shoes, slip on the peace that comes from being ready with good news. And don't forget the shield of faith to stop the devil's fiery arrows, plus the sword of the Spirit, which are the words of His book. Pull on your helmet to protect your vision and clear thinking. Finally, don't forget to speak to the Spirit, (existing in Aura's company,) so you discover purpose in everything.

MYSTERIOUS 🦄 SCOTLAND

IN AUDIOBOOK FORMAT

AVAILABLE FROM AMAZON
AUDIBLE AND ITUNES

Made in the USA
Las Vegas, NV
30 March 2025

20306758R00239